THE
End
OF THE
Sky

SANDI TOKSVIG

CORGI BOOKS

CORGI BOOKS

UK | USA | Canada | Ireland | Australia
India | New Zealand | South Africa

Corgi Books is part of the Penguin Random House group of companies
whose addresses can be found at global.penguinrandomhouse.com

www.penguin.co.uk
www.puffin.co.uk
www.ladybird.co.uk

First published by Doubleday 2017
This edition published by Corgi Books 2018

001

Text copyright © Sandi Toksvig, 2017
Cover artwork © David Dean, 2017

Typeset in 11/16 pt Sabon by Jouve (UK), Milton Keynes
Printed in Great Britain by Clays Ltd, St Ives plc

A CIP catalogue record for this book is available from the British Library

ISBN: 978–0–552–56660–5

All correspondence to:
Corgi Books
Penguin Random House Children's
80 Strand, London WC2R 0RL

MIX
Paper from
responsible sources
FSC® C018179

Penguin Random House is committed to a
sustainable future for our business, our readers
and our planet. This book is made from Forest
Stewardship Council® certified paper.

To Deej, my travel companion

Follow Slim Hannigan's Journey

LINE OF
ORIGINAL EMIGRATION
TO THE
PACIFIC NORTHWEST
COMMONLY KNOWN AS THE
OLD OREGON TRAIL

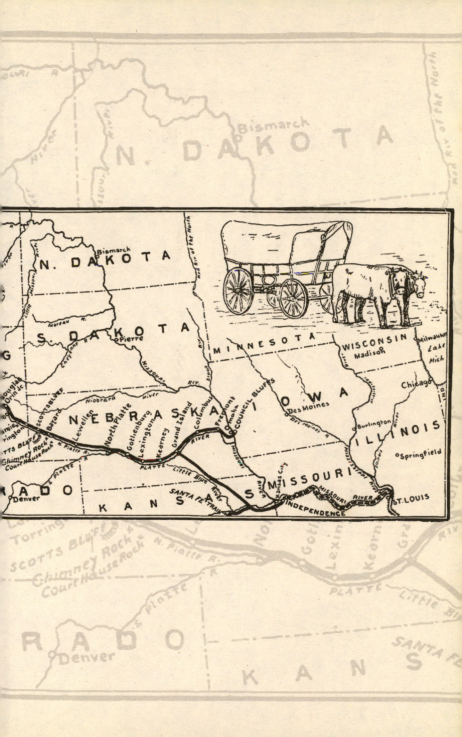

I have been to the end of the earth,
I have been to the end of the waters,
I have been to the end of the sky.
I have been to the end of the mountains,
I have found none that are not my friends.

Navajo proverb

CHAPTER ONE

Sometimes you remember a moment so clearly it is as if you have a painting of it. I was sitting with an Indian man. Actually, that's not right at all. I have a big tale to tell you and I don't want to start by making a mistake. He wasn't just any Indian man. He was a Choctaw, and that matters. It's wrong to think all people are the same even if at first glance you think they look alike. My little brother Toby thought all the Indians in America would be scary but that certainly wasn't true. There were lots of kinds of Indians, just as there are lots of kinds of all sorts of people everywhere you go, and you need to pay attention to detail. Da taught me that.

'The Choctaw are a great people who have fought to keep their identity.' That's what my friend Louise told me. I don't really know what that means except that they had a tough time, just like we Irish did.

It was early morning, a bright morning, and I was waiting

outside Weston's Wagon Shop in the town of Independence, Missouri. I suppose I should paint a bit more of a picture for you. I mean, *I* know everything that happened but you're just catching up. Well, it was spring, 1848, and I was thirteen years old. My big brother, Henry, and my friend Jack were inside the shop buying us a wagon. It was a particular one called a Weston Wagon, which the advertisers said would 'never wear out'. That was good! We had a long trip ahead of us.

I wanted to go into the shop too, but Henry was older than me and he had started trying to boss me about. 'If Jack's coming in, then someone has to stay outside to keep an eye on the cart. You stay put.'

I don't know why I listened to him. No one seemed at all interested in our old farm cart. It had come all the way from Ireland and was quite battered by now, but I stayed beside it just the same. I think the fight had gone out of me. I'm not sure I cared about anything.

'What you got there, girl?' A large woman in a bonnet the size of a barn stood in front of me. Her huge hat came between me and the sun and the world went dark.

'Sorry?'

She pointed to the cart and the giant piece of metal which stood on it. 'What the heck you got there? Some kind of monster?'

'It's a printing press. It makes newspapers and . . . posters

2

and books. My Da made it, and my Uncle Aedan. Uncle Aedan's a blacksmith. In Ireland.'

I realized I still felt excited about the press. It was a wonderful thing, but instead of being impressed the woman scowled at me.

'You Irish?'

I nodded.

She shook her head. 'Damned Irish get everywhere these days.' She turned to leave and I heard myself shout after her:

'It's the printing press which will help bring democracy to the United States! You wait and see!'

And for the first time in ages I grinned. It's what Da would have shouted, I was sure.

Then it hit me again. Da was no longer with us. There was just us Hannigan kids now, and we had no idea really what we were doing, or what lay ahead.

I don't know why I remember that particular morning so well. Maybe it was the small book I was holding. Jack and I had just finished printing it. Writing made me feel better somehow, so I had put down the story of how we came to be in America.

'But it's not finished!' I protested to Jack, my gentle giant of a friend, when he said we should print it.

'I know,' he said, 'but it's a start.'

It *was* a start, but I couldn't imagine the tale ever being finished. There were too many things I didn't know – like what had happened to Da. He was missing and I could hardly understand how the whole world was just carrying on anyway. And not just carrying on but doing it with such energy.

It seemed to me then that if I could have flown into the sky and looked down, I would have seen that Weston's on that day was the busiest place on the planet. That spring, hundreds of people were getting ready to head out to the prairie. Have you heard of the prairie? It was once the wildest bit of land. Thousands of miles with nothing on it, but you had to walk across it if you wanted to seek your fortune in the wild west of America. Customers from every land in the world were coming and going as they got ready for their trip. From inside the wagon shop you could hear the steady bang of the blacksmith's hammer. Wagons were being built, and horses and oxen were having their metal shoes put on. It was a sound which made me homesick because it reminded me of my Uncle Aedan's forge back in Ireland. I wanted to cry, but I think I was running out of tears. I was such a long way from home.

I was sitting on a hay bale abandoned at the side of the road on the corner of streets called Liberty and Kansas. Perhaps the hay had fallen off some passing wagon. I was so busy thinking that I didn't even notice the old Indian man arrive.

'You are young,' he said, looking at me, 'yet your face is old.'

I don't think I replied. I thought he was probably right. I was just a kid but I felt old. I carried on sitting, but so too did the man. Indeed, he sat so still that after a while it caused me to look up in case something had happened. Under a wide-brimmed black hat, his eyes smiled at me in silence. He had grey hair and a lined face of deep brown. I knew he was an Indian. Back then people told terrible tales about them, but he seemed nice. To be honest I was too tired to feel frightened. I think I thought that all the worst things in life had already happened to me. After a moment though, I felt I ought to say something.

'My brother Henry ... and my friend Jack, they're buying a wagon so we can carry on. Jack's done drawings of what is wanted,' I explained.

The man nodded. 'You go west,' he said as if he were simply stating a fact.

He was right. We were about to head west in a covered wagon, just like the hundreds, maybe thousands of others in the town. My unexpected companion sat looking at our cart and its heavy load for a long time without saying a word. I think it made me uncomfortable.

'It's a printing press.' I felt I ought to explain. 'You use it to ...'

He smiled as if he didn't need my explanation. 'Yes.'

I carried on anyway: '... tell stories. Make books and newspapers. We're going to make a newspaper. In a place called "Oregon".'

The old man sat so still and silent that I felt I needed to

say something else. In my family there were so many of us that I wasn't used to such quiet.

'My Da made the press himself with my Uncle Aedan back in Ireland.'

'Ireland,' he repeated as if he liked the sound of it. 'You wear funny boy's trousers,' he added.

I looked down at my trouser legs. They *were* funny, I suppose. Not just that I was a girl wearing trousers but that I was Irish and my clothes were silk with Chinese patterns. Such a lot had happened.

Now I nodded. 'We're going to Oregon, and I'm hoping I'll have a horse. If I have a horse, I will need to wear trousers, although maybe not these ones.'

This seemed sensible to the Indian gentleman, who said no more about it.

I'm not sure how an old Indian man and I ended up washed against each other in the sea of people streaming through the town of Independence that morning. You would have supposed there were no quiet corners where a conversation might even have taken place. Certainly no one else seemed to have time for a chat. Noise erupted from every living thing, and everyone was busy being, well, busy. Bearded men in boots and long coats with hoods hurried past, jingling coins in their pockets, while Mexican fellows in bright colours called out in a strange tongue as they herded dozens of braying mules. Their unbelievably wide straw hats hid their faces as they pushed along the noisy animals. Smoke spilled out from the men puffing on foul-smelling cigarettes rolled in what looked like the husks of corn.

Giant wooden wagons – some carrying sacks of wool or the hides of animals, others filled with people of every age and size – were trundling along everywhere. They creaked and groaned with the weight of their burdens as whooping riders on ponies galloped between them, racing through the mud to get a drink at Colonel Noland's tavern. There they leaped down to drink cheap, strong whiskey called 40 Rod, slapping each other on the back and calling out, 'Are ye for Oregon or California?' Herds of cattle lowed in the distance, and every minute, it seemed, new people were arriving from the east, excited by the promise of a new and better life.

I looked at the passing crowds. We had been travelling for a long time and I already knew you could tell something about a person just from their clothes. The Germans looked smarter than the Irish. The men wore neat felt hats and the women had embroidered aprons over their skirts. We Irish usually looked poorer, wearing whatever we had rather than what we actually wanted. The Choctaw man had leggings which were like trousers made from buckskin except there was a separate piece for each leg. They had fringes down the outside and were tied onto a belt, over which hung a long flap of deerskin. The flap fell down in front and behind. On top he wore a plain rough shirt and round his neck a bright red piece of cloth. Like me, he had no shoes. I looked down at our two pairs of bare feet – his brown, long and thin, mine short and stubby but brown too from the dirt in the street. You couldn't tell who we were from our feet, I thought.

'What will you call your newspaper?' he asked.

I had thought a lot about this. 'I like the name "Chronicle",' I answered immediately. 'We had a paper before . . . in New York . . . that was called *Éire Nuacht*, which means "Irish News", but I'm thinking we should try and sell to more people by making news for everyone.'

'"Chronicle",' repeated my new friend as if the word pleased him. 'And your name?' he asked.

'My name is Slim Hannigan,' I said. 'And you?'

'I am Nashobanowa,' he replied quietly.

'Nashobanowa,' I repeated, enjoying the sound of his name as much he had liked the word 'Chronicle'. I nodded. 'Does it mean anything?'

'Mean?' repeated Nashobanowa.

'My Da says it matters what words mean.'

He smiled. 'Nashobanowa is "walking wolf", but I am old. I don't walk so much any more.'

'Slim just means "slim",' I said.

He pointed to the small book I was holding. 'You have a story.'

'Yes,' I mumbled, embarrassed that the story wasn't finished.

As we sat there, a tall man walked past having a debate with his friend about which wagon train to join. It was something almost everyone in the town talked about. This man had a drawling way of speaking which I was learning came from one of the American states down to the south.

'But I don't want to join a train with a bunch of suckers,' he was protesting.

'What the heck are suckers?' demanded his friend.

'You know, people from Illinois. Suckers – like the bit of a tobacco plant you don't want.'

'Better than going with pukes.'

'What are pukes?'

'People from Missouri.'

'Why pukes?'

'You been to Missouri, right?'

They walked on still discussing who they might travel with.

I sat for a minute thinking about the adventure that lay ahead. I thought about Ma and Da and how much I missed them. All I wanted was to travel with them.

Still my new friend sat just waiting.

'May I see?' asked Nashobanowa, pointing to my printed pages.

'It's not finished,' I explained.

He shrugged and smiled at me. 'The end of a story is always hard to find.'

I handed him what I had written so far.

FROM IRELAND TO AMERICA
A Tale by Slim Hannigan

Printed by Slim Hannigan and her friend Jack on
a printing press made by Patrick & Aedan Hannigan

It's hard to know where to begin. I mean, I know perfectly
well that a story ought to begin at the beginning. It's the
obvious place, but it's often hard to know exactly where
that might be. There's always a bit that happened before
the beginning and a bit that happens after the tale is told,
which might just add something to the end. It's like a
journey. There is the moment when you set off on a trip,
but the part where you get ready to go is important too.

Perhaps my tale is no stranger than any of the thousands of stories of those who made a new life for
themselves in America in the 1840s. My name is Slim
Hannigan and I come from a small town in Ireland called
Ballysmaragaid. It's a tiny place which we Hannigans
called home until the great famine came. That was in
1845. That was the year everything changed.

There were six of us then – Ma; Da; my big sister,
Bea, who was sixteen and thought herself quite the
lady; my older brother, Henry, who was fourteen and

liked to settle things with his fists; then me, eleven, and finally my little brother, Toby, who was eight.

We didn't have much but we had enough land to grow potatoes. No one in our village had much money so everyone pretty much lived on potatoes, but that year the crop in all the fields got a terrible disease. It was dreadful because suddenly there was no food. You can't imagine a famine till you've lived through one. We had absolutely nothing to eat from our fields and nothing even to sell to buy food. We were so poor we didn't even own our own land. Our neighbours were the same. In our village almost everyone we knew rented their land from a landlord who didn't live in Ireland. The landlords were English, and ours was called Lord Cardswell. He lived in London, but he also had a grand house in Ballysmaragaid called Cardswell Manor. When the potatoes failed and we had nothing to eat, it wasn't long before we had to do something desperate.

Now you'll think it strange, I'm sure, but my little brother Toby had a pet pig called Hamlet who he loved very much. When things got very bad Da took the poor creature to market. No one was happy about it and I remember Ma waiting at home for Da to return with some money so they could get some food and pay the rent, but Da, well, he never does things quite like other people. Instead of getting us something to eat and a few coins he came back with a big box of silver letters. He'd bought them with the money from the pig. He told us he had met a printer who was going out of business. Da said it was as though he'd had a 'date with destiny'.

We had no food, but Da was always cheerful. He said the box of letters was going to 'change the world'. He explained that he was going to make something called a printing press and start a newspaper which would spread the word about how awful everything was. He believed that a newspaper would help the starving Irish by giving people information. If the world knew how bad it was, then someone would help us.

My big brother, Henry, wanted to change the world too, but not like that. He didn't want to use words. He wanted to fight. He thought Da was foolish and gradually he became more and more angry.

Our landlord, Lord Cardswell, didn't help us even though we were starving. Instead he carried on asking for our rent once a week, but he didn't do it in person. He sent a terrible man called Parker Crossingham to do it. Parker Crossingham was what they called an 'agent'. He worked for the landlord and he didn't much care how he got his money or what state we were all in. When we were all weak with hunger, he still came banging on the door demanding that we pay, but of course we had no money on account of Da getting the silver letters for the pig instead of cash.

Da refused to give up and began making a printing press for his letters with my Uncle Aedan. Everyone was in a dreadful state in Ireland, but Da was certain it would help. Henry had had enough. He was furious with Da, saying that no writing would ever be enough to make a difference. For Henry there was nothing to do but fight, so he joined a gang of boys and men called the Ribbonmen, who were battling the English landlords. It all turned very ugly. Parker Crossingham was so angry he tore down our house, and Henry got into so much trouble that in the end we had to run away from Ireland and head for America. We had no choice. Henry was going to be arrested and sent to Australia as a convict. If we hadn't run away, we would never have seen him again.

We decided to go to a place in America called Portland, Oregon, because Da's other brother, Niall, already lived there. It is as far west in America as you can go without falling in the ocean. Uncle Niall had written and said it was wonderful.

Leaving your home causes quite an uproar and I have found out all sorts of surprising things. It turned out that Ma wasn't Irish at all but English, and that her father was none other than our own landlord. Ma and I went to Cardswell Manor to ask for help, but the only person who was kind was Esther, Ma's sister, who I hadn't even known existed. It seemed that years ago Ma had fallen in love with Da, but he was very poor and Ma was very rich. Ma's family didn't approve, but she loved Da so much she refused to give him up. This made her father cross and he wouldn't see her after she married Da. They hadn't spoken for years, so when Ma and I went to get help it didn't go well. Lord Cardswell still wanted Ma to come home and not be with Da, but she loved Da too much for that. I thought we would end up with nothing, but Esther secretly gave us a small bag of money and some food, and with that we set off to Dublin to find a boat to America.

We sailed away on a terrible old sailing ship called the *Pegasus*. It was a shockingly bad thing and an awful journey. It took weeks to get across the sea to America. Lots of people died. So many, in fact, that they called the boat a 'coffin ship'. The woman in the next bunk to us, Kate Kavanagh – her tiny baby passed away and was buried at sea. A lad of seventeen called Liam Byrne lost both his brothers. Others got very sick, including my big sister, Bea, and a lovely sailor who I became friends with called Jack. I hadn't realized when we left home that Ma was having a baby. I think she must have been awfully weak from all those months of not eating properly because when the baby, my little sister Hero, came along, Ma didn't survive. She died at sea and never saw America at all.

It was the worst thing that ever happened to me, well, all of us. Da missed Ma so much that he went to pieces and stopped speaking. He was so sad and it made life very difficult. Da had carefully hidden the bag of money we got from Esther. Now we couldn't get him to tell us where it was, and we couldn't find it. We found ourselves in New York City with no money, a baby to feed and no parent to tell us what to do. My sailor friend Jack and I had become good friends. I think he fancied an adventure because now he left the boat and came with us. Jack was very strong, so he pushed the heavy cart with the printing press. Thank goodness. Without him we would have had to leave it behind and it was all we had. Liam Byrne, the boy from the boat who had lost his brothers, lent us a little money, and slowly we began to make a life. We had never intended to stay in New York City, but we had no money to travel on to join Uncle Niall in Portland, which was thousands of miles away.

We needed to make some money so, with the help of some new American friends, Jack and I got to work with the box of letters. We started a newspaper called *Éire Nuacht*, which means 'Irish News', using Da's press. We printed news about people who had just arrived; there was a column to help people find family members who were missing, and advice about how to manage in the big city. It was good and people wanted to buy it. A few cents at a time we made a start on gathering the money for our trip west.

Meanwhile we lived in a dreadful room in a place called the Old Brewery – me, Bea, Hero, Toby, Henry, Da and poor Kate Kavanagh from the boat who I bumped into by chance one day. A man who had been with us on the *Pegasus* had sold her a ticket to take her all the way to her sister in California. It had cost Kate all her money, but when she tried to travel the ticket turned out to be a fake. So she stayed with us too and looked after my little sister.

I think we started to get used to life in the city. Da slowly got better. He began talking again. He made friends with Kate, and I know that helped. One day Toby found a pig in the street, He was sure it was his old friend Hamlet. He taught the new pig to do tricks and they were both so happy. Bea also loved it in New York, and we might have stayed if it weren't for Henry getting us into trouble once more. Da says my big brother is like 'a moth to a flame' when it comes to getting into a scrape. I know Henry wanted to help, but he chose a funny way of doing it. He began stealing to get us money and was arrested for it. We got him out of prison and back to the Old Brewery – only to find that the Dead Rabbit gang were after him and the Byrne boy, Liam. Henry and Liam had thought they could make money by gambling but it hadn't worked out. Now they both owed lots of money to the rough gang who were chasing after them to get it back. It was terrifying. Henry was in so much trouble. Even more than he had been in Ireland. Now it wasn't about him being arrested; it was that he might be killed.

A Chinese neighbour called Mr Liu helped us escape through a tunnel dressed in Chinese silk trousers and tops. He thought the men who were after us would be looking for an Irish family and not a Chinese one. We managed to get to the dockside on the Hudson River in the dead of night where we caught a ferry heading south – me, Da, Kate, baby Hero, Bea, Henry, Toby (and the pig, of course), Liam, and Jack with the cart holding our precious printing press. We loved New York but once more we had to leave our home in a hurry and set sail.

The ferry was very wide and had a huge iron chimney. Steam billowed out as the two great paddle wheels began to turn to take us away. We were tired and frightened and it was hard not to be suspicious of everyone else on board. Why were they leaving the city so early in the morning? What did they make of the large and odd-looking Chinese family who huddled together against the cold? Most of the passengers were men. A lot of them were chewing tobacco and spitting the juice on the deck, where it lay in great brown puddles. We had read about travelling to Oregon in Uncle Niall's letters, but he had written about a trip made with wagons pulled by oxen. He had told us about the prairie and about herds of buffalo and dangerous Indians but never mentioned steamships. I knew things were bad that day as we left New York, but somehow I thought it would all work out. I had my family. Da was back to his old self. We had Kate to look after the baby and I had my friend Jack. I thought it would be all right. Even with all our trouble I felt safe. How wrong I was—

Nashobanowa finished reading what I had written. He put the printed pages down on his lap. He didn't speak, but instead picked up a piece of straw off the bale and began sucking on it.

'I don't think all Indians are dangerous any more,' I explained hurriedly. 'It was what we were told.'

He nodded.

Just then Henry came out of Weston's. He was frowning and seemed in an awful rush. 'Come on, Slim. We've to hurry.'

I stood up. 'Henry, this is Nashobanowa. He's a—'

'Choctaw. I am Choctaw,' said Nashobanowa, putting out his hand.

'It's a tribe of Indians,' I explained.

Henry quickly shook hands with him and then said, 'Yes, well, we haven't the time now. We must hurry. Come on, Slim!'

'Where's Jack?' I asked. I wanted Nashobanowa to meet my friend, who had helped me do the printing.

Henry grabbed a handle of the cart and indicated I should take the other. He began pushing almost before I was ready.

'Jack has to finish in the wagon shop,' he muttered.

I waved goodbye to Nashobanowa and ran to help my brother.

'I have your story!' shouted the old man, waving the pages in the air behind me. But there was no time to go back. Henry was rushing along as best he could, considering how heavy the cart was, and I had to keep up.

'What's the hurry, Henry?' I panted.

'We have to get organized. We have to leave before the snow comes.'

I looked at the bright blue spring sky and was confused. 'What snow? It's spring.'

'In the mountains.'

'What mountains?'

Henry was exasperated with me. 'You don't know anything, Slim, so just do as I say. We have to leave Independence within the week and we're nowhere near ready.'

I stopped pushing and stood still in the mud street. 'We can't leave, Henry. We need to wait here for Da.'

Henry was blind in his right eye and he was on the wrong side of the cart to be able to see me. Now he turned and looked straight at me.

'Slim,' he said quietly, 'you have to stop this. Da is dead.'

CHAPTER TWO

S howing Nashobanowa what I had written so far made
me realize how much of the story I had left out . . .

I could still the feel the cool planks of the wooden deck on the
ferry as we waved goodbye to New York for ever. I remember
Bea was crying. For someone who had never wanted to leave
Ireland she had grown very fond of the big city. Henry and
Liam Byrne had sat together on a narrow bench huddled
against the wind. They didn't look up as we left. We wouldn't
have had to leave if it weren't for them and they knew they
were in deep trouble. Da stood with Kate. He was holding
baby Hero and they were talking quietly. Jack had already
gone up to the top deck. He loved boats, and nothing would
stop him finding out how this one worked.

The ferry took us through narrow straits past the places
in New York called Staten Island and Brooklyn, which we

had first seen from the bow of the *Pegasus* all those months ago. Now we were out on open water as we steamed across Raritan Bay to a different state entirely. I had learned that there were thirty states and that this one was called New Jersey. We landed somewhere called South Amboy, and there we saw something amazing – a monster steam machine standing on a set of metal rails. I think I was both startled and afraid. The machine was huge! So long, and with great shining iron wheels taller than me. The wheels were joined together by vast beams of metal. The main body of the engine was made of gleaming wood like a giant barrel to which all manner of brass pipes and equipment were attached. At the front of the whole thing was a vast triangular piece of metal sticking out across the rails. We none of us dared go near it.

'What is that?' whispered Henry, backing up a little.

'I think that's a . . . what do you call it . . . a "railway train",' suggested Kate uncertainly.

A train! I had never seen one before; well, none of us had. I'd only heard of them. You have to understand that there were no trains at all in Ireland, and hardly any in America.

'A railway train!' I repeated. 'Did you ever?'

Da gave a great sigh of delight. 'That is not just a railway train. That is the beast of wonder that is to take us west.'

'We're going to get on that?' I whispered, terrified and excited at the same time.

'I don't think so,' said Liam, who in no time had gone from a tough guy to a fellow who couldn't stop shaking.

'I think' – Da looked at the monster machine carefully – 'that we go in there!' He pointed to a carriage pulled behind the huge engine, then shook his head in amazement. 'Did you ever think you would live to see such a thing?'

Toby said nothing. His mouth hung open in amazement, while even Hamlet the pig, who never noticed much except food, came to a halt by his side.

'What do you do?' I asked in disbelief at the size of the thing.

'You climb aboard, I imagine,' answered Da. He was the first one of us who dared to move closer.

'I think it looks like something designed to kill you, not take you anywhere,' whispered Henry.

Even Da took a moment to catch his breath before saying, 'Come on now, everyone, you've Hannigans in your party. We can do this! Why, given enough steel and a furnace, we might have built our own train!' Da moved towards the giant thing with a determined expression. Toby and Hamlet followed slowly behind him.

Even Toby, who has the loudest voice on the planet, had gone quiet. 'Will this go all the way to Oregon, Da?' he whispered, as if afraid the thing might hear.

Just then a man wearing a uniform of black trousers and waistcoat with a white shirt and black string tie called out, 'Tickets for Philadelphia! Tickets for Philadelphia!'

Da introduced himself to the fellow, who said he was the 'conductor' for the train and could sell us tickets.

'We'll be wanting to go to Oregon,' said Da, 'but you don't go that far, do you?'

'Nowhere near,' replied the man. 'No trains which go that far. Can't imagine there ever will be.' He took his cap off to scratch his head. 'Long way to Oregon. I reckon you'd need to get to Pittsburgh first. I think you can get there by the canal. Furthest we travel is to the great city of Philadelphia – though why anyone would want to travel on from there is a mystery to me. Philadelphia is where the Founding Fathers of these United States signed the Declaration of Independence in 1776. It is the very birth-place of America and the future of this great nation. Who wouldn't want to live there?'

'Do *you* live there?' asked Da.

'I do indeed,' said the man with pride.

Da bought the tickets. When we first arrived in New York we had borrowed money from Liam. Now he had nothing and it was us who lent him his fare. I felt sorry for him. He was not having a good time. Everyone was cross with him, but Bea was especially furious. She wouldn't speak to him or even look at his face. She blamed him entirely for making Henry misbehave again and us having to leave the big city.

'Here's your ticket, Jack,' said Da, but Jack had other ideas.

'I'm not going on that thing,' he declared, setting down the handles of the cart on which he pushed our printing press. He spread his legs wide like I'd seen him do when he had to steady himself on the big sailing ship in a storm. He looked as though he would never move again.

'Well, if Jack doesn't want to . . .' began Liam, clearly delighted that someone else was afraid.

I laughed. 'Liam Byrne, you're scared!'

'I'm not!' he declared.

Suddenly I knew how to get him moving. I pointed to somewhere behind him. 'Look!' I called. 'There's a member of the Dead Rabbit gang!'

Liam shrieked and tried to hide behind Jack.

It was only when I laughed that he realized he was being teased.

My baby sister began to cry and Kate tried to comfort her.

'You shouldn't joke, Slim,' said Kate as she rocked the baby. 'We shouldn't laugh about it. Those men might still be after us.'

The conductor looked at us suspiciously when he heard this, obviously hoping we weren't going to cause trouble.

'Why you folks dressed as Chinese?' he asked. 'You don't look Chinese up close.'

'Patrick!' whispered Kate, afraid.

'Why!' declared Da as if there was the simplest explanation. 'We work . . . we work . . .' I could see he was trying to think of a good story. His face lit up as he announced, 'We work in the circus! And such a circus as you'll never have seen before. It may be, Mr Conductor, that you have seen horses do great tricks! Perhaps even an elephant! But where in all your born days have you ever seen a pig who can do such marvels?! It's all based on Chinese magic, which we learned many years ago while travelling the Orient in these very clothes! Look and marvel!'

Da winked at Toby, who immediately got Hamlet to walk on his back legs. The two of them had quite an act worked out by now. Toby was amazing with animals and he had taught Hamlet all sorts of tricks. My little brother got a ball out of his pocket and chucked it in the air for Hamlet to catch on his nose and throw back. Then Toby knelt down on one knee and the pig jumped over it before sliding to a halt on his bottom. The conductor was impressed but I don't think he had noticed Hamlet before, and now started discussing how much it would cost to take a pig on the train.

'It's three dollars each to take you to Philadelphia, but

we've never had a pig before. Plus you've that huge metal thing on the cart. No one has ever asked to take such a thing with them on a train before. Maybe the pig is all right, but I think your cart and whatnot on it are too heavy,' declared the man.

It was a terrible moment. We had come too far to leave our printing press behind.

I couldn't stop myself from speaking. 'But this – this machine – this printing press is just like . . . Philadelphia. It is the future of our great nation! We are going there to make newspapers and books! To bring . . . what do you call it . . . ?'

'Literacy to the poor,' Da chipped in.

'I thought you were going to Oregon?' said the conductor.

I laughed. 'Until we heard about Philadelphia. Right, everyone?'

I turned to my family and glared at them to agree with me.

Suddenly an unmistakable New York voice boomed out from behind us, declaring, 'What a thing!' A very tall, very thin man, carrying more bags than you might think one person could own, was rushing along the platform. 'What a thing!' he repeated, dropping one of his bags and promptly tripping over it. He fell forward, and only our handcart stopped him landing flat on his face. Jack reached out to steady him and the man looked up, grinning.

The fellow then held one hand up in the air with the thumb of the other tucked into his waistcoat pocket and tried to stand still as if he were about to have his portrait painted but he was too excited and kept fidgeting.

Bea took a loud breath of annoyance, and I don't blame her. He was quite the dandy, and a bit too pleased with himself. He wore a beautiful dark suit with a fine white shirt, a black-and-grey-checked tie with a great fat knot at his neck and the most luxurious emerald-green tartan silk waistcoat I had ever seen. It was like a field of Ireland round his middle. His brown hair was parted at the side but it was so curly that it refused to lie down. He kept order on his face by having the neatest of beards, which was permitted only to grow beneath his jawline. He had a pair of wire spectacles, and a fine silver chain hung around his neck, disappearing in a great curve into a waistcoat pocket.

He tried to calm himself as he stood there, but he was almost breathless with excitement. 'A printing press and now this!' He gestured to the train. 'Well, I . . . Who could imagine such a thing! I mean, I've tried. I've read about them, you see.' He turned to Da to explain. 'But you have to actually stand here and see the size of it to—'

Suddenly he turned as if we were all at a public meeting and he was making a speech. 'Ladies and gentlemen, and indeed boys and girls, who . . .' He took a second look at us. 'Well, who appear to be from the Chinese community . . .' He looked more closely at Bea. 'And yet the red hair makes this unlikely . . . Be that as it may, I wonder how many of you are aware that in this very moment *you*' – he appeared to look each one of us in the eye before continuing – '*you* are in the presence of the future?'

'What's he talking about?' whispered Toby.

'The train!' breathed Da, delighted by this turn of events.

The man began to march up and down alongside the giant engine. 'I suspect not even our fine conductor here, a man clearly equipped for this job of supreme importance . . .'

The conductor was delighted with this compliment and beamed at everyone.

'. . . not even our fine conductor can truly appreciate the glories of this wondrous machine. This is the *John Bull*, and this is the machine which will change the face of America for ever. Why, one day we shall barrel across the Great American Desert on tracks laid as far as the eye can see. We shall be powered by such steam that we might arrive in California in weeks – yes, weeks, not months! Can you imagine such a thing? And here's a story which will convince you of the power of the human mind. I read about this in a book' – he waved his arm towards our machine – 'obviously printed on a fine printing press such as this ... I read that every piece of this glorious invention ...' The man patted the side of the train just as the driver tested her head of steam and a very satisfying belch of smoke made the train itself seem pleased with his praise. '... every piece was built in England. She came over here all broken up into hundreds of parts, and no one thought to send any instructions. Anyway, we had good old American know-how. The man who put her together had never even seen a train, but he built this beauty in just eleven days.'

Da nodded. 'Just shows what you can do if you make your mind up. I should have liked to meet such a fellow.'

Now a porter appeared with more bags and cases. A large wooden box slid towards the floor and our excitable new friend leaped forward to save it.

'No! No, no, no! Lenses, my dear fellow! Yes! Mind the lenses!'

The man's name was Cornelius Stringer and he was, he told us, 'a scientist, an inventor and a man of the future! New York City born I may be, but I am westward bound. I have come to help found a great nation!'

'We had the same thought,' enthused Da, 'hence the printing press.'

'But the conductor man doesn't want to let us take it with us,' I explained.

Cornelius looked as though he might faint. He put his

hand to his chest and took a deep breath as if even the thought of the press being left behind made him unwell. He turned to the conductor and seemed barely able to whisper, 'Why ever not?'

The conductor gave a sort of sucking sound as if it were all very difficult.

'Never seen such a thing. Don't know the price of it. I am only the conductor.'

Cornelius' eyes widened in shock. 'Only the conductor! Only the conductor! My dear fellow, you are in America, the land where we hold certain truths to be self-evident: that all men are created equal, that they are endowed by their Creator with certain – what is it? No! Yes ... ! Unalienable Rights, that amongst these are Life, Liberty and the pursuit of Happiness' – he clapped the man on the shoulder – 'and the right for you to run your train as you please! You, sir, are not a conductor; you are the very cornerstone on which these United States have been built!'

Kate smiled and whispered to Da. 'I think, Patrick, that you may have some competition here for being the King of the Blarney.'

'What does that mean?' whispered Toby.

'That Da can tell a tall tale when he wants to,' I replied.

Blarney or not, it worked, and without further discussion the conductor, who now saw his job in quite a different light, helped Jack load our precious machine onto the train. No one wanted to 'stand in the way of progress' when Cornelius was around. Now, not only was the heavy press coming with us, we were not going to have to pay for it.

'Come on, Jack!' I called.

Jack helped heave the cart aboard and was so busy with it I don't think he noticed he was now on the train himself. A sudden look of panic crossed his face. 'No, wait!' he cried.

I was busy trying to get Jack to sit down, which meant I almost missed the laughter that came when everyone noticed Hamlet the pig snorting with delight as he stepped onto the train on his forelegs.

Henry shook his head. 'It's like having another little brother,' he said crossly.

'What time do we leave?' Kate couldn't get enough miles between us and our New York troubles.

The conductor tipped his hat to her. 'Eleven a.m. sharp, ma'am. Eleven a.m. every other day, come rain or shine, and eleven a.m. back the next day. We pride ourselves on punctuality on the Camden and South Amboy Railway.'

There were two passenger cars. They were a bit like the inside of a New York omnibus but bigger. Each one could hold about forty people, and the seats, instead of stretching from end to end, were placed across the carriage with an aisle up the middle. There was a door at each end and we piled on with excitement. Each place held two people, but everyone, including Hamlet, wanted to sit by the window to look out.

The driver, with a peaked cap pulled low over his face, stood behind the engine, ready to begin our journey. Jack sat in a corner with his hands over his eyes. I think he was sure he would pass away on this giant boiler.

'It's not natural,' he kept repeating.

The driver had a helper who was already on board, standing by a great pile of wood, which he kept feeding into the furnace, making the flames hotter and hotter. The driver pulled on a cord and a dreadful shriek sounded from the steam whistle, making all of us jump. Even Henry gave a little yelp, which we teased him about. There was a great deal of jolting and the sound of metal forcing itself to move was so loud that no one could speak. Slowly the wheels of the *John Bull* began to turn. There was no hurry at first and you could feel the engine really strain. I held my breath – I think we all did.

It was very slow to begin with, but once we were under way we began to pick up speed. I was terrified and held on for dear life, but Cornelius Stringer had no fear. He put his head right out of the window into the wind. Hamlet was next, shoving his little pink face into the breeze and letting the wind flap his ears up so high he appeared to be flying.

'Give it a go!' Cornelius shouted, helping me towards

the open air. Suddenly I could feel the tremendous excitement of our adventure. I gripped the side of the window and slowly dared to put my head out. The air flung itself at me and my heart pounded, but it was wonderful to go so fast through the countryside.

The only person who didn't like it at all was Jack. He looked ashen-faced and kept saying things like, 'It's too fast! Surely we'll all die!'

But we were fine as the train clattered across the wooden timber that held the metal tracks in place. Every now and then there would be another blast from the steam whistle as the driver warned anyone in the way that we were coming. I'm not sure anyone could have missed us. The noise was amazing and sparks of fire fluttered around the top of the chimney like fireflies dancing. Soon our clothes were covered in fine ash and we had smoke-filled eyes, but nobody minded. As we dashed past trees and fields, heading south, none of us could speak. I couldn't believe how quickly we were travelling. The conductor called out place names as we went. 'Cranberry!' 'Windsor!' 'Florence!' 'Fish Town!' But none of them were for us. In an astonishing seven hours we travelled seventy-five miles to the town of Camden, which lay in the state of New Jersey.

'Seventy-five miles in seven hours!' exclaimed Cornelius. 'It would take days on foot or by horse! I can hardly get my breath from going so fast. I must make a note! A note!' He took a small black leather book and a silver pencil from his pocket and began scribbling. I watched him writing and knew I should do the same. I got out my notebook from Nashobanowa's daughter Emily and began writing too, but the rattling of the train made most of my notes unreadable.

We were all still shaking when we got off. The conductor helped us unload. Cornelius' many bags and boxes were carried to a waiting wagon. There were so many the wagon wheels sank into the dirt under the weight. Cornelius shook each of us firmly by the hand and Hamlet by his front leg.

'A pleasure! A true pleasure!' he kept repeating. 'And where to now, Hannigans?' he enquired.

'We're for Oregon,' I said proudly.

Cornelius smiled. 'Well, of course you are. You are a forward-thinking family, anyone can see that, and Oregon . . . Why, Oregon is the very future of this great country. For myself, I've to stay here in Camden for a while. There's a physician called Isaac Mulford in town whom I am keen to meet. I've one or two thoughts about ether which he might like to discuss, but then – on! I too shall venture forth. It's been a pleasure. A memory to cherish, my friends!'

Cornelius bowed low, then kissed both Bea's and Kate's hands before hopping up next to the driver of his wagon and yelling, 'Forward to the future!' Even as he drove away, we could hear him exclaiming with delight to the driver about something or other. For a moment we stood in our little group, watching him leave in silence. Bea gave a small sigh.

At last Toby spoke. 'Is Oregon far now, Da? How do we get there?'

No one was sure, but we knew we needed to find out. Despite what the conductor had said there was no time to stop and admire Philadelphia, which lay just across the waters of the Delaware River.

'If we can get here so quickly, then so too could those ruffians from the Dead Rabbit gang if they really wanted to,' Kate whispered to Da. 'We should keep going.'

'I'm sorry,' muttered Henry for the hundredth time while Liam looked away and said nothing. Henry hung his head in shame.

It wasn't just Kate who wanted to put as many miles between us and New York as possible.

Da cuddled Hero, who was half wrapped in his Chinese jacket. 'We must keep moving,' he agreed.

Jack was so relieved to get off the train that he hurried to find someone to help us.

'We have to get to a place called Pittsburgh,' he explained to a black man with a large cart and two horses who had been delivering beer. 'Can you take us?'

The man was suspicious at first.

'Where you people from?' he asked.

'Patrick!' warned Kate – she could see that Da was about to explain about the circus again.

'It's a long story,' muttered Da from under his little silk hat. He gave the man some money and we all climbed aboard while Jack walked alongside with the cart.

The man was called Joseph. I sat squeezed in between him and Kate at the front. Joseph liked to talk.

'Great city, Philadelphia,' he told us. 'A black man can even own a business and make something of himself. I met a man called James Forten once. He's gone now, but he made sails for a living and was richer than most white folks.'

I couldn't understand why he told us this.

'Can't *anyone* own a business?' I asked. I had had a business in New York and I was only a child.

'Not if you're a slave,' he explained.

'Are you a slave?'

He shook his head and smiled. 'I was, but now I'm a free man making my own way.'

'What's a slave?' asked Toby.

Joseph laughed. 'Every child ought to have no idea what the word "slave" means.'

'It's when a man is owned by another man,' explained Da behind me.

'Can anyone own anyone in America?' I asked. 'Could someone own me?'

Da laughed. 'As if anyone could own you, Slim.'

Joseph shook his head. 'It's only black people who can be owned by white people, and then only in some of the states here in America. Where we are now is called a "free" state, and every man, black or white, may do as he pleases, but there are places where no black person, man, woman or child, is free.'

'That's terrible,' I said.

'Yes it is,' agreed Joseph firmly.

Despite being in trouble Henry couldn't help saying, 'Lord Cardswell owned us.'

'You know nothing about him, Henry,' said Da sharply, and Henry knew enough to be quiet. But I was desperate to know more about the old man I had met up at the big house with Ma.

'Tell us, Da,' I pleaded, 'about Lord Cardswell. He was Ma's father, wasn't he? So he's my grandfather, but if he was, then why did we never meet him? And what about Esther? She was Ma's sister, but how come . . . ?'

I had so many questions I wanted to ask Da, but my head was getting too foggy to think. My voice trailed off.

'You're tired, Slim. Rest now,' said Da softly.

The lack of sleep from the night before, the worry over Henry while we were in New York, and the excitement of the ferry and the train had all been too much.

The small wagon jogged along and my head began to droop. Without thinking I rested my cheek on Kate's shoulder.

'Ssh!' she soothed, reaching out to stroke my hair. I drifted off, and for one brief, wonderful moment I thought that she was Ma.

Next it was time for another boat, this time on the Pennsylvania Canal. The new one was nothing like the *Pegasus* or even the Camden ferry. It was narrow and not very big: only about forty feet long and eleven feet wide as the water we were on was not a real river at all. It was what was called 'a canal'.

'Man-made,' explained Da, 'which is why there isn't much of it. I mean, imagine digging this.'

It didn't matter that the water was so small and flat; it instantly turned Jack back into a happy sailor. Where he had been afraid of the train, now he strutted towards the boat.

'Come on, let's get aboard!' he called, leading the way. 'Got cargo needs loading!' he called to one of the crew.

Jack leaped aboard, making friends with the men who worked the boat, and got the printing press lowered onto the deck with no trouble at all.

After the train, the boat was incredibly quiet because there was no engine. Instead it was pulled by three horses who walked ahead attached to the bow by long ropes: two in the front and one behind ridden by a man with a whip. Having been in such a hurry before, now we had no choice but to make our way gently across the state of Pennsylvania, slowly heading west.

'A heck of thing,' boasted the captain. 'Used to take twenty-three days to get from Philadelphia to Pittsburgh. Thanks to this here canal, I shall have you there in four.'

It was crowded on board and we were all exhausted. I don't remember much about that bit of the journey except that in the night we stopped at a town to let people on and off, and I saw the lights of an omnibus waiting to take passengers to an hotel. In the distance we could hear laughter and the sound of people enjoying themselves.

'They are at home, those people. I wonder what will be home to us?' said Bea as she stood looking out with Kate. Henry didn't seem to like Kate, but I could see that Bea was glad to have a friend. I liked her too, and knew how much we needed her for my baby sister.

We travelled on. I remember when day broke Da pointed out the first range of hills as we headed towards what the captain said were the Allegheny Mountains. Toby got very excited about the frogs, whose croaking sounded like a chorus of deep-voiced singers endlessly following our journey. Jack helped him jump off onto the canal bank and catch one.

'I'm going to have lots of animals!' Toby declared,

triumphantly holding up his slimy new pet. 'I'm going to be the king of animals!' he boomed, loud enough for every frog in America to hear him. He then set about teaching his pig to get along with the frog.

We passed lots of new settlements, some with log cabins, some with frame houses, and others made of anything the people had been able to get their hands on. We saw walls made of old boards, bits of blanket and even a wardrobe.

'This place will be as big as New York one day,' predicted someone, and we laughed.

We glided into a long tunnel, and for quite a time could see nothing except the dimly lit bricks above our head.

There was an old man with a big beard and not the cleanest of clothes who was travelling by himself. He said he had been out west before, and he shook his head at the thought of us going. In the gloom of the tunnel, lit only by a few oil lamps, he began warning us.

'Injuns,' he said darkly. 'You can't trust 'em. Can't trust 'em at all. They'll kill any white folks they see.'

'Not if I have a gun,' declared Liam, who seemed a little braver when it was dark.

'You will not have a gun, Liam, if I have anything to say about it. You're lucky we didn't leave you behind,' said Da firmly.

The old man gave a short laugh. 'Gun ain't gonna help

you,' he declared, his voice low and menacing. 'You won't even see 'em coming when they decide to get you!'

These dark words caused lots of the women, including Bea, to start sobbing. It seemed to me that we had had enough tears on this trip to float to Oregon.

'I don't believe a word of it,' I said crossly. 'Why would the Indians want to kill us?'

Hero began crying, and it was to that sound that we emerged from the tunnel onto what looked like a large, pleasant lake. Here the air was so still that you really couldn't believe any danger lay ahead at all. The water made a mirror picture of the trees and land that surrounded it. It calmed everyone down. Later I would hate all boats and the water they sailed on, but then it seemed so nice.

'It's like my box,' said Jack, looking out across the still waters. He got out his only possession. It was a box that his father had given him and which our Chinese friend, Mr Liu, had said was magic. It was not very big – about the size of a brick – and beautifully decorated with a delicate picture of a river passing by a small group of green trees with great wide brown trunks made out of many tiny pieces of different coloured wood. At the foot of the trees stood a man. Jack was right. It did look a bit like the water we were on.

Ever since Mr Liu had said the box was magic Jack

had spent part of each day turning it over and over in his hands.

'Where is the secret, Slim?' he asked for the hundredth time. 'What is the magic?'

'I don't know,' I replied, 'but what a story it will make when we find it.'

'You can write it,' said my friend with a smile.

I smiled back. 'And you can print it, Jack.'

We had been quietly gliding over the flat water when we heard the loud sounds of steam and heavy machinery.

Jack went pale. 'Train!' he said, sounding afraid.

'You did fine on the train, Jack,' soothed Kate.

'Quite the man of the future,' agreed Da.

Jack liked the idea of being a man of the future, but nevertheless he stared anxiously ahead, looking to see what was making the noise.

We were in a wild part of the world with no towns or villages yet. It seemed deserted, but all the same we could hear wheels turning, engines cranking and ropes straining. A cloud of dark smoke belched from an unseen smokestack somewhere on the hillside on our right. Then, through a break in the trees, we glimpsed the front section of a boat slowly moving up the steep slope of a mountain! A boat on land going up a mountain! What was even stranger was that the boat appeared to be climbing under its own power.

'We're about to go over the Allegheny Mountains,' the captain announced. 'Just a few years ago that would have taken three days, but now we're going to do it in six hours!'

'How?' asked Jack nervously.

I don't think it's there any more, but when we made the journey over the mountains it was by something called the Allegheny Portage Railroad. It was an incredible thing. We all got off, and the canal boat was split into two pieces and loaded by a big group of men onto a flat truck which sat on railway tracks. Ropes ran from the truck up the hill to a shed where a steam engine could be heard throbbing. A signal was given, and the men jumped onto the roof of the boat as it was slowly pulled up to the engine shed. We walked behind, marvelling at the sight of a boat going up a mountain. The same thing happened on five separate levels as we went up and up to the very top.

Sometimes we were allowed to ride on the canal boat and sometimes we walked. On the way up we passed through an incredible tunnel, nine hundred feet long, where two tracks ran through solid rock, then we were pulled by a steam tug, and even passed over a river valley on something called 'a viaduct', which was like a bridge filled with water. I don't think Jack could quite believe each new way of moving forward. Boats passed us going the other way loaded with salted pork, smoked beef, dried tobacco, wheat and finished leather.

'Goods are going east,' commented Da, 'but it's people who are heading west.'

We stopped for lunch at a stone tavern called the Lemon Inn. We had been on a lot of boats, so it was odd to be in a house again. The parlour was beautiful, with red carpet and gold wallpaper. Bea took out the fine fan she had been given as a present in New York – the one with the wonderful painting of the fountain at City Hall – and sat at a table pretending she was a lady. Liam had not said a word since Da had told him off, but I saw him looking at her.

'I thought you liked Liam,' I said to Bea.

'You are too little, Slim,' she replied. 'You don't know anything.'

I wondered how long he would continue to travel with us.

The air was cooler and clearer up in the mountains and everyone started to relax. I think even Kate was beginning to be less worried that we had been followed. Da stood at the corner bar in the Lemon Inn with the other men from the boat and had a drink. He looked so funny in his Chinese clothes, but the barman seemed used to travellers of every kind and never said a word.

When we left, Da was smiling. 'Do you know Charles Dickens had a drink in that very bar where I was just standing? He drank there not four years ago! Imagine if I had walked in and he had been standing there.'

'Who's that?' asked Toby.

Da made a sound of exasperation and pretended to smack Toby on the head. 'Only one of the greatest writers who has ever lived. He wrote a book a few years ago called *A Christmas Carol*. Marvellous tale of ghosts, and a lesson for us all about being kind. Perhaps your Uncle Niall has a copy we can read when we arrive.'

Da stopped in his tracks and I thought he was going to weep.

'Niall!' he repeated with wonder. 'I'm going to see my brother again. How marvellous is that?' Kate smiled at him and he smiled back. I think he was beginning to enjoy having another grown-up to chat to, to discuss things with. He turned to me. 'A brother is a wonderful thing, Slim' – he looked at Henry – 'with the possible exception of your own brother, Henry, who is the work of the devil himself.'

Henry looked away, ashamed, but Da grabbed him round the neck and pulled him in for a big hug.

'Ah, go on with ya!' he said, ruffling Henry's hair.

I remember it all felt a bit more normal. I thought maybe it was going to be all right. That we would get to Oregon and have a lovely life with Uncle Niall and eat all that food they had there. I began to believe that the hand-drawn map that Uncle Niall had sent us in Ireland and which I still carried in my pocket would one day take us up the lane to his Oregon house.

Coming down the mountain on the other side, clinging to the boat, was much more scary. It was very steep and neither Bea nor Kate could look at what was happening. I thought we were brave. Some of the other passengers were too afraid and walked the whole thirty-six miles instead.

'No need to worry,' called the cheerful captain when he saw Kate looking so anxious. 'We use wire rope. Installed it two years ago. First of its kind in the whole United States. Imagine that! Rope made of wire!'

'It's a modern world!' declared Da, delighted by each new discovery.

I think Kate was sure we might slip anyway, rushing down the mountain to be dashed into a thousand pieces at the foot. Da reached out and held her hand and she seemed to like that. At one point Liam stood up to look out just as the wire rope jolted a little and he fell forward onto the floor. A small silver box slipped out of his pocket and slid forward to stop at Da's foot.

Da reached down to pick it up. 'What's this?' he asked.

Liam turned bright red. 'It's nothing. Just a matchbox,' he said gruffly. 'It's mine!'

He put out his hand to take it back, but instead Da brought it up to his eye for a closer look. He frowned as if he couldn't make out what he wanted to see.

'There's a crest on it. Some engraving. I can't read it. What does it say, Kate?'

Liam tried to snatch the box back, but Da handed it to Kate, who looked closely at the engraving.

'It says "Cardswell",' she said after a moment.

'Cardswell?' I repeated. 'Like Lord Cardswell? Our . . . grandfather?'

Da nodded. 'It's his crest.'

'What does that mean?' I asked.

'Rich people have a sign for themselves. Shows how important they think they are,' sneered Henry.

Kate handed the box back to Da, who weighed it in his hand.

'Where did you get this, Liam?' he asked quietly.

Liam looked as ashamed as I had ever seen him.

'I . . . I . . . I pickpocketed it down at the docks,' he admitted.

My father looked pale. 'Which docks?'

Liam could see he was in trouble but he didn't know why. 'In New York,' he replied. 'Where the boats come in with the Irish.'

New York? Why would something belonging to my grandfather be found at those docks?

'What does "pickpocket" mean?' asked Toby – too loudly, as usual.

'He stole it from someone's pocket,' I explained.

'Whose pocket was it in?' persisted Da.

'Maybe it was Lord Cardswell,' I suggested, excited at

the idea that my grandfather might be here in America too. 'Perhaps he's come after us! Maybe he feels bad about not helping Ma when she went to see him. He has lots of money. We'd get to Oregon easy.'

'Could it be him?' wondered Kate.

Da grabbed Liam by the arm. 'What did the man look like?' he demanded.

Liam shrank back, looking worried. 'I don't know. A fella. Tall, with a top hat. He had a cigar.'

Da leaned forward. 'Anything else?'

Liam thought for a second. 'I don't remember. Oh, wait! He had a black cloak with the most amazing red lining.'

I gasped. I knew exactly what that meant. I had only seen such a cloak once in my life. Both Henry and Bea looked pale.

'You're sure it was the docks in New York?' whispered Da, hardly daring to ask.

Liam nodded. Da let him go; he didn't say anything, but we knew what he was thinking.

A black cloak with an amazing red lining. A matchbox engraved with the name *Cardswell* in his pocket. It could only be the terrible man who had burned down our house and tried to have Henry arrested. The man we had fled Ireland to escape.

It was Bea who dared say his name. '*Parker Crossingham,*' she whispered. 'He's here. He's in America.'

Just then the carriage we were riding in came to a halt with a slight bang. Bea gave a little shriek and Henry stood up, looking terrified.

'What are we going to do?' he cried.

No one had an answer. The only thing we knew for certain was that the Dead Rabbit gang were not the only ones who might be after us.

CHAPTER THREE

When we got to Pittsburgh I think everyone was relieved. The boat docked in the midst of a confusing mixture of the backs of buildings and crazy stairs leading who knew where. We were beginning to understand that it was the usual picture in towns along the banks of any water, whether it was a river, a sea or a canal. After the quiet of the canal it was overwhelming to be surrounded by streets and shops and the sounds of people everywhere going about their business. Smoke hung in the air from factories making iron, brass, tin, steel and glass. There had been a great fire in the city a couple of years before, and now the place was being rebuilt. Welsh voices were everywhere. We found out that lots of them had come from a place called Merthyr Tydfil in Wales after they had their own troubles with landlords.

'We could stop here,' said Bea hopefully, who had had enough of travelling a long time ago.

'We're going to Oregon,' Da said firmly.

Steamboats lined the wharf, arriving and departing.

'Not another boat!' groaned Toby.

'Don't complain, lad,' said Da. 'We've a long way still to go.'

The canal-boat captain had shown us a map of America. Before we came I don't think we had any idea how big the country really was. We had travelled about four hundred miles west from New York to Pittsburgh, but there were still thousands between us and Uncle Niall. Now we needed to get to a place called St Louis.

'St Louis is your starting point for Oregon,' explained the captain. 'You got boats can get you to St Louis, but after that I hear you're on your own. No real towns west of there. Just a lot of desert.'

'How far?' asked Da.

The captain shrugged. 'To St Louis? Got to be six hundred miles at least from here. You want to find a boat to take you along the Ohio River and then up the Mississippi,' he explained.

Jack nodded. 'We need another boat,' he repeated. 'I can find that.' And he headed off to look at boats while we tried to gather our few things together.

The Pittsburgh shoreline was packed with people of

every kind. There were all those working on the boats, along with the passengers, but there were also gamblers wandering about between missionaries who handed out pamphlets and complained about boats sailing on a Sunday.

'Sabbath breakers!' the missionaries called out to anyone who would listen.

'Where you from?' was the main question we were asked.

'Ireland,' we would say.

'Where you heading?'

'Oregon.'

And all the old-timers would shake their heads.

'You ain't even had the tricky part of the trip yet,' they would say. 'You wait till you stand on the edge of that prairie with nothing but miles of nothing ahead of you. You gonna wish you never left home.'

They didn't know that we had had no choice.

Baby Hero began to cry and Kate soothed her, saying, 'It's all right, my lovely, don't you worry now, my little one.'

For some reason this made Henry mad.

'Don't say that!' he yelled unexpectedly. 'She's not your baby!'

Kate looked hurt and immediately handed my little sister to Bea before wandering away. I thought she was going to cry.

'Right, Hannigans!' called Da, gathering Bea, Henry, Toby and me to his side. He looked serious. 'We've come a long way, but we have much further to go so we need to make some decisions. Let's start with Kate. I'm not going to have her travelling with us if anyone is unhappy about it.' Da was staring at Henry, who looked away. 'We would not have been able to feed or manage Hero without Kate's help,' he continued. 'So I say she comes with us and that no one complains. Are we all clear about that?'

Everyone nodded, although Henry did not look happy.

'Well, Hero's not her baby,' he muttered.

Da's voice softened. 'We are where we are, Henry, and everyone must do their best. Your Ma would want you to be nice and she would want Hero to be loved. She's a baby and you are a man . . . well, nearly . . . and she needs you.'

Henry looked down at his feet, his face bright red.

'So go and apologize to Kate,' suggested Da.

I thought Henry was going to refuse, but after a moment he shuffled over and mumbled something to Kate. She put her hand on his arm and I saw him give the slightest of smiles. Then he frowned again and shuffled back to us.

'Right – Liam . . .' continued Da, looking over to where Henry's friend stood alone on the quayside.

'He's not our responsibility,' declared Bea. 'He's the one got us into trouble in the first place.'

'But he's all alone,' I protested, 'and we have each other.'

We could see Liam begin to chuck stones at passing boats.

Da shook his head. 'Liam! Stop it!' he called out, before turning back to us.

'He's nothing but trouble,' sighed Da, 'but I think he's *our* trouble. Anyone disagree?'

No one did.

'Da?' said Henry, who since his telling-off had sounded more like the boy he used to be. 'What are we to do about Parker Crossingham?'

I think we could all see that Henry was frightened. Da put a hand on his shoulder. 'Let's have the worry when we need to. He's not here, and right now all we need to do is keep moving.'

Then Da went over and took Liam to one side.

'What's it to be, Liam?' he asked. 'Will you fall in with us and behave, or do you want to shake hands here and say goodbye?'

Liam stared at his own feet. 'Henry got into trouble too,' he muttered.

'Yes,' agreed Da, 'but Henry is my son, so he's coming with us whether he likes it or not.'

Liam muttered something so low that Da couldn't hear him.

'What did you say?'

Liam looked up for a second. 'I don't have anyone.'

Da tried to be kind. 'I know. You lost both your brothers and I feel for you. We all have our sadnesses to live with, but you're young, Liam. You have your life ahead of you and I'm happy for you to fall in with us, but there will have to be some rules.'

Liam didn't answer so Da carried on.

'There'll be no pickpocketing or trouble of any kind,' he insisted, 'and I'll keep the silver matchbox for the money you will cost us.'

Liam nodded and quietly handed it over. After that he followed along as quietly as Toby's Hamlet, doing as he was told and trying to stay out of Da's way.

Jack returned from enquiring about boats for us. He was beaming. 'I've asked around and all the lads say that the Ohio can be a dangerous river. They reckon the only steamboat worth considering for the next stage is a mighty craft called the *General*.'

'Good work, Jack!' said Da with a smile. 'You lead the way!'

We followed him and I realized we'd never discussed whether Jack should stay with us. It was just happening anyway, and I was glad.

Following my giant friend wasn't easy. All along the two- or three-mile waterfront, barrels, sacks and crates blocked the way, creating lots of narrow, twisted passages which were nearly impossible to get through. The noise was incredible. Black deckhands sang while they worked, whistles blew, smokestacks erupted with dark clouds, the waters churned, and everyone tried to shout louder than the next man to be heard. There was rubbish everywhere. Great crowds gathered round the steamboat boards discussing the price of tickets, which had been written up in chalk. Passengers made their way to clerks' offices to buy tickets. Well-wishers waved their hats, and flags blew in the breeze as the great boats backed up, straightened and moved out into the river. With all hands on deck, paddle wheels turning and the singing of the crew, it was a glorious sight.

The *General* looked a wonderfully large boat after the one on the canal. I thought at last we would be able to relax a little as we journeyed on. It couldn't possibly be as bad as the *Pegasus*.

'We'll be all right on this, Jack,' I enthused, looking up at the new boat. I smiled at my friend and then teased him. 'As far as I know, there are no more mountains to go over on a train and scare you half to death!'

'I wasn't scared, Slim,' he declared. 'I was just pretending to . . . to make you feel better.'

I punched him lightly on the arm and he grinned.

Jack went to find out where the cart would need to be loaded and I waited with Da.

'You never asked if Jack should come with us, Da,' I commented.

'We need him,' replied Da. 'We need him for the printing press.'

'Yes, but that's not the only reason why we—'

'Don't worry, Slim. I'll pay him for his service when we get to Oregon.'

'His service?' I repeated.

But Da was already off to find the clerk who was selling the tickets. I didn't like what Da had said about Jack. Jack was my friend. He wasn't our . . . I didn't know what to call it . . . slave.

'How much?' Da asked the boat clerk while the rest of us stood behind him waiting. The man took a long look at our strange Chinese clothes and turned away.

'The boat's full,' he declared without even looking at his papers to check.

Da started to move on to the next clerk, but I think Kate gave him a look because he turned back and began repeating the story about us being dressed like this because we were in the circus. As usual with Da, once he had started, the story became more and more elaborate. Now not only were we marvellous acrobats but we had with us 'Jack, the strongest man in the world!' He got Jack to lift me and Toby above his head, and then Hamlet the pig outdid himself by walking backwards on his hind legs to catch a biscuit while balancing Toby's frog on his nose. It made the clerk laugh and he realized perhaps he *did* have room after all.

'Deckers or wooders?' he asked.

We didn't even know what that meant. It turned out that for twenty-four dollars rich people got a proper cabin all the way with all their food. The poor, however, lived on deck, so they were known as 'deckers'. They paid eight dollars for no shelter and no food at all. Children were half price. The men, however, could sign on as 'wooders'. The *General* had a great steam engine which was fired with wood. If they helped load wood along the river, then the clerk would knock a dollar off the fare. Da signed Liam, Henry, Jack and himself up as wooders on the spot.

'I can wood!' protested Toby in his loud voice.

'Only if the wood comes in splinters!' teased Henry.

'I can help too!' I almost shouted.

The boys all laughed. 'Don't be ridiculous, Slim. You're a girl! Girls can't do that sort thing.'

I was so angry. 'I'm as strong as any of you!' I yelled, clenching my fists with rage and practically jumping up and down.

I heard a woman getting on the boat say to her husband, 'That child's mother ought to calm her down. Why, she's not even wearing a dress.'

Kate moved quickly to put her arm round me. 'Come

on now, Slim, sure you and I will be plenty busy with the baby,' she soothed.

I didn't want to be busy with the baby, but Hero didn't seem to notice how furious I was. She put her arms out for me and I had no choice but to take her. She was starting to smile a lot and it was hard to stay mad.

'Your Ma would be proud of you,' whispered Da as the clerk handed him the tickets. 'Do we go all the way to St Louis?' he asked.

The clerk sucked on his teeth and gave a deep sigh, as if he had had enough of foolish questions from people travelling with no idea at all. 'Stop at the falls,' he drawled.

'The falls?' said Da.

The man nodded. 'Ohio Falls. Right by Louisville. Water drops twenty-four feet down over rapids. Got to change boats there. Get one the other side.'

Jack had chosen well. The *General* was perfect. She was bright white, with two large paddle wheels on either side, each of which was covered by what was called a 'guard' – a sort of wooden case on which her name was painted in black and gold. At the very top of the ship, sitting on the roof of the upper deck, was a small room with many windows. This was where the boat was steered from. Two iron chimneys towered over a long black roof covered with scorch marks from the engine.

There were two decks. The upper one for the rich had a railing all round it, and in the centre were cabins for sleeping, as well as a bar for the men and a parlour for the women. It wasn't anywhere near as fancy down below where we were. The lower deck had no railing and no cabins. It was for cargo and for people with not very much money. People like us.

We made a space for ourselves on the open deck as best we could. It was late spring and the river was rising fast as ice from the winter thawed. Da and Kate made a sort of nest for us behind the giant pile of wood on the forward part of the deck. It was near the furnaces, so I think they thought we might keep warm.

I can't say it was comfortable, but we were getting used to that. Hero had it best as she was small enough to sleep tucked inside the carpet bag Mrs Liu had given us. She lay snugly with her head on Ma's piece of Irish turf, which we had brought wrapped in a cloth all the way from home.

I stood next to Da as he watched goods being loaded. He was playing with the silver matchbox he had taken off Liam. He turned it over and over in his hand.

'Do you think he will come after us, Da?' I asked. 'Parker Crossingham?'

Da smiled at me. 'What can he do to us here, Slim? It's America. Land of the Free!' He wouldn't talk about it after that.

There seemed to be three people in charge of the *General*. There was the clerk who had taken the money from the passengers, the captain who shouted orders and a man called 'the pilot'. As we pulled out of the wharf, the captain stood at the window of the little room at the very top of the boat calling out orders to the crew below. Huge black clouds puffed out of the two giant black metal chimneys as we backed out into the river. There was a lot of shouting, with the men running to stop and start the paddle wheels on opposite sides to steer us out into the main flow of water.

Jack loved the Ohio River.

'Nothing straight about this water,' he said with delight. 'Not like that canal. Look, Slim!' He pointed ahead. 'The water just winds round and round, flowing where it likes and carrying us along. That pilot will have work to do.'

Once we had left the city the pilot was in charge. He was the man who knew the river. He had short hair and a great sweep of moustache, with the bluest eyes I ever saw on anyone. He wore a neat blue woollen jacket with brass buttons, but he also had the fanciest shirtfront you could imagine – all ruffles, worn with a diamond breast pin, and kid gloves and patent leather boots. On the back of his head was a very smart peaked cap with the word PILOT embroidered in gold.

'He's a legend on the Ohio river,' Jack said admiringly, 'the crew say he's king of these waters.'

His name was Boisseau, I think, but everyone called him 'Chief'. It was said that he could steer a steamboat full of goods and passengers across just twenty-four inches of water.

'I'll get you safe down to the falls,' he declared.

It was good that he was so confident. Even I could see that the river was not easy. It had great sandbanks which could stop a steamboat midstream. We quickly learned that the trick for the pilot was to stay as close to the banks as possible, where the water was calmer and the current not so strong. Night and day he called out for the crew to lift the heavy metal shaft on one of the paddle wheels to stop it. Then they would run across the deck to throw a lever to start the other one and we would change direction. Bells would ring from the pilot house and the crew would run. No sooner had we gone one way than the bells would sound again to go the other way. It was just like going from side to side in the wind on the *Pegasus*, but much louder.

In fact, everything was loud. At night we passed lots of boats like ours. It was amazing because all of them had a great belly of fire which spat and roared out into the dark. In places, the river had hardly any water, so during the day there were constant shouts as someone checked just how much clearance we had. No one wanted to get stuck on a sandbank. A piece of lead on a string was lowered from the deck and the 'leadsman' called out the distance it had dropped into the water before hitting sand.

'Mark three! Quarter less three!' you would hear, and the pilot would change direction. Sometimes the river was so shallow that they just used a pole to check the depth. At night the pilot would send men out in a small boat to search for the deepest water while he watched from the pilot house with a spyglass. They would carry a paper lantern with a candle fastened to it, so the pilot could still see the signal as the crewman raised an oar to show where the *General* could move forward. I remember those nights.

'Block all lights on board,' called the pilot. Heavy tarpaulins made of canvas would be wrapped round the furnaces. Even the cigars of the men on the cabin deck had to be put out so that nothing disturbed the view from the pilot house. There weren't that many towns along the way in those days and it was dark. The starlight would throw heavy shadows over the shoreline, making every tree branch appear solid. Sometimes grey mist smudged all shapes and you could see nothing but gloom.

Despite all the checking, occasionally we hit a reef anyway and the boat would have to force its way over the bar of sand beneath us. Every bit of power would be needed from the engines, and the boat would shift and jerk as the pilot tried to steer her. Sometimes it was impossible, and the *General* would mount an obstacle before plunging ahead, out of control. It could be a mile or more before he could steer her properly once more. It was really tricky work, but all the time he stood on the top deck smiling, his bright blue eyes shining.

Da admired him. 'There's a man who loves his job,' he said.

Every thirty miles or so we would pull in to the bank, and all the men who had signed up to help with the wood went ashore to 'wood up'. It was hard work. Each man had to carry six or seven logs, each one four or five feet long, over their shoulders.

'I can't,' moaned Liam as he tried to heave a particularly large piece of wood onto the deck.

'I've got it!' cried Jack, grabbing the load off him and jumping on and off the boat as if it were nothing. Jack was so happy that I began to worry he might never leave the boat. That he might leave me instead.

Liam saw Da coming back with more wood and went back to work.

While the wooders worked, we 'deckers' went ashore to get what food we could. It was always very expensive. Everyone along the shore was busy trying to make money.

One day Bea and I were buying food when we met a cowboy riding past on his horse. He had the smartest white hat, silver guns and a black horse that he just nudged with his knees to get it to do what he wanted.

He caught me staring at him. 'Morning, little one,' he said, touching the brim of his hat with his finger.

'Wow!' I sighed.

We watched him ride away as if he hadn't a care in the world.

Bea laughed. 'You going to marry a cowboy like that one day?' she teased.

I shook my head. 'I'm not going to marry a cowboy,' I said, my mind made up. 'I'm going to *be* one!'

We ate a lot of things we had never tried before, like deer meat and Indian corn cakes. Sometimes there were buckwheat cakes, pancakes, wheaten bread and skimmed milk or buttermilk for sale. There was a man on the open deck who never bought anything. All he wore was a pair of trousers. He had no shirt or shoes.

'Aren't you hungry?' asked Kate.

He smiled and said, 'I sold most of my clothes to pay for the trip. I can't afford food.'

Kate felt sorry for him and gave him some of ours.

'What the hell are you doing?' exploded Henry. 'That's not yours to give, Kate.'

'Henry!' said Da. 'You'll kindly remember where you're

from. We're Irish, so we share what we have, and don't you be talking to Kate like that.'

There were about a hundred passengers but only one cooking stove on the lower deck, so Kate and Bea were always in a queue to use it. I liked the river, but some things were not nice. We had a bucket of river water for drinking and another for going to the toilet, but we got used to it. Nothing was as bad as the *Pegasus*.

The crew also slept on the open deck. Their meals were served in iron pots with a piece of hard biscuit to use as a spoon. Mostly they ate the leftovers of cabin passengers. You'd hear the cry 'Grub pile!' and the next thing you knew there would be forty men all clawing at the large pots. The crew were a mix of Irish, who complained loudly about everything, and slaves who just ate quietly.

A few slaves were not working but being transported to St Louis in chains. I'd never seen human beings chained up before. The heavy metal cut into their ankles and they could hardly move. It was horrible. I tried to talk to them but their master shooed me away.

'No one should be in chains,' I said to Henry.

Henry agreed and the old anger came out in him. He couldn't keep it to himself.

'What happened to all men being created equal?' he shouted across to the man in charge of the slaves. 'You should be ashamed of yourself.'

The slave owner was a big fellow who immediately moved as if to punch my brother.

Henry squared up to him, holding up his fists and calling out, 'Go on then! I'm ready for you!'

Da stepped between them. 'It's all right,' he said to the man. 'He's just a boy. Let him be.'

The man spat on the deck. 'Your *boy* should shut his mouth.' He turned and walked away, and Da had to put his hand on Henry's shoulder to stop him from following.

'It's good that you are passionate about things, Henry; just mind it doesn't get you into more hot water.'

The river was busy with traffic and we saw lots of other boats steaming along. There was everything from grand ships, where you could hear music entertaining the rich people, to just a rough raft of logs lashed together by people too poor to make the passage any other way. I remember standing at the railings, looking out with Da.

'It's incredible, Slim,' he said, 'these rivers so far from home. It wasn't that long ago that their surface was ruffled only by wild animals or the occasional gliding of an Indian canoe. Now look. Look at those boats carrying the produce of one of the most fertile regions of the world. It's remarkable. It's a privilege to be part of it.'

And I did feel that then. I loved the trip. I loved the curving shorelines covered with low hanging trees, colourful shrubs and flowers, even the smell of the burning wood in the furnaces mixed with the whiff of fresh paint, tar and oil on the deck.

'Surely no one will ever be able to find us?' whispered Kate one night, and I think we all agreed. There were many miles now between us and New York.

After three days we reached a place called Cincinnati. It was quite big but it's not one of the towns that I recall. In my mind's eye I see the white churned water, the passing current against the bow and the flocks of birds that seemed to follow us above. An American flag fluttered from the stern of the boat and I was so proud to be a new citizen.

Not everyone was quite so content. Liam and Bea had a falling-out. One night I heard her say, 'You leave me alone, Liam Byrne. I am not interested. I don't want your attention and I never will. You're a rotten fellow and I'm sorry to say there's no hope for you. Da should never have let you come along.'

I couldn't hear what Liam replied but he was very angry. Kate got up and took Bea away while Da told him to calm down.

I hardly saw Jack as he kept himself busy doing jobs that should have been done by the crew. He was so strong that the captain was forever calling out, 'Hey, Jack, pull that rope for me, will you? Jack! Get that light, will you?'

I missed him, but life on the river was never boring.

There was always someone or something passing by. We got used to waving to other boats, so when the *Pearl* steamed up behind us everyone ran to the side of the boat to wave. She was about the same size as the *General*.

We weren't the only boat with a pilot famous for guiding his boats safely in all weathers. The *Pearl* had one too.

'There's going to be trouble,' said Jack, coming to stand beside me and look at the other boat.

'Why?' I asked.

'Their pilot hates ours. They both want to be king of the river,' he explained.

Our boat seemed to slow a little to allow time for the *Pearl* to get alongside us. I think we all knew that a race was going to start. Our pilot stood in the pilot house staring as the *Pearl* now tried to sail past him. He gripped the rail with clenched hands and immediately called for the engine fires to be stoked. There was no way he was going to allow another boat, especially this one, to pass. The crew knew their own reputation was at stake and now they began running to do their jobs. The wooders all dashed to help feed the fire. We all felt we belonged to the *General* now, so Henry, Jack, Liam and Da were quick to help. Steam belched from the engine and the passengers on both boats began hanging over the rails shouting encouragement. The race was underway.

Each pilot tried to get the best of the river, the fastest

part of the current. They both wanted the same patch of water and began steering as close to each other as possible, so close that they brushed against each other and there was a great bang. Several passengers fell to the deck, including Kate, who had been holding Hero.

She picked herself up, shouting, 'Patrick!' and ran to put the baby back in the carpet bag to keep her safe.

Da was busy with Liam, Henry and Jack, helping to put wood on the fire. They were all covered in soot and supposed to stay at their posts, but Da leaped to help Kate while the boys ran to the side of the boat to have a look.

'Go on with you!' shouted Liam at the *Pearl* as she raced alongside.

'You'll never catch us!' yelled Henry, and they both began screaming and banging the rail with their fists as the boats separated and once more raced on.

'Sandbar ahead, Chief!' called the man on lookout at the front of the boat, and the pilot sounded the bells to turn the *General* hard to the right. Jack sprinted back to the furnace to load more wood on the fire. The flames leaped high, lighting his face in orange and red. The *Pearl* moved left towards the centre of the river at the same moment, and once more the two huge steam vessels cracked into each other. This time the wooden guards, which protected the paddle wheels on both ships, locked and we sped through the water with the boats tangled together.

It was crazy and I thought both pilots had lost their mind. We roared on round a curve and past the town of Louisville. It was all anyone could do to hang on. Louisville was where we were supposed to change boats but our pilot wasn't thinking about that. He would not give in. The *General* was still attached to the *Pearl*. There was a terrible crunching sound as the wood tore and splintered.

The pilot yelled to the deck below, 'Stoke the fires! Stoke the fires!'

Jack and the crew threw more and more wood into the furnace, and once again steam poured from the engine. Round another bend, and now the Ohio Falls were ahead. You could hear the roar of the water, but still the pilot would not stop. Small islands of rock swirled past us, and just as we reached the great drop of the waterfall the pilot of the *Pearl* lost his nerve and tried to pull away. There was a terrible wrenching sound as the boats finally separated. The *Pearl* held firm and managed to stay back, but the *General*, that great steamboat with us on it, plunged down the falls.

We fell fast. Everything and everyone on deck flew about. I hit my head on the railing and only Henry's quick thinking stopped me from flying into the water. He grabbed me as I slipped past and pulled me back into the boat. Kate and Bea clung together and were only stopped from being thrown into the river by Jack's giant body. He stood with his arms and legs spread out, clinging onto the ship and making a sort of human net for them. At one point the carpet bag holding Hero escaped from Kate's grasp. It slid across the deck. No one was close enough to stop it moving towards the edge of the boat. Another great shudder and the bag with my baby sister in it bounced against a crate. I screamed but no one could hear me over the roar. Jack was too busy holding onto Kate and Bea to notice. Toby and Hamlet banged into the great woodpile. The bag kept sliding along the deck towards the railing. Just as it reached the edge I saw Liam flying through the air. He fell with a great thud on the wooden deck and put his arm out with all his might. The bag was over the rail and about to plunge into the water as he grabbed it by the handle and pulled it back. Liam tried to get to his feet but there were violent splashes of water all around us. He lost his footing and just managed to throw the bag safely to Jack before falling to the deck once more. Jack clutched Hero, and I was so relieved she was safe that I dared to look around and was just in time to see Da fly from the deck out into the wild river.

'No!' I cried as if it was the last word I would ever say.

The breath was taken from my body but there was no time to think. I clung to the railings for dear life as the *General* flattened out at the foot of the falls and the impact made her spin round and round. I saw Liam get up and try to hang on, but there was one more furious jolt of the boat and he too flew across the railings and out into the Ohio.

It was miles before the ship was steady again. Miles before I could get to the captain and beg him to turn round, to look for my father. By then both Da and Liam had disappeared.

CHAPTER FOUR

'We have to go back,' I sobbed, but the captain would not listen. He was furious with the pilot. Goods and passengers had been lost overboard and all he could think about was the insurance. We didn't stop anywhere for anyone to get off, and the further we travelled the more impossible looking for my beloved Da seemed to be.

'Where are we going, Jack?' I asked, bewildered.

Jack shook his head in despair. 'The crew say the captain has fallen out with the pilot over what happened. He won't stop now till we get to St Louis. Someone said there are courts there and I think he'll have him arrested.'

On we steamed. Even the people who had missed their stop at Louisville were made to travel on.

'Henry! Make them go back!' I pleaded, and he tried. He tried his best but it was no use. It was too much to bear.

Everything on board was chaos. Kate had banged her head and it needed bandaging.

Toby didn't seem to understand what had happened. He was sobbing and kept saying, 'I've lost my frog! I've lost my frog!'

'It can swim,' I heard Bea shout at him. 'I can't believe you're worrying about a frog!'

Bea never shouted. Everything was wrong. I went back to the spot on the deck where I had last seen Da. I don't know if I thought he might suddenly reappear. Maybe I had been mistaken. That was when I found his penknife and the small silver matchbox. They were wedged into a crack in the wooden deck. Everything must have emptied out of his pockets as he fell. I picked them up and looked at the knife. I knew then what it felt like to have your heart break.

We could none of us even cry we were so shocked. I had had enough. I didn't want to go anywhere and now I hated everything about the journey. Everything was ugly. The trees along the shore were stunted and even the banks were low and flat. No wonder there hardly seemed to be anyone living here. The birds stopped following us and the sun shone with a new, unpleasant heat. We turned off the wretched Ohio River and up another called the Mississippi. Where the two rivers joined looked like a dismal swamp where some half-built houses were rotting away. The miserable Mississippi was the worst water we had seen: slimy, like an enormous ditch of liquid mud. It was wide and the current was strong, but huge logs and sometimes whole trees joined together in the water to block our way like great rafts. The tangled roots looked like matted hair and the swirling water made me think of snakes. We kept hitting floating timber and I felt so terrible that each bang on the hull made me wish we would sink.

We arrived at St Louis a few days later. No one had listened to us. No one had looked for Da. No one had even tried.

The pilot was arrested and everyone said he would pay for what he had done but we didn't care. We had lost both our parents and now we were alone.

'Where are we?' wept Toby, clinging onto Hamlet.

'St Louis,' replied Jack.

I don't know what we would have done without him. It was Jack who helped us ashore, got everything unloaded and then stood by the gangway to the boat.

'Slim . . .' he began.

I put my hand up. I felt sure he was going to tell me that he was joining the boat crew.

'No, Jack,' I said with all the energy I had left. 'You are not going to stay with that terrible boat. I am your friend and that is not a good idea. I know that you like the water but this is not happening! You are coming with us. I can't . . . can't manage without you.'

I began to sob.

Jack put his arm round me. 'It's all right. I told them no, Slim,' he whispered. 'Please, don't cry.' He stroked my head and I knew how much I needed him.

'What is to become of us?' wept Bea.

Kate's head was bleeding again and Bea was trying to stop it.

'I need your hankie, Henry,' said Bea through her tears.

'Kate's not our concern,' muttered Henry, but Bea held out her hand until he reluctantly pulled his handkerchief from his pocket.

'Everybody stop crying!' he exploded as he handed it over.

We all went quiet. I looked at what was left of my family. Henry was shaking with rage, Kate was bleeding – it wasn't serious but it needed looking at – Bea was dealing with Kate, Toby was still crying and Jack stood silently waiting, holding Hero. I tried to calm myself. I knew someone needed to take charge. I looked around. We appeared to have landed in the centre of the world. I had thought New York was busy, and Pittsburgh too, but St Louis was quite overwhelming. There were horse-drawn stagecoaches everywhere you looked, as well as the big heavy wagons which had massive floors curving up to stop the cargo spilling out. Men on horseback weaved between the carts, while poorer men, women and children on foot carried all they owned in the world on their backs.

We stood right in the middle as people from all over the world milled about us. Sheep, cattle, pigs, horses, mules and turkeys wound their way past us, brushing my shoulders and legs while men shouted to keep their flocks together.

'Letters for Oregon!' called a man. 'I'm taking letters to Oregon.'

Da had written to Uncle Niall in Oregon from New York to say we were in America, but no one could be sure of any letter actually arriving.

'Should we write?' whispered Bea, her eyes wide with fear.

'I don't know,' said Henry, irritated. 'Don't ask me! I don't know anything.'

Groups of slaves looked down at the ground as they were moved along the road.

'Raised these slaves myself,' explained a fat white man in a straw hat to someone he had just met. 'Good stock. Couple of them worth a thousand dollars a piece. You mark my words – in a few years they'll be worth more.'

Henry and I both looked at them but never said a word. The fight had been knocked out of us.

'Welcome to St Louis!' called out a woman carrying leaflets. 'Gateway to the West!'

Gateway to the West – what did that mean? It made it sound as though no one wanted to be here. As if everyone was just passing through and heading somewhere else.

'Isn't this where we head for Oregon, Henry?' I asked.

'I don't remember,' he snapped. 'Stop asking me questions!'

We stood lost and bewildered as the crowds washed around us in great waves. People were arriving by horse and stagecoach, or just walking. It didn't matter how you arrived or how rich you were – everyone who got to St Louis was tired and dusty. The air was filled with the strong smell of animals, and all around us were people and places selling everything you could think of. We just stood there amongst the constant din of languages – French, Spanish, English, several different Indian tongues we had never heard before, southern drawls and Yankee twangs.

Steamboats crowded the cobblestone levee. Maybe a hundred and fifty or more were docked side by side, sometimes nearly touching each other and often two or three deep. I felt so lost. There were endless crowds calling out.

'We're heading west!'

'I want to see the sights!'

The sights? I wondered.

Boys hired by hotels screamed about their 'favourable room rates' while grabbing bags so passengers had no choice but to go along with them. Others hawked the latest newspapers, sold fried cakes, fruit and nuts. This was not like Dublin or even New York, because Indians were everywhere. They rode by on tough-looking ponies while others loitered about by the docks amongst the trappers with 'coonskin caps' who were trying to sort through great mounds of buffalo skins.

Bales of cotton piled on top of one another formed high temporary walls, which made it difficult to get anywhere, while barrels of whiskey and molasses, crates of heavy machinery, travel trunks and carpet bags were shoved in every available corner as if the whole world was on the move. No one bothered us. It must have been clear to everyone that we had no money.

Large, elegant town buildings rose up from the shore like seats in a theatre. It was quite the place, but I didn't care about any of it. None of us moved. I knew I had to do something.

'We have to go back,' I said determinedly. 'We have to go and look for Da.'

'And Liam,' added Bea quietly. I think my big sister felt bad that she and Liam had had words. He had fallen overboard saving Hero. Bea had never meant to be mean to him.

Kate was trembling and pale. 'Slim's right. We can't just leave him there. He wasn't that far from land. Surely there must be some hope.'

'It's too far to go back,' said Henry.

He was right, but we didn't know how to go forward either.

'I want to find Da, but what if we go back and find Parker Crossingham instead?' declared Henry. 'What shall we do?'

'We need a boat,' said Jack. 'If we had a boat I could go back. I never met this Parker Crossingham. He wouldn't know me.'

'Good idea!' I said, glad that we were making a plan.

But Jack asked around and no one would help us. No one believed that Da could have survived.

'Over the falls, you say? Crazy pilots on those steamboats. Think so much of themselves. Nobody gonna come out of that water alive.'

'That man with the letters to Oregon!' pleaded Toby, standing in front of Henry. 'Let's find him and write to Uncle Niall.'

Henry almost pushed Toby out of his way. 'A letter would take months. Don't be an idiot.'

Hamlet didn't like Toby being pushed and began snorting and butting Henry in the bottom.

'Stop it!' yelled Henry. 'Stop it or I'll . . . eat you!'

'Everybody calm down!' I insisted. 'We need to think.'

In fact, it was Hero who decided what we should do next by beginning to cry.

'We'll need somewhere to stay,' said Kate. 'It's getting late.'

Kate wasn't much older than Bea, maybe five years, but

I think she felt that she ought to take charge. There were no other grown-ups left. Bea had pulled Kate's hair back into a bun to get at the injury on her head. It made her look older. Everything in her face looked strained. I could see she was trying to be brave.

'I'll go and find a room for us,' she said, her voice quivering, 'Bea, you keep the baby.'

'It's not safe,' protested Bea. 'Henry, go with her!'

'I'm not going with Kate!' he protested. 'I'm sorry, Kate, but I have to stick with the family now! I'm the man!'

Bea turned on Henry. 'You shut up. Kate is family.'

Henry went bright red, but still he replied, 'Not to me she isn't.'

'I'll go,' muttered Jack. 'I'll go with Kate.'

Jack stood next to Kate. He was such a giant beside her that I was glad she had his protection, although I didn't want him to leave us.

'It's all right, Slim,' he said. 'We can do this. Don't you worry. I'll be right back.'

Kate was weak and took Jack's arm as they headed up into the town. Us Hannigan kids were left alone with nothing but our precious cart: big sister Bea rocking baby Hero, big brother Henry, little Toby, the pig and me. The five Hannigan kids without Ma or Da.

Henry looked at me with his one good eye. He didn't look so much 'the man' now.

'What are we to do, Slim?' he whispered.

I couldn't answer. I couldn't even make something up like Da would have done. I had no idea what to do next. I looked at my brothers and sisters in our ridiculous Chinese clothes. Whatever we did, I realized we needed to find something else to wear. What had once hidden us now made us easy to find.

When they returned, Kate and Jack had found a room in a terrible part of town where there was nothing but billiard parlours and saloons. There was constant shouting and fighting in the street, and even though it was nearly evening, you knew the noise was never going to settle down. It was awful but we were getting used to awful. At least it was cheap. We sat in the small room not speaking. Everyone was silent. I wanted to pray but we weren't that sort of family. I didn't think Da believed in God, but now I wanted to. I wanted someone somewhere to be looking after us.

It was Jack who stirred first. 'We need food,' he said. 'Henry?' He looked at my brother, slumped on the floor.

'Yes,' agreed Henry, getting to his feet. 'Food.'

It was something simple that we could all focus on so we nodded, although I don't think anyone wanted to eat – I didn't.

'We'll go and find food.'

'Don't you be messing about, Henry Hannigan,' said

Bea, trying – I think – to sound like Ma. 'Don't you be going out and not coming back.'

Henry looked shamefaced at being reminded of his behaviour in New York. 'Bea!' he pleaded as tears fell from his one good eye.

She couldn't bear to see it and looked down at the floor.

'We won't be long,' said Jack as they headed out of the door.

He was as good as his word and he and Henry weren't gone long, but they both looked glum when they returned. Henry handed out bread and milk and then took me to one side to whisper, 'Word has come up river that a man's body has been found washed up from the falls.'

My heart gave a terrible thud. 'Liam!' I said, and then felt bad, but I couldn't think for one moment that it might be Da. 'I'm telling you, Henry, I would know if Da was gone from us,' I declared. 'I would feel it.' I didn't believe my wonderful father could possibly have left us for ever without me knowing it. I know Henry thought I was ridiculous but I would not be persuaded that Da was dead.

Each morning for a week after that we woke up in that terrible room in St Louis and Henry would say, 'We should make a plan.'

'There is only one plan,' I would answer, 'and that's to see if there is any news about Da.'

We would all head out into the streets and ask anyone we could find for news about the men who were lost at the Ohio Falls, but no one seemed to know anything. The body that had been found belonged to someone else. It wasn't Liam or Da.

One evening Kate and Bea sat on the bed counting out our money. It was something they did a lot. We had so little of it and needed to be so careful. Baby Hero was happily clapping her hands in Kate's arms. She had no idea how sad we all were and she certainly had no idea that she was about to decide what we would do next.

'We should take a vote,' said Henry suddenly.

'About what?' I asked.

He looked around at all of us. 'Whether we stay here or move on.'

'Move on?' asked Kate, biting her lip.

Henry nodded. 'To Oregon. There's nothing for us here.' He looked at me. 'I know Slim won't like it, but if Da is' – he looked away and continued – 'if Da is alive then he'll follow us to Uncle Niall's. He knows that's where we're going. He'll find us there but he might not find us here. We should vote.'

I couldn't bear the thought of giving up, of turning our backs on Da. I got up and moved towards the window, looking out as if I might suddenly see him. As if he might suddenly save us.

'You go if you like but I'm staying here,' I said.

Jack had been sitting on the floor. He got up slowly. He was so big that the small chest of drawers shook. He walked over to stand beside me.

'I do what Slim says,' he said firmly.

Henry shook his head. 'I'm not asking you, Jack. I'm asking the family.'

'If we're voting, Henry, then everyone gets a say,' I said, just as firmly.

Henry looked at me as if he might start a fight but then said, 'I vote we go.' He clenched his jaw and moved to stand on the opposite side of the room by the door.

Bea watched it all from the bed. Now she got up and took Hero in her arms. She swung our baby sister up onto her hip as she got to her feet.

'I'm with Slim,' she declared. 'I want to find Da. Besides, I don't want to do any more travelling. I'm done. Why can't we just settle somewhere? St Louis is as good a place as any.' She came to stand beside me.

'Toby?' I said.

Henry laughed. 'He doesn't get a vote. He's too little.'

I turned on my big brother and reminded him, 'This is America. It's a democracy. We all get a vote, whoever we are.'

'What about the slaves?' Henry challenged me.

He was right but this wasn't the time. 'Toby,' I said, 'what do you want?'

My little brother had grown since we left Ireland but he was still only ten. He looked anxious.

'Does Hamlet get a vote?'

'No,' replied Henry, irritated. 'The pig is not voting. This is America, not some fairy story. Now vote, Toby.'

Hamlet moved to Toby's side. It was clear they were going to vote together. My little brother's face crumpled as his answer choked in his throat. 'I don't know,' he managed. 'How do I know what to do?'

Kate smiled at him and said softly, 'Do what your heart tells you.'

Toby looked at all of us and then, hanging his head, he and Hamlet went and stood with Henry. 'I want to be with Uncle Niall in Oregon,' he mumbled.

'Kate?' asked Bea.

Kate shook her head. I could see she didn't want to choose, but at last she slowly stepped to Henry's side. 'Your father Patrick is one of the kindest men I ever met. I think he would want me to try and look after you. I think we need to move on and try to find your uncle.'

We stood on opposite sides of the room – three on each side. Jack, Bea and me voting to stay. Henry, Toby and Kate to leave.

'Well, there is no decision,' I began. 'It's three against three, so . . .'

Just then baby Hero, who had been in Bea's arms,

turned her little body and put her arms straight out to Kate. It had become clear that Hero had no idea that Kate was not her mother. Our own Ma had died the day Hero was born. The baby gurgled and gurgled until Kate had to cross the room to take her. Jack and Kate, both of whom had become part of the family since we sailed from Ireland, stood on opposite sides – Jack with me and Bea, Kate with Toby, Henry and now baby Hero.

Kate smiled as we all looked at Hero.

'Looks like it's four against three,' she commented.

And thus it was that my baby sister decided what we should do next.

Perhaps it was the right decision. There was nothing for us in St Louis. All we were doing was spending what little money we had.

'I'm not going unless I get to wear trousers,' I decided.

We found a place that sold old clothes. Kate chose plain dresses for herself and Bea, and trousers for me and the boys. The woman who sold them had a large sunbonnet for sale with roses made of pink fabric decorating it. Bea loved it.

'Try it on,' urged Kate.

'We can't afford it,' muttered Bea, but she tried it on anyway. How Bea loved it. I thought it looked awful – much too girly – but it obviously made her very happy.

'I think your Ma would have wanted you to have it,' Kate said quietly.

Bea's bright red hair seemed to weave itself amongst the flowers. It did look nice. She smiled a little, and that at least was good.

As we were leaving I saw a bright red handkerchief with white spots on it. I picked it up.

'That's a neckerchief,' said the shop woman. 'Sort of thing the cowboys wear.'

I loved it, and when Kate bought it for me I nearly burst with delight. I put it round my neck, sure I looked quite splendid.

'You shouldn't have trousers,' Toby said to me when I tried some on. 'You're a girl.'

'That may be,' I agreed, 'but if we're going to Oregon then I shall need to ride a horse.'

I thought about the cowboy with the white hat Bea and I had met. I wanted to be one of those, and I was sure I needed a horse.

'And where will you get a horse?' asked Henry. 'As if we have money for that!'

Jack asked around and everyone he spoke to said that we needed to travel on from St Louis to a place called Independence.

'I'm sorry, Slim, it's by another boat,' said Jack. 'But there are no waterfalls.'

We boarded another steamboat for another week. I don't remember what it was called. I didn't care any more. All I know is that there were another five hundred miles of river. Yet more water heated boilers so steam could push the paddle wheels churning against the hard driving current of the light-catching liquid mud known as the Missouri River. I looked back to St Louis from the railing thinking it was where Da would have stood. Kate came over to join me. She had become so much part of the family that I suddenly couldn't imagine her not being with us. I thought about her losing her baby, who had died on the boat, and wondered if she was glad to be with us too.

'I won't give up on Da,' I confided.

She put her arm round my shoulders and squeezed gently before saying, 'Believe in hope, Slim.'

The boat was loaded with so many goods that the river water lapped up over the edge of the lower deck. Here the upper deck didn't hold the rich; instead it was covered with large wagons heading for a place in the south called Santa Fe. The hold was crammed with things. Everywhere you looked there were piles of saddles and harnesses, boxes, barrels, tents, and a herd of mules and horses. I'm sure everyone thought Hamlet was something we intended to sell.

In that untidy mess it was impossible to overlook the incredibly neat Honeyman family. Everything about them suggested that they had money and that they were on the wrong boat. There were three of them – mother, father and a small son called Algernon. How Bea loved them. She became all silly and dreamy.

'Look at that dress!' she said, staring at Mrs Honeyman. 'It's the brightest pink I've ever seen. And the collar and cuffs so white and clean! It's like they've been made from . . . I don't know, a cloud!' She sighed. 'And what about Mr Honeyman? Surely those are the softest white hands in the world? His tie is so perfect and that white collar so high it almost tips his head back so you can admire his neat beard and his hair – why, that parting could have been drawn by a sharp knife.'

She went on like that for hours, boring me to death. Algernon Honeyman was about Toby's age but he couldn't have been more different. He wore a bright blue suit, also with white collar and tie. He didn't play or mess about like the other boys, but spent his time sitting neatly at his mother's side.

'I swear the whole family has stepped out of a beautiful shop window on Broadway!' said Bea dreamily.

The Honeymans didn't chat with the other passengers but we could often hear Mr Honeyman say to his wife, 'Fear not, my dear, we are bound for the El Dorado of the west!'

'Is that a place?' asked Toby, but I had no idea. It's the sort of thing Da would have explained.

Kate tried to make friends but they didn't want to. It was clear we were not quite good enough. All we learned was that the Honeymans were from Cincinnati, where Mr Honeyman had had what he called 'huge success in business'. Now they were heading to Oregon, where he was sure even greater riches lay. At night we could hear them talking.

'We are leaving our comfortable home,' fretted Mrs Honeyman.

'For the comfort of something even grander!' soothed her husband.

Not everyone was excited about the journey ahead. One old sailor smoked his pipe on deck all day and would repeat to anyone who would listen, 'Oregon fever! Ridiculous. I'm telling you, if you love your family, if you love good food and a night's rest and if you don't want to make a fool of yourself, then stay home.'

There was another man travelling on his own who was very anxious. His name was Bob and he was full of stories about the bad things Indians did.

'I have to go . . . I have to go to Oregon,' he would tell anyone who would listen. 'I have to go because my wife died and her family is from there and she made me promise to go tell them. She asked me when she was dying. I shouldn't have said yes. There are Injuns, loads of Injuns.'

'We've heard these stories before,' I tried to say. 'And Indians are people, the same as us . . .'

But he wouldn't listen. He shook his head.

'You don't know the Injun. I tell you, he can change hisself into the shape of an elk. You won't never know they're near. I read it in the paper. You might be all corralled up nice and tight and think no one can get you, but that Injun who wants to kill you can sneak up looking just like an elk and then he can pass amongst your horses . . . and he'll cut the ropes where they are tied until he has loosed a great part of them, then he'll throw off his disguise, mount a horse, and with the most hideous whoops and yells he'll put the horses to flight. No guard can stop him, you'll have no horses to ride away and soon he will be joined by hundreds of his villainous comrades in their terrible war paint. You'll be dead in your beds afore morning!'

Bob had so many stories like that, we started calling him Nervous Bob. I'd just try and smile when he started off on another tale. I thought it all sounded ridiculous, but the stories frightened Toby. My little brother would sit staring at a group of Kansa Indians travelling with us and whisper, 'They don't look like elk to me.'

Henry came up behind us. 'Ssh! I'm sure it's not true, Toby,' he said calmly. 'Not true at all. People don't turn into animals . . .'

Hamlet walked past holding a biscuit on his head.

Henry smiled. '. . . even if your animals seem to turn into small people. Don't you worry about it.'

Toby hugged Henry and ran off after his pig. I looked at my big brother. He did seem to be growing into a man. He had quite a beard now, and although he would never see again out of his right eye, at least the skin had healed around it.

We stood looking out at the muddy waters passing below us. I kept hoping that Da might magically appear. I sat on the deck, took his knife out of my pocket and began carving a heart in the wood. Da had done the same on the trip from Ireland – carved his and Ma's names in a heart.

'Whose names you gonna put in there?' Henry asked, but I knew I didn't need to answer.

On the shore we had begun to see signs of the great western movement that was taking place. Parties of emigrants, with their tents and wagons, were camped on open spots near the bank, on their way to the place where everyone 'jumped off' onto the Oregon Trail – the town of Independence.

For a long time Henry just stood silently watching them. At last he said, 'It's all my fault, Slim. Maybe we would have stayed in New York with Da if it weren't for me.'

'We were always going to Oregon, Henry. Da wanted to see his brother so now we have to do it for him,' I said quietly. 'We are on our way and we'll not give up. We are Hannigans. You and me, Henry, we can do this together.'

He looked at me and slowly he put out his hand. I shook it solemnly, and in that moment we made a bond that was never broken.

CHAPTER FIVE

It was late April 1848 when we arrived in Independence, Missouri. The last stop before we headed out onto the prairie. It was what everyone called the 'frontier'. Beyond the town lay miles of nothing. The town itself was not huge, but it was full of the kind of pandemonium we were now getting used to. Animals bawling and braying, powerful black men lifting things that looked too heavy for anyone, people quarrelling, children getting lost and parcels going missing.

I was thirteen now, but small for my age, and I felt even smaller in the crowd. The streets were busy with all manner of Indians in blankets, Mexicans in wide hats, hunters in buckskin, townspeople in tall beaver hats and long frock coats, and emigrants wearing any home-made thing they could afford.

'You'll need the right equipment,' Nervous Bob had

told us when we explained how we were to journey on to Oregon. 'It's thousands of miles across the desert. You best get yourselves to Weston's Wagon Shop on the corner of Liberty and Kansas. I hear they're the finest.' He shook his head. 'Not that that will help you if you get attacked.'

It's funny he should say that because that was how I came to meet my Choctaw Indian friend Nashobanowa. And so here we are, back where I started my story. It turned out that Weston's Wagon Shop was the one everyone recommended to get a wagon that would see you across the plains. Independence was full of people who had no idea how to get ready for their big trip, but Henry and Jack got as much information as they could and began making plans.

'What's that?' I asked as Jack sat drawing page after page of diagrams and sketches while Henry sat beside him pointing and making suggestions.

'These are all the parts of the wagon we're going to build,' Henry explained.

There would be no more boats to travel on, but Jack treated the wagon design as if he were making a new kind of ship for the sea. He did lots of drawings with arrows, leading to a whole dictionary of new words.

'The wagon shop will put together what's called "the running gear",' my big brother explained.

'The what?' I asked.

'It's the wheels and the bits and pieces that hold them

together. Look here' – he pointed to Jack's drawings – 'the wagon will have four wooden wheels, each of which will have an "iron tyre". The wheels are in pairs, and each one will have an axle to turn round on.' Henry pointed to the underneath of the wagon in one of the drawings. 'This bit of wood is the . . . what is it, Jack?'

'The "reach",' explained Jack. 'It connects the front and the back of the wagon, while the "hounds" is the bit in the middle that holds the whole thing together.'

'And this piece?' I pointed to a bit sticking out from the main frame.

'That's the "tongue",' said Jack.

Henry frowned. 'I think they call it that because it sticks out the front,' he explained. They both seemed to have learned such a lot in a short time. 'It's the piece of wood that attaches the wagon to the animals.'

All this, apparently, would be put together by the men at Weston's, although Jack and Henry would make the 'bed' or wooden base of the wagon themselves because that was cheaper.

'We'll only have one wagon so we need to get it right,' said Henry. 'You may not be able to sink in the desert, but it's just the same as having the right ship. If we get our wagon wrong, then we'll never make it to Oregon. Jack's design is brilliant.'

Jack was more pleased than I had ever seen him. I

looked at my huge friend. He was the biggest young man I had ever met, and also the gentlest.

'What about animals?' asked Toby. 'Won't we need help with those?'

Henry nodded. We would need all the help we could get.

Once more we had found a small room in the busy town. It was even smaller than the one we'd had in New York or even the one in St Louis. There were seven of us and only one bed. Bea, Kate, Toby and Hero slept in it, while Henry, Jack and I were on the floor.

Almost as soon as we got back from Weston's, Henry and Bea started fighting. They'd been doing it since we lost Da. I think Bea didn't like Henry trying to take charge. Mostly what they fought about was money. Everyone said a family going west needed between $125 and $150 for all the equipment and supplies. We didn't have anywhere near that much, and deciding how to spend what we did have was not easy.

'You weren't there, Bea!' yelled Henry. 'I was talking to the men in Weston's. If we're going to get to Oregon, we need so much more than we realized.'

'That may be,' replied Bea angrily, 'but you don't count the money.'

Bea had emptied Ma's small velvet bag of all its coins, which now lay in neat piles on the bed. 'I've been over it a hundred times,' she continued, 'and there isn't enough.'

Henry began pacing, which is what he did when he was anxious.

'The journey to Oregon takes months. They say there are hundreds of miles of desert where there is nothing to buy because no one even lives there. We have to take everything with us.'

Kate was holding baby Hero, patting her on the back and quietly singing to her.

'Take a breath, Henry,' she suggested calmly. 'Bea's just trying to help. Why don't you both make a list of what everyone suggests, how much it costs and how much money we have? Then we'll just have to see if we can cross off anything we can manage without.'

'Why don't you mind your own business?' snapped Henry.

Kate had finally had enough. 'Because this *is* my business!' she replied, standing up to him. 'Like it or not, Henry Hannigan, we are stuck with each other, so let's just try and work together instead of fighting.'

I hated the quarrelling so I crawled under the bed for some peace. The mattress above my head sank down near my face where Kate was sitting playing with the baby. I could hear Hero giggling on the bed. She had no idea what was happening – maybe that was best. Then I heard Henry sigh. The mattress sagged some more as he sat down next to Bea.

'They say you need two hundred pounds of flour,' he

began, 'but I don't know because then I heard someone else say it was six hundred.' Henry frowned, his face looking more and more like Da's.

'How much is flour?' asked Bea.

Henry bit his lip. 'Well, I've seen it for two cents a pound.' He was not good at maths. 'How much would that be if we got two hundred?'

Once Henry and Bea had been through everything, it was clear we didn't have anywhere near enough money. They started bickering again and Hero began crying. It was awful. I could feel myself getting angry. This shouldn't be happening. Where was Da? Why didn't he come and save us?

'Newspaper,' said Jack. 'We could make a newspaper, like in New York!'

I wanted to cry, but instead I lost my temper. I think everyone was surprised when I leaped out from under the bed shouting, 'I don't want to make a newspaper. I don't want to go to Oregon! I just want to find Da!' The whole family looked at me, astonished, and I knew I might cry so I ran out of the room.

I didn't know where to go. I ran through the streets until I found myself out of breath outside Messrs Wilson & Clarke, a 'general furnishing store for westward expeditions'. The store had a wooden porch and I sat down on the steps and leaned against a wooden post. There was a slight breeze and I heard something flutter over my head. I looked up and saw a poster nailed to the wood.

It read $600 REWARD! in bold letters, and then listed the names of six RUNAWAY NEGROES, the owner saying he would pay $100! for each if they were found. There were descriptions of them like '*long under lip*' and '*stiff in the left ancle*'. The whole idea of putting a price on a person was horrible, but it gave me an idea. We could make a poster for information about Da!

I was so excited that I ran back to the room where Bea was now on her own. She frowned at me as if I might cry again, but I had no time for that now.

'Bea, can you draw Da?' I panted. 'I mean, his face, so it looks just like him?'

'I think so,' she replied and got her pencils out.

It was a wonderful drawing, and later Jack and I set about making a poster with Da's face and information about how to find us if anyone knew where he was.

We printed a load and put them up all over the town. As the first one came off the press, still wet with the ink, Jack held it up and stared at it.

'I'd like a poster . . . for my Da,' he said quietly.

Jack had never wanted to talk about his family, apart from telling me his father had given him his magic box.

'Is he alive then?' I asked.

Jack shook his head. 'No. He's dead. I saw him die. I just want a picture. I want Bea to draw a picture. It would be nice.'

'Who looked after you?' I asked. 'When he died?'

Jack looked away. 'My uncle was supposed to . . . He sent me to sea.'

'How old were you?'

He shrugged. 'Maybe ten.' He looked at me. 'When my father died,' he said, 'he gave me the box and said he would look after me in Oregon, but he can't, can he?'

I didn't know what to say.

Jack went back to printing. It was clear he didn't want to talk any more.

I was just nailing one of the posters to a post outside Wilson & Clarke when I bumped into my Indian friend Nashobanowa again.

He looked at the picture of Da and said, 'Missing?'

I nodded. 'Yes.'

'I too am searching,' he said. 'My daughter. I go from town to town looking. Now I look here.'

'How long have you been here?'

'A week maybe. Not long.'

'Why is she missing?' I asked.

Nashobanowa sat down on the wooden step outside the shop. It was clear he was going to tell a story.

'Life for my people, the Choctaw, is hard so I sent my daughter to school far away. A boarding school. To learn what I do not know. How to have a better life, perhaps. Wheelock Female Seminary – it is for Indian girls. They changed her name. Emily. They called her Emily and gave her new clothes. Soon her head was full of things I did not understand and she did not seem like my daughter any more. I was angry with her. When she had learned everything, she was supposed to come home, but she stayed and married a teacher, a white man.'

It made me think about my mother and Lord Cardswell. He too had been angry with his daughter because of what she chose. I knew what Da would have said. That we were all the same no matter how we looked.

'I wanted her to help the Choctaw people, not the white man, so I turned her away when she came to see me, but now I am old and I am sorry.'

He looked as sad as I felt. 'She is beautiful. She can play piano. I think she came here to Independence,' he explained, 'but I'm not sure. I want to see her. I am old,' he repeated. 'I want to say goodbye but I cannot find her.'

I had more posters to put up round the town so Nashobanowa and I walked along together.

'Do you have other children?' I asked.

He nodded. 'A son.'

'Is he a chief?' I had heard about Indian chiefs in great headdresses made of feathers.

My new friend gave a slight laugh. 'No, he's a lawyer.'

'A lawyer?'

'Yes. From Cumberland University.'

No one on the steamboat who had talked about Indians had ever mentioned this – that there were Indian lawyers. The thought made me very happy.

'Do you think, Nashobanowa, that if there are Indian lawyers then maybe there could be girl cowboys?'

'You want to be a cowboy?'

I nodded and he smiled at me. 'I think, Slim, you could be whatever you want, but why a cowboy?'

'I've seen them. They can go anywhere they want on their horse. I would like that. I would like a horse.'

He nodded. 'Yes, a horse is good.'

Nashobanowa was nothing like the stories about Indians in the local papers and from Nervous Bob.

I told everyone about Nashobanowa's missing daughter, and Bea said, 'Perhaps we should make a poster for her as well?'

'I bet lots of people are missing someone,' commented Kate. And that's how we went into the poster business.

We put up an advertisement saying we could help find anyone who was missing, and soon we were getting orders from all sorts. Bea would do drawings of the missing person based on a description and then we'd get paid for printing a poster and putting it up.

We got into quite a routine. Jack and I would print at night and then Nashobanowa would meet me in the morning to walk around the town while I put up posters. Bea had sat with him and got him to tell her about his missing daughter. He talked about her in such detail that when the drawing was done it was almost as if Bea knew her. I think it was the best picture I had ever seen her do. Nashobanowa could hardly speak he was so touched.

'It is like she is with me,' he said. 'Thank you, Bea. Thank you, Slim. Even if I do not find her, then I will always have her with me in your drawing.'

He taught me such a lot, those mornings we spent together.

'See there, Slim,' Nashobanowa would say as he pointed to some Indians with shaved heads and painted faces. 'They are Sacs and Foxes, but those ones with turbans, they are Shawanoes and Delawares.'

I learned that the Wyandots from the far north in Canada dressed like white men, while the Kansa tribe wore ordinary woollen trousers but from the waist up were covered only by a blanket or buffalo robe. The Kansa men also wore trinkets in their ears and had shaved part of their hair, except the bit in the middle of the head, which was gathered into a long plait, hanging down their back.

I suppose he and I must have looked strange together, but I missed Da so much and Nashobanowa missed his daughter, so I don't think we cared what anyone thought. Meanwhile Henry and Jack spent the days trying to build the bed of the wagon. It was to be four feet wide, ten feet long and two foot deep to fit on the wheel base Weston's were making. Most people made this part of their wagon themselves. We couldn't afford to buy wood so they were always hunting for anything they could find to use. One day they came back with a large wooden board advertising 'Thayers Slippery Elm Lozenges' which had fallen from the side of a store.

'Look what we found!' said Jack excitedly.

'Are we going to sell lozenges as well as posters?' asked Toby, who was too little to really understand any of it.

'Oh, Toby, never mind what it says!' exclaimed Henry. 'Look!' He tapped on the advertising board with his knuckle. 'This is a great piece of wood. We can use it to make the back of our wagon.'

I thought it seemed a crazy idea, but what did I know? I was learning new things every day.

All anyone in Independence talked about was what you might need for a long trip west, though hardly anyone agreed about anything. Some people said that heading west was no problem. That there was nothing to it.

'Women can make the trip, that's how easy it is!' said a

man trying to persuade Jack to drink whiskey in the 'Name Your Pizen' saloon.

Others said no one should head west at all because it was too dangerous. As well as tales of terrible massacres by Indians, they mentioned even worse ones by some kind of people called Mormons who I had never even heard of.

'So you're going to see the elephant?' said a cowboy I met outside the steepled brick courthouse in the town square.

'The elephant?' I repeated.

'That's what they say – head west far enough and you'll see the elephant,' he replied.

'A real elephant?'

The man shrugged. 'No idea. Ain't never been that far.'

Lots of people mentioned the elephant, but no one seemed to know whether it was an actual elephant or something imagined. Others we met were not quite so fanciful. They told us how much flour, bacon and eggs we would need. What kind of tools to take and what kind of clothes.

'A milk cow is useful,' said a man outside a harness shop. 'You can drink the stuff and any you have left over can be put in a bucket at the back of your wagon to churn butter while you walk. Of course, if you don't like butter you can always eat the cow.'

'A cow?' said Henry. 'Where are we going to get a cow? Bad enough travelling with a printing press and a pig,

never mind adding a cow. Anyway, a cow is a girl and Bea
will only want to get it a bonnet!'

I'd had no idea there would be so much advice or that
a lot of it would make no sense to me.

'Don't bother to bring a cook stove,' said an old trapper
with a finger missing. 'You can pick one up anywhere for
free between Forts Kearney and John.'

I had no idea what he meant.

Every day we learned more and more about the journey
ahead.

'I met a man says we need to make about fifteen miles a
day if we're going to avoid the snow in the mountains,'
Henry said one evening. I had forgotten about the snow
until now. 'They say the snow can come early in the autumn,'
he went on. 'If that happens, then there won't be enough
grass to feed the livestock and they'll get sick and slow us
down.'

Toby was not having any animal get sick so he started
insisting that we leave soon.

'Good luck with the thunderstorms!' everyone said.
'You ain't seen one of those till you seen one in Kansas! It's
like we invented 'em.'

There was a lot of debate about what animals ought to
pull the wagon. Some people suggested mules while others
were clear that oxen were best.

'An ox is slower,' said a man who had been out west

and back twice, 'but patient and half the cost. Might take fifteen days longer than a mule but they don't mind the prairie grass and Indians won't steal 'em. The Injuns care nothing for an ox but they'll steal a mule every chance they get.'

'Indians don't steal!' I protested, but the man laughed at me.

Bea and Kate were busy trying to learn how to cook the sort of food everyone said we would need.

'You want to make hardtack,' explained a woman they met at the grocery store. It was a kind of biscuit made of flour and water. Kate and Bea made pounds and pounds of them and let us all have a taste.

'They say they'll last a really long time!' said Kate, looking really pleased.

I choked on the horrible thing. It was awful.

'I think they last a long time because no one will eat them,' said Toby, spitting his out.

We learned that we were called 'movers' and that we needed to join a 'wagon train', which is what they called a group of wagons travelling together to keep safe. Bea made a list.

For Our Trip
600 pounds of flour
30 pounds of hardtack

200 pounds of bacon packed in bran to keep it fresh
50 pounds of rice
15 pounds of sugar per person in India rubber bags to
  keep it dry
15 pounds of coffee per person
5 pounds of tea
Half a bushel of cornmeal
Half a bushel of dried beans
A bushel of dried fruit
2 pounds of baking soda
10 pounds of salt for each adult
Molasses and lard

'Is that everything?' asked Henry.

I looked at the list and shook my head.

'That's just the food.' I checked my notebook. I'd been making notes about what people told us. 'We also need rope, tools, tin plates, cooking pots, clothes, candles, bedding, things to cook with, something to keep water in, matches, blankets . . .'

'And maybe some shoes,' added Jack, who liked the idea of them.

'Shoes?' boomed Toby. 'I'm not wearing shoes.'

We had none of us ever had shoes but we were about to walk a long way and Kate thought it was a good idea.

'And schoolbooks,' she added firmly. 'Your Da would

want you to do your reading.' She chose a set of *McGuffey Readers*, some brand-new poetry by an American called Edgar Allan Poe and a copy of Shakespeare's plays.

Kate got us all some second-hand boots and I didn't like them. Actually, I don't think any of us liked them at first. The leather pinched as we walked.

'They make my feet feel trapped!' moaned Toby, and he was right. My toes felt squashed.

'I can't walk properly!' I complained.

'Don't be ridiculous,' said Henry, tying up his laces and then standing up and immediately falling over. Bea laughed, which made him angry. Kate was the only one who had worn shoes before.

'You'll get used to them,' she said, 'and you'll be glad out there in that desert.'

'I'd like a horse,' I kept saying, but Bea just told me to 'Shush! We've no money for such a thing.'

Bea did think it might be a good idea to buy some gifts for any Indians we might meet. 'To keep them friendly,' she explained.

'I think they're already friendly,' I replied, 'but my friend Nashobanowa could help you if you want.'

So Bea and I went shopping with him.

Toby was afraid to come with us.

'But he's an Indian,' he whispered when he saw him. Just then Hamlet ran straight to Nashobanowa and sat down right in front of him, looking very happy. Nashobanowa crouched down and stroked the rather large pig.

Toby slowly moved towards my new friend. 'You like animals?' he asked.

Nashobanowa carried on stroking Hamlet before saying, 'If you talk to the animals, they will talk to you and you will know each other. If you do not talk to them, you will not know them. And what you do not know you will fear. What one fears one destroys.'

Toby liked that. When Nashobanowa stood up again, Toby quietly took his hand and we all walked along together.

'I'm sorry,' said Toby. 'I thought you would be scary.'

Nashobanowa thought about this.

'The Indians you meet will probably want to help,' he told us, 'but perhaps you won't speak their language so you could show them you are friendly with a gift.'

'What if they aren't friendly?' he asked.

Nashobanowa smiled. 'Conquer a man who never gives by gifts, subdue untruthful men by truthfulness, vanquish an angry man by gentleness and overcome the evil man by goodness.'

He helped Bea choose bolts of red and blue cloth, narrow red, blue and green ribbon, bright handkerchiefs, boxes of beads, cans of dry paint in different colours, and a large bundle of tobacco.

Jack had the idea of taking a bag of metal nails with us.

'We might need to make something,' he suggested. How right he would prove to be.

Kate's head had taken a long time to heal. The cut was deep and sometimes it would still bleed. In the end Bea had to sew it together. It terrified her, but we had no money for a doctor. Nashobanowa helped her. He showed her how to heat the needle in a candle flame to make it safe. Jack held Kate steady but she was very pale.

'Wait,' she said, and then she looked at me. 'Slim, you take Toby out for a while. It's best.'

I was glad. I didn't want to watch.

After that, Bea kept telling Henry that some money needed to be put aside for a few basic medicines to take with us. We didn't want to waste any of our precious coins so I asked around. Some of the old-timers said that 'A box of "physicking pills", a box of castor oil, a quart of best rum and a vial of peppermint essence mixed with a glass of brandy will cure most ills.'

The newspapers had lots of advertisements for all sorts of fancy medicines like Connell's Magical Pain Extractor, which claimed to 'magic away all manner of bruises and burns', Hewes' Nerve and Bone Liniment, Indian Vegetable Elixir, and Spohn's Head Ache Remedy, which could cure headaches, 'either nervous or bilious'.

'Here's something called Dr Sweetser's Panacea,' said Jack, reading aloud, 'Listen to this – it cures "eruptions of the skin, spine disease, rheumatism, melancholy and falling sickness".'

'That sounds wonderful,' declared Toby. 'It's a wonder it can't pull the wagon as well!'

And we all laughed. It was unexpected. I think we had thought there would be no more laughter.

Bea didn't care about the advertisements. She wanted what Ma would have bought – pain-killing laudanum, castor oil for digestive trouble, quinine for malaria, camphor for cholera and citric acid for scurvy.

The man she bought it all from said we should also take 'a sharp knife to do service for surgery if necessary'. That was not something any of us could imagine so we didn't bother following his advice.

'We'll need a gun,' said Henry.

Even though all the cowboys I had seen carried a gun, it had never occurred to me that we might have one.

'What for?' I asked.

'Hunting,' he replied. 'For fresh meat.'

'And to kill Indians,' added Jack.

'We are not going to kill Indians,' I said sharply. 'We don't need a gun. We won't know what to do with it.'

Henry looked at me and smiled. 'And weren't you the one who shot a lion in New York?' he teased. It was true. I had shot a wooden one in the mouth and won a penknife for Da. The knife lay in my pocket now and made me think of him as I walked around. Perhaps I needed a gun as well as a horse.

Bea and Kate made the wagon cover. It was sewn out of double-thick canvas and made watertight with a coating of linseed oil. Jack made a frame for it out of long thin hickory boughs about as thick as a man's finger and bent into loops. These held up the cover like a sort of tent over the wagon, just high enough for someone to stand up in the middle. The sides were tied to the wooden bed and the whole thing could be closed by a drawstring. On the inside of the cover Bea sewed some storage pockets for her medicines.

I spent all my free time seeing if anyone arriving had word of Da. Our posters were a big success and lots of people found who they were looking for, but there was still no news of him. I asked every new person I met, but no one had heard of a man lost at the Ohio Falls.

Ours weren't the only posters. They were the only properly printed ones, but there were notices everywhere about all sorts of things. I remember one morning Jack stopped in front of a sign pinned up outside an office. He read aloud, '*For Sale – a LIKELY negro girl 17 years of age – of good character – sound mind and body. Any person wishing to purchase can get information by enquiring at this office.*'

Jack surprised me by suddenly tearing the piece of

paper down. 'It's not right,' he said loudly. 'No should own someone else. Not ever.'

It was the sort of thing Henry would have done but I had never heard Jack give such a strong opinion. He threw the paper into the street and I thought for a moment he was going to go into the office and complain, but he walked on muttering, 'It's not right.'

I watched Jack's retreating back and wondered about him. I still wasn't sure why he was coming to Oregon. I hoped it was because we were friends but I also knew it was something to do with his father and the magic box – though I had no idea what.

All Toby talked about was the animals we would need, and he practically dragged Nashobanowa along to help us choose. I think there must have been as many animals as people on the move in Independence. Maybe more. The town was full of long trains of oxen strung together pulling huge tented wagons, destined for some Santa Fe trading expedition. They would move past while the drivers cracked their whips and made a great noise. Farmers would come into town to sell oxen but few of them were in good condition or well trained.

'You need young animals,' said Nashobanowa, and took us to meet a man he trusted.

'There are people who won't sell to you because you are Irish,' he said, 'but this man is fair.'

'Are there people who won't sell to you?' I asked.

He smiled. 'My dear Slim, there are people who don't know that the Choctaw man even exists.'

As soon as we got to the yard where the oxen were for sale Toby ran to the animals and began looking them over. He ran his hands up and down their legs and across their backs as if he had been buying them all his life.

'What the heck?' said the man who was selling.

Nashobanowa held up his hand and declared, 'Small boy knows animals.'

We let Toby finish. Finally he pointed to the ones he liked best. I looked at Nashobanowa. He agreed with Toby and everyone was impressed.

Henry paid for four oxen who would work in two pairs pulling our one wagon. It was cheaper than horses or mules because we wouldn't need a complicated harness. Oxen were attached to a wagon with just a wooden yoke – a loop of wood which went round the neck and then joined each creature to their pair with a wide beam of wood. An iron ring in the middle joined them to the pair behind and then to the wagon. There were no reins to steer them, but one of us would have to walk alongside cracking the whip like a pistol shot.

Our four young animals looked fit, but they had never pulled anything before, and when the man who was selling them brought them out into the barnyard they went sort of mad. They were huge and quick to lash out with both their heels and their horns. No one dared go near them. The man we bought them from said he could 'break them' for us. It was all costing money but we had no choice. After a day or two he claimed they were ready to try and draw the wagon.

Henry and Jack had only just finished building it and they were so pleased with themselves. They couldn't stop grinning as they pulled and pushed the wagon by hand into the oxen's corral. None of us had been allowed to see it while it was being built.

'Here it is!' cried Jack with delight.

Nashobanowa, Bea, Toby, me and Kate, who was holding the baby, had been made to stand with our eyes shut while they revealed their great creation. Now we opened them and I don't think any of us knew what to say. It was a wagon, all right, but it did not look like anything we had ever seen before.

'There's never been a wagon like it,' declared Jack.

And that was true. I knew it was going to be made of odd pieces of wood like the advertising sign; I just didn't know how odd. The whole wagon was the most curious collection of scrap wood. There were signs for beer and cigars, a steamship and even some kind of large balloon people could travel in.

'What do you think?' said Henry, all puffed up with pride.

Toby tried not to laugh.

'Toby!' warned Kate, also trying not to smile. She managed to say, 'I think it's magnificent.'

Nashobanowa smiled. 'It is a blessed creation,' he said.

'I think it'll be the talk of the prairie,' said Bea, giving a tiny chuckle.

I nodded because I couldn't think of anything to say and didn't want to hurt anyone's feelings.

Now our strange wagon had to be attached to the new oxen. The four creatures stood with Toby and grumpily allowed the yoke to be put on.

Once the oxen were attached together, the farmer opened the corral gate. Henry got up onto the seat at the front of the wagon and put his hand on the brake lever that stopped the front wheels turning.

'You be careful, Henry,' called Kate, who was standing with Bea a little distance away, holding Hero up to look.

Meanwhile Jack stood beside the animals.

'I've a small whip, if we need it,' Henry called to him.

'You won't need a whip. We are not using a whip,' protested Toby.

'It's just to encourage them,' said Henry, bouncing up and down in the driver's seat, ready to get going. I'd never seen him so excited since we left Ireland all those months ago.

Well, no encouragement was needed. As soon as Henry released the brake and the animals saw the open road they were off, running like crazy. They had no idea where they were going. I think they just didn't want a wagon chasing after them.

Henry did his best to keep control. We raced after him as he pulled on the reins while shouting, 'Whoa!' to no effect whatsoever.

First the oxen raced to the right-hand side of the street so fast that Henry was flung about. Somehow he kept his seat and violently pulled the reins to the left to stop the wagon hitting a small cart. Then the oxen raced to the left side of the street, and it went on like that, with Henry and the wagon lurching at top speed from one side of the street to the other.

We could hear Henry constantly calling out, 'Whoa! Whoa!' and Jack yelling, 'Stop!' but it didn't help. In fact, rather than calming the huge creatures the shouting seemed to enrage them, and they sped along even faster. A large wooden slogan for beer from the Empire Brewery flew from the side of the wagon and nearly knocked me over.

Now we were all shouting, trying to stop the chaos, but it was only when Toby raised his voice that the oxen suddenly seemed to pay attention.

'That will do!' yelled Toby. I don't know whether it was the way he said it or just how loud his voice was, but the beasts suddenly appeared to be frightened into coming to a halt. We were all out of breath and delighted that the mayhem had stopped.

We were less delighted to see that the out-of-control animals had turned our strange wagon into the front garden of a beautiful little frame house painted green and white. They had ploughed through a lovely lawn and come to a stop by the front porch. Everyone except the animals was shocked. Indeed, the oxen acted as though nothing at all had happened and slowly began eating a rather fine flower-bed as if lunch had been served. We ran towards our wagon and I knew there was trouble ahead.

CHAPTER SIX

Henry was shaking. He had only just managed to hold on and avoid being flung from the wagon.

'Well, that went quite well,' he said quietly as we approached. The two of us laughed together. I was panting from running. I was relieved he was all right but I knew we had to go and apologize to the owner of the house.

'It'll be fine,' I said, although I wasn't at all sure it would.

A young woman with long, sleek black hair pulled back in a ponytail came out onto the porch and looked at our animals grazing on her plants.

'Hello,' I managed, trying to look friendly.

She smiled at us and then at the animals eating her garden. 'I've always thought tulips looked delicious,' she said. 'I'm Emily.' And she put her hand out to me.

Now Bea came running up to help. As she did so, she gave a great gasp and then laughed with delight.

'Nashobanowa!' she called up the street where the old man was slowly making his way towards us.

I realized what was happening. I knew this woman. I mean, I knew her face.

'Do you play the piano?' I asked and she nodded, looking confused.

'You're Nashobanowa's daughter!' I declared.

And indeed she was. We could hardly wait for him to arrive. I ran back and took his hand.

'We found her, Nashobanowa. We found Emily!' I cried, but he didn't seem to think it was amazing at all.

'The animals led you there,' he explained calmly. 'We are all on a path.'

Now Emily saw him and ran into his arms. How happy father and daughter were to see each other. We were all crying and laughing. We were delighted for them and it was so good to be part of something so happy for a change. Toby jumped up and down in excitement and the oxen were just as happy, still eating the flowers.

'My child, my child,' Nashobanowa kept repeating as he held Emily tight.

'I'm sorry if I let you down,' Emily kept saying to her father.

'You chose a different path,' Nashobanowa replied, 'that is all. Now I am here once more to walk beside you.'

He hugged her again. I was so happy for him, but how I

wished we might find Da one day. That the animals might take us to him too. I imagined myself running to him just as Emily had run to her father, and tears came to my eyes. I was so pleased for them and so sad for myself.

Nashobanowa seemed to realize this because after a while he turned and put both his hands on my shoulders and said, '*Yakoke*, Slim. It is Choctaw for "thank you".'

Emily wanted us to stay, but there was no time for visiting. May had arrived, and both Jack and Henry were anxious to get started.

'We have to leave Independence,' Henry declared for the hundredth time, the day after our new animals had reunited Emily and Nashobanowa, 'and get going or we'll never get over the . . .'

'. . . mountains before the snow comes! I know, Henry,' I said. 'I have been listening, you know.'

For some reason Henry trusted me to go and buy the gun he'd talked about.

'I need to fix the wagon,' he said. 'You're the only one us who has ever fired a gun, Slim. You go.'

I'd only ever fired a gun at a fair and it wasn't even a real bullet, but I was so pleased he trusted me. Bea and Kate were busy with the packing so Bea gave me the money and I went alone. I wanted to do something by myself.

The man in the shop didn't seem to worry about me being a girl.

He chewed tobacco and kept spitting on the floor.

'Oregon, you say? You gonna need a rifle – five pounds of powder, I'd say, and twenty of lead. I got a nice Springfield flintlock musket. Been used so you know it works.'

He handed it to me to hold. It was very heavy and I had no idea if it was any good, but I pretended I did this strange sort of shopping all the time. I turned it over in my hands. Then I nodded and said I would take it. He went to get the powder and lead I would need, so while I waited I looked around. On a low shelf sat a pair of revolvers like all the cowboys wore on their belts. I couldn't resist picking one up to see what it felt like. It too was heavy, but I thought I could manage it. I lowered my right hand, holding the gun to my side, and then pretended to pull up quick to shoot something.

'That's a Colt.' The man surprised me by coming up behind me. I quickly put the gun down but the man picked it up again.

'Old and scuffed, but a pistol's better for shooting buffalo from a horse. You like it?' He held the gun out to me and I couldn't resist taking it. I nodded and knew then that I was about to buy a pair of revolvers as well.

Nashobanowa teased me when I showed him.

'Are you going to fire those from your horse?' he asked.

I grinned. 'We can't afford a horse.'

He smiled. 'Well, at least you have boots and trousers.'

Nashobanowa got me some rope and made a kind of belt for me to stuff the pistols in round my waist. Then he ruffled my hair and told me to aim straight.

Henry was mad at me for spending so much money.

'What were you thinking, Slim? I said *a* gun – not three guns!'

I liked the feeling of the pistols in my new belt so I stood my ground. Besides, I was tired of Henry thinking he could always be in charge. 'I earned the money,' I said, 'so I can spend some of it if I want.'

'Yeah, well, those pistols better be useful or I'll shoot you myself.'

'Henry . . .' Kate started to speak but he walked off, too angry to listen.

We didn't have time to argue further because we needed to hurry and pack all our belongings into the wagon. There was a wagon train meeting soon outside town. I knew because I had printed a poster about it. A big group of people leaving Independence for Oregon and California were going to head off together and we planned to go with them.

Our new wagon had seemed large while it was empty but it quickly filled up. There was supposed to be a narrow space in the middle so you could move around and get things out but we hadn't managed that at all. We had tried to be careful about what we took with us but by the time we had packed our stores of bacon and flour, rice and coffee, brown sugar and hardtack biscuits, plus all the tools and cooking equipment, the wagon was full to the brim.

'Where are we going to put the printing press?' asked Jack.

'Where are we going to put me?' asked Toby.

It was clear that no one would be riding on the wagon except sometimes maybe Kate and the baby. There would be a lot of walking by everyone and somehow we would have to push the printing press in the old handcart too.

'But it's two thousand miles!' exclaimed Bea. 'Surely we have to leave that here?'

Jack and I wouldn't hear of it. The press had already served us so well and we both somehow knew we would need it in our new life.

'I can manage,' Jack assured everyone.

Hamlet the pig seemed to like our new ox servants. He happily ran between their legs and rubbed up against them while the packing was going on.

'We should name them,' said Toby.

'What for?' scoffed Henry. 'They're not people. They just . . . work for us.'

'Like servants?' asked Bea, laughing. She looked at Hamlet and continued, 'Then you should give them servant names. Who are the servants in Shakespeare?'

Kate had a look in the book of plays she'd bought.

'I've got it,' she declared. 'We'll have two Dromios at the back with a Balthazar at the front, and the biggest ox' – she pointed at him – 'he can be called Malvolio.'

'He's not very clever,' said Toby, who was really getting to know our new beasts.

'Neither was Malvolio,' declared Kate, snapping the book shut with a grin. 'Actually we none of us know what we're doing so he can lead the way.'

'Da will like those names!' boomed Toby, delighted. I hugged him for not saying that Da might never know.

The wagon had a wooden bench seat at the front and we agreed that Kate and Bea would take turns to sit there holding Hero with their feet on the 'jockey box', a wooden box with a lid containing all our tools and Jack's iron nails.

It was 3 May 1848 when we finally said goodbye to Independence and headed out into a new life, a life which we couldn't have imagined.

'We'll find Uncle Niall,' Henry kept saying.

'Make a new home,' said Bea.

'Da will find us there,' I insisted.

Every few moments a wagon trundled past, already on its way, with children's faces peeping out from under the covers. Inside were piled all the possessions a family could carry as they turned their faces to the land of golden promise far beyond the Rocky Mountains. We didn't have much – a printing press, a carpet bag and a piece of turf from Ireland, but as Kate said, 'We have each other.'

There were all sorts of people. I remember one quite fat old woman who seemed to be going it alone. She was riding a tired-looking horse and holding a faded umbrella.

'Are you all right?' called Kate.

'Meeting my family along the way,' she replied cheerfully. 'Ain't this fun?'

She rode off smiling and waving to everyone.

'Might be some fun to watch Henry drive the wagon,' muttered Bea and we all tried not to laugh.

Henry and Jack had repaired the wagon after its unfortunate first outing. Since then they had been practising driving. It was getting better. The most helpful thing was that everyone had quietly agreed to let Toby be in charge of the animals. There was no question that, even though he was young, it would be best.

'In you go!' he called so confidently that the ox team, led by Malvolio, quietly allowed themselves to be attached to the wagon. I don't think any of the oxen were very happy about pulling a wagon but at least they had stopped running off.

Nashobanowa and Emily came to say goodbye. He was so happy to have his daughter back.

Nashobanowa had been so kind. He smiled as he put his hand on my shoulder.

'Be strong when you are weak, my friend,' he said, 'and be brave when you are scared, but never forget to be humble when you are victorious.' He pointed at the sun above. 'We call the sun *nanpisa* – the one who sees. Have respect for the sun. It has the power of life and death. Don't hold talks on cloudy days. Wait for the sun. Everyone is more honest in the light.'

Emily gave me a book. It was brown leather, but when I opened it the pages inside had no writing on them.

'There's nothing to read.'

She smiled. 'Then you'd better get writing.' She put her hand under my chin and lifted my eyes up to meet hers. 'You are going on a great adventure, Slim. Write it down so that one day it will be like I went with you.'

'It's time!' called Henry.

Kate climbed up onto the wagon and Bea handed her the baby. Toby took up his place beside Malvolio. Jack picked up the handles of the old cart. Henry walked behind where a bucket containing a mixture of tar and tallow to lubricate the wheels dangled from the rear axle. I gave Nashobanowa a final hug.

'Come with me?' I pleaded. 'You would know what to do.'

He smiled. 'I wish I had one more adventure in me but I am old, little one,' he replied.

'Not in your heart,' I said, and he laughed.

'Now you sound like a Choctaw. Listen to your own heart, my young friend, and you will know what to do.'

'Come on, Slim!' yelled Henry impatiently.

I let go of my friend with sadness and then ran to walk beside Toby.

Toby had a head full of fears.

'Jack read that there are five thousand Mormons at the Kansas River and that every man is armed with a rifle, a knife, and lots of pistols,' he told me anxiously. 'Do you think they will kill us?'

'Why would they bother with us?' I asked. 'No, Toby, the Mormons don't care about us, but I bet the Kansa Indians are already dressed as elk and out to get us!'

He shot a look at me. 'Are they?'

I was sorry I had teased him. 'No,' I replied firmly, 'they are not. They are our friends. Just like Nashobanowa.'

We all turned to wave to Nashobanowa and Emily, and even baby Hero almost seemed to wave her little hand to say goodbye. We turned away from the town and I think we all sighed at the same moment.

It was Jack who said, 'Let's begin.'

And so we took our first steps west.

I dropped back to walk with Bea.

'It's a year,' she said quietly.

'What is?' I asked.

'It's a year since we left Ireland. A year today,' she replied, before adding, 'We had Ma with us then.'

A year. I had lost track of time. I got Da's penknife out of my pocket and opened up the blade. We were walking behind the wagon, and taking the knife I marked a small line on one of the pieces of wood that made up the wagon bed.

'What you doing, Slim?' asked Bea.

'Keeping track of time from now on.'

I think we all felt sad and not a little scared, but then baby Hero pointed to something and began laughing. She had a great laugh, and although she couldn't speak she seemed to find most things in life funny. We had no idea what she was looking at, but she couldn't seem to stop giggling. It set us all off and we were still chuckling when we got to the edge of the town.

As we passed the last house in Independence, Malvolio came to a halt by himself, which meant the other oxen paused too and the wagon stopped moving. Hamlet stood still beside him. It was as if the animals were taking it all in.

For the first time we could see out across the prairie. For a moment all of us fell silent until Kate whispered, 'No towns.'

'Wilderness,' agreed Jack.

'Thousands of miles of nothing,' I muttered.

'Wild buffalo,' said Henry.

'Snakes,' murmured Bea.

'Mormons and Indians,' added Toby, before he flicked the whip in the air and we moved on.

I looked over my shoulder one last time. I don't know if I thought Da would suddenly appear but it was all I longed for.

CHAPTER SEVEN

Summer was on its way when we left Independence. The grass was growing. It was nearly six inches tall and the spring flowers were in full bloom. As we left I saw Bea almost stumble as she too turned to look over her shoulder. I knew she missed Da, but the truth was that everywhere we went on our journey, my big sister always looked back. She never wanted to travel on and now she longed to stay where we were. I think anything even slightly familiar was better than the unexpected which always lay ahead.

'Do you think we will come back?' she asked as we left the town behind. I could see Henry was doing his best to look confident. He walked along as if he were showing everyone that setting off on a two-thousand-mile journey was something he thought nothing of.

'Of course,' he replied with a slight swagger. 'Why, when we are very rich someone will carry us back.'

'They'd have to be big like Jack,' remarked Toby.

I took Bea's hand and squeezed it. I knew that, of us all, she was not designed for the trip.

Jack seemed the most delighted, even though he had the toughest job. I had once tried to push the handcart with the printing press by myself so I knew how heavy it was, but he sauntered along as if we were simply off on a summer picnic.

'Look at this!' he kept saying. 'And that! What's that?' he cried, pointing. The journey seemed to have brought him to life in an unexpected way.

'It's just a rock,' laughed Henry.

'A rock!' sighed Jack. 'Oh! And over there! What is that?'

'A jackrabbit!' said Toby, happy to help.

The small rabbit popped up out of the grass, scared and scampering with long leaps to get away.

'A jackrabbit!' Jack repeated as if he would never tire of what he saw.

'When did you first go to sea, Jack?' asked Kate.

'I was ten, I think,' he replied.

'And how old are you now?'

Jack frowned. 'I might be eighteen.'

How odd not to know how old you are, and how glad I was right then to have something as simple as a family who remembered my birthday.

Even though lots of people were heading west it was

still quite a sight to see wagons loaded with a family's entire life, because when we crossed a deep stream opposite a few rough houses and the usual saloon, the whole population came out to watch us pass.

An old woman doing laundry at her washtub on a porch called out to us in the local accent, 'Be you gwine to California?'

'No. To Oregon!' we sang back with one voice.

'What is this place?' yelled Henry.

'Mason City,' shouted a man drinking beer.

Kate's eyes widened. 'They call this a city?' she marvelled quietly, looking at how small the place was.

Despite my best efforts and even despite knowing Nashobanowa, Toby still talked about being afraid of Indians.

'. . . and if they catch you they cut the top of your head off. It's called scalping . . .' he said breathlessly. 'And—'

'And that would be terrible, Toby,' said Henry seriously. 'Of all of us you can't afford to lose the top of your head because you are already short enough.'

We all laughed but Toby didn't find it funny. The truth is, the only Indians we saw in the beginning were down a long lane at a schoolhouse belonging to the Methodist Mission. A group of Kansa Indians were gathering on wooden benches under the trees for a religious meeting. They were half dressed in their native clothes and half in white men's, while their horses waited patiently, tied to the sheds and fences. The minister called for us to stop and join them but we couldn't delay. We were due to join a large group of wagons to form a train twelve miles outside Independence at a place called Elm Grove and we didn't want to miss it.

I don't know if you know, but no one made the trip west on their own. It wasn't safe. Even so, there were plenty of folks who were fussy about who they travelled with. A group of five stout wagons pulled by mules passed us as we walked. The wagons looked expensive with the wood painted in gorgeous green and yellow paint. Across their canvas tops someone had written in bold letters OREGON OR BUST! They were much quicker than us and the people waved and jeered as they went past.

When we saw the other wagons I think even Jack and Henry realized just how much smarter-looking they all were. None of the wood of our wagon bed matched and it wasn't painted at all. Our second-hand rifle hung from straps on one side, but one fastening was made from an old belt and the other from some frayed rope. It was not at all professional-looking. On the other side of the wagon dangled an old water canteen Jack had been given by some drunk steamboat man, a very battered compass that Jack had found but that I wasn't sure worked, and Bea's sunbonnet, which I wished she'd keep inside because it was too fancy for me.

None of that mattered though when we looked around.

Mother Nature did her best that day to cheer us along. It was a beautiful spring morning, with the earth and the sky competing to look at their best. There was green everywhere. All the trees and saplings were budding into fresh leaf and there were hundreds of flowers. Robert Weston at the wagon shop had given Henry directions to Elm Grove and we felt confident as we followed a narrow track through some woods. The red clusters of the maple blossoms and the rich flowers of the Indian apple were everywhere and the chequered sunshine was lovely. Bea wanted to stop and pick flowers to press but Henry had learned too much about the trip ahead to let her.

'A day dawdling in Kansas spring flowers can mean disaster three months later,' he quoted, and we moved on. It was hard to imagine snow on a day like that, but everyone who knew anything about this trip had warned us that timing was everything. You had to get over the mountains before the snow came or you would never make it.

The weather was about to become our tricky companion. I don't think any of us had ever thought how much it mattered before. We had all heard Kansas people brag about their thunderstorms and they didn't exaggerate. We had only gone about five miles when the blue skies suddenly disappeared. Sharp and never-ending flashes of lightning accompanied by the loudest and most frightening thunder appeared all around.

Hero screamed and Malvolio stumbled.

'Jack, help me!' cried Toby as the four oxen tried to pull in separate directions. Jack put down the cart and ran to steady the animals.

'Get in the wagon!' called Kate, but there wasn't time. Within moments we were all drenched to the skin. Diagonal sheets of rain fell with a heavy roar and rose up again in such a violent spray from the ground that we couldn't see where we were going.

'We have to stop!' insisted Kate.

'No!' shouted Henry, who I don't think would have done what Kate said anyway. 'We can't run the risk of missing the wagon train at Elm Grove! We cannot do this without them.'

So we tried to keep moving, but the rain was so heavy and out of nowhere streams rose so rapidly that we could hardly get across them. We had only gone about a mile when we got stuck in mud. Kate and Hero had to get down from the wagon while we all tried to raise the wheels. The four oxen were young and had never seen anything like this.

'Come on, come on!' coaxed Toby, trying to get them to work together, but they didn't seem to have a clue. Instead of working in pairs, all four tried to pull away from each other. Malvolio snorted and bellowed as if terrified. He tried to pull to the right while the Dromios banged into each other and Balthazar slipped his yoke to the left. The wagon, pulled in every direction possible, just sank deeper into the mud.

Bea began to cry. 'Please, can we go back? I can't do this. I just can't.'

'Come here,' called Kate, putting her arm round her while trying to shelter Hero from the rain.

Henry and Jack pulled and pulled on the yoke to try and move the animals.

Henry was beside himself with frustration. He practically jumped up and down, yelling, 'We are *not* getting stuck here! We are *not*!' He shook his fists at the sky as if that might help.

Jack turned to me, his hair slicked down over his forehead. He was soaked. 'Now what?' he asked.

I knew I should do something but I couldn't think what. It was beginning to look as though we were never going to travel further than five miles from town. Just then I saw a black man with well-trained oxen coming down the road. I ran towards him through the pelting rain.

'Hello!' I called. 'My name is Slim and we need your help and you look nice so I expect you will help because my brother is going mad and we have to get to Elm Grove before everyone leaves because we can't do it on our own and anyway if we're late the snow will come and—'

The man put up his hand and laughed. 'All right, all right, little one. You could have just said "please".'

'Please,' I said quietly, and he nodded down at me. The man was kind and knew what he was doing.

'I got it,' he called, hitching his team of oxen to ours so neatly that the wagon was immediately drawn out of the mud. He waved goodbye, wanting nothing but to help.

'That is a kindness to remember,' said Kate as we waved back through the rain.

'We are set afloat again!' called Jack, grinning.

Kate smiled and turned to me. 'Of all of us Jack seems the most excited. Do you think perhaps he wonders if he might learn something about his father when we get to Oregon?'

I hadn't thought of it but it made sense.

Toby put his arm round Malvolio's neck. He pointed towards the departing man who had helped us and whispered into the ox's ear. 'You need to learn to do that!' he urged. 'Like those proper oxen.'

At last the heavens calmed. We came out of the shadow of the trees into a broad light and saw for the first time the green ocean-like expanse of prairie. It stretched, swell over swell, to the horizon. It was beautiful but it was endless.

'To the end of the sky,' said Bea, overwhelmed.

Our collapse into the mud and out again had caused all our neat packing to come undone. By the time we stopped for the night there were sacks of food and all manner of cooking utensils in a great jumble inside the wagon. We also hadn't thought about needing to get to our supper when we first packed up. Now we had to move heavy boxes and sacks before we could find our flour and bacon, and the pans and dishes we needed. Everyone set about putting it right but we just got in each other's way. In the end Henry was exasperated.

'Right! That will do!' he declared, and took charge of getting everything unloaded so we could start again. The flap of canvas that acted like a door to the back of the wagon was thrown open over the wagon sheet, and out all our possessions came.

'You make a fire,' said Henry to me.

'I don't know who made you the boss,' I grumbled, but it wasn't the time to argue. Toby sorted the animals and then came to help me gather firewood.

'Look at these big pieces!' he called, pleased with himself, as he held up a couple of small round logs. 'I'm a wooder like Da!'

'They look a good start for a fire,' I agreed. Toby had been upset about the animals not doing as they were told and he needed some praise.

We had matches, but the rain had got to some of them so it took ages to get the fire going. It was only once the thing was lit that I remembered the silver matchbox in my pocket. I took it out and looked at it. It definitely had the Cardswell crest on it. I had seen it up at the big house. I turned the box over in my hand. Liam had said he'd found it in New York. What did it mean? Could Parker Crossingham really be after us?

Kate filled the iron kettle from a nearby stream and placed it on the logs, but as soon as the fire was going the kettle rolled on the logs, turned over and put the whole thing out. There was smoke everywhere, and by the time Kate and Bea managed to cook some eggs the food was covered in ash. I hadn't noticed before how much Bea looked like Ma, with her curly red hair and the way she bit her lip as she tried to clean the ash off the supper so we could eat. She was doing her best, but how I wished Ma were with us to take charge. I tried to imagine my mother cooking at the fire in our little house in Ireland but I realized the picture of her was getting fainter. She seemed further away every day and I wanted to cry, but Kate saw me and shook her head.

'We've too far to go to have tears just yet, little Slim,' she said gently.

'Where are we going to sleep?' asked Toby when we'd finally eaten our burnt food.

'In the wagon of course, you idiot,' replied Henry.

'I'm an idiot, am I?' said Toby, who was weary. He pointed to the back of the wagon and we all looked. It was so full with all our things that there wasn't room for anyone.

'I can make a tent,' said Jack, pulling out a piece of tarpaulin. 'Come on, Henry.'

We were all tired and a bit irritable and I don't think Henry wanted to do anything, but he didn't want Jack showing him up. The two of them made a sort of makeshift tent using the side of the wagon to hold the cloth, but the space they made was small and we all had to squeeze in together. No one was happy and this was only our first day. I don't think I had realized until then how hard it was going to be.

Jack snored and Toby kicked. The others said I slept with my arms and legs out and took up too much space. I didn't believe them, but no one had a good night. Our clothes were still wet and we had not eaten well.

'This is hopeless,' I muttered.

'We shall do better tomorrow,' said Kate soothingly, but as soon as the sun rose there was chaos. Toby hadn't tied the animals up properly and they had all wandered off. Perhaps they had seen what lay ahead, and rather sensibly thought that they preferred to turn back for home.

'I didn't think they would leave me,' sighed Toby, genuinely hurt and surprised by the oxen's lack of loyalty.

Henry and Jack got them back and Toby gave Malvolio a particularly stern talking-to.

'You're supposed to be in charge,' he said firmly to the ox, who looked at him blankly with big brown eyes.

Then we realized that none of us could quite remember how to hitch the oxen up again. There was endless toing and froing, with Malvolio being the least helpful of the animals. It appeared as though he hadn't a clue what we wanted him to do. He was a huge animal and we couldn't think how to get him to do as he was told.

'A rope!' suggested Jack.

'Good idea,' said Henry, trying to loop a rope round Malvolio's neck so that he and Jack could pull him into place.

'Got him!' cried Jack, giving a great tug, but instead of forcing the creature into the yoke it just threw Malvolio to the ground with great force.

'Oh!' cried Toby, horrified.

Malvolio struggled on the ground for a short while before rolling up his eyes and lying there as if he were dead.

'No!' screamed Toby, jumping up and down on the spot.

'Oh my!' cried Bea, covering her mouth with her hand while Kate hid Hero's eyes. The boys were horrified and couldn't move. I ran to cut the rope with Da's knife, but still Malvolio lay there not moving or apparently breathing.

It was a disaster. We couldn't possibly manage with just three oxen. The wagon was too heavy.

Toby ran forward crying out, 'No! Malvolio!'

'Maybe we can go back and get another,' whispered Henry.

'We've no more money,' replied Bea.

'Could we manage with three?' I asked.

Henry shook his head. 'We'll have to go back and—'

Just as we thought we would have to return to Independence, the giant animal slowly opened one eye and looked around. Kate began to laugh.

'What's so funny?' demanded Toby, putting his little hands on his hips in fury.

'He's messing about with you,' Kate said, still laughing. 'That big fella is fine. He's just enjoying the drama.'

She went over and stood in front of Malvolio where he lay on the ground.

'Come on, you big brute, you get up and behave yourself,' she said sternly. 'It was just a bit of rope. You are not dying. We've no time for this.'

Malvolio looked at her for a moment, snorted and then, almost embarrassed, got to his feet and allowed himself to be quietly hitched to the wagon.

'I expect it's like children,' said Kate. 'Maybe if you speak to him firmly, Toby, then he'll behave.'

Toby put his hands on his hips and then wagged his finger at Malvolio. 'Well, I never! You naughty boy!' he scolded, which made us all laugh. He looked for all the world like he was trying to be Malvolio's father, except he wasn't even as tall as the animal's head.

We needed to get going. Everyone carried on re-packing the wagon. Bea stood at the back wrestling with a large cooking pot called a Dutch oven, saying, 'Well, it was in the wagon before, so it must fit in here somewhere.'

A wagon packed with goods rolled past driven by two tough-looking men.

'Where to?' called Jack to them.

'Santa Fe,' they shouted.

Bea started to call out to them for help, but Henry was furious and wouldn't let her.

'We cannot keep getting help from others. We have to do this ourselves!' he shouted, suddenly losing his temper. 'Otherwise the time will come when there is no help and what will we do then? We've no Da and . . .'

Henry stood there, shaking with rage, and I thought he was going to cry. I felt so helpless.

'It's all right, Henry, we'll manage it,' Kate said soothingly, and quietly went on getting us sorted. I don't know what we would have done without her.

Lots of people passed us but we asked no one for anything. Our pride meant that we were ages getting going, and by the time we reached the wagon train we were already quite tired.

It wasn't all bad. The clouds of the previous day had broken and the day was perfect. The young grass of the prairie, refreshed by the heavy rains, appeared in its tenderest green. The delicate early flowers were everywhere and the view was magnificent. Our only problem was that the earth was still muddy, and every now and then a spring of water would burst from the ground. These scared Malvolio each time. Clearly he was not going to be the bravest of beasts. At first it upset Toby, but soon we were all laughing at our ox's fear.

'Just our luck to get a really dumb animal,' Henry remarked, and we all thought it was funny.

Mostly everyone walked. At first sitting in the wagon had looked the easiest part, but we soon learned that no one really wanted to ride. The wooden wheels had no springs attached to them and the whole bed shook and jolted over every stone and dip in the land. It wasn't at all relaxing as you had to hang on if you didn't want to be thrown off.

We'd been looking on the horizon for the wagon train for ages, but in the end we heard it quite a while before we saw anything. All these years later I can still recall the terrible hubbub as we approached the gathering wagons. Some people had already been there for a day or two and made quite a camp. They were cooking or sitting beside the wagons, talking while their cattle fed on the broad prairie. A few women were washing pots and pans and everyone was trying to dry their clothes, soaked from the pouring rain of the past night.

You have to remember that there were no roads of any kind then, so the trail we followed – the Oregon Trail – was . . . well, it was like a rope frayed at both ends. There were so many ways to join. Almost as many ways to begin as there were travellers. We had all started our trip from so many places. There were 'movers', who had already travelled thousands of miles from Ireland or England or Germany, but there were also those who had started their journey from just down the road. All the journeys no doubt began at a kitchen table where a family had decided to seek a better life than the one they were living.

There were maybe forty or more wagons gathered that spring day in Elm Grove. Some families were rich – they had two or three wagons – while others, like us, had just the one. Lots of them had written their names on their wagon covers. Others had slogans or something they wanted to say painted in bright colours for the world to see.

There was a wagon called *Prairie Bird* and another called *Tornado Train*. An ancient-looking one had *54° 40' or Fight* written on it in bright blue, although I didn't know what it meant. Others had sayings like *Never Say Die* or *Patience and Perseverance*, while another made clear the owner's feelings with the words *The Eleventh Commandment – Mind Your Own Business*. There were two wagons of men not destined to be neighbours, for one read simply *Oregon* while the other had *California* splashed in bright green across the wagon cover. I thought it looked great.

'We should have a name,' I said, and Kate agreed.

'How about *The Elephant's Eye*?' she suggested. 'We're up high in the wagon. Must be as high as that elephant.'

'What elephant?' asked Toby

'The one everyone says we're looking for,' explained Jack.

'I didn't know there was an elephant,' said Toby anxiously.

'I don't think it's real,' soothed Kate.

'We don't even know what the elephant is,' scoffed Henry, who was finding fault with everything.

'Stop being so grumpy, Henry,' I scolded.

Kate pulled Toby in for a hug. 'I bet we'll know the elephant when we see it,' she said, 'and what a wonder that will be.'

'I like the name,' declared Bea.

'Me too,' I said, and Jack nodded in agreement.

Bea set to work using some of the paint we had brought as Indian presents. Soon she had painted what she thought an elephant might look like in soft grey and the words *The Elephant's Eye* in bright red across the wagon cover. Even Henry agreed that it looked splendid.

Throughout the campsite everyone was packing and unpacking, trying to work out what they truly needed.

If we had thought *our* wagon was full, we were amazed at what some people had packed. They had honestly left nothing behind. They had all the usual things, but also brooms and brushes, ox shoes and horseshoes, pieces of fabric and leather, boxes which rattled with glass beads, rings and bracelets, pocket mirrors, calico vests, boiled shirts, anvils, dining tables and chairs, wardrobes, bookcases and enough kitchen equipment to start a restaurant.

It turned out the *54° 40' or Fight* was owned by the man we had called Nervous Bob. He was the one we had met on the steamboat to Independence. The one who thought Indians could disguise themselves as elk. He didn't seem to have calmed down at all and kept wandering around asking what anyone in the wagon train planned to do if there was an Indian attack.

I was only a kid but I was pretty sure there was no plan. I guess we were about a hundred people, but out of that hundred no one seemed to be in charge. All you could hear was a lot of grown-ups arguing and calling out. We weren't the only ones who knew nothing about tying animals up properly. Travellers seemed to be herding up lost creatures everywhere you looked. There was a lot of chatter, but not, I thought, much sense. I don't know what we had expected. Someone like a captain to tell us what to do, I suppose.

'Look!' called Bea, pointing to a wagon a short distance away. It was magnificent. Easily the finest wagon we'd ever seen. It was solidly built out of beautiful wood which had then been painted the prettiest blue and white. The wagon cover was immaculate and it had *Oregon – the Whole or*

None written on the side in professional neat writing. None of that, however, was what drew our attention. Trying her best to stay seated at the front was a woman in a dress of such bright pink that none of us could have mistaken who it belonged to.

'It's the Honeymans . . .' Kate said, smiling. 'From the boat!'

Mr Honeyman was still getting the hang of driving and he pulled up a little shakily. Kate wanted to say hello, although I wasn't sure why.

'They weren't very friendly before,' I muttered, but I followed Kate as she wandered over.

Mrs Honeyman and her husband looked as immaculately dressed as ever, but their son, Algernon, had managed to get a tiny tear in the trousers of his bright blue suit and was being made to sit in the back of the wagon in disgrace. They were perfectly polite but, as I had predicted, not exactly pleased to see us.

'We shall need a full cup of courage,' declared Mrs Honeyman.

Nervous Bob wandered past and couldn't have agreed more.

'No one is listening to what I am saying!' he complained, but Mrs Honeyman wasn't either.

'I had no idea you couldn't buy things along the way,' she continued. 'What a lot of things we needed!'

The Honeymans' wagon was piled high with bright shiny new things. It was clear no expense had been spared.

Mr Honeyman stroked his perfect beard.

'By all accounts it is an uncertain and dangerous trip,' he declared, before turning to his wife and saying, 'But I tell you, my dear, where other folks have gone we certainly can go.'

'They say there are "castles of shining gold the other side of the mountains",' said Toby, smiling. He had just heard that from someone and thought it sounded marvellous.

Mr Honeyman nodded and said in a low voice, 'We shall simply need to make the best of everything.'

'Indeed,' agreed Mrs Honeyman, spreading a white tablecloth on the grass to show that they were busy. She reached into the wagon for some china plates for them to eat their supper off.

Lots of people were trying to be positive about what lay ahead.

'No malaria,' said one man with delight.

'No snows to keep you trapped in your cabin,' said another.

'Bumper crops, and so much grass they say the livestock don't never need no hay.'

'Out in Oregon I can get me a square mile of my own land!'

More wagons joined all the time. We were a long way

from being the last. A preacher was trying to gather everyone for a final prayer meeting. He was called Reverend Eli Goudy, and he and his wife, Parenthia, were 'Off to bring the Book of Heaven to the Indians!' as he kept telling us. Or rather he tried to. The Reverend had trouble with his breathing and we often had to wait mid-sentence for him to finish a thought.

'Off to bring . . .' he would begin, and then start wheezing while everyone wondered what he might be planning to bring. His wife couldn't see well and wore very thick glasses, but she had got them second-hand, so they were less than perfect.

'I doubt they'll be much help to the Indians,' whispered Kate.

'Or even themselves,' added Bea.

The Reverend stood with his Bible held aloft in one hand and began to speak, but it took for ever.

'If we have the temerity' – he coughed, and we all waited – 'to turn our backs on civilization and face the—'

'Indians?' called out someone helpfully.

'Dangers?'

'Long distance?'

We all wondered what the Reverend thought we were facing, but it turned out to be the 'far-off mountains, then we shall need to be bold but not reckless. Let us recall the great journey of Moses as he led . . . as he led . . .'

There was an even longer pause punctuated with terrible wheezing.

'Led who?' shouted an Irish voice impatiently.

'I think it was the Israelites,' called another. 'Isn't it always them Israelites heading for the Red Sea when your man Moses is leading?'

'Moses leading the way?' called out a man in a red flannel shirt. 'Who voted for him?'

'Religion is all that sustains us,' the Reverend finally went on.

'There's water too,' called out someone who was enjoying a big drink of the stuff.

The whole wagon train gave up paying attention and went back to getting ready.

It seemed that Reverend Goudy and Parenthia were planning to convert the Flathead Indians up in the mountains to the east of Oregon.

'Why them?' asked Toby, who was now interested in all Indians. 'Is it because they have flat heads?'

Parenthia didn't seem to speak. Kate tried to make friends with her, but she just bent her head and turned away.

'I think every time she has something to say her husband calls on God to keep her busy,' Kate remarked.

'Why are they coming with us?' asked Toby.

'For safe passage,' answered Kate. 'Same as everyone else.'

Toby looked confused. 'What do they need us for? Won't God just protect them?'

'No one can protect us,' said Nervous Bob, who was passing by.

Most of the women were busy changing into short so-called 'washdresses', putting away their flowery straw hats in their wagons and putting on Shaker bonnets and thick buckskin gloves. Bea watched them. We didn't have anything to change into. We had got new clothes in St Louis but there was only one set each.

'One day, Bea,' I promised, 'you shall have those fine dresses we saw in New York.'

While Bea longed for fancy dresses, another woman in the train was getting rid of hers. I was just passing the wagon called *The Eleventh Commandment – Mind Your Own Business* when I nearly got hit on the head by a flying blue hooped skirt that was being thrown out. The woman doing the ejecting was called Louise. She wasn't at all happy.

'Darn fool idea!' she kept repeating. Then she saw me. She pointed straight at me and yelled, 'Pantaloons! Are you a girl wearing pantaloons?'

'Yes,' I said slowly, wondering if she meant my trousers.

'Good for you!' She jumped down from her wagon and slapped me hard on the back.

Louise seemed old to me. Maybe she was in her fifties. She didn't seem to care that I was just a kid because she carried on.

'If Jeni thinks I'm going to wear a hooped skirt across the prairie just for pro-piety, she has another think coming. I am wearing a pair of pants and be done with it.'

Louise was amazing-looking. Beautiful really. Very tall and thin. She had incredibly dark, almost black, hair which shone in the light. There was a single streak of white in it which started at her forehead and swept back over her right ear like a lightning flash. Mostly she hid the white streak under an old battered cowboy hat. She had intense dark eyes, and under her thin shirt you could see how strong she was. She was travelling with two other women, Jeni and Jeni's mother, Mrs Meadows. Jeni was about Louise's age but was very small and very round. They made an odd pair. While Louise was dark, Jeni was pale, with long blonde hair that hung right down her back. She wore a round red cap with a black knob on top, a scarlet Scottish plaid coat with fringes, a large bright red skirt and hob-nailed shoes. In the corner of her mouth hung a little black pipe which seemed to stay there with no effort on her part.

'It's going to be marvellous!' Jeni declared as many times as Louise repeated that the whole trip was 'a darn fool idea'.

Louise stared down at Jeni, who looked up at her. A tall thin woman with a small round one.

'They're like something out of a nursery rhyme,' whispered Kate, coming up behind me. 'How your Da would have loved them.'

I smiled at Kate. I was so glad she was with us. She helped keep everyone calm. I just wished Henry could be nicer to her.

Louise was keen to make friends. She spotted Kate nursing Hero and came over to chat.

'Darn fool,' she repeated, nodding towards Jeni, 'would not hear "no" about this trip. Sold everything at auction so we'd have the money, but my sister Fanny' – Louise lowered her voice and went on confidentially – 'she secretly bought back my fine Dutch plates. I've sewed them inside Mother's wagon featherbed.'

She pointed to the back of her wagon, where we could just see an old woman lying asleep.

'That's Jeni's mother, not mine. She ain't right, but Jeni won't hear of leaving her behind. Says the climate in Oregon will cure her right away.' Louise lowered her voice again and whispered to me and Kate, 'Between you and me, I reckon the plates will make it but her mother won't. Damn shame. Damn shame.'

There were a few Indians hanging around while we waited to set off, and nothing pleased Louise more on our whole trip than the sight of a huge young brave strutting about in the old worn-out hoop skirt she had thrown away.

Henry was pacing up and down.

'What are we waiting for?' I asked. 'Are there more people coming?'

Henry shook his head. 'A guide, apparently. Some fellow called James Long. I had nothing to do with it but he's been hired by the train. Bob says as no one had made the trip before we have to have someone who knows the way. All I know is we have to pay and we've little enough money as it is.'

'He's a hunter from a little French town near St Louis,' explained Louise, who seemed to know the most about what was going on. 'They say he's been working in the Rocky Mountains since he was fifteen selling buffalo meat.'

When he arrived, he looked like he knew what he was doing. Henry actually looked pleased, and even Nervous Bob calmed down. I think James was about thirty. Six foot tall and good-looking, with a jaw so large it might have been modelled on one of the mountains we kept hearing about. It was huge, with a great dimple in the middle. He wore a white blanket coat, a broad felt hat, moccasins, and deerskin pantaloons ornamented along the seams with long rows of fringe, and rode a tough-looking grey Wyandot pony. A knife was stuck in his belt, while a bullet pouch and powder horn hung by his side. His rifle lay before him, resting against the high pommel of his saddle.

James was not a man of many words, but as soon as he arrived he did make a short speech. First he touched his fingertips to his hat in greeting, which I had begun to learn was something all the mountain men did.

'Good morning, all. My name is James Long and I have undertaken to take you on a route which is easy, safe and expeditious.'

The word 'safe' was very pleasing and a lot of people murmured about how good that sounded.

'Now I would ask you all, especially the lady folks, to be prepared. There are no roads west of here. Just a trail – a trail first made by wild beasts, then Indians, mountaineers and trappers. It is an ancient network created long before anyone thought of the word "emigrant".'

James paused and looked at us.

'Now, one or two have asked me about the Indians,' he continued.

Both Nervous Bob and Toby nodded.

'Not a big danger in my experience,' continued James. 'Spring has just sprung and the grass is only just beginning to sprout so Indian ponies are still thin from winter. Even war has a season so they need to fatten them before they can attack. We won't need to concern ourselves until at least Fort John. Right, follow me.'

And without further warning he wheeled his pony

round and headed off, expecting us to follow.

It was clear that James Long knew the way but he was not interested in helping us organize ourselves to get there. He didn't seem to think that was his job, so no order of how we were to leave had been arranged. Once James gave the word that we were leaving, everyone tried to be quick and get to the front. I think we all thought being as close to the guide as possible would be the best position, but that move was a disaster. A general shambles followed as hardly anyone was familiar with their wagon or their livestock and lots of the animals were as uncontrollable as ours. We all got tangled up with each other.

Toby hurried to keep up, his voice louder than anyone else's. The noise was fantastic. To be honest, the whole hopeless departure made us feel better. We weren't the only ones who didn't know what we were doing.

By the time we set off there were 72 wagons, 130 men, 65 women and 125 children. There were all kinds of people – Germans, Hollanders, Frenchmen, Englishmen and Irish of course. A jeweller, a stonemason, a couple of blacksmiths, lawyers, teachers, a cabinet maker and any number of farmers. Between us all there was a mountain of goods. We had food for six months, rope, harness, spare rifles, pots, pans, clothes and portable compasses, and it all made a noise as we clattered over the uneven ground. It was a sound I was to become very familiar with. Above the noise of tin plates clanging in the backs of wagons you could also hear a lot of laughter. Jeni and Louise had two milk cows called Daisy and Gert who followed along behind their wagon, attached by a length of rope. Even they looked as though they were happy to be off.

'How nice everyone seems,' said Bea.

And we did feel then that, despite our many differences, we would all get along.

James led us across the highest 'divides' or prairie swells, avoiding the dips created by the streams. It was quite a sight to see for the first time the white tops of so many covered wagons dotting the landscape.

'Looks like lots of ships!' Jack beamed.

At noon we stopped to rest near a little creek full of frogs. It was a lovely place, and everyone set about lighting fires to make hot drinks. I got out my leather book from Emily and began to write about the journey. What sounded like thousands of young croakers and insects filled the air with their noise and there was a lazy feeling of calm. Small birds came hopping along the ground, feeding, while some sang cheerily from the tops of bushes. Kate and Bea got out a few crackers and herring from a small barrel.

I remembered Ma showing me how to find food in the woods when we didn't have any potatoes and I thought how she would have loved learning about all the creatures around us.

The people in the train started to get to know each other. We quickly settled into a routine. As we walked, the women in particular would drop back a wagon or two and chat. Bea often walked behind Louise and Jeni's wagon. I liked them too and would often find myself tagging along. Mrs Meadows couldn't walk and the trip was tough. She never complained, but she looked pale and tired. She couldn't eat because her body hurt so much and she was much too thin. The women had made her as comfortable in bed as possible, but she jolted about over the rough ground so Bea and Jeni would chat where she could hear them. Jeni knitted during every spare moment and Bea would often hold the wool for her. The women helped each other with all sorts of things. You would often see a woman a little way off holding out her apron to shield another from view as she excused herself.

Louise had a fine horse which she rode up and down the line, shaking her head at 'this darn fool idea'. I knew she wasn't really as grumpy as she pretended because she took time to teach Jack about the birds we saw. 'That's a meadow lark,' she explained to him as we heard a mellow whistle in the air. He cocked his large head to one side, listening. 'And that sort of gurgle?' she continued. 'Those are blackbirds.'

He loved it, and soon he was pointing out what he had learned to me.

Jeni had a horse too, but it was always tied to the back

of their wagon. When Jeni wasn't walking she sat up front on the driver's seat, sucking on her small pipe, knitting and telling anyone who got close enough how wonderful it was all going to be. I liked her cheerfulness.

'I'll tell you how good the climate is in California,' she would begin, before taking a suck on her pipe and continuing. 'Why, I heard tell about a man who lived in California to the age of two hundred and fifty!'

'Two hundred and fifty?' Toby called out, wide-eyed with amazement. Kate wandered closer, holding Hero against her shoulder.

Then Jeni would tell a long story about California being so good for you that a man not only lived to be two hundred and fifty years old, but when he died they put him in a coffin and at the funeral he sprang back out because he was too healthy for heaven!

As Jeni spun these stories, Louise would call out, 'Don't think I can't hear you, Jeni: fillin' folks' heads with nonsense.'

Jeni would ignore her and carry on with her tale, her knitting needles clicking as she spoke.

'What happened to him after that?' I asked, determined to write the story in my book so I could tell Da. I knew he would want to hear it and I refused to accept that I wouldn't tell him one day.

'Well, the old man had no choice but to submit to his

fate,' said Jeni thoughtfully, 'and to live out his appointed time. So, you see, we're all going to live for ever.'

'Live for ever!' scoffed Louise. 'That's if we get to California. Don't get sick and die on the way.'

'We are not going to get sick,' said Jeni reassuringly.

'Might get attacked!' shouted Nervous Bob, who had been listening.

'We are not going to get attacked!' said Jeni.

No sooner had the words come out of her mouth than we heard a tremendous hollering behind us. We all turned to look, and saw a great string of horses galloping at full pace. There must have been forty or fifty of them carrying a band of Indians towards us so fast that in a moment the entire wagon train was in a panic. Nervous Bob gave a scream that sounded just like a girl and began jumping up and down on the spot, unable to run away. I didn't want to panic. The Indians were our friends, but as the horses galloped towards us they kicked up a storm of dust which looked like it would swallow the whole train. The earth shook with the thundering noise and it was hard not to feel frightened.

Our guide, James, tried to get the wagons turned into a circle for protection, but no one really knew how to make their ox teams do as they were told, and anyway Bob seemed to be in everyone's way. Animals went in all directions, women screamed for their children and men began running to stand by their families. Between us we carried enough equipment for a war. Most of the men had a rifle slung across their saddles, but many of them, including Jack and Henry, had no real idea how to use them.

I reached for my pistols but my hands were shaking and I realized I had no idea how to fire them. I also remembered that I had never loaded them with bullets.

'Henry, get the rifle!' shouted Bea.

Henry ran to grab our rifle from the side of the wagon, but it was tied on and he couldn't get the rope undone. By the time he had hold of the gun, he found out how heavy it was and it slipped from his grasp. He turned to grab it, got the butt of the rifle caught between his legs and fell over. He jumped up quickly and held it to his shoulder, but he looked terrified of firing the thing. Not that he would have the chance anyway. I was pretty sure it too wasn't loaded.

The Indians got closer and closer, whooping in their dust cloud, which made it impossible for us to shoot at them even if we'd known how.

'Get behind the wagon!' shouted Kate.

'I told you! I told you!' yelled Toby, desperately trying to get our oxen to move up behind the Honeymans' wagon. Louise grabbed a gun and Jeni ran to be with her mother. Jack dropped the cart and raced to help Bea into the back of the wagon. Bea tripped on her skirt hem and fell forward. Jack tried to help her up and got in the way of Kate, who was running to our wagon so she could hide Hero in the carpet bag. Toby looked trapped between the four oxen while I stood frozen in place. Henry, still fumbling with the gun, tried to run over to me but he fell forward and dropped the weapon.

I could see that the braves racing towards us were from the Kaw or Kansa tribe. I could tell by their leather leggings and buckskin shirts decorated with porcupine quills and fancy beadwork. Their hair was cut to the scalp except for a thing like a rooster's comb on top of their head, coloured red. Even on horseback you could tell that they were tall. They were impressive and a bit scary. Suddenly one of them held up his hand and the descending horde stopped in their tracks. Some made their horses rise up on their hind legs and continued whooping. That was when Nervous Bob fainted. No one moved to help him. Not even Reverend Goudy, who talked a lot about neighbours and being nice. Instead he rushed to hide with his wife, Parenthia. Everyone in the wagon train was terrified. Everyone except James. He calmly rode his horse out from our group and held up his hand.

'Hold your fire!' he commanded. 'Nobody shoot!'

'What's happening? What's happening?' called Mrs Meadows from inside her wagon, where she couldn't see.

'It's all right, Mother,' soothed Jeni, trying not to sound as terrified as everyone else.

'Everybody calm down!' insisted Louise.

Slowly the Indian in charge approached. He was old, but there was no question that he was the chief. All the other braves moved to let him through. His head was also shaved and painted red, and from the tuft of hair remaining on the top dangled several eagles' feathers, and what James later told me were the tails of two or three rattlesnakes. His cheeks too were painted red, while green glass pendants hung from his ears. There were several large necklaces of traditional shell beads on his chest, which I knew from Nashobanowa were called *wampum*. He was an impressive sight.

James stepped forward and shook the chief's hand.

'What do you want from us?' he asked politely.

'Slim Hannigan,' the great Kansa man replied. 'I wish to see Slim Hannigan.'

He said my name but I didn't think I had heard properly.

Kate gasped and held onto me tightly. 'No! You stay where you are, Slim.'

James turned to the wagon train. 'Which one of you is Slim Hannigan?' he called.

I just stood there, frozen to the spot, and managed to say, 'It's me. I'm Slim Hannigan.'

'No!' cried Henry, scrambling to pick up the gun. 'Don't speak!'

'Slim!' called Bea.

James rode his horse over to me.

'It's all right. It'll be all right,' he said. 'Come on now.'

I nodded and slowly moved forward. Kate didn't want to let go. She gave a slight gasp as I walked towards the Indian chief. I inched forward until I was standing in front of his horse. I looked up into his face. The sun was behind him and he seemed almost to shimmer in front of me. He had an amazing collar of grizzly bears' claws around his neck. What did he want with me? I had no idea what was happening or why.

CHAPTER EIGHT

I knew Henry was frightened too but he ran to my side. He was holding the rifle again, and I knew he wanted to protect me, but I also knew he didn't know how to fire it. I could almost hear his heart pounding.

'I'm her brother,' he managed. 'You can speak to me.'

I looked at the chief's face.

'I think it's all right, Henry,' I said. 'I don't think they mean us any harm.'

'No indeed,' agreed James.

James took out a small pouch of tobacco from his coat pocket and handed it to the chief, who looked pleased. Out of the corner of my eye I could see Louise get Nervous Bob up and move him to her wagon.

I looked steadily at the Kansa man. He seemed enormous, sitting high up on his horse. He looked down at me from a great height. He was very impressive, but somehow

I knew he didn't mean to frighten me.

'You are Slim?' he asked in a deep voice.

'Yes,' I said. 'Are you a Kansa chief?'

He nodded and then waved his hand at one of the braves behind him. A young Indian, who was no older than Henry, leaped down from his own horse and moved to bring forward a beautiful stallion which I hadn't noticed until then had no rider. It was what they call a 'paint horse', a beautiful black creature which looked as though it had been decorated in patches with a can of bright white paint. It had a white face and then another great splash of white along one side and up over its back. The horse snorted and pranced as it was led forward.

The chief smiled. 'For you,' he said to me.

I was confused. 'The horse? It's for me?'

'From Nashobanowa. My brother. You help him. He says you go to Oregon and need horse.'

I didn't know if Nashobanowa was his actual brother or not, but I did know I was being given the most amazing gift. It was unbelievable, but here was the horse I had wanted.

'Well, I never,' declared James. 'Ain't that a thing.'

I didn't know what to say. 'But you are Kansa and he is Choctaw,' I said foolishly.

'He is still my brother,' said the chief.

I looked back at Kate and Bea, and they were standing together grinning. I looked at Jack, who was almost laughing he was so pleased. Toby gave a small cheer from where he stood with Malvolio, and even Hamlet stood up on his hind legs as if to clap. The rest of the wagon train all had their mouths open, looking amazed. Most of the men had been holding rifles at the ready, but these now slowly dropped to their sides.

'I don't know what you've done to deserve it,' continued James, 'but go on, young woman, collect your gift. It's all right.'

Henry nodded. 'I think it's fine,' he said quietly. A great beam of a smile broke out on his face.

I moved towards the beautiful horse, which whinnied and pranced as I approached. It had leather reins with a tiny bit of silver decoration and an Indian saddle made of two pieces of soft tanned hide sewed together and stuffed with hair or grass. There were short stirrups, and the whole thing was held on by a long piece of rawhide. The young brave handed me the reins and the horse brushed its soft lips against my head. I fell in love instantly. What a creature! He was so beautiful!

'Thank you,' I said. 'Please say "*yakoke*" to Nashobanowa. It is Choctaw for "thank you". *Yakoke* very much indeed.'

The Kansa Indian chief raised his hand again, and without seeming to tell his horse what to do he wheeled away to leave. Then he looked back and called out to me.

'Nashobanowa said the horse is called' – he stopped for a moment to think and then said – 'Chronicle. The horse is called Chronicle.'

Then with a great whoop the chief rode off, leading his men off at the same fantastic speed as before. Dust flew in the air, and soon they had all disappeared into the landscape as if by magic.

James looked at me. 'Hannigan? You're Irish, right?'

I nodded but I couldn't speak.

He smiled. 'You know the Choctaw sent money to the Irish?'

'When?' I asked.

'Last year. When they heard you were hungry. The tribe sent money to the Irish.'

I didn't know that but I knew Nashobanowa's people shared what they had and I wasn't surprised. I wished I had known. I wished I had thanked him. How odd that the Choctaw had thought of us when we were in Ireland. From now on I would always think of them.

Dozens of people gathered around me. The whole wagon train was amazed by what had just happened.

'Got to keep my eye on you, little one,' declared Nervous Bob. 'Friend of the damned Indian.'

'Astonishing!' said Louise, impressed.

No one was more astonished than me. I had my own horse. An Indian horse called Chronicle.

'He's beautiful,' cried Toby, and Kate rushed to bring Hero down from the wagon to have a look. Bea thought the silver on the reins was 'perfect' and Jack just kept clapping me on the back while Henry quietly put our rifle back on the side of the wagon.

Not everyone was pleased. In fact, quite a lot of people in the train were angry about what had happened.

Nervous Bob felt it proved his point about the danger we were all in. 'What if they had wanted to attack us?' he demanded.

'I guess you could just faint again!' laughed Louise, and I'm afraid we all joined in.

'But they didn't attack us,' I said. 'They were nice. They're Kansa. They're kind people. Just like the Choctaw. When we were all hungry in Ireland, they . . .'

But Bob wasn't listening. The arrival of the Indians had caused great fear and I think everyone realized how disorganized we were. Now some wanted us to elect officers for the wagon train and others said that we should stop travelling so that we could practise moving the wagons into a giant circle for protection.

In the end nothing was settled. James was not interested in the conversation, and as usual he just set off and everyone had to rush to follow. It was the now-familiar chaos, with children snatched up by their mothers and men endlessly trying to get any animal they owned to do what it was told.

175

I stood with Jack and my new horse.

'He's beautiful,' he said, echoing Toby.

I nodded and then whispered, 'But, Jack, there's just one thing – I don't know how to ride.'

And I don't think Chronicle was all that used to being ridden. I had thought you just got on and then off you rode, but all day long I got on and *fell* off. Chronicle was big and strong, but it seemed almost anything could frighten him. If something blew across his path in the wind or a jackrabbit jumped, then instead of swaying or shying side-wise he would just quickly squat on his back legs and I'd slide off.

'You're not holding on tight enough,' said Henry bossily.

'Oh well, you try!' I replied, irritated.

Henry got on Chronicle, and I was secretly pleased when he only managed a yard or two before my new horse decided a crack of Louise's whip in the distance was frightening. He sat back down, dumping my brother on the ground. It made Henry very grumpy and he never tried again.

Toby thought it was hilarious. 'I don't know who's more afraid of the world: Malvolio or Chronicle.'

It was true. We seemed to have two huge animals, both of whom found the prairie terrifying.

'Do you want me to help you, Slim?' asked Toby, who really *did* think he was the king of the animals, but I wasn't having my little brother teach me anything.

176

'I'm all right,' I insisted.

Bea had to get some liniment out for my many bruises. She used it a lot. Poor Jack's hands were in a terrible state from pushing the printing press on our old Irish farm cart. He was strong but it was very hard work.

As I tumbled once more to the ground, Kate helped me up. I think she could see I was ready to give up.

It was Kate who made me get back on Chronicle one more time.

'You can do this, Slim,' she said. 'I've seen you be determined. Now you need to do it again.' She reached out and pushed my hair back from my forehead.

James, who I think was impressed that I'd got a horse from an Indian, tried to reassure me. 'Ten days of carrying and he'll settle down gentle,' he said. 'He just needs to get to know you.'

That night I sat aching and trying to get enough light from a blazing fire to fill in my journal. The stars overhead were bright, and the movements of the people and animals from the wagon train flickered through the fire smoke. There were a few Irish in the wagon train, and you could hear them singing and carrying on. It was a funny thing about the Irish: they seemed to like to stick together. But Kate didn't like all the drinking so we kept to ourselves.

'I don't want Henry to get caught up with the ruffians,' she confided in me and Bea. 'He's doing so well lately.'

I knew Kate didn't want to upset Henry, but that night she suggested, 'We don't need to spend time with anyone but ourselves.'

We did what she said. I think it felt nice having someone look out for us. Kate was right, of course. Henry had been in enough trouble and no one wanted that to start again. How we missed Ma and Da to tell us what to do!

'Do you think Da would . . .' I tried one night, but Henry told me to be quiet and no one else seemed to want to talk about him.

Despite Kate's advice Bea couldn't quite manage to keep to herself. She loved company, especially fine company. Louise and Jeni had a very grand tent which they would put up each night, and Bea took to visiting for a cup of coffee. Jeni's mother, Mrs Meadows, sat knitting at these gatherings. It turned out that she had once been quite the lady in London and Bea loved to hear all about the parties and the dresses. The old lady also claimed she could see into the future. When they had all finished their evening coffee, she would take the empty cup with its bits of coffee grind at the bottom, turn it upside down and look for scenes of Indians in pursuit or covered wagons on the trail.

'I see California for you, Bea,' declared the old woman.

Bea shook her head. 'I think the coffee grounds are mistaken, Mrs Meadows. We're all off to Oregon.'

I can still picture myself one evening going to check that

Chronicle had enough grass and walking past the open flap of the women's tent. Jeni and her mother had proper chairs they'd brought with them and Bea was sitting on one. She sat as if she were quite comfortable in someone's fine house and it made me smile. She always wore Ma's old hair clasp now and her bright red hair looked almost like fire against the white of it. How I wanted the life for her that she deserved. A fine house with roses round the door, linen on the beds and a fireplace not just for cooking. Each night I took Da's knife and made a small mark on the wood at the back of the wagon. I already had a lot of markings and I wondered how many there would be before we finally had a home of our own.

We got used to being on the road pretty quickly. Once a week the Reverend and his wife would try to get everyone to stop for the Sabbath but mostly we just carried on. At night a lot of the women and children slept on packing boxes in their wagons. Everyone else made what bed they could on the ground – a blanket, a piece of canvas, an India rubber cloth or even a buffalo robe.

As soon as the day broke James would start calling out 'Arise, arise!' to wake everyone. Immediately the mules would start making a terrible noise which no one could sleep through. I'm difficult to wake but no one can ignore a mule.

Henry's voice would be next.

'Come on!' he would call to us. 'Lots to do! Bea – breakfast. Toby – sort the animals. Jack! You and Slim get the wagon packed again!'

Despite the hustle and bustle of everyone getting ready you could still hear prairie birds. They seemed to be everywhere.

'Cowbirds, kestrels, sparrows and larks,' Jack would tell me. How he enjoyed repeating what he had learned from Louise, and how he loved all the animals and birds we saw. His great face would light up at the sight of the smallest creature on the plain and he wouldn't rest till he had found someone who knew what it was called. I think some people just made up names to keep him quiet.

One night, as darkness fell, we began to see lightning flash on the horizon and it wasn't long before the thunder rolled. A high gale could be heard sweeping over the prairies some moments before it struck us. Everywhere members of the wagon train were busy. Men were brushing and currying the stock, oiling the wheels of their wagons and endlessly reloading the camp equipment. I couldn't be bothered with cooking but someone had to. Kate and Bea were trying to make bread. Kate had a small book with instructions which she was reading aloud from.

'*When baking bread on the prairie, the utensils can be of the most simple and primitive kind,*' she read aloud. '*All you need are two sticks inclining over the bed of coals, one*

end thrust into the ground, while the dough is twisted in a
spiral form round the other.'

'Spiral form?' Bea asked, bewildered, as she wiped her hand across her face and covered it in flour. 'What on earth is that?'

While they were cooking it began raining and blowing violently. Our fire was extinguished by the downpour, and our dough almost turned to batter. At last the rain came down without stopping and we all had to hide under the wagon, where we ate bread that was black on one side and soft on the other.

There was silence as everyone ate.

'Well, what do you boys think of our first effort at making bread?' asked Kate, trying to be light-hearted.

'I think we should call them "sinkers",' said Toby. 'If you ate one of these before you went swimming, it would surely make you sink.'

'How rude!' Bea exploded, and then we all laughed because it was true.

The lightning blazed almost continuously for hours. Jack said he had once seen fireworks in Dublin, though this was grander. The lights were amazing, but once more we felt we had to swim through the night rather than sleep.

The next morning the now-familiar cry of 'Catch up! Catch up!' meant it was time to get moving, and at about 6 a.m. we set off once more. Each day was much the same.

We travelled for five hours, walking sometimes alone, sometimes with others, while the younger children played, running in and out of the wagons, making trouble, scattering around and getting lost. Then we would rest and eat before starting again at about 2 p.m. Then it was another four hours till we camped for the night, having usually covered at least fifteen miles, sometimes as much as twenty. The pace was slow, partly because most people were walking and partly because the oxen would not hurry. Toby was always exhausted from driving them. It wasn't just because he was so young. I watched all the other drivers struggle too. Keeping the beasts in line was a trial to anyone's patience.

I spent my time trying to see if Chronicle had settled down at all but I kept being disappointed. I would walk with him, holding his reins and stroking his soft nose before trying to get on, but I always ended up back on the ground. Henry would laugh at me, which made me even more determined. I had no idea how, but I was going to make that magnificent horse my friend.

While Chronicle continued to be grumpy, Algernon Honeyman seemed to take to life on the road. Slowly he began to escape his mother's attention. Mrs Honeyman had decided early on that the trip was not for her. Whenever I was near their wagon I would hear her repeating that she wanted to 'go back home' and that it had been 'a terrible mistake', and warning Algernon not to play with the other boys on the train as they were 'not nice at all'. But whenever he could Algernon ignored her and ran off. In fact, more often than not, if there was a commotion, he would be at the centre of it.

We didn't see many people other than those we travelled with. Sometimes very large contractors' wagons passed us, heading for Santa Fe with goods, each carrying a couple of spare axles lashed under their bodies, to be used if one gave way on the difficult ground. We would wave but no one stopped. Everyone just kept moving.

'How far is it, Henry?' I asked. 'To Oregon?'

He shrugged. 'From here? James Long says maybe not quite two thousand miles but there's no way to know for sure.'

I looked back over my shoulder. It had become a habit to look each day for Da.

Then Henry surprised me by saying, 'You could leave a message, you know.'

'What do you mean?'

'Print some more pictures of Da and leave them along the way. If he's behind or someone knows something, well, then they'll know we went this way.'

I knew he thought Da was dead, but it was kind of him. That night Jack and I printed some more posters and I began leaving them behind at regular intervals. There were no towns or even settlements any more, so I pinned them to trees or left them on the ground, held in place by rocks. It made me feel better.

At some point we crossed the Missouri state line and headed into an area known as the Louisiana Purchase. Or, as James called it, 'unorganized territory'. I only knew because Louise took her hat off, turned east and waved it above her head, shouting, 'Goodbye, America!'

'Old fool,' replied Jeni, smiling.

The line was important and everyone knew it, for now we were heading into an unknown country.

'It's a lawless place,' sighed Jeni, going back to her knitting.

'Indian territory,' said a worried Mrs Honeyman, although I wasn't sure why. So far the Indians had been nothing but kind.

Ahead lay a trek across trackless plains and over lofty mountains. The grown-ups all seemed anxious.

'We must ever be on the watch for enemies,' explained Nervous Bob when I asked him why he sat up at night.

'Who?' I asked.

Bob sighed. 'That's the trouble with enemies, you just don't know.'

We forded a small creek and soon found ourselves on a magnificent prairie inside Indian territory where there were no armies or sheriffs to protect us. I think mostly we were all glad of each other's company, although some people started to become grumpy and silly. Two men died in a fight. The Reverend held a service and they were left on the trail, buried side by side.

'They never got on,' said Henry.

Kate shook her head. 'Idiots. Now they're destined to be together for ever.'

I had heard that people might die on such a trip but it had never occurred to me it might be from something so stupid. If there wasn't fighting amongst our own wagon train, then it was with strangers we happened to meet. We often saw other groups making the same journey. It was a difficult trip, but instead of helping each other our guide, James, decided it was a matter of pride to get ahead and 'not eat their dust!'.

Most days there was a great flailing of bullwhips and loud quarrels as everyone tried to get in front. Louise called it 'jockeying for position'. I thought I'd seen enough of such silliness when we were on the *General*, but there wasn't much entertainment and I think people found it hard not to get caught up in it.

'Wagons ahead!' would be the call if anyone saw a train in front of us. Immediately some of the men in our train were so determined to get round them that they would fan out and do anything to get past. Then we lost any sense of being an even slightly organized train and ended more as a great bustle of wagons and people roughly heading in the same direction. Sometimes we would pass a train, and then while we were stopped for lunch or 'nooning' we would see them coming again. One of the men would jump up, saying, 'We earned the road too dearly to let them pass again!'

There was one team from Missouri who battled with us like that for days. James Long was just like our old steamboat pilot. He couldn't bear for anyone to beat us. One night he even made all us get up in the night to get round the Missourians. We managed it and everyone was happy but it was all pointless. We hadn't had enough sleep and walked so fast that the animals were exhausted. We ended up having to let the creatures rest as the Missourians passed once more and waved.

'Oh no!' cried someone. 'They passed us.'

'It seems foolishness to me,' I said to Louise.

'Men are not always sensible,' she agreed.

Louise seemed to know what she was doing. She could load her rifle in the blink of an eye and all her animals did as they were told. She strode about in her men's trousers and looked so confident. Even though she and Jeni looked old to me, nothing stopped them getting all the chores done and done quickly. Jeni was brilliant with an axe and could split logs better than anyone, while Louise rode her horse out to the plain as if she were flying. We got used to the fact that the sound of her gun firing meant she had found some supper. I began to think it might be nice to hunt some meat.

'I want to learn to do that,' I confided to Jack.

'Ask Louise to teach you,' he suggested, but I was too nervous to ask so he did it for me.

She came over one evening and stood in front of me saying, 'Jack says you want to learn to shoot.' I blushed and nodded. 'Well,' she continued, 'seeing as how you have your pistols in your belt every day, you might as well know what you're doing. I'd hate you to shoot me or Jeni by mistake.'

Louise began giving me lessons – first how to clean and look after the gun, then how to load and fire. The bang it made was so loud I didn't really like it. Louise was patient, but I soon realized that here was another thing I wasn't very good at. In the end I avoided her when she offered to help. I was embarrassed, so I didn't ask her about my horse either. I wanted to ride Chronicle so much, but my pride meant I ended up trying to work it out by myself. Louise was so sure and fast on her horse and James Long never seemed to give any instruction to his at all, yet it did just what he wanted. I had seen several cowboys in Independence and had imagined that I would be just like them once we were out on the prairie. I had everything I had hoped for – a fine horse, two splendid pistols, trousers and leather boots. I pictured myself sailing across the prairie on the back of my beautiful stallion, but instead of that he and I were hopeless together. Anything might set him off – a jackrabbit running in front of us or, honestly, a leaf blowing the wrong way – and my magnificent horse would put his head back, sit down and I'd slide to the ground. Kate had said I should keep trying and I knew she was right, so I got up out of the dust time and time again and back onto my exasperating horse.

I was embarrassed to be so useless so I took to riding a little way off from the train. I didn't want anyone laughing at me. One afternoon I was concentrating hard when a lumbering yellow creature suddenly appeared out of nowhere. I don't think I even bothered to wait for Chronicle to sit down. I knew it would happen so I leaped off into the dust and landed right at the feet of a stranger.

I say 'feet'. The truth is, I landed at the 'foot' of a stranger, for this man had only one leg.

CHAPTER NINE

Sometimes people joined the train for a while. They would seem to come out of nowhere, a frayed part of the rope, and suddenly be part of the moving parade of people. I had landed at the foot of an ancient-looking man with one normal leg and one made entirely of wood. He was what Da would have called 'a stranger to a razor'. His white beard had been allowed to grow until it stopped halfway down his chest. The hair on his head was equally white and out of control. He had a cart pulled by a single mule. The cart was made of so many pieces of other people's wagons that it was impossible to work out how it held together. It was his big yellow dog that had caused Chronicle to leap with fright.

'Good morning, good morning, good morning!' called the man in a surprisingly smart voice, before declaring, 'I say, better grab your horse!'

Chronicle was trying to make his usual escape. Not only did he still not like being ridden, any moment he could he turned back the way we had come. He seemed to have no interest in going to Oregon at all.

I got quickly to my feet and chased after my naughty horse. I grabbed his reins and decided I had done enough riding for the day.

'Dog!' called the man as he made a clicking noise, encouraging the mule to head for the wagon train. 'Come along, mule,' he said.

I ran to catch him up, pulling Chronicle along beside me. The man managed to walk just fine but I couldn't help looking down at his wooden leg.

'Yes, yes, just the one leg!' He beamed as if most people were extravagant for having two. 'Lost the other one in the war, you know. Battle of Waterloo. Against Napoleon?'

I shook my head.

'What are they teaching these days?' he exclaimed. '1815. I was a mere child, of course, but even a British child could see off a Frenchman!'

'You're English?'

He nodded. 'Wretched leg used to hurt anyway,' he continued. 'Bayonet wound, you know, so I'm glad it's gone.' He banged his wooden leg against the side of his cart. 'This thing causes me any trouble, why I just make another! Honestly I'm as sound as a . . .' He looked down at me. 'Is a dollar sound?'

I wasn't sure. 'I guess.'

'And your guess,' he declared, 'will do me.'

The train was stopping for our midday meal. He waved to Kate, saying, 'Name's Buddle! Colonel Buddle actually, but Buddle will do.'

Kate came over to say hello.

He was a most unusual fellow. Toby pulled on my sleeve and went to whisper to me.

'I know,' I said. 'He's only got one leg!'

'No, look!'

Toby pointed to Buddle's shoulder, where a bird appeared to be sitting. It looked like a real black crow but on closer inspection you could see that it was dead and stuffed.

With his small cart and mule Buddle seemed to carry almost as many things as we had in our whole wagon. He wore a red flannel shirt, belted around the waist like a dress, a single moccasin on his real foot and Indian trousers made of buckskin. He smoked a pipe and always muttered, '*Sacré enfant de grâce*,' when his mule refused to do what it was told.

'What's the dog called?' asked Toby.

'Dog,' replied Buddle.

'And the mule?' asked Toby a little more hesitantly.

Buddle snorted. 'Don't be ridiculous, boy. What does a mule want with a name?'

'You could call him "Mule",' suggested Toby. 'Our oxen are called Dromio One and Two, Balthazar and Malvolio,' he explained.

'How very smart,' said Buddle, and I suppose it was.

It seemed Buddle had been in the fur trade but he told us there wasn't work there any more.

'I arrived in these United States when the beaver hat was quite the fashion, but sadly it is no more,' he told us.

'Where are you going?' asked Bea, as politely as if we'd met for tea at Astor House.

'Heading west,' declared Buddle. 'There's adventure in the old man yet. Thought I'd see what there might be out there.' He waved his arms in the general direction we were heading.

Dog and Buddle and Mule soon slipped into our march as if they had always been with us. I don't know what the bird was called. 'Bird' probably.

At first the novelty of seeing new sights kept us going. I spent every spare moment either writing about our trip or trying to make friends with Chronicle. Mostly he and I just walked along with me leading him by the rein. So far the land had not been too rough, but after a few days we split with the Old Santa Fe Trail. We had often seen wagons piled high with goods travelling alongside us. Now they all swung south-west towards Santa Fe while we emigrants continued to head west. I think we were sorry to see them go. We felt much more alone.

We had all been excited at the beginning of the trip. At first we would all lie at night chatting under the stars. By now, however, darkness falling just meant that we went to sleep exhausted. We did get better at a few things. The whole wagon train knew how to pull all the wagons round into a circle to make a corral. The tongue of each wagon was placed on a rear wheel of the one in front of it to make a kind of fort. This meant we could keep the oxen inside the corral and have each other for protection in case of attack.

We began to learn things that would soon be second nature to us.

'How do we know which way to go?' I asked Louise.

'Every day it's the same,' she replied. 'Sun gets up in the east and goes to bed in the west. We're heading west so we want the sun on our backs in the morning and right in our eyes all darned afternoon. Some things you can just depend on.'

'*Nanpisa*,' I said. Louise frowned and looked at me. 'It means "the sun" in Choctaw. We need to pay attention to the sun.'

'You are a surprising child,' murmured Louise.

Whether the sun shone or not, each day my battle with Chronicle continued.

'I don't think he likes me, Toby,' I moaned. 'Every night I have to tie him up so tight or by morning he's trying to escape and turn back for home.'

'Maybe he's not happy. Maybe he wants an Indian brave on his back and not a little girl,' suggested Toby.

All Henry practised was grabbing the rifle and firing it. I think he was upset that the one time he had reached for it he had made such a mess of things. He became obsessed.

'We don't have Da,' he kept explaining, 'and I need to be able to look after you all.' He pointed to my pistols. 'You keep at those lessons with Louise, Slim.'

Henry was right but I didn't like the pistols at first. One of the men at the front of the train had accidentally shot himself in the foot while carrying a gun in his belt and I had lost my nerve. I didn't like the idea of losing part of my foot the way that man had. Despite Louise's lessons I packed my pistols away in the wagon. Now I didn't even ride my horse or carry a gun.

'Hopeless cowboy,' I muttered to myself.

We walked for miles and miles and yet the prairie didn't seem to get any smaller. Each morning it spread out before us as far as the eye could reach, bounded only by the blue wall of the sky. The green swells of grass and the flowery slopes were unending. They rolled ahead of us until they faded from sight in the dim distance.

'Isn't it wonderful?' breathed Jack as he stood admiring the view.

Hundreds of flowers decorated the velvety carpet of grass.

'Wild pink verbena, and that one with the blue bean-like blossom, that's wild indigo,' explained Louise. 'Look, there's larkspur!'

The flowers were so beautiful it was impossible to imagine that unpleasantness lay ahead, but there were hints of it. Already we were a little tired of the salted meat we had brought and Henry began talking about 'going hunting'. I think he was jealous of the wonderful smell of roast meat that drifted from Louise and Jeni's fire each night. They always offered to share but Henry was too proud to take any.

'I'm not too proud,' said Toby, and I agreed, but Henry wouldn't let us.

We began to see more and more wolves. At night they gathered to howl and during the day they skulked near the cattle, just out of rifle shot. James Long's horse stepped in a badger hole and had to be put down. One night Bea screamed until almost everyone in the wagon train came running. Louise was only half dressed but she had her gun ready to use.

'What is it?' yelled Jeni, running after Louise, her hair pulled up in a night-cap.

Henry and Toby were putting the animals out to grass and Jack had gone to help James with something. Kate was sitting by our fire rocking Hero. I ran past her to the wagon shouting, 'What's happening, Bea?' but Bea just stood in the back of the wagon screaming, pointing at her sewing bag. I thought she'd gone mad.

I could hear the Reverend complaining from inside his wagon, 'This noise is intolerable.' But he didn't come to help. Lots of other people ran towards us, but no one could work out what was the matter. Bea just kept making a horrible sound and pointing at her bag.

'Be quiet, Bea!' I yelled. 'It's just sewing. How dangerous can it be?'

But Louise saw what the problem was. 'I got ya!' she bellowed and then fired at the bag. It made us all jump. Now I thought she must be crazy too, but then she reached into the bag and pulled out a very long, very dead snake. She had shot its head right off.

'Pretty dangerous, I'd say,' she commented as the dead reptile swung in her hand.

'Can we keep it?' asked Toby, excited at the thought.

'We are not keeping a dead snake!' said Kate firmly.

'We're not even safe in the wagon,' Bea kept sobbing as Kate calmed her down by putting the kettle on.

'Think of the tale you'll have to tell one day,' said Kate. 'You'll be sitting with your sewing bag and have to explain why it's got a great gunshot hole in it. Who wouldn't want to hear such a story?'

The whole event made me think that I should try again with my pistols. Maybe it was true. Maybe we really didn't know who our enemies were.

From every mud puddle and stretch of marsh you could hear the bellowing, croaking and trilling of hundreds of frogs competing with the insects which buzzed around us. We got used to pulling a cup of water from a pool, only to find a handful of tadpoles swimming in the bottom of the cup.

Some days we marched for hours without seeing another living thing. Sometimes we'd walk with Jeni and Louise. Jeni lent her horse to James Long now that his had been put down. That meant she was always by her wagon. Sometimes the two women would make us play a game.

'Who can see anything at all beginning with the letter "A"?' Jeni would begin.

Toby, walking along behind us with Malvolio, would call out, 'An ox!'

'That doesn't count, young man, and you know it!' Louise would shout back, but Toby never tired of the joke.

Mostly we yelled out things that were on a wagon or a

person because there was nothing else to see. Jack was thrilled if we could point out at least a crow or a raven to break up the monotony.

'What shall we do tonight for wood and water?' became the question everyone asked about an hour before the sun set each night. It was a daily problem. There were more than two hundred people in the wagon train. Everyone needed food cooked over an open fire, and both people and animals needed water. Some nights it would almost be dark when at last someone would spot a dark green speck far away on the swell of the prairie. It was usually Jack. All his years as a sailor meant he was used to looking at the horizon from the helm.

'There!' he'd cry, and we'd all rush towards what we hoped was a tree, beneath which might lie some water.

If Jack was right, we would all pitch camp and Kate would rush about getting out our tin cups, iron spoons and the coffee pot. All along the wagon train it was the coffee pot which came out first. Coffee was what everyone drank. I didn't like it at first but soon it became something to look forward to.

I'd make the fire with my silver matchbox and then Kate would roast the coffee beans in a skillet. After that the beans all went in a bag and Jack would crush them with the handle of our axe. Toby or Henry would bring water and fill the coffee pot. The crushed beans would be dumped in and set on the fire to boil. Louise taught us to throw egg-shells in the pot to settle the grounds but others used to tie a rope to the pot and swing it in circles to move the coffee grounds to the bottom. It didn't matter how you made it: Toby didn't like it at all. We kept trying to get him to drink it but he would screw his face up at the slightest sip.

'Tastes like mud,' he would complain.

One night we had found a particularly good spot with lots of pools of water. For once it wasn't raining and there was a gorgeous sunset; the red glow of the sky was reflected in the nearby water. Kate was playing with Hero by the fire and it almost felt like a picnic. My little baby sister was growing up. She was crawling about so fast now she had to be watched all the time. Bea was 'visiting' with Mrs Meadows and Toby was checking the oxen once more, which was how he spent most evenings.

Henry stood beside the wagon with the rifle over his shoulder. He reached inside and grabbed my pistols.

'Let's go hunting,' he said to me and Jack.

I didn't want to. I was afraid of the bang of my pistols and I was hopeless at riding my horse. I was pretty sure hunting was a terrible combination of both those things. So much for me being a cowboy!

Henry could tell what I was thinking. 'All right, we can

walk,' he said, 'and I'll bring the rifle, Slim, so you don't need to bother with a gun.'

'I've seen some prairie hens over that way,' said Jack, pointing. He led the way towards some bushes in the distance, with Henry behind him carrying the rifle and me dragging along behind. I felt bad about being so useless.

I knew about prairie hens as we'd seen a few. They were like a sort of thin brown striped chicken and the boy ones had a bright orange lump at the neck. Soon the ground became tricky to get across. There were large clumps of very tall grass with great gaps in between which weren't easy to walk through. It was easier for Jack with his long legs and he kept having to help me. Henry followed behind. At last we came to the edge of the bushes where a wide stream of water about three inches deep was slowly making its way over a bottom of sleek mud. Jack reached for my hand, and as he did, he brushed some water willows growing along the edge. This upset a huge green bullfrog, which gave a furious croak. It jumped off the bank with a loud splash, throwing water up at Jack. You might think that after all his years at sea he wouldn't mind a bit of damp spray, but he leaped back as if Henry had fired the rifle at him and fell backwards onto the bank.

Both Henry and I laughed. 'What's the matter, Jack? It's only one of Toby's frogs,' I said.

'I don't like water,' he muttered, getting up again.

'But you're a sailor,' I protested.

Jack looked almost cross. 'I like being *on* water, not *in* it.'

'You're scared of it!' teased Henry, and he was right. Our great big friend who had sailed the world's oceans didn't actually like water.

Jack looked really upset. 'It's all right,' I soothed. 'I have a horse and can't ride. We all have our ways.'

This particular pool of water looked harmless enough. It was shallow and full of living creatures. More frogs, these ones small and spotted, followed the example of their leader, and three tiny turtles, no bigger than a dollar, tumbled into the water.

'Snake!' shouted Henry, pointing to a black and yellow one that glided out from the bank and slithered across to the other side.

We all scrambled away as fast as we could and headed for some rising ground covered with trees and bushes. Henry was leading, when suddenly he stopped and began swinging his hat violently around his head, and lifting first one foot and then the other without moving from the spot. He kept looking down at the ground for something and then glancing up.

'No! I . . . hey!' he began shouting.

He looked as though he had gone mad.

Jack and I ran forward to see what the trouble was and heard a droning sound, as if twenty beehives had been overturned at once.

'Look!' cried Jack, pointing above Henry's head.

It wasn't bees. The air above was full of large black insects in a state of great commotion. Like a sort of beetle but flying.

'There!' yelled Jack.

'And there!' I echoed.

Hundreds of the dark bugs were flying towards us just above the tops of the grass blades.

'Run!' shouted Jack and he began sprinting away from the clouds of insects. Henry was fixed to the spot so I grabbed his hand and pulled him away. He didn't seem hurt, just out of breath and dazed.

One of the bugs landed right on his nose. He went to hit it with his hat but bashed his nose instead.

'Ow!' he cried.

'Don't fight them,' I shouted. 'Run!'

I wasn't waiting any longer. The horrible bugs were all around us now. I hoped Henry would have the sense to follow. We must have run for about half a mile before we finally left the wretched flying creatures behind. We were all out of breath.

'We're never going to see anything to shoot at this rate,' huffed Henry, embarrassed to have been defeated by something as small as an insect. Just then a flock of prairie hens rose up from a nearby bush.

'There!' shouted Jack.

Henry had no time to think. Still shaking from his encounter, he raised the rifle to his shoulder and fired. The gunshot threw him back on the ground and the small flock of birds instantly flew off, flapping hard. One bird, however, seemed to have been injured.

'I think you got one!' shouted Jack, but the creature was not finished yet. It carried on trying to get away so Jack chased after it and we chased after him. The bird had been wounded by Henry's shot but it still managed to keep fluttering from his grasp. Jack was so focused on what he was doing that he didn't realize he had reached the bank of one of the pools. He put his hand out for the hen, grabbed it, and in that moment he and the bird fell into the water. Luckily there was a willow sapling just where he went down and he managed to grab hold of it. He emerged from the water shaking but still holding onto his prize bird.

Henry and I were jumping up and down with delight. 'Well done, Jack, well done!' I cried. 'You conquered the water *and* caught some dinner!'

Jack stood there, soaking wet and shivering and trying to smile, but I could see how much the water had frightened him. 'I still hate it,' he managed to say.

Henry reached out his hand. 'Come on, big fella. Don't you worry, I'll get you out.'

When we got back with our prize, Kate was sitting with Toby and Bea by our fire. We told our tale and she laughed as Jack mumbled about how much he hated water. Just as he was getting to the part where he fell in the pond, he suddenly stopped and clapped his hand to his cheek. We began to hear sounds as if bullets were humming over our heads. Something rapped me sharply on the forehead, then on the neck, and I felt as though I was being scratched at with small claws.

'It's the bugs!' yelled Henry, who had had quite enough of them for one day.

I saw Jeni, by her fire, jump up.

'Dorbug!' she shouted.

We could hear Louise reply, 'They won't hurt you, you old fool!'

I don't think they *did* want to hurt us, but they were horrible. We all scrambled into the wagon even though there wasn't really room for us all, and tried to close the covers.

Kate pulled out a blanket for Jack and tried to get him warm.

'I am never going in water again,' he declared, shivering.

'You'll be glad you did when you taste that hen tomorrow, Jack,' Kate soothed.

I looked at my big friend from the sea. We had all had enough of water. It was water that had claimed Ma when she was buried in the great ocean, and water that had taken Da from us on the Ohio River. But we had no idea of the trouble water was still to cause.

CHAPTER TEN

The first thing I saw in the morning was Kate by the fire holding our frying pan at arm's length. In our rush to get into the wagon the night before, the pan had been left by the fire and now the bottom of it was covered with the wretched dorbugs. Dozens more lay shrivelled and scattered amongst the ashes. But we had no time to worry about that because a cry went up from Toby.

'The animals!' he yelled.

Chronicle and the oxen had been turned loose to feed, but now they seemed to have joined a whole band of others, including mules and a milk cow, making an escape. All of them appeared to have agreed on a plan to run back to where we had come from. About twenty assorted animals were running as fast they could manage. Some of them had been 'hobbled' overnight, which meant having their front legs fastened together with a rope, but that didn't stop them trying to hop away as fast as possible. I was ashamed to see that Chronicle was right out in front, leading the charge.

Men and boys ran after them, dashing through the tall grass and mostly running into each other as they tried to cut the herd off. Everyone was yelling. Buddle kept shouting advice, the Reverend and his wife got on their knees to pray and the Honeymans shook their heads, but there seemed to be no plan whatsoever.

Nervous Bob just stood looking helpless, shouting, 'The Injuns will get them, the Injuns will get them!'

Toby was running along behind all the men, crying, 'The animals won't stop if you scare them!'

Louise's horse had not joined the escaped gang so she saddled up and raced off to try and help.

Jeni stood watching. 'I think all those animals want is to get back to town,' she declared.

'So do I,' sighed Bea. We had been travelling for weeks now and she had had more than enough. 'I wouldn't be at all surprised if none of them come back.'

'I think the animals are more organized than we are,' said Kate as she tried to stop Hero putting one of the dead dorbugs in her mouth. She was nearly a year old now and liked to crawl towards anything within reach and try to eat it.

'Slim, take Hero please?'

I picked up my baby sister but I didn't want to. It wasn't that I didn't like her. It was just that I wanted to be the one saving the day on my horse instead of babysitting while Chronicle caused trouble.

It was Louise who managed to get some sense into what was happening. She galloped towards the herd, which she managed to head off, and moved them back towards the wagon train. By now the escaped animals were frightened. Their pawing and rearing up caused a great dust storm to erupt around them. The men were all yelling and Toby was right in the middle of it all. He was so small that his head didn't even come up to the shoulder of the horses, and suddenly he disappeared.

Bea had just poked her head out of the wagon when she saw what was happening.

'Toby!' she yelled, and Kate gave a great gasp as we lost sight of my little brother.

There was dust everywhere and the bright sun shone down, making it difficult to see. Then, in a great shaft of light, we saw him. Toby had caught Chronicle by a rope trailing from his bridle and, even though my brother was small and the horse quite tall, Toby had leaped onto his back and managed to ride in front of the remaining runaway animals. Chronicle had no saddle, yet Toby controlled him and forced all the escaping creatures to slow down. He had clearly learned a thing or two from watching Louise. Now the two of them were in charge of the chaotic herd.

'Whoa! Whoa!' Toby called out in his unnaturally loud voice.

'Easy now!' shouted Louise, and the oxen and mules and horses all began to calm enough for the crowd to catch up and grab them. The animals were driven back to the train with lots of curses and sounds of irritation. Some of the animals had cut themselves on their hobbling ropes while others were out of breath and steaming with sweat. Toby was quite the hero of the hour but he had no time for anyone's praise.

'Where's Malvolio?' he called out as he slid off Chronicle's back.

We all looked around – until Kate began laughing and pointed under the wagon.

Malvolio had clearly not liked all the commotion and was now lying as far under one wheel of the wagon as he could get, trying to hide his big head and looking out at us with only one eye open.

'Maybe you should have Chronicle,' I said quietly to Toby. 'He behaves for you.'

Toby shook his head. 'You just have to tell him you're in charge. Remember what Nashobanowa said: *If you talk to the animals, they will talk to you and you will know each other*. Tell Chronicle what you want and you'll be all right.'

I looked down at Toby and thought how odd it was that I was taking advice from my little brother, but then there was nothing about this trip that anyone could have expected. I decided it couldn't hurt to follow his advice. He seemed to have the most extraordinary skill when it came to animals, so I took Chronicle from him and walked away from the wagon.

I passed Louise, sitting drinking coffee with Jeni. Jeni was fussing about, but Louise sat calmly as if nothing had happened.

'Listen to your brother,' she called out to me. 'Let your horse know you need him to help you. Make friends with him.'

I carried on walking with Chronicle, and once we stood alone on the prairie I pulled my horse's head down level with my mouth.

'I need you to help me, Chronicle,' I whispered. 'I need you to never do that again. Please don't run off because I need you to get us all to Uncle Niall. Then I promise you can have a whole field to yourself and as much grass as any horse could manage.'

Chronicle just stared at me with his huge brown eyes, and in that moment I had had enough. I had no more fight left in me. If he didn't want to be my horse, then I would just give up. I let him go. I dropped the reins and sat down on the ground, sobbing. The world was finished for me and I couldn't do any more. I sat hunched in a little ball, weeping with all my heart, and then I felt something on my neck. It was Chronicle. Rather than running off he was nuzzling me with his soft white nose. Gently he pushed me as if he were trying to get me to stand up. I looked up at him and knew he meant well but I felt hopeless. I took hold of his reins, and slowly we walked back to the wagon train.

I think Algernon Honeyman was jealous of all the attention Toby got because that night he picked a fight with him. Toby stood his ground and got a black eye for his trouble. Mrs Honeyman blamed Toby and said he was not to come near Algernon again, but we all knew the truth about what had happened.

It was late the following morning before we were back on the march. Kate cooked the prairie hen and I never ate anything more delicious in my life. We were all tired of the salty meat we had brought with us from Independence.

Not a breath of air stirred over the open prairie. The clouds were like light piles of cotton, and where the blue sky was visible it looked hazy and fit only for anyone who wanted to sit still for the day. The summer heat was beginning to rise and the sun beat down on us as we crept slowly over the endless plain. *Nanpisa.* The animals hung their heads as if ashamed of their morning's adventure. I tied Chronicle to the back of our wagon and even he seemed a little embarrassed.

The day had already been difficult and everyone was tired when we reached our first big river. So far we had crossed only small streams but now we faced something much greater. We knew we must be heading towards water because large trees showed the way. Trees only grew where there was water. There were tall sycamores with a patchwork of brown bark, as if they had been painted by the same person who had given Chronicle his splashes of white and black. Wide cottonwoods like huge umbrellas of green also lined our path, and an occasional elm, standing more majestic than the rest, tempted some of the younger boys, led by Algernon, to try and climb high in the branches.

As we approached the river we all stopped to look. It was very wide and very fierce.

'No choice but to go across,' yelled James as he rode up and down the line on Jeni's horse. 'Halt here. We need to check the depth and the speed of the current before we make our way.'

'What happens now?' asked Jack, clearly frightened by the fast-moving water.

'We might try and ford it,' explained James, 'but if it's too deep we'll have to float.'

'What does that mean? Ford?' asked Toby, worried about the animals.

'Walk through it,' explained Louise.

Reverend Goudy's wife, Parenthia, had been walking with Kate. She looked very anxious and began pacing up and down at the water's edge.

'Isn't there a bridge?' she asked anxiously.

'It's the wild west,' soothed Kate. 'There's been no one ahead of us to build bridges.'

Jeni laughed at the idea and called out, 'Maybe you can get your husband to part the waters like Moses did with that sea!'

Toby's pig, Hamlet, had made friends with Buddle's yellow dog called Dog. They played together all the time, and somehow they had both managed to get amongst the oxen, which didn't help. Malvolio clearly didn't like the look of this and was trying his best to turn round. Toby called out for Jack to help him hold the animals steady but Jack was hiding behind one of the trees.

'I can't do that, Slim,' he said, pointing at the river. 'There's too much water and no boat.'

'Maybe we should wait till the water is calmer,' wailed Mrs Honeyman, who was also becoming afraid.

'Stop your nonsense,' snapped Louise, helping Mrs Meadows out of the wagon to go across. The old woman was very frail and it was hard to see how she would make it.

'We have to keep moving,' said Henry, repeating his most common fear. 'We can't delay or we'll never get over the mountains before the snow.'

I walked along the bank to see what was happening and found James sitting on the ground with an old Indian. They were passing a pipe of tobacco between them as if they had all the time in the world. The old Indian man was explaining that he loved the white people but that he liked tobacco even more. At this James handed him a small pouch of the stuff and the man beamed. An old squaw was cooking something on a small fire, and even though I knew we needed to keep moving, no one seemed to be in a rush. Up above their heads three buzzards were sitting on the limb of a dead sycamore. Their ugly heads were drawn down between their shoulders and they seemed to be keeping an eye on us all.

They probably saw the rest of the tribe approach before we did.

'Injuns! Injuns!' cried Nervous Bob, running to get behind a tree.

I looked up and saw a whole parade of men, women and children, some on horseback, some on foot, but all looking poor and wretched. There were old squaws on thin ponies with sometimes one or two wide-eyed children sitting behind them, clinging to their tattered blankets. Tall young braves on foot with bows and arrows in their hands and girls in scarlet cloth and glass beads marched along. Most of them didn't even look at us as they passed. One old man riding a tough shaggy pony stopped near our wagon. The horse was in a terrible state, with its mane and tail knotted with burrs, a rusty bit in its mouth and just a string of rawhide for reins. The old man wore a buckskin frock, which, like his fringed leggings, was well polished and blackened by grease and wear. An old handkerchief was tied around his head. He carried a rifle but it rested across his saddle as if it were rarely used.

He looked at me. 'Food?' he said simply.

'They're hungry, Kate,' I said.

She nodded and reached into the wagon for some bread we had made the night before. We were getting better at making it and this batch didn't look too bad. He took it, nodded and rode on.

Even though Reverend Goudy and his wife were heading west to go and help the Indians, Parenthia seemed very nervous about actually having anything to do with them.

'Why did you do that?' she asked Kate. 'Why did you give them bread?'

'They look hungry,' Kate replied. 'Haven't you come to save them?'

'Not these ones,' replied Parenthia, and turned away.

Nervous Bob was shaking. 'You shouldn't encourage

them,' he declared slowly, coming out from behind the tree where he had been hiding. 'You'll cause trouble for us. Why does no one listen to me?' Suddenly he stopped speaking and took a deep breath before he pointed at us and said, 'You Hannigans are on the side of the Indians! They give you a horse! You're going to help them!'

'We will help anyone who needs it,' I declared. 'They are good people. All that is the matter with them is that they are poor.' I was so angry I thought I might cry. 'They lived here first. We should be nice to them, and you should . . . you should be ashamed of yourself.'

'Mind your manners, Slim,' muttered Kate, but when Bob had gone she patted me quietly on the back.

I could tell Bob didn't trust us. After that he started hanging about watching us. It wasn't long before one of the Indian women came and asked for some flour and Kate gave her that too. Bob was beside himself but Kate wouldn't listen. Later the Indian woman came back.

'I told you!' shouted Bob, appearing out of nowhere. He pointed at the squaw as she walked towards our wagon. 'They want everything we have. Beggars!' he screamed.

But the woman had returned to bring Kate some shell beads. She smiled and handed them over. We couldn't talk to her.

'She's saying thank you,' said Kate.

'Well, I say watch out,' muttered Bob.

Kate was not happy with him. 'It's their land that we are crossing,' she protested.

'But we will make it ours,' he replied.

Louise was passing and shook her head. 'That man should never have left New York,' she commented.

Toby watched the Indians walk slowly away. 'They don't look at all scary,' he admitted.

'Where are they going?' I asked Buddle, who stood watching with his stuffed bird on his shoulder and his dog by his side.

'Probably begging in the nearest town.' He shook his head. 'A noble people. It's a terrible thing that has happened to them.'

After an age of sitting and smoking with James Long the old Indian took him to fetch two dugout canoes, which the tobacco had helped the Indian 'remember' he owned.

Now James got everyone working. He showed the men how to dig ramps down the steep banks of the river while others built a raft by laying timbers crossways between the two canoes. This would be for the wagons to get across, but first the livestock had to swim over.

'The animals will follow a leader,' explained James, 'so we need the biggest of them to lead the way. Toby was thrilled when this turned out to be Malvolio. He did look very strong, but Toby's pride didn't last long. Malvolio got into the water without too much trouble and set out for the other shore, but something spooked him and he changed his mind halfway, turning back in a great loop.

'No, Malvolio!' shouted Toby from the riverbank.

He started to get into the water but Henry held him back.

'There's too many, Toby,' he cried.

The other animals did indeed follow a leader, and now they all turned round and headed back towards us. There were men waist high in the river trying to direct them.

'That way!' shouted Toby, pointing to the other side of the river. 'Malvolio! What are you doing?'

Algernon Honeyman stood near Toby laughing. He didn't seem to understand how dangerous it all was.

'Not so good with animals now, are you, Toby Hannigan?' he called, sniggering and pointing.

No one could get the animals to head in the right direction. All the men could manage was to guide them downstream and back towards the bank where they had started. There were men shouting and cracking whips all over. Soon all the oxen were just swimming in a circle and getting nowhere. The cattle were becoming tired and it wasn't long before they tried to climb on each other's backs to get out of the water.

Toby was starting to cry. 'They'll drown!' he cried.

The animals struggled back to the shore, but then some got stuck in the mud and began bellowing.

'Ropes and spades!' ordered Toby, running to get our spade from the wagon. Now everyone was frantically digging and trying to pull the exhausted animals free by tying ropes to them and pulling. Jack pulled with all his might while Henry and I dug mud with our bare hands to get them out.

At last all the animals were safe. Everyone was exhausted and filthy, but we were still on the side of the river where we had begun.

'Catch your breath,' ordered James, 'and we'll try again.'

Toby, who was covered in mud, leaped to James's side. 'Someone needs to lead the leader,' he said breathlessly. 'The leader can't swim on his own.'

James nodded. 'Yes, but not your ox, Toby,' he declared.

Toby was disappointed, but Malvolio had disgraced himself, so this time a smaller ox, which belonged to Nervous Bob, was chosen to lead the way. Bob was beside himself with worry but no one listened to him. A rope was tied to his ox and two men led it into the water. The river ran fast and none of the animals liked it. They snorted as they were brought to the bank, tossed their horns and balked, until men on horseback with whips forced them forward. Meanwhile the entire wagon train surrounded the herd and made all the animals swim after the old Indian in a canoe. It was an astonishing sight – a great wedge-shaped mass of cattle with big-eyed, anxious cows and small calves at the back.

Buddle led his single mule and cart down to the river-bank. As soon as the animal saw the water he reared up. As the mule fell forward, he lost his footing and plunged down into the flowing stream. The ropes and straps which held him to the cart broke and the whole thing was flung into the river. Now everything Buddle owned was caught by the moving water. We all scrambled to grab what we could as Buddle and Henry pulled the poor mule back to safety.

Toby was busy all day with everyone's animals. I've never seen a little boy work so hard. His loud voice soothed and persuaded frightened creatures and everyone wanted his help.

Henry stood looking at him as we waited to get our wagon across.

'He's loud, isn't he?' said Henry.

'He's the king of the animals,' I replied.

Henry nodded. 'Yes, I do believe he is.'

I think it made Henry look at him in a different light. This was not our annoying little brother but an important member of the wagon train.

It took a day and a half to get everyone over the water, and despite all our efforts it was a sad time. Some of the cattle got stuck in the sandy riverbank, which had been so trampled that it became, as Buddle said, 'just like quick-sand'. I didn't know what that meant but I did know that the more the poor creatures tried to get out, the faster they seemed to sink into the mud. A few were dug out with pick and spade and pulled free, but others were so deeply stuck that they had to be abandoned. Their cries were terrible to hear. In all, three horses and twenty cattle were lost to the river that day. Toby was inconsolable and wept in Kate's arms.

The wagons were next. They were wheeled aboard our makeshift boat one by one and ferried across with oars and ropes. It took a while for everyone to work out what they were doing. The Honeymans had been keen to get their wagon on first. They hadn't helped anyone else so no one much wanted to help them.

'I'll pay ten dollars!' shouted Mr Honeyman loudly, waving green banknotes in the air. Someone took the money but in their rush almost overbalanced the boat and Algernon was tipped into the water. He lost a boot in the swirling river and after that had to walk barefoot.

'Not so good at walking now, are you, Algernon Honeyman?' called Toby, but Kate told him off for not being kind.

Once on the other side all the teams of animals were doubled up to help pull the wagons up the opposite bank.

Buddle's mule and cart were saved but most of his things were gone. Getting the printing press across was the hardest of all and I don't think anyone except our family thought it was worth it. The old cart it stood on was beginning to look as if it wouldn't make it but we had nothing else we could use.

At last it was time to begin to move the many people in the wagon train. Anyone who could manage it had to walk waist high through the water, while some of the children, baby Hero and old Mrs Meadows were taken across on the raft. Poor Mrs Meadows was not well. She could hardly manage to move, and getting her onto the raft caused her terrible pain.

'The trip is too much for her,' sighed Louise.

The weight of all the traffic caused the raft to snap on the last journey, and the wood it had been made of drifted off down the river. No one minded.

The whole train was safely across. The only person still on the wrong side of the river was Jack. He had helped everyone pull their animals free. He had been so brave and strong, pulling on the ropes, but now he stood shaking his head at the thought of wading across. He was like a big frightened ox himself. No one had enjoyed getting across the river but he really hated water. Now he was the one who needed my help.

'Idiot,' declared Nervous Bob. 'Big man like that frightened!'

'Just because you are big does not mean you can't be afraid,' replied Kate, whose jaw was tense with worry about Jack. She wasn't that much older than Bea but her face looked strained. I thought how much older she looked than when we had first met her all those months ago.

Some of the men began jeering and calling Jack names across the water. Others suggested that we move on and just leave him behind.

'Kate!' I cried. 'We have to help him.'

'Of course we do, Slim.'

'The canoe!' I pointed to the Indian man who had been letting us use it. It stood ready to paddle but he shook his head as if his work was done and began to leave.

'Kate!' I moaned.

'What would Nashobanowa tell us to do?' she asked quietly. I couldn't think. She smiled. '*Conquer a man who never gives by gifts.*'

Kate reached into the back of our wagon and pulled out a length of bright red material. She took it to the old Indian and gave it to him as a present. Then she pointed to one of the dugout canoes. Now he nodded.

Kate walked over to me where I was standing beside Chronicle.

'I've borrowed one of the canoes. I'm going to get him,' she announced, but just then Hero began to cry and reach for her.

'It's all right, Kate,' said Henry, smiling at her for the first time that I could remember. 'We can do it. Come on, Slim.'

You'll think me silly, but after my first conversation with Chronicle I had taken to chatting to my horse.

'I'm scared,' I whispered as I held my face against the side of his. It felt soft and he blew a little warm air on me, which felt nice.

'Slim! Come on!' yelled Henry, and I swear Chronicle gently nudged me towards the water.

Henry and I paddled back to Jack. We had watched the Indians use a canoe and tried to copy what they had done.

'You paddle one side and I'll do the other,' instructed Henry, steering from the back with his oar. The current in the middle of the river was fast. It was what had taken the horses and cattle whose lives were lost.

We could hear faint voices carrying across the water as we struggled across. 'Coward!' shouted someone. 'Scaredy-cat!' called another.

Jack stood trembling on the shore. 'I'm sorry, Slim, Henry.'

'It's all right,' I said quietly. 'You don't have to get in the water. You're all right on a boat. You like a boat.'

'But this one is so small,' said Jack, shivering. 'It's so close to the water.'

'You'll be fine,' I assured him.

Jack was right. The canoe was small and he was very large. We quickly discovered that we couldn't get all three of us in it.

'I think it's even too small to take me and Jack,' said Henry. 'You'll have to do it, Slim. I'll wait here,' he suggested. 'You take Jack and come back for me. Jack, you paddle at the front, and Slim, you sit at the back and use the oar to steer when you get in the current.'

Henry got out onto the bank and Jack had to be persuaded into the boat. He did paddle, but he also shut his eyes the whole way across. I was terrified, and it took all my strength to steer us safely across. Jack almost fell out of the boat onto the other bank, where Bea and Kate were waiting.

'Slim . . . you . . .' Kate began, but I was already heading back for Henry. I think if I had stopped I would have thought about how frightened I was and not been able to do it. Now I was on my own, having to both paddle and steer. The water swirled around me, and suddenly the current took hold of the canoe and spun it in a great circle before forcing me fast down the river.

'Use the paddle!' shouted Henry. 'Hold it steady behind you and use it as a brake.'

I tried that, but the pressure of the water against the oar made me feel as though my arms would never be able to hold on.

'You can do it, Slim!' I could hear from someone.

Suddenly the current seemed to release me, and with a quick stroke I was out of the fast waters in the middle and heading once more to Henry. He stepped waist high into the water and grabbed the boat as the stream threatened to whirl me away once more.

'I got you!' he yelled, pulling himself into the boat. Henry was soaking but he grinned at me.

'Well done, Slim, well done!' He beamed and I felt myself flush with pride.

Henry picked up the spare paddle, and together we made for the shore, where the family all stood waiting anxiously with Jeni, Louise and Buddle. As we got to the other bank Henry got out and I was so pleased that I stood up to cheer, only to find myself toppling into the water. I went under in a great heap, and it was Chronicle who reached in and gently grabbed the back of my trousers with his teeth so I could steady myself. I pulled myself out. Both Henry and I were now soaked but our family and friends didn't care. They rushed around us, with Kate bringing blankets and all of us hugging and laughing.

'Thank you, Chronicle,' I mouthed to my horse, but he turned away and pretended nothing had happened.

Reverend Goudy stood by the riverbank and insisted we all thank God for our deliverance. Everyone was exhausted but the whole wagon train stood silent as the Reverend raised his arms and proclaimed, 'We are like the children of Israel in the wilderness, but we remember that the' – he wheezed for a bit before continuing – 'that the everlasting arms are underneath us at all times, holding us up and—' Just then he raised his arms for emphasis, lost his footing, and he too fell backwards into the river.

'Well, maybe not holding us up all the time,' commented Louise, and I'm afraid we all laughed. We needed to. We were not even halfway through our incredible journey, and already everyone was so tired they could hardly speak.

No one said it, but the truth is, I had been thoughtless getting so wet. I had forgotten about the matches in my pocket. The silver box was fine but the matches inside were ruined. Now we needed to borrow fire from someone else each night and I was very cross with myself.

The train of wagons stretched out as once more we were on the move. A few more families had joined us over the last few days. Jack counted and we were now more than eighty wagons. We were quite near the front. I walked along with Chronicle and Buddle.

'How far back to the last wagon do you think, Buddle?' I asked.

He looked back to the final wagon, which seemed so small. He squinted in the sun and then declared, 'Must be at least a mile.'

'How does James know where to go?' asked Toby as he coaxed our team of oxen along.

Buddle pointed ahead. 'There's the sun, of course, but if you look carefully you can sometimes see faint wheel tracks in the grass. Get used to looking for signs of others. Always know the lay of the land as you head into battle.'

He was right. Here and there you could see a band of grass had been pressed down before by wagon wheels.

'That means other folks been this way afore us,' agreed Louise.

'I like that,' Bea called from the wagon, where she was having a short ride. 'I like that others have been here before. I don't want to be alone out here.'

Bea was not the only person worried about being alone. We were in the middle of nowhere, and guarding was about to become a big issue for us all. Nervous Bob had talked about little else since the start of the trip, of course, but as we headed into the land of the Otoes, everyone was worrying about the Indians.

'The Otoes are a small, peaceful tribe,' said Louise, trying to get everyone to be calm, but even James said this tribe liked to steal cattle.

'We'll need a guard at night. Two-hour shifts for every man each night,' he announced.

This decision caused yet more uproar. I wasn't sure why. So far all the Indians we had met had been very nice.

Occasionally a few Indians would follow the wagon train, but all they ever wanted was coffee and biscuits. Kate, and sometimes Jeni, would feed them and then they would go away again. Though it made Bob furious.

There was a lot of arguing between the men about who should guard and when. Despite all the bickering Bea seemed happier. The landscape was beautiful and she took to drawing it each time we stopped. She said even the finest coloured pencils couldn't compete with the loveliness of the bright green grass, flecked as it was with red, blue and yellow wild flowers. We found the verbena and the indigo plant in large quantities, and also a species of wild geranium. James showed us a plant called the prairie pea, which had a fruit the size of a walnut. It tasted nice – a bit like a green pea – and if you ate them raw when it was hot, it made you less thirsty.

Finding enough to drink was a daily problem. Jeni and Louise's two milk cows, Daisy and Gert, had been providing lovely milk for Hero, and Jeni really loved them. One day we were all marching along as usual when one of the cows suddenly fell down in the road.

'Daisy!' yelled Jeni.

The poor cow just lay there and wouldn't get up again. Even Toby couldn't persuade her.

'Poor Daisy is tired, Jen,' said Louise gently. 'It's too much for her.'

Jeni began crying, but Louise said it was kind to let her go.

'Slim,' she said to me. 'Take Toby away.'

'No!' cried Toby, but I took him by the arm and made him get in our wagon for a while. We were inside, crushed against some boxes, when we heard a rifle shot. Toby jumped and tried to get out but I held onto him.

'It wouldn't have been kind to make her keep walking,' I said, but my little brother was so upset.

'*I'm* tired, but no one is going to shoot *me*,' he wailed.

The next day there was fresh beef. Louise and Jeni insisted we had some. I'm afraid it was delicious but Toby wouldn't eat any. He shook his head and asked for bread instead.

One time we passed another wagon train. It was smaller than ours. Just ten wagons, all belonging to the same family. The Walkers of Missouri were led by Christopher Walker and his wife, Sophie. They had several sons and daughters, all of whom were heading west. The Walkers had a lot of cows and other stock with them. They were nice. They offered to sell a cow to Louise and Jeni, but Jeni said she couldn't go through looking after a new one and maybe losing it.

One evening Jack and I found a water hole to go fishing in. We had to be patient, but after about two hours we had caught fifteen small fish. Buddle had lost all his cooking things in the river so now he cooked with us. I liked what he made. It didn't matter what it was, he called it 'mess' and it was always delicious. That night he stirred up the fish with some wild onions. I think Kate was glad of the help. She didn't really like cooking. We shared it with Louise and Jeni. We ate most of our meals with them and Mrs Meadows now. Everyone was too tired to worry about anything except getting fed and moving on.

'Where are you from, Kate?' asked Louise while Kate made bread.

I realized I didn't know. I knew Kate was Irish but I had never asked her about what life she had come from. I was ashamed that I hadn't paid more attention.

'Dublin,' she replied, smiling.

'Do you have family?' asked Jeni.

'My sister in California and my father . . . he lives in the place in Dublin where I grew up. They call it "The Liberties". He's a fine man but I . . . disappointed him.'

'Did you have a grand house?' asked Toby.

Kate nodded. 'Yes, we did. What makes you say that, Toby?'

Toby pointed to the bread, which was burning. ''Cos I don't think you did a lot of cooking.'

We all laughed.

I liked all of us sitting together round the fire. Louise, Jeni, Mrs Meadows and Buddle as well as the rest of us.

'Jack nearly stepped on a snake today,' I told them.

Jack looked embarrassed. 'There's no need to tell everyone, Slim!' he said, sounding a bit cross.

'You tell us, Jack,' urged Kate, smiling.

He looked down but managed to explain, 'It was about three foot long, with a sort of triangular head and a thick body.'

'Dark brown, nearly black,' I added.

Louise nodded. 'Sounds like a moccasin snake. Poisonous, but they don't usually bite people' – she paused – 'unless you threaten them.'

'They sound worth keeping clear of,' remarked Kate as Buddle served out the last of the delicious fish.

Later that night the moon and stars shone and all seemed calm. The cattle were feeding and campfires blazed everywhere you looked. Men, women and children were talking, playing and singing. We could hear the whole Walker train carrying on and having a party in the distance. It felt safe and happy. Some people had been anxious about the Otoe, and as no guards had been arranged they had driven the animals up close and attached them to their wagon by chains. Hero had fallen asleep on Kate's shoulder and I was standing stroking Chronicle. I could see Bea washing up the dinner plates in a bucket. Jeni and Louise had left some time ago to help Mrs Meadows to bed. Just then there was a terrible cry from a wagon on the other side of the corral.

'Injuns! Injuns! Injuns took our cattle!' yelled a boy's voice. It was Algernon Honeyman calling from a distance.

'Where's Henry and Jack?' I called.

'They went to get water!' shouted Kate as she and Bea raced to get Hero and Toby into the wagon.

I could see Sophie Walker gathering her many children and herding them into the wagons. Louise leaped from her wagon, her gun ready to defend us all.

'I need to stay with the animals!' protested Toby, almost kicking Bea in his temper.

'Toby, get in the wagon!' she demanded, grabbing him and speaking more forcefully than I had ever heard.

'Come on, Slim,' called Kate, but I could see our rifle hanging from the side of the wagon and thought we ought to have it to protect ourselves. I ran and grabbed it, but I hadn't really had much to do with it and it was heavier than I thought. As I got it, I fell forward and the gun went off. I hadn't realized Henry had taken to leaving it fully loaded since the first time he'd had such trouble with it.

Reverend Goudy was a few yards away and fell down

shouting, 'I've been shot by Indians!' and soon there was the most almighty roar as everyone else leaped up and reached for any weapon they could find.

Nervous Bob could be heard shouting, 'They shot the Reverend! They shot a man of God!'

I thought I'd killed him and was sure that this was a very quick way to go to hell. I dropped the gun and couldn't move. Louise ran towards me carrying her gun.

'Get in here, you young fool,' she cried, practically scooping me up and throwing me into her wagon along with Jeni and old Mrs Meadows. She climbed in after me and quickly closed the wagon covers.

I was breathing so hard.

'I think I killed the Reverend!' I cried.

'Ssh, now,' said Jeni. 'Hasn't he got God looking out for him?'

Jeni put her arms round her mother, who was somehow managing to sleep through all the commotion. We sat still inside the wagon, listening and waiting to see what would happen. After a while Louise poked the end of her rifle out through the wagon covers to have a look. She seemed so calm.

'Aren't you scared, Louise?' I whispered, amazed.

Jeni answered for her. 'Oh, she'll be scared all right, like a long-tailed cat in a room full of rocking chairs, but you won't ever get her to admit it.'

Louise chuckled. 'Still as a graveyard out there. I'm going to take a look.'

Slowly Louise climbed down from the wagon just as Henry and Jack returned with water. Jack was leading Algernon Honeyman by the arm.

'Did you see any Injuns?' called Jeni from the wagon.

Henry shook his head. 'No, and neither did Algernon, did you?' he said to the Honeyman boy.

Jack shook his head. 'He was mucking about with one of the Walker boys. I don't think he knew we saw them.'

'I was just having some fun,' muttered Algernon, trying not to laugh.

'Fun!' Reverend Goudy appeared in the gloom, shaking with rage. He grabbed Algernon and began smacking him round the head. 'I could have been killed!' he yelled. The Reverend seemed to have gone crazy.

'Sorry about that!' I called out quietly.

'Are you not shot?' Louise asked him.

'No, I am not shot!' yelled the Reverend. 'But I am going to kill this child!'

'Stop!' said Henry, stepping between Algernon and the furious man. Louise put her hand on Reverend Goudy's arm and tried to calm him down. Algernon was beginning to look ashamed.

'I'm sorry,' he said as his parents came towards him.

'Now, Reverend, I agree that boy ought to go to hell,'

Louise said, 'but I don't think it's your job to send him there any quicker than the good Lord intends.'

Now everyone was gathering to find out what had happened.

'It's not my fault,' claimed Algernon. 'The other boys . . . they dared me to yell that Indians had taken the cattle. It was just a prank. We thought it would be funny to scare Bob.'

Algernon got into terrible trouble, and Mrs Honeyman couldn't stop sobbing because Louise had said her boy was going to hell. Slowly everyone got down from the wagons.

Louise looked at me. I was mortified that I had nearly killed the Reverend.

'Now will you let me teach you to shoot right?' she asked.

I nodded. Firing the gun like that had really scared me. I wanted to protect us all, but I truly didn't want to hurt anyone. I was shaking at the thought of what I had nearly done. I knew I needed to learn what to do.

Calm had returned to the camp when Jack asked, 'What's that noise?'

'I think it's my mother snoring,' sighed Jeni. 'How that woman can sleep through—'

'No!' shouted Jack, suddenly pointing into the distance. 'There! Ship on the port side! Ship on the port side!' We all looked at the horizon and saw the oddest thing. Something just like a ship was moving towards us very fast. It couldn't possibly be a ship, yet it had a white sail and was barrelling across the desert at great speed. We had no idea what it was. All we *did* know was that it was heading right for the wagon train.

CHAPTER ELEVEN

It was crazy. There we were in the middle of the prairie, yet it did look exactly as though a ship was coming straight for us. It had two white sails and a flag hoisted above a low deck, but it didn't make any sense. We hadn't seen any water for hours. All around was nothing but miles and miles of plain hilly land covered in rough grass. I had never seen anything move so fast, and yet there were no animals helping it along. As the strange 'ship' got closer, you could see it was a wagon, but a wagon with sails which were billowing in the wind and causing the wagon to barrel along on four large wheels. There appeared to be a man steering in the front, whooping and yelling and trying his best to take charge of the giant sails which were causing the thing to go so fast. It was clear that the driver didn't have the control he had hoped for. I was sure he didn't want to hit us, but no matter what he tried, the wind-powered wagon kept coming straight towards us.

We all ran to get out of the way.

'Hamlet, move!' yelled Toby.

Toby's pig lay curled up, sleeping with Buddle's dog by one of our wagon wheels, and it looked as though both pets were going to be run over. Toby's cry woke Hamlet, who squealed and tried to push Dog with his great pink nose to wake him, but it was too late.

'It's going to hit our wagon!' shouted Jack, but at the last moment the crazy machine swerved to the left and ran straight into the middle of the Honeymans' fine wagon. The tongue of our wagon was attached to their rear wheel, and our entire home, with everything we owned, spun to the side with a great crashing of barrels and goods inside. Malvolio and the other oxen had been attached to the front by a piece of rope. Now they tried to run away and caused the wagon to spin once more.

'Hero!' yelled Kate, for my baby sister had been asleep inside in her carpet bag.

We all rushed to the back of the wagon and looked in. All our things now lay in a great jumble and we couldn't see Hero anywhere.

'Oh dear God!' cried Kate, racing to move everything out of the way. We threw sacks of food out onto the ground, and Henry and Jack lifted great barrels as if they weighed nothing. Then we heard a giggle.

'Hero?' called Jack, and lifted a sack. There, sitting in a great pile of flour, was baby Hero, entirely white from being drenched in the stuff. She looked up at us and clapped her hands as if she had never had more fun. The flour had softened the blow from the strange ship and she was completely unharmed.

Kate grabbed Hero, and the poor child nearly suffocated from all of us trying to hug her, we were so relieved. Soon we were all covered in flour but no one cared.

A loud groan came from the next wagon.

'The Honeymans!' I cried, and we all raced to see what had happened to our neighbours.

The wind-powered wagon had made quite a mess. It had crashed firmly into the Honeymans' home and made a large crack in the side. As for the strange sailing ship, it had entirely fallen to pieces and the driver now lay face down, quite senseless on the ground. Bea was first to his side, and as she turned him over to see if he was alive we saw that he was wearing a magnificent emerald-green waistcoat.

'Cornelius Stringer!' she exclaimed.

It was indeed the great scientist and inventor we had met on the train from New Jersey. He had been knocked out, but now he slowly opened one eye and looked at Bea.

'I have died and the angels have come to fetch me,' he announced with complete certainty.

We gathered round. It was definitely Cornelius. No one could have forgotten that waistcoat, although it was now made grubby by the dust he had landed in. His curly hair looked quite mad and his spectacles were missing, but it was him all right. If he thought for a moment that Bea was an angel, then it wasn't an idea which lasted very long. Bea stood up and hit him across the top of the head as she did so. Her sympathy had not lasted long.

'Bea, what are you doing?' I said, shocked by her behaviour, but she was in a terrible temper and wouldn't be stopped.

'What the heck do you think you are doing, Cornelius Stringer?' she demanded, ignoring me and almost stamping her foot.

'Why, I'm harnessing the very power of the planet,' he declared, leaping to his feet with surprising speed considering what had just happened. 'My gratitude is unbounded to that power. It extends to Aeolus himself, the god and ruler of the winds, who transported me here! Juno asked him to release the winds, as I'm sure you know, although I have to say he did it with an enthusiasm that my original plans had not quite envisaged.'

Bea stood with her hands on her hips, absolutely furious.

'You're trying to kill us is what you're doing!' she exploded. 'You could have hurt my baby sister!'

Hamlet squealed to remind everyone he had been in danger too. Bea nodded. 'And Toby's pig!' she added.

It was a terrible telling-off and Cornelius should have been ashamed, but instead he looked at us, shook his head as if he could not believe what he was seeing, and slowly smiled.

'Well, never mind Aeolus! If the Fates are not remarkable,' he said, 'it's the horde of Hannigans. How delightful.' He smiled and gave a slight bow. 'I would take my hat off to you but I have no idea where the infernal thing has got to.'

Cornelius' top hat had rolled some distance and Toby ran to fetch it before going to calm the animals.

Everyone was talking on top of each other when suddenly we heard Buddle yelling, 'I've lost my leg! My leg!'

For the first time Cornelius looked pale. He ran to see Buddle lying on the ground. His leg was completely missing. 'Oh my, the poor fellow!' exclaimed Cornelius.

'It's not a problem,' called Henry, who was enjoying a drama which was not his fault. 'He never had that one in the first place.'

Buddle held up the many pieces his wooden leg had broken into.

'I can make another!' he cried happily.

'He had a wooden leg,' I explained. 'He'll be fine.'

'Splendid, splendid!' declared Cornelius, before whispering, 'I'm glad about the leg but . . .' He took another look at Buddle, who was now sitting up grinning. Cornelius pointed to a pile of black feathers lying nearby. 'Was that your bird?' he asked quietly.

Buddle nodded. The stuffed black bird he always carried on his shoulder had been knocked clean off.

'Was it a pet?' Cornelius enquired hesitantly.

Buddle nodded again.

Cornelius went very pale. 'I'm so sorry. I . . .'

I had got so used to Buddle walking about with the stuffed black bird on his shoulder that I had stopped noticing it. Now I realized that Cornelius thought he had killed it.

'Buddle should tell him the truth,' I whispered to Henry.

He shook his head and sniggered. 'No, this is much funnier.'

Mrs Honeyman was standing, shocked, beside their damaged wagon, leaning on her husband.

'That looks bad,' said Henry, going to inspect it. 'See, the beautiful paintwork has a great crack in the middle and there's a tear in the cover.'

'You, sir, will purchase me a new wagon!' Mr Honeyman yelled. 'I shall be recompensed.'

Cornelius knew he was in trouble.

'Indeed, indeed!' he said, moving towards them. 'I was just dealing with the bird and the . . . leg.'

We all moved closer to hear what he would say. I hadn't had a lot to do with the Honeymans while we travelled so I don't think it was till then that I noticed the change in them. Mrs Honeyman was still wearing her pink dress, but I noticed for the first time that neither the cuffs nor the collar were white any more. Mr Honeyman was almost purple with rage. His tie had come undone and he kept shouting about the price to fix his wagon.

Cornelius held up his hand. 'Sir, madam,' he began, 'all scientific advancement has its cost and today, sadly, you have borne the expense of my marvellous experiment.' He looked at his own wrecked wagon and their damaged one. 'Indeed, a lesser man might say that today you literally stood in the way of science, for I believe my wind machine was doing well until your own transportation stood in the way.'

'What the hell were you doing?' demanded Mr Honeyman, shaking with fury.

'A wind wagon!' declared Cornelius, throwing his arms out to the sky. 'I was harnessing the very wind to take me across the prairie. Can you imagine the delight of such a thing? The wind in your hair . . .' He stopped speaking when he realized that Mrs Honeyman was not at all pleased with the thought of wind in her hair.

Cornelius had not had enough money to buy either mules or oxen in Independence so he had decided to make

244

the journey by rigging sails to his wagon. He had done well for quite a number of days, until a great gust of wind had caused him to lose control and driven him right into us. He was sorry, but more interested in the science of what he had been doing than anything else.

'Worry not!' he declared to the gathered crowd. 'I believe I can rebuild this.' Then he began gathering up the splintered remains of his invention.

'You will not,' fumed Mr Honeyman. 'If anything wants fixing, it's our wagon. You will make it right or I will . . . I will . . . sue you!'

'What does that mean?' I asked Buddle, who was quietly laughing about the whole thing.

'Take him to court. Lawyers, judges, that kind of thing,' he replied.

'Do we have those?'

Buddle shook his head. 'Not out here. Mr Honeyman has money but that doesn't mean he's not a fool.'

Cornelius tipped his hat back on his head with a quick flick of his hand and moved to help the Honeymans.

'Let us not trouble the courts when remedy is at hand.' He smiled, winking at Bea, who turned away, still furious but also blushing. Cornelius began to examine the damage to the Honeymans' wagon as James Long joined the group, shaking his head. 'We ought not to dally. Time to head out.'

Everyone began to leave, but Buddle, now without his

leg, needed our help and Kate said we couldn't just leave the Honeymans behind.

'Remember the man who got us out when we were stuck in the mud?' she said. 'Well, he was a stranger and he helped us. We'd help them if they were strangers, but the fact is we know the Honeymans and we need to do what we can.'

No one argued with that. Louise and Jeni got Buddle into his cart but he couldn't steady himself enough to drive.

'I'll need a new leg,' he said matter-of-factly.

'Never mind your leg!' yelled Mr Honeyman. 'I need a new wagon. This man' – he pointed in fury at Cornelius – 'has ruined my home!'

'Buddle, do you mind if we fix your leg later?' asked Henry politely.

Buddle shook his head. 'I was ready for a lie-down anyway,' he said, smiling.

Then, despite low protests from Cornelius, parts from the broken wind wagon were used to help make the repairs to the Honeymans' broken home. A new axle had to be fitted, and Jack astonished everyone by first removing one from Cornelius' broken wagon and then lifting the Honeymans' heavy wagon bed up all by himself to make the change. The end of the train was passing and a carpenter stopped to help, and then a blacksmith. I think everyone had more respect for Jack after that. Kate and Bea cut Cornelius' 'sails' to make a patch for the cover, which had been split in the accident. Jack's bag of nails proved to be very helpful indeed.

Cornelius never stopped being cheerful, even though he was clearly in trouble.

'No modern development was ever popular!' he chirped as he rolled up his sleeves and worked as hard as anyone to make things right. 'Why, I have travelled on a railway train with the delight that is the Hannigans. Who can forget that it was only a few years ago that the governor of New York himself said railway travel was impossible? He said he believed the Almighty never intended that people should travel at such breakneck speed, and yet travel we can. Why . . .'

I could see Mrs Meadows and Jeni falling for his charm. Even though his arrival had been upsetting he had a knack for making friends.

'He's like Da, don't you think, Bea?' Bea nodded and a tear came to her eye. She turned away. I knew I missed him every day, but I hadn't thought about how everyone else was feeling. I loved Cornelius being able to turn a bad moment into a good one, but it was so like Da that it hurt.

'My wind wagon is the future,' Cornelius assured Mrs Meadows. 'And it's only the beginning. I tell you, there's a fellow called Rufus Porter plans to fly emigrants all the way to Oregon hanging – I think *hanging* – from balloons with propellers driven by steam engines.'

'Stuff and nonsense,' replied Louise, but she smiled and went to make him a hot drink.

Cornelius insisted on having a proper funeral for the bird. Buddle went along with it, and as the poor stuffed thing was placed in a grave he sang a few words from a regimental song while winking at me.

'British army!' Cornelius declared, delighted. 'How marvellous! I once spent a glorious evening at the Honourable Artillery Company in London. We drank to the king's health so many times we damned near ruined our own!'

The two men laughed and I could see that Cornelius was going to be with us for a while.

He had a large wooden chest with him which had survived intact. Somehow he persuaded Louise and Jeni to let him heave it aboard their wagon in exchange for helping them with their livestock and driving.

'I can fetch wood and water for you as if made for the job,' he promised.

The Honeymans' wagon was fixed up as well as everyone could manage. It no longer looked quite the smart affair that had started out the journey, but it went along all right. Jack, Cornelius and Henry had done their best with the new axle, but even so one wheel sort of limped a little. It meant that the wagon gave a slight hiccup as it moved, but at least it could still travel.

Buddle couldn't drive his cart, so Kate said he would have to come in with us. His mule was tied behind our wagon while he bumped along inside. Buddle's old cart had to be left behind.

'I don't mind,' he said cheerfully. 'Didn't have anything to put in it anyway! Lost everything in the river, which now seems like a blessing!'

The abandoned cart was quite big.

'I could put one of my posters with a picture of Da on it,' I suggested to Henry, but he didn't want to talk about our Da either. It was too painful. I pinned a poster on the cart anyway. Maybe someone would come past and see it. Cornelius and Louise watched me, and later I saw Cornelius talking to Kate.

That day, when we stopped for 'nooning', our midday break, Cornelius joined us for our lunch of salted meat. He said quietly to me how sad he was to hear about Da. He shook his head over what had happened.

'A fine fellow,' he kept repeating. 'A fine fellow. A sad tale, to be sure, but I wouldn't write the man off yet. He was made of stern stuff, your Da.'

'You wouldn't "write him off"?' I repeated, hardly believing what I'd heard. 'You think he might still be alive?'

Cornelius looked at me. 'You believe it, Slim, don't you?'

I nodded.

Cornelius put his hand on my shoulder. 'Then let's you and I believe it together. When thoughts are too awful to think, well, then I just don't think them.'

I thought about that a lot as we moved on. Perhaps Da was behind us, as I hoped. I suspected I was the only one who even dared think so, but perhaps he would catch us up and everything would be how it should be again. I believed he would because I couldn't bear to think anything else.

We had become quite used to life on the road now. Since the Walkers had joined with their ten wagons, others had come along too and there were a lot of us setting off together each day. So at 4 a.m. James had taken to firing his gun in the air to get everyone up. It was much quicker than shouting. The women made breakfast, which was usually bacon or corn porridge, while Buddle liked to turn out little flat breads called 'johnny cakes', which were made of flour and water. Meanwhile the rest of the men and older boys saddled the horses and got the oxen.

Once I'd lit the fire I helped Toby yoke Malvolio and his team. The oxen had surprised everyone by becoming as gentle as kittens. Malvolio would quietly step into his place without Toby having to say a word, and always got a hug for it. I still hadn't ridden Chronicle, but at least he had stopped trying to run away. You might think it silly but I'd chat with him each evening. About Da and things I didn't think I could tell the family, like being scared or tired. It was almost as if he understood and he even seemed pleased to see me each morning.

'Morning, Chronicle!' I would call, and he would turn to make a low whinnying sound. As I untied his rope from the wagon wheel, he would turn and nuzzle me with his soft mouth.

'Did you sleep well?' I would ask, putting my arms round his neck to whisper, 'I miss Da too much to sleep all through the night. I keep thinking he might come.' Chronicle would almost nod his head as if he understood, and I loved the warm feeling of his gentle breath and the softness of his mane.

'Come on, Slim, enough with you and your horse!' Toby would call.

Toby was brilliant in the mornings, and between us all we could hitch the wagon in less than half an hour if the weather didn't turn against us.

Louise began giving me shooting lessons again, and this time I was determined. When there was time she would set up a target and get me to practise aiming at it.

'Go on, Slim, draw and shoot,' she'd shout as I took aim at a bottle on a distant log.

I got pretty good, and began to be more daring. I began to carry both pistols with me once more. Jack was brilliant at knotting any rope into something useful and he made me a better sort of belt to tuck them into.

Lots of people had new skills now, but even so the wagon train setting off each day was still a mess. It was mostly to do with the order of the wagons as we travelled. There were nearly a hundred wagons by now and no one wanted to be at the back because the dust was the worst there. Everyone fought to be near the front. A few people did try to make a plan, but any new idea always ended in one or more men punching each other. Kate told Jack and Henry to keep out of it.

Most days we didn't ride right behind the wagon in front but alternated to the left or right to keep out of the cloud of soil their wheels threw up as they drove. We must have been filthy but possibly not as grubby as Buddle. No one had yet been able to find a piece of wood the right size to replace his leg, so in the morning he needed help to get into our wagon, where he rode each day.

Buddle had lost almost everything, but every night he made a camp for himself out of grimy and ragged old buffalo hides stretched over a frame of poles. One side was open, and at the side of the opening hung his powder horn and bullet pouch, along with a long white pipe which he smoked at night. Reverend Goudy and his wife came by Buddle's tent one night with their Bible and tried to talk to him. Buddle never really washed himself or his clothes and I think it upset them.

'We have here the way to Heaven,' they declared, holding out the 'Good Book' to Buddle, but he didn't answer. Instead he just sat sucking on his pipe.

I don't think the Reverend was very impressed.

'I refuse to save him. God can't make me. It's too much!' we heard Parenthia exclaim as the wheezing Reverend led her away.

Once Louise had taught me to fire my guns she began teaching me other things. It was she who taught me how to scrub my teeth with the ragged end of a stick and how to make the best butter. Kate would bargain for milk with the women in the train who had a few cows. Sometimes they wanted a piece of cloth in exchange, but more usually it was some medicine from our cabinet.

I think my best lesson was how to make fire without matches. Jeni knew about plants, and one afternoon she gathered something called cat-tail, which grew near the edge of ponds and streams. They had brown tops and she gave them to Louise.

'Look here, little one,' Louise would say as she started teaching me something. She took a knife from her pocket and split open the brown part of the cat-tail. She held it out to me.

'It's fluffy inside!' I said, surprised.

Louise smiled. 'So you take all the fluffy part out and keep it to one side,' she instructed me. 'Next we're going to need a bundle of dry grass. You can go get that while I sit here and drink my tea.'

I gathered the grass and brought it back. First Louise made a small pile of the fluffy cat-tail, then she piled the grass over the top of it.

'Now you need a rock like . . .' She looked around. '. . . this!' she cried, triumphantly picking up a rock the size of her fist. 'Put a piece of the cat-tail on the rock and rub the back of your knife back and forth against it.' She moved a knife quickly in this way until sparks jumped from the rock. She kept going until there were enough to cause a tiny flame in the fluffy plant stuff. Louise blew on it until she thought it was hot enough and then used the flame to set fire to our bundle of grass. It wasn't long before we had a real bonfire.

'No matches,' she said with satisfaction.

I had to practise, but once I knew how I never needed matches again.

We were all learning skills. With Buddle's help Kate mastered bread-making. He had cooked a lot in the army.

'Army marches on its stomach,' he would say as they baked together.

Now the rolls were sweet and light, and Kate began taking instruction in the mystery of cooking with the great iron pan known as a Dutch oven. Jeni was used to using one and was happy to explain. It was a big heavy metal thing with a lid that you could either hang over the fire or bury amongst the embers with its short legs keeping the base above the burning wood. It made wonderful food, and every night we began to look forward to dinner.

It was good that we had something to look forward to because the rain continued to follow us. On many a day a black curtain of clouds shaded the entire heavens with the exception of a narrow fringe of yellow light behind us in the east. It was as if we were leaving daylight behind. Some days the rain fell without stopping, accompanied by loud continuous peals of thunder and flashes of lightning so vivid as to light up the entire scene. On the days it didn't rain the mosquitoes came out to attack us. I didn't know which was worse – being bitten or being soaked. Still we marched on, trying to make sure we covered twenty miles each day. Working out how far we had gone was done by counting the number of turns of our wagon wheels. It was a tiresome job which usually fell to one of the women at the back of the train. Sometimes it was Bea, though she was no good at it as she found it difficult to concentrate. A red flag was tied onto one of the wagon wheels and she had to count how many times it went round. These were then added up, and someone, usually Buddle, could work out how many miles had been travelled.

It gave Bea a headache. All she wanted to do was look at the landscape and draw what she saw. Cornelius knew this, and after just a few days with us began working on a new invention. Every moment he got he was pulling things out of his wooden chest and muttering. He did drawings and calculations while he gathered bits of old clock and even made a couple of cogs out of wood. None of us could work out what all the pieces might make, but slowly he put them together and began making a sort of 'counting' machine.

'Ladies and gentlemen!' he said one evening. 'Try not to get overexcited but I give you' – he made the sound of a trumpet blowing with his lips – 'the Beatrice Hannigan Roadometer!'

He held up a strange-looking device which looked like the inside of a clock.

'This machine is the future!' he declared, his eyes shining with excitement. 'Why, it will turn tedium into triumph! And more importantly it will relieve Miss Hannigan of the need to ever count anything but her blessings!'

Cornelius bowed to Bea, who couldn't help smiling back. It was a marvellous thing which he attached to the hub of a wagon wheel.

'I have been exact in my measurements and the whole machine will turn once every ten miles. That means I can use it to calculate exactly how far we have travelled down to the last quarter-mile. All we have to do each evening is check the roadometer and we shall all know that we are on track to reach the great glory that is Oregon!'

'California!' called someone.

'Or indeed, as you say, California.'

There was no one on the train who didn't come to admire the new roadometer. James Long thought it ought to be on every wagon train and that Cornelius would 'make big money!' but he seemed uninterested in making his fortune.

'It's the science that matters,' he said.

I loved all the strange things Cornelius had in his wooden chest of wonders.

'What are these?' I asked him one day as he searched for something.

'Ah, those are a marvel.' He took out a small band of what looked like material, but it felt strange and you could stretch it. 'It's called a "rubber band",' he explained.

You probably have them all the time but we had never seen anything like it. No one had. It was literally a band of rubber, which seems so simple, but you could use for all sorts of things. Cornelius took two of them and a Y-shaped stick and made me and Toby something called a 'slingshot'. He carved some notches in the handle so it didn't slip in the hand and then fixed two rubber bands, one to each side, with a piece of leather, to form the sling which you put a stone in and could shoot at anything. We couldn't stop shooting at things as we walked along.

'See if you can hit that bush over there!' I'd cry.

'I can hit that, no trouble,' Toby would boast. 'I can even hit the top left branch with the bright green leaf.'

And he could as well. Toby got really good at using it. From quite a distance he could hit whatever you named.

'I'll bet on Toby,' Henry would say.

'I'm with Slim,' Bea would call, and we'd fire away.

When I wasn't playing with my new slingshot, my favourite thing was to walk Chronicle up to the very front of the train and stop to look back.

'Look at that, Chronicle! Isn't that something!' I'd say.

The line of scattered wagons creeping slowly along as if they had risen up from the horizon was an amazing sight. I would look back and I could always spot Mrs Honeyman's bright pink dress and then look along for the grey elephant on our wagon cover. Everyone trudged on. The Honeymans were no nicer to us than before, even though we had helped them, but everyone else felt like family now.

From a distance you could see how uneven the ground was but not how soft and muddy. Often we had to stop and cut down big bits of brush and trees to throw into the muddy ravines so that the animals and wagons could pass over them. The oxen got more and more tired as the wagons often got held up in mud holes or at the crossing of small streams. Sometimes wagons had to be let down the banks with ropes, and then the teams were doubled, sometimes even quadrupled, in order to draw them up on the other side.

James refused to take charge. 'I'm just the guide,' he would say, so once we arrived it was usually Louise who rode up and down counting to see if everyone had made it to camp. She would often find some wagons had been left behind and a party would be formed to go back and help them. Some were delayed in mud or because some part had broken and they couldn't continue without repairs. Sometimes it was near midnight before everyone arrived.

The chaos continued until one night Buddle had had enough and declared that an election would be held, whether anyone liked it or not, so that we could have leaders to organize the wagon train and parcel out chores. He built a large campfire and called all the men to take part.

'What about Louise?' I said. 'She's been doing all the work.' But no one listened. No women were allowed to join the chat.

There was a lot of shouting, and someone threatened someone else with a knife, but in the end we had all sorts of 'officers'. There were a lot of daily decisions to be made, but that's not what the new officers talked about.

At the first meeting Buddle, who had been elected Captain, declared, 'We need a code of laws.' Immediately he was interrupted by Reverend Goudy.

'Nonsense! We already have a code of laws given to us by the Creator of the universe which is found recorded' – he stopped to cough and it was a while before anyone found out where the code was recorded – 'in the breast of every man.'

'You're just cross because no one voted for you to be an officer,' said Buddle angrily, but it was no good. A lot of people in the train couldn't read, but they knew about the Bible and thought that the Reverend must be right, so they voted not to have particular laws for the journey but to 'trust in the ones from God'. This meant nothing was actually done to help manage moving everyone along.

'Do you think the animals getting on the great ark were in such disorder?' Cornelius wondered aloud as we tried to get our wagon into the line one morning. 'Do you suppose Noah himself sighed and sucked on his teeth as the elephants and giraffes wandered about the place?'

'I expect the elephants and giraffes were more organized,' replied Bea, and then looked away.

I noticed Kate looking at Bea and smiling, and wondered what was going on.

Even though a lot of the travelling was the same day after day, Cornelius was the only one who never seemed to get bored. He spent a lot of the time getting very excited about any large pieces of wood he came across.

'What about this?' he would call out to Buddle as he held up a large log or branch with great delight.

Buddle would look from the seat on our wagon, put his head to one side as if thinking, and then reply, 'It's not quite right.'

Cornelius was trying to find something with which to make a new wooden leg for Buddle, but wasn't having a lot of luck.

'The man is impossible,' muttered Cornelius.

'Buddle is looking for a new leg,' Bea reminded him, 'not something to put on the fire.'

Mostly everyone was getting along, but one early evening, as we were all settling into camp, Nervous Bob climbed down from his wagon and found that his horse was missing. He was certain it was stolen, and even more certain that it was our fault. He came straight to us.

'You Hannigans have been feeding the Indians. That's why they won't leave us alone.' He pointed at Kate. 'It's all your fault.'

Kate shook her head. 'Please, don't start again, Bob.'

'Start again?' repeated Bob. 'I'm not the one who fed them in the first place.'

Henry moved towards Bob, and Jack stood up, ready to help.

'Leave Kate alone and go on back to your own wagon,' he said calmly.

I thought Bob was going to hit him, but instead he left,

shaking his fist at Kate as he went back to his wagon, the *54° 40' or Fight*. That night at the men's meeting Bob stood up, full of fury.

'We need to show those damn Indians who is in charge here,' he fumed.

'Maybe your horse just found you annoying and ran away,' said Buddle.

Bob was not listening. 'We need to get a rope and capture an Indian horse,' he said. 'Show them that we mean business.'

Toby, Cornelius and I stood on the edge of the circle listening.

'What does *54° 40' or Fight* mean?' asked Toby.

'It's to do with maps,' explained Cornelius. 'It's the number on a map which shows the northern boundary of the great region known as Oregon. The numbers on a map are a marvellous thing; why, they—'

'I think he's more interested in the fight part,' interrupted Toby.

Bob kept insisting that the wagon train should steal an Indian horse. The idea caused an uproar.

'We haven't even seen any Indians!' cried Buddle, exasperated.

'That doesn't mean they aren't out there!' exclaimed Bob. 'They can hide, you know!'

'Like elk,' whispered Toby.

'The Indians are no danger to us, but they might be,'

declared Reverend Goudy. 'If Bob starts causing trouble, he'll upset the Indians and they'll attack.'

'The Reverend is right!' cried another man. 'We *do* have an enemy and he is right here in the camp.'

'It's Bob!' said another. 'Bob is the enemy.'

Nervous Bob had never made friends with anyone on the train. He was, well, too nervous, and it didn't take long before all the men decided that Bob was actually encouraging an Indian attack. They all voted, and the next morning he was made to leave the wagon train. I'd never seen a man so angry. I can't say we had liked him, but we all felt sorry that he was being made to head out into the wilderness on his own.

'But he didn't do anything,' said Toby, watching him ride away.

Henry agreed. 'It was just talk.'

'People are afraid,' said Kate.

And they were. The talk was all about Indians. Bob might have left, but some of his ideas stayed and some of the talk was silly. A lot of families in the train had dogs, who used to bark in the night when the wolves howled. Now someone suggested that there should be a law in the wagon train against dogs.

'The dogs bark and howl and they let the Indians know where we are. We should kill them all,' one man suggested.

'Yes, but they also let us know if anyone is coming,' said Toby.

No one could agree, but a couple of dogs were killed anyway. Then the dog owners started carrying guns and saying, if any man should kill their dogs, they would kill him, regardless of the consequences.

So another vote was held by the men and it was decided the dogs could stay. Toby was also worried that any killing of pets might include Hamlet, and he took to letting Hamlet and Dog sleep together near Buddle so they might protect each other.

I watched all the arguing and discussion from a distance, shaking my head.

'You all right, Slim?' asked Kate, coming up behind me with Hero in her arms.

'I don't get it,' I said. 'All the arguing.'

Kate pulled her shawl tight around the baby against the night air. 'Well, I suppose you could say it is democracy in action.'

'Democracy?' I said. 'That's when everyone gets a vote, no matter who they are?'

Kate nodded.

'Then why don't *you* get a say?' I asked. 'Why don't Louise or Jeni? Louise knows more than any of them.'

Kate gave a small chuckle. 'This may be a new world, Slim, but it's still a man's world.'

'I'm going to complain,' I decided, but Henry stopped me.

'They'll make us leave the wagon train, Slim, like Nervous Bob. We can't manage on our own.'

'But it's not right,' I fumed.

'Let's just get to Oregon, and then I promise you can have all the say you like,' he assured me.

Maybe Bob had been right, because the next morning a few more animals were missing. Maybe the Indians had taken them. I was relieved to see Chronicle still grazing nearby but Louise and Jeni had lost Gert, their last milk cow, and others had lost cows too.

'If there are Indians, then I think they're Shawnee,' warned James. 'If I'm right, they're fierce warriors. They fought with the French at their trading posts till the French gave up. We shouldn't confront them.'

'Well, someone is taking the cows. We'll lose every animal in the place if we're not careful,' muttered Buddle, beginning to wonder if Bob might have been right after all. 'There is nothing for it but every man in the camp must stand guard, taking turns, whenever we stop.'

'He's right!' agreed one of the men. 'Supposing a hundred Indians should jump up out of that ravine, all yelling and flapping their buffalo robes like they do? Why, in two minutes not a hoof would be in sight.'

'I would imagine that if there are a hundred flapping Indians and we've just the one guard, then it won't be much of a defence,' said Cornelius quietly, 'although I admit I should like to see that many Indians flapping.'

Buddle was too busy planning to listen.

'Our whole system is wrong,' he went on. 'It is totally unmilitary. Why, the way we travel, strung out over the prairie for a mile, an enemy might attack the foremost men, and cut them off, before the rest could come up. We've no guards and we camp in disorder.'

Plans were made, and soon all the men had to sign up for a rota of guards posted each night for two hours at a time. Buddle was in charge, and the men lined up at our wagon to sign up. Toby got in the queue.

'What are you doing, you little squirt?' sneered one man.

'Signing up. With the men!' declared Toby, and now all the men laughed. I had been ready to sign up too and was glad I hadn't.

Not everyone was nice any more.

A few people began to be horrible to Kate as if what had happened was her fault, and it hurt me to see it.

'That woman is a menace,' said Reverend Goudy to me. 'You should stop travelling with her.'

'She's our friend,' I replied.

'She is no friend to the wagon train. She shouldn't have given food to the Indians,' he said sternly. 'They don't understand kindness. They were born not to be trusted.'

'I thought you were going to save the Indians,' I said, confused.

'Not these ones,' he said. 'They're not worth saving.'

That night there was another dreadful storm. The air grew heavy and the sky darkened. The birds went silent, as if every creature on the prairie could feel it coming. There was a fresh damp smell on the wind, warning us that a blustery night was about to succeed the hot clear day. We had camped on a high swell of the prairie, at the foot of which a small stream ran through the clumps of rough grass. It was getting dark and Toby had turned the animals loose to feed.

'Batten everything down,' said Jack, who still sometimes spoke like a sailor. 'It's going to blow.'

He pointed at the sky, and you could see it had changed totally. Even the prairie looked black under the shadow of the clouds. The thunder soon began to growl at a distance. A lone wolf moved near the camp, its large grey eyes searching for food. Buddle aimed his rifle at it from the back of our wagon but it skulked away. The storm began with just one small cloud, but it wasn't long before it was blazing with what Buddle called 'the whole artillery of the heavens', and everyone rushed for cover. There was torrential rain, hail and very sharp lightning. In less than two hours the water was a foot deep all over the campsite and we all crowded into the wagon with no supper. We sat crushed together.

'I only have the one leg, so how is it that everyone seems to manage to sit on it?' complained Buddle as we shifted around, trying to get comfortable. Even Hamlet seemed to be shoving for space. He kept snorting and pushing me with his nose. It wasn't until I started getting annoyed with him that I realized the pig was trying to tell me something. 'Where's Toby?' I cried. We had all been in such a rush to get in, no one had noticed that Toby was missing. It was Hamlet who had noticed. Wherever the pig was you could usually find my brother, but now Hamlet sat squashed next to a barrel by himself.

'I don't know!' replied Kate with a note of panic in her voice.

'I haven't seen the young fellow for a bit,' said Buddle.

There was nowhere for him to hide in the wagon so he had to be outside.

Henry sighed. 'I'll look.'

As he opened the cover and got out of the wagon, the wind howled so much we thought it would tear us all to pieces. Rain lashed in and Hero began to cry. Kate sang to her, but I could see she was frightened. We had had enough of storms for a lifetime.

Henry was back in no time. 'I can't see him. I can't see him anywhere.'

'I'll come with you!' I offered, moving towards the opening.

Henry shook his head. 'No, it's too dangerous. Jack, will you help me?'

Jack got up and squeezed past everyone. He nodded at me as if to say it would be all right, before climbing out of the wagon. Now both he and Henry disappeared into the storm.

I don't know how long we sat there: Bea, Kate, Hero, me, Buddle, Dog and Hamlet. The wind ripped at the cover and the rain fell in great sheets. Hero wouldn't stop crying and poor Hamlet jumped every time there was thunder. Buddle tried to hold him, but the poor pig was terrified and Dog began to howl. I didn't have a watch so I didn't know how long we sat there. I began counting the lightning flashes, which lit up the inside of the wagon. After I had counted ten I said, 'Henry and Jack have been gone for an age. What if something has happened to them?'

'There's nothing we can do,' said Bea. 'We have to wait.'

But I just couldn't. We had lost enough people for one family and I wasn't about to let us lose any more.

'*Be strong when you are weak; be brave when you are scared . . .*' I mumbled to myself.

'Are you all right, Slim?' asked Kate.

I looked at her and knew what I had to do.

'Are you scared, Kate?'

She nodded as another lightning flash lit her pale face.

'Nashobanowa said,' I explained, 'that I should be strong when I am scared.'

I reached for our bullet pouch and began loading my pistols.

'Slim, what are you doing?' asked Bea with panic in her voice.

'I need to go and help!'

'No!' she insisted.

'There are wolves out there,' I said. 'The boys could be in trouble.'

I finished loading and shoved the pistols into my rope belt.

'No, Slim!' insisted Kate. 'Nashobanowa didn't mean you should risk your life!'

Buddle sat watching and saying nothing, until he quietly murmured, 'Do what you have to do, Slim. You're a brave girl.'

I nodded and moved quickly. Both Bea and Kate tried to grab my arm but I was quick and clambered out of the wagon. The rain was so fierce I could hardly see. I stood there, not sure which way to go, when I felt something nudge my shoulder. It was Chronicle. I hadn't ridden him for weeks, but now he nudged me again. I didn't know if I could trust him. He had no saddle on. It was madness, but I untied his reins from the back of the wagon, reached for his mane and pulled myself up onto his back. I was ready for him to send me straight back down to the ground, but instead he stood patiently waiting. I was blinded by the storm, and a great flash of lightning nearly unseated me, but Chronicle stayed steady for me. I couldn't see anyone around who might help, and the boys were missing. I had no choice. I picked up the reins and pressed my heels gently into Chronicle's sides. He led us out of the corral just as the wolves began their dreadful howling.

The storm was so fierce that I couldn't see anything, but Chronicle set out as if he hadn't noticed it was raining enough to drown us. It felt more like wading through a river than taking a ride, but still my amazing horse moved forward. My heart was pounding, though Chronicle kept a steady pace. I could feel his ribcage expand and contract against my legs and how strong he felt. I was scared, but he gave me the courage to carry on.

'*Be strong when you are weak*,' I repeated out loud, though the storm was so loud my words disappeared into it.

It was so dark that I was almost glad of the massive lightning flashes as they gave the only light to show the way. In one brilliant flash I thought I saw a crowd of men heading towards me. I reached for my gun, but then the sky lit up again and I saw it was the cattle huddled together. I could see no sign of the two men who were supposed to be guarding them. I couldn't remember who it was supposed to be.

'Cornelius?' I called out. 'Reverend Goudy?'

There was no answer. I doubt anyone would have heard me even if they had been nearby. The only sound that carried above the weather was the howls of wolves, which echoed through the wet night. Sometimes even that died away and all I could hear was the rain and my heart pounding.

The lightning flashed again, and this time I *did* see someone up ahead near some oxen. Whoever it was seemed to be trying to drive them away. I urged Chronicle on. It wasn't someone I recognized, but it didn't look like an Indian either. I pulled one of my guns out of my belt, but Chronicle, who had been so steady, now stopped by what looked like a great rock.

'Chronicle! Come on!' I urged, nudging him with my heels, but he wouldn't move. I wiped the rain from my eyes, and with horror realized it wasn't a rock at all but Henry lying on the ground. Thank goodness Chronicle had seen him. My brother was struggling to get up and couldn't seem to catch his breath. I jumped down to him. I had to put my face right beside his so we could hear each other. Even then it was difficult.

'He came from my blind side,' he wheezed, almost bent over with pain.

'Are you hurt?' I cried. I couldn't lose someone else I loved.

'I'll be fine,' managed Henry, 'but . . .'

'No!' I moaned. 'Has something happened to Jack and Toby?'

Henry almost sobbed. 'I don't know. There's a man, a bad man. I couldn't see his face, but they've gone after him. I told them not to, but he was after Malvolio and Toby wouldn't listen, so Jack went with him.'

Henry frowned and I saw that blood was running down the right-hand side of his face.

'Henry, you're bleeding!'

'Never mind that, Slim.' He looked at me as if he couldn't make up his mind and then asked, 'Are your guns loaded?'

I nodded.

He sighed and collapsed back down on the ground.

'I can't manage it, Slim. You have to go and help them. There's no one else. They went that way.'

Henry held up his hand and pointed, but it had all been too much for him – in that moment he passed out.

'Henry!' I cried, but he lay limp on the ground and I didn't know what to do. I didn't want to leave him, but somewhere out there in the dark were Jack and Toby, and they needed me too. I checked that Henry was breathing, took a great breath of my own and leaped back onto Chronicle. My horse needed no encouragement to turn and head in the direction Henry had indicated.

We rode as fast as the slippery, muddy ground and

rushing water would allow. I thought I would fall off at any moment, but somehow Chronicle kept his footing and we carried on. My eyes hurt from the strain of peering into the dark. I don't how Chronicle knew the way or how long we travelled, but at last I saw Jack's tall image in the distance. He was running, and I thought I could see Toby standing beside the giant shape of our ox, Malvolio.

That was when I saw the man with a gun. The rain was still pelting down, but there was no question that he was pointing the gun right at Toby. Jack was running, and he was nearly at Toby's side. I think the man heard either me or Jack because he turned to look and raised his gun. Jack threw himself through the air in front of Toby just as the man fired. There was a sharp sound and a bright flash of fire, and Jack fell to the ground.

CHAPTER TWELVE

Chronicle raced forward and skidded to a halt between the man and where Jack lay on the ground bleeding. My wonderful friend had tried to save Toby's life and the bullet had hit him instead. Toby dropped to his knees beside him.

'Oh, Jack!' I heard him cry.

Now the two of them were hidden from the man by my horse. I strained my eyes in the dark and the rain, and realized it was Nervous Bob. He turned and pointed his gun straight at me. I had stopped thinking about what I was doing and instead pulled both pistols from my belt and aimed them at him.

'Leave them alone!' I called.

Bob was shaking. 'I didn't mean it, but now . . . now I have to shoot you too.'

'Slim!' cried Toby, frightened.

Bob looked around. 'You alone?' he demanded.

'The others are coming,' I lied. 'Lots of them.'

Bob shook his head. 'I don't think so.' He sneered at me through the pouring rain. 'A girl! Quite the cowboy. That's who they send out to protect them? It's pathetic! They'll learn. They should have listened to me.'

He raised his gun, and in that second I knew I was going to have to shoot him. I clutched my guns. This was not at all the same thing as firing at a mechanical lion, as I had done in New York. The pistols shook in my hand but I had to protect the others. I moved to squeeze the trigger, when suddenly there was a sharp noise and Bob's weapon flew out of his hand at the same time that there was the loud flash of fire from his gun. I swear I felt a bullet whistle past my ear. Without any instruction from me Chronicle rushed forward and knocked Nervous Bob to the ground.

I looked to the right and saw Cornelius Stringer racing towards us. His curly hair was wet through and it lay flat against his head. In his hand he held one of his slingshots. It was Cornelius who had knocked Bob's gun away using a stone and his clever rubber bands.

'Keep your guns on him,' shouted Cornelius as he reached into his own jacket pocket.

I kept my shaking pistols pointed at Bob as Cornelius pulled the terrible man's hands tight behind his back and fastened his wrists together with rubber bands.

I jumped down from my horse to Jack's side. He was bleeding and his breathing was shallow.

Toby was crying.

Jack could hardly speak. Blood was pouring from his leg.

'I'm so sorry, Slim. I tried to protect Toby, but he wouldn't leave the animals.'

'I'm sorry,' sobbed Toby. 'They needed me.'

Malvolio snorted in agreement and pushed his head gently against my little brother. I pulled my red neckerchief off and held it against Jack's wound.

'Hold this,' I cried, and he clutched it against his body.

'We can't stop here,' yelled Cornelius over the roar of the storm. 'We have to get Jack to the wagon. Where's Henry?'

'He's hurt too!' I shouted back.

Somehow we managed to lay Jack across Malvolio's back. Our great ox, who had once been so much trouble, now did exactly what Toby asked and gently carried my poor hurt friend.

'I'll find Henry!' I cried, getting back on Chronicle.

'Can you manage by yourself?' shouted Cornelius.

I nodded, absolutely confident that Chronicle would look after me.

I raced off while Toby and Malvolio brought Jack with them and Cornelius pushed a now silent Bob in front of him.

I found Henry. He was awake now. He was in terrible pain but he managed to stand.

'Oh, Slim! You found them!' We hugged in the rain. 'What happened?' he cried, but there was no time to explain. Henry was weak and the storm wasn't letting up. It took all our strength to get my big brother on Chronicle's back. Henry had to pull himself up and he groaned in pain. Chronicle stood patiently, as if the terrible weather wasn't raging all around us. At last Henry was on his back and I got up behind him. We might easily have got lost in the confusion but my amazing horse seemed to know the way without thinking. I clung onto Henry, who swayed as we slowly made our way back.

It seemed to take for ever to get back to the safety of the corral. I could see Kate and Bea at the back of the wagon looking out, beside themselves with worry. Henry and I got there just as Toby arrived with Jack lying across Malvolio's back. Cornelius was just behind him, pushing Bob along in front.

'Jack's been shot!' I shouted. 'And Henry . . .'

'I can manage,' muttered Henry. 'Look after Jack.'

Cornelius tied Bob to the wagon wheel and I ran to wake some of the men to help lift Jack into the wagon. The rain was easing off now and I managed to get a fire lit so that Kate could boil some water. Louise and Jeni heard the commotion and came running to help.

Jeni took Henry to her wagon to look after his wound while Buddle called out instructions.

'He'll be fine,' Jeni called back firmly, but Bea and Louise were less certain about Jack. He was bleeding badly.

'Buddle,' Louise said, 'you served in a war. You must know about bullet wounds.'

Buddle bit his lip and sighed. 'I'm afraid there's nothing for it. The bullet will have to come out. We can't stitch him up with that inside.'

Bea nodded and Louise looked worried. 'Do you have a scalpel?' she asked.

'I'll need your knife, Slim,' said Bea.

Now Bea took charge. She shooed me, Kate, Hero and Toby off to Louise and Jeni's wagon. I didn't want to go.

'I can't leave Jack!' I cried. 'He's my friend.'

I couldn't stop shaking and I didn't want to sit still while Jack was in such trouble. Kate looked terribly pale and Toby began to cry. I think he believed the whole thing was his fault.

Henry lay in the dark of Jeni and Louise's wagon with a bandage round his head while Mrs Meadows gave him sips of tea.

Our wagon was close by and the sound of Jack crying out from the pain was terrible. We sat crowded together.

Kate was furious with me. 'Slim, you shouldn't have gone off,' she kept repeating. 'What were you thinking?'

I could see how upset she was. 'I'm sorry, but I did manage. Chronicle looked after me. Looked after us all.'

Kate was so upset she couldn't hold Hero and gave her to Jeni. 'And what were you thinking, Toby?' she demanded, almost shaking my little brother and then pulling him in close for a hug that looked as though it would never end. 'We can get more animals but we can't get more of you!' she said angrily.

'I knew someone was after Malvolio,' Toby tried to explain, 'and I couldn't let it happen. He's—'

Outside the wagon Hamlet squealed and scratched to be let in.

'There's no room for a pig in here,' said Jeni determinedly.

Toby repeated, 'Malvolio's—'

'I know,' said Kate, shaking her head. 'He's family.'

'Will Jack . . . ?' Henry began to ask, but he couldn't finish the sentence. We could none of us imagine life without Jack.

'He saved Toby's life,' I said. 'He's family too.'

By now everyone in the wagon train was up and wanting to know what had happened. It turned out that no Indians had stolen anything. All the animals had been taken by Bob.

When Jack's operation was over, Buddle called the wagon train together.

'How is he?' people called out. Everyone liked Jack.

Buddle shook his head. 'No way of knowing. The bullet is out. Now we have to hope for the best.'

Cornelius untied Bob from the wagon wheel and brought him forward. Bob hung his head.

'You shot Jack!' I yelled, running forward. I think I would have hit him, but Cornelius scooped me up in his arms and held me back.

'Whoa, little one, let everyone have their say,' he soothed. 'We know what he did.'

Bob tried to explain. He said he'd been so angry at being sent away that he had decided to teach everyone a lesson for not listening to him about the danger of Indians.

'But there was no danger,' said Buddle sternly.

'No,' admitted Bob, a little shame-faced, 'but there could be and you should have listened to me.'

'So Bob was the one who took all the animals?' asked Toby.

Louise nodded. She was calm but she was also angry. Now she took charge. She sent two men to round up the missing animals before declaring, 'I'm afraid we need to make an example of Bob. We cannot have treachery in our midst. He will have to go.'

Even though the men hadn't wanted any women to help make decisions, now everyone nodded. Without further discussion it was decided that Bob should be sent away with nothing but the clothes on his back.

'Please!' he said. 'I won't make it!'

But the decision was made.

'You will go, and you will go now, with nothing,' said Louise. And Buddle, who was in charge, nodded in agreement.

We watched Bob go and I felt uncomfortable.

'No one was listening to me,' he protested. 'I was trying to teach you a lesson!' But everyone turned away and went back to their wagons.

'Do you think he meant well?' I asked Louise as we watched him go.

She turned to me and said quietly, 'A frog does not drink up the pond in which it lives.'

I looked at her and thought how much she sometimes sounded like Nashobanowa.

No one had slept much because of the storm and then all the excitement, so James announced we wouldn't leave until lunchtime the next day. The storm took a while to blow over, and everyone waited till it was safe to go and look for some animals which were still missing. I saddled up Chronicle properly and rode out to help round them up. We worked quickly and easily together and, even though it had been a terrible night, I did smile because I knew that at last my wonderful horse and I were now friends.

Soon all the livestock were returned, including Louise

and Jeni's milk cow. Toby couldn't bear harm coming to any creature, so when he saw Gert trotting home he yelled, 'Yippee!' in his very loud voice. It turned out that this was too much for Chronicle. He had been so brave in the rain and with all the shouting and guns firing, but Toby's bellowing finished him off. He sat down with a loud bang and I fell off behind him. I don't think I have ever seen my family laugh more. I looked up from the ground and started laughing too. We had been through a lot. I don't think anyone else from the wagon train could understand our laughter, but it was how we managed things together.

The storm had caused its own damage. Two oxen had been killed by lightning and we all had repairs to make to our wagons, so in the end it was not till the next day that we set off again.

I brushed Chronicle down and had a long talk with him.

'Thank you for saving them,' I said, and he nuzzled into my shoulder.

Louise was watching. 'I think it's the saddle,' she said.

'What is?' I asked.

'I think your horse doesn't like the saddle. Try riding him without.'

And I realized that Chronicle had been fine in the storm and the rain and the lightning but there had been no time to put on the saddle. Now I got back on him bareback. He whinnied and waited patiently for me to do whatever I wanted. He was like a different horse.

Louise smiled. 'We all have our own little ways,' she said.

Meanwhile Buddle went mad organizing. He'd had enough of chaos, and after the stormy night I think everyone was now prepared to listen. Our entire company was divided into four sections, with a leader appointed for each to supervise their order of march. We were so proud when Henry was put in charge of ours. He couldn't stop beaming and from then on did nothing but check on everyone at all times. Regular guard duty was established. Everyone had been frightened as much by the storm as by the thought of Indians, and now they all wanted rules about everything.

Whiskey was banned except as medicine. Laws were made about card playing and gambling. Everyone in the train was required to take care of the sick. It was agreed that anyone who died would have their possessions divided between the wagons closest to them and that anyone who decided to leave the train would have to give up all their belongings except clothing. Mr Honeyman objected to all these things.

'I am not sharing my possessions!' he fumed, but no one was listening.

Now that he had the chance Buddle began to make

everything military and the next morning he woke us with a bugle.

'Dear Lord,' sighed Louise. 'The man managed to lose everything else but kept hold of that wretched bugle!'

Buddle was taking it all very seriously. He had shaved his beard and even tried to comb his hair.

'I think people should call me Colonel,' he declared, but I think everyone thought he was going to far. Nor were they interested when he suggested that we should march. It was too hot.

'Why should we march?' they complained. 'The man rides in a wagon all day.'

'He's only got one leg,' Toby reminded them.

'Well, when *he* marches, *I* will,' said someone.

Buddle was military-mad now. I think he would have liked it if the cattle marched in step too. Mr Honeyman refused to go along with the train because of the new rules, so he and his wife and Algernon rode some distance away to the side.

'We're moving too slowly,' complained the Reverend and his wife.

There was a vote, and for the first time the wagon train split into two parts – one fast and one slow. Henry was adamant that we should be quick, but Bea worried that Louise and Jeni would have to be in the slow part of the train because of Gert, the milk cow, but no one was telling those women what to do. I think the whole family was glad when they joined us in the speedier half. The slower group chose a new leader and we were pleased that James Long carried on as our guide. Cornelius was still with us as his chest of wonders was on Louise and Jeni's wagon. Buddle was also in the fast group, along with the ten wagons of the Walkers, and Reverend Goudy and Parenthia, who had caused the split in the first place.

Before we set off we had to get rid of more things from the wagon to make room for the wounded. Buddle still hadn't found a new leg so he went in Louise and Jeni's wagon while we made a bed in ours as best we could for Jack. The bullet was out but he was weak.

'Lost a lot of blood,' explained Buddle. 'Just have to hope the wound doesn't get infected.'

'Might he die?' I whispered to Bea, terrified, but she wouldn't answer.

Henry was recovered, although his head hurt, but he was busy with his new duties so I raced about doing his chores as well as my own. When I was done, I found him standing next to the printing press.

'Slim! Come here.' I went and stood by the old cart which had come all the way from Ireland. I knew what he was going to say but I didn't want to hear it.

'We can't manage it,' he said quietly. 'You know that.'

Jack had been pushing the press along for hundreds of

miles, but no one else was that strong and there was no room in the wagon. We would have had to get rid of all our food to get it in.

I couldn't bear it.

'But we need it,' I cried. 'We're going to bring democracy and print newspapers and . . .' I began to sob.

Henry was right. There was nothing we could do but leave the printing press behind, though it hurt me so much. It was like abandoning my father all over again. I felt I had let Da down. I couldn't even look as we rode on, leaving it standing alone in the middle of nowhere. No one would know what it was. No one would know why it mattered.

We were a much smaller group when we set off again. We were supposed to be quicker, but the heavy rain had saturated and softened the ground and travelling was more difficult than usual. The day was at least bright. The prairie air was fresh and filled with the lovely smell of countless spring flowers. Every little blade of grass hung with drops of dew.

'Like jewels swaying in the gentle breeze!' declared Cornelius, putting his head back and raising his arms as if to hug the whole prairie. I knew he was trying to make me feel better.

'How much further, Buddle?' asked Toby for the millionth time.

Buddle shook his head. 'Long way still. Not reached Independence Rock yet.'

'We've travelled forty marks so far,' I said.

'What does that mean?' asked Toby.

'I scratch a mark on the wagon for each day we've travelled,' I explained. 'There's thirty-five so far.'

'And in five days we'll have forty days and nights,' said Cornelius. 'Why, it's a Biblical journey.'

I hadn't wanted the wagon train to split up, but the truth was, we were quicker than before and it was easier to organize. James Long carried on leading us west, and soon the storm clouds cleared and a bright rainbow formed ahead. It was a perfect arch.

'That is the most brilliant presentation of all the colours of the prism I have ever seen,' sighed Cornelius, and Bea agreed. She got out her coloured pencils to try and capture it and they both smiled. She knew he had saved us all the night before and she was grateful.

Louise showed us how to find wild onions, and that evening Kate made quite the dish, cooking them up with bacon in our Dutch oven.

'Eat, Jack,' she encouraged as she tried to spoon a small bit of the delicious food into his mouth, but he couldn't eat.

He whispered something so I leaned closer to hear.

'How are you managing the printing press?' he managed.

'Ssh!' Kate replied, and he lay back and slept.

Jack was very unwell and I know Kate was worried but she didn't say so. Instead she clapped her hands and declared, 'Well, time for some school, I think!'

She got out the books she had brought from Independence and gave me and Toby some lessons. We quite enjoyed doing something new for a bit. I realized how tired I was of the endless travelling. We never did anything but chores and walking. I liked taking some time to look at books. Kate handed Henry our book of Shakespeare, and he surprised everyone by sitting for ages and reading out loud. Mrs Meadows was lifted down from her wagon, and she loved being in the sun, listening. Jeni enjoyed it too. She sat cross-legged on the ground, knitting while Henry read and read. When I was released from my books, I sat and cleaned our guns. They might not have been fired all that often, but the rain had made them rusty and now I wasn't taking any chances. Cornelius was showing Bea how to use something called a microscope to look at the veins in a leaf. She loved it, and set about doing drawings of what she had seen. Meanwhile all around us folks lay on the grass, smoking and telling stories.

A few jumped up when an Indian, two squaws and some children came into the camp. Everyone was still nervous, but Kate smiled, and Louise held up her hand calling out, 'It's fine. They mean no harm.'

The Indian man was very tall and rode a handsome pony while the women and their families walked. He spoke good English and said his name was John Wolf. The small group set about making a camp of smoke-coloured skin tents raised on sticks about two feet off the ground. John wore a medal bearing a picture of Thomas Jefferson, who had once been President of the United States but was now, Cornelius told me, long dead. Kate and Louise both gave them food.

The women had moccasins for sale which they wanted to trade for meat. Soon quite a few people were wearing Indian shoes, including Cornelius, who declared they were 'like walking on clouds'.

Not everyone was walking on clouds. Jeni's mother, Mrs Meadows, was very frail and getting frailer. Jeni and Louise fussed over her constantly. The old lady wasn't the only person heading west to try and improve their health. Apparently there were American towns where every autumn a fever struck and lots of people died. Louise and Jeni had come from such a place.

'She needs the sun, the great California sun that every-one talks about. That will make her better,' Jeni said as she tried to make her mother more comfortable. We were all finding the journey difficult but Mrs Meadows struggled more than most. She was too old to walk or ride a horse so had to travel on her bed in the wagon all day, where she was jolted about and could hardly rest.

We moved on over the high rolling prairie. In the far distance we could see the narrow dark lines of timber, which we now knew lined small watercourses, stretching far away until lost on the horizon. Some of the slopes looked almost like parks with their rows of trees but we hardly saw a living thing amongst them. The only relief in the great expanse was our own white-topped wagons, and the people and animals belonging to them. Mile after mile we wound slowly over the hilltops and through the hollows, becoming almost blind to the land in front of us.

Despite all the rain, water for cooking and drinking was becoming difficult to find. For many days the wagons had groaned up a long slope where water was scarce, so you can imagine our delight when at last we reached the Platte River. From a distance it looked wonderful. A wide green ribbon, lazily winding through the middle of the broad shallow valley.

'Water!' everyone shouted, and ran towards to it, but it was so disappointing. In lots of places the Platte was not so much a river as simply moving sand.

'You'd have to chew this water,' grumbled Buddy, 'if you wanted it to do you any good. I swear it flows upside down.'

The river was full of little creatures Toby called 'wiggle tails'. He hated them and tried to scoop them out of his water cup.

'Urgh!' he said loudly.

'I thought you were king of the animals,' Henry teased. 'Do these poor little ones not count?'

Kate ruffled Toby's hair, saying, 'All little ones count, Henry, but that doesn't mean you want them in your tea.'

'Don't be too nice to the wiggle tails,' I said, 'or Toby will start naming them all and we'll be here for ever.'

We had brought Jack out to lie by the fire. I looked at him to see if he thought it was funny too, but his eyes were glazed and he paid no attention. I couldn't bear it, and tears came to my eyes. I turned away so he wouldn't know how worried I was.

We needed to drink from the river, but you had to boil the water to stop the wiggle tails wiggling about. Some people filtered it through a cloth, while others dug a hole two to four feet deep in the sandy soil near the riverbank and used that water. It all added to the time the journey was taking.

Bea found one still wriggling in her tea and shrieked. We were all sitting with Louise and Jeni and I think it gave Mrs Meadows a fright. Louise took the cup from Bea and gently pulled out the wiggle tail.

'Look how tiny it is,' she said, holding up the small thing. 'It must be so afraid of you.'

Cornelius showed us what it looked like under his microscope. It was quite a creature, and I think we had more respect for them after that.

That night I found Louise standing at the edge of the river. I went to speak to her, but she held up her hand as if she did not want to be disturbed. As I turned to go, she said quietly, 'Honour the sacred. Honour the Earth, our Mother. Honour the Elders. Honour all with whom we share the Earth: four-leggeds, two-leggeds, winged ones, swimmers, crawlers, plant and rock people. Walk in balance and beauty.'

I stopped and watched the water flow past with all the things living in it hidden from view. I liked what she said. When Chronicle and I rode together now, that was balance and beauty, I thought. I wasn't in charge of my horse; instead we worked together.

After a long moment Louise looked at me and said, 'You are sad, Slim.'

I nodded.

'Your printing press.'

'My Uncle Aedan and Da made it. I felt . . . like I was leaving part of Ireland behind. Part of my family behind. Like I let them down.'

Louise nodded. 'There are many ways to do good in this great new country,' she said. 'Now you're just going to have to find another.'

When I went back to the wagon, Bea called me over.

'I washed your neckerchief, Slim,' she said, handing me the red cloth I had been so proud of. 'You don't look right without it.'

It was so kind and I was pleased to put it on again.

'I love you, Slim,' she said.

'I love you too, Bea.'

We never talked about love now that Ma was gone. I don't know why Bea said that. It wasn't like her but it felt nice. Maybe we had come too close to losing yet more people we loved. Every day we trudged over the endless waves of hills. The land was bleak. The light sands, driven by the gusts of wind, drifted across the dry plain, filling the atmosphere and colouring everything with a grey coating of dust.

We had seen none of the legendary buffalo yet, but there were plenty of signs of them. The path along the river had regular grooves running from the water to the sand hills at right angles to our wagon train.

Buddle pointed to them from the back of our wagon, where he was getting bounced about.

'It's the buffalo make those hollows,' he explained as I rode behind on Chronicle. 'They make 'em going to the river to drink.'

The ruts were worn into the soil as smoothly as if cut by a spade. It made the road rough and the wagons moved with a constant rocking motion. Old Mrs Meadows was quite ill with it and I hated Jack being shaken about.

Though we saw no living buffalo, we saw plenty of dead ones. Their skulls lined the side of the road. They were white and picked clean, and other travellers had turned them into a sort of post office. People wrote messages for those following behind and placed them on the buffalo skulls. There were notices about trouble with Pawnee Indians or general information about particular companies travelling ahead. Kate wrote out a message and placed it on a stick by a large skull.

'What does it say?' I asked.

'It tells anyone who might know us where we are going and that we are well,' she replied.

'Do you mean Da?' I asked. 'Do you think he will come?' My voice was raised in hope. But she walked on carrying Hero. 'Do you think he is alive, Kate?' I called after her, but she wouldn't answer.

Despite the poor water, following the Platte River was good. At least it was quite level. It made a sort of natural roadway heading in the right direction. Soon water was not our only problem though. The trees became scarcer, which meant there was no firewood for cooking. For the first time we began to search for what Buddle called 'buffalo chips', which he said were fine for cooking.

Louise showed us. And once you started looking you

could see that there were piles of the stuff all over the place. Toby was delighted and grabbed great armfuls.

'This is much easier than chopping wood!' he said, delighted at how easy it was to collect. 'Where did it all come from?'

Louise grinned. 'Out of a buffalo's bottom,' she replied. 'Buffalo chips are just buffalo manure left to dry over many years.'

'Manure?' repeated Toby. 'What's that?'

'Poo,' laughed Jeni.

Toby immediately dropped everything he was carrying, and I didn't blame him.

'Poo!' he shrieked, as appalled as I was, and indeed that was what it was. Dried poo. It stank, but once the chips were dry they burned well and gave a strong clear heat, which oddly, considering where they had come from, did not smell at all.

Collecting was a dirty business but Cornelius thought it splendid stuff.

'Isn't nature a wonder to provide just what we need out of the bottom of what is really a large cow?' he declared. 'Much better than wood!'

'Unless you're still wanting a new leg!' yelled Buddle from the seat of Jeni and Louise's wagon.

Bea hated the stuff.

'I can't cook with this,' she insisted. 'How can I make supper with heat from . . . from . . .' She couldn't say it.

'Poo!' laughed Toby.

Cornelius swept in front of her and posed with one hand in his waistcoat pocket and the other waving above his head.

'Think of it as *bois de vache* instead,' he suggested brightly, 'which is French for "cow wood".'

Despite this rather fine name it took Bea ages to cope with cooking over poo. Mrs Honeyman was beside herself at the thought of collecting such terrible stuff and went for some days without a fire at all.

Jack slowly began to mend but he was weak. An infection got into his leg, and three times a day Bea would make us stop so she could clean it. The fear of death was with us as we walked. I was terrified of losing anyone else. I knew I couldn't manage it. One morning Kate stopped to read the rough writing on a plank which had been half in the soil. It had crude lettering which read:

Mary Ellis
Died May 7th 1845
Two months old

Kate, who had been so strong for us all, began to sob. It made Toby worry.

'Why are you crying?' he asked. 'You didn't know her.'

'Off with you now, Toby!' instructed Bea, putting

her arm round Kate. Kate had lost her own baby on the boat to America. We never talked about it, but I knew that was who she wept for. That same day we passed a man pushing a wheelbarrow. In it was a headstone on which was carved the name *Julie Birtwood*. Kate gave him water.

'My wife,' he explained. 'She died on the prairie. We lost everything, but I promised her a headstone. I promised,' he muttered, and walked on, trudging west. We tried to get him to ride with us but he could not or would not change his mind. I watched him struggle and thought how hard this journey was; how much we all loved our families.

It was always exciting to meet someone on the trail, but now, for the first time, we began to meet people who had given up on their journey and were heading back to St Louis.

Buddle called them 'turnarounds', and the first of them made everyone anxious. They still had a few oxen and a couple of wagons but it was a sad group who walked towards us.

'Why are you going back?' Toby asked them outright.

'Nothing but bad luck ahead,' said one of the men. 'We lost our cattle to wolves.'

'Then some of our people died,' explained a tired-looking woman. 'One man was killed by the Pawnees.'

'And about a week before, Dakota Indians attacked and stole all our best horses,' added another woman.

'We just want to get back alive,' said the leader of their wagon train. It made one or two in our group question what we were doing, but Louise wouldn't hear of it.

'They're exaggerating,' she said. 'They just feel bad about giving up so they're making it worse than it is.'

That sounded like it could be right but a lot of people were scared. 'We will not be swayed,' Buddle boomed, and we marched on.

Mosquitoes began to plague us in great swarms. They bit every living thing and the animals hated it. Louise lit fires of sagebrush to try and keep the pesky insects away.

Soon even the wagons began to suffer. The wheels were made of wood, with an iron band or tyre round the outside. The atmosphere was so dry that the wood shrank, which meant the tyres became loose. Cornelius showed us how to put a wedge between the tyre and the wheel for a temporary repair, but soon many wagons were limping along. Buddle called a halt for the day and even James, who was always pushing us forward, could see it had to be done.

Everything was unloaded and the wagons 'jacked up' to take the wheels off. Then the iron rims were removed and the wheels soaked in the river overnight to make them swell again. Great fires were built so that the men could heat the iron rim red hot to make it expand. Then it had to be slipped back on the wood and the whole thing dipped back into the water to make the two parts sit tight. It was delicate work. Let the rim cool too much and it wouldn't fit. Too hot, and it charred the wood.

The Honeymans' wagon was in more trouble than most, but they continued to move along by themselves away from the main train. Cornelius had a spyglass and could see them struggling with their wheels.

'We should help them,' he said.

'Not you, Cornelius,' said Bea. 'They don't trust you. You're the one who ran into their wagon, remember?' But the rest of us went over to lend a hand. Algernon had got no better. The once neat boy was a ragged mess now. His long trousers had torn into shorts, he had no shoes and he was filthy. He didn't help at all as Henry and Louise set about dealing with the wheels on the patched Honeyman wagon.

We were all with them for a couple of hours, and by the time we left the wagon was ready to roll again. I'm sure they were grateful but they couldn't bring themselves to say so. Just as we were leaving Algernon tried to steal Toby's slingshot from his pocket.

'Hey!' yelled Toby, and chased off after Algernon, who ran away laughing until he tripped and cut his chin. Then he was crying. Mrs Honeyman had seen none of it and blamed Toby.

Henry was furious. 'We are not helping them again!' he announced. 'Never!'

Still we followed the never-ending Platte. Some days we had no choice but to cross the wide river. The path we were following would become impassable and James would lead us to the other side. He showed us how to attach the wagons and teams to a chain which extended the entire length of the train. Men waded through the river alongside the oxen, sometimes clinging onto ox yokes and swimming. Some places were so deep that everyone had to swim and the wagons floated, held in a line by the chain. I was glad Jack didn't have to deal with it; he lay asleep, restless and fevered in the floating wagon.

Louise was good with water.

'Never try to go straight across a stream,' she taught us. 'Get in the water and head across. You'll feel a current try to take you. Let it, and then follow it up or down till you hit another, then follow that up or down, and so on till you reach the opposite bank.'

It was a good lesson, for the river was unpredictable. In some places the hoofs of the oxen were hardly wetted by the thin sheet of water; but the next moment the river would be raging against their sides. Buddle lay in Jeni and Louise's wagon watching Henry struggle with the mule in the water.

'Wretched creatures!' he cried. 'Damned if they don't prefer drowning to swimming.'

None of it was easy. Once again the Honeymans tried

to go it alone. Mr Honeyman drove his team of oxen and the wagon into the river and did well to get across, but he was just pulling out when his team broke loose and both the wagon and the animals backed into the water. It began to be swept away. Mrs Honeyman ran to help, but the fast river caught her pink dress and pulled her along. Algernon began screaming on the bank as Mrs Honeyman swept right past where we were standing.

'Henry!' yelled Kate, but Henry had had enough. He stood just watching, refusing to move.

'They'll drown!' shouted Kate once more.

CHAPTER THIRTEEN

'Henry!' screamed Kate. She ran over and shook him with both hands. 'This is not who you are. You are not this person. You are Patrick's son and you will save those people. You will not disappoint your father.'

Henry looked at her and I could see shame on his face at the mention of Da's name.

He took a deep breath and yelled to Toby and me to help. Cornelius and Louise joined us as we all dashed to the river.

'Make a human chain,' shouted Henry. 'Cornelius, tie yourself to a tree and then hold everyone steady.'

We all held hands and made a chain out into the river, with Cornelius acting like an anchor for everyone to hold onto. Henry managed to grab Mrs Honeyman and pass her along the line to safety. Now we all rushed forward to grab the wagon and guide it ashore. I heaved at it along with everyone else. There were no longer any jobs that were just for the men. I could feel how strong my arms had become. I was sorry the Honeymans were in trouble but it felt good to be able to help.

Mrs Honeyman wasn't breathing, but Louise turned her onto her side and banged her on the back. Great heaves of water flew out of her mouth and she began to cough and shake. Algernon was terrified and cried for his mother, while Mr Honeyman sat soaking wet with his head in his hands.

'Thank you,' he said. After that they never left the wagon train again.

We travelled on and began to get an idea of how hard everyone had found the journey ahead. We weren't the only ones leaving precious things behind. We started seeing abandoned furniture that people on the trail ahead now thought too hard to carry with them. There were ancient tables, well waxed and rubbed, even massive bureaus of carved oak.

'Beautiful!' sighed Kate.

'From someone's home,' whispered Bea.

Perhaps the fine furniture had come all the way from England, but now it had been abandoned to crack in the heat that bore down on the prairie. Bea was so sad but Buddle couldn't have been more delighted.

'Look at this!' he cried, pointing to a massive table with

elaborately carved legs which finished as giant lion's claws. 'Why, it's the very thing,' he declared, showing Cornelius.

Cornelius smiled and nodded in agreement. 'I believe you may be right, Mr Buddle. Henry,' he called out cheerfully, 'we shall need a saw!'

Henry helped to cut the leg off the table, and it wasn't long before he and Cornelius had fashioned the most marvellous replacement for Buddle's missing limb. Now the old colonel marched at the front of the train, bringing the claw of his new leg down with a great thump each time he took a step. He whistled as he walked and it made all of us feel better.

We needed things to cheer us because everyone was exhausted. Even those who had been in perfect health when we left were now weak. Reverend Goudy was no longer the only one with a cough. The endless dust had left both Jeni and Toby struggling to catch their breath and the poor water had caused epidemics of diarrhoea in the whole family.

Cornelius checked his 'roadometer', muttering, 'Four hundred and twelve . . . Add on the bit before I invented the machine . . .' He looked up and smiled. 'I reckon we're well over five hundred miles from Independence!'

'Is that all?' cried Bea. 'But that means we have hundreds more miles to go.'

She began to sob and Cornelius watched helplessly.

'We're about eighteen hundred miles from New York, if that helps. If you look at a map of America, we're more than halfway across.' But she was too tired to listen.

The ground had become quite rough and very wild. Our road lay along a narrow ridge. At the top of a hill James halted the train. Everyone was silenced. The view was amazing. You could see green hills for miles around. Before and below us the river wound its way through broken hills and meadows, behind us the undulating prairie.

'This is Windlass Hill,' declared James, 'and we've no choice but to go down.' There were still about two hours of daylight left, but he insisted we wait until morning to try and get down it. It was clear we were going to need to take our time. The hill went almost straight down like a cliff.

I sat with Jack. He was awake more and more, and he wanted to know what was happening. He knew about windlasses.

'We use them on ships,' he explained, so weak he could hardly speak. 'It's like a drum attached to the deck. You wind rope around it, so you can let it out slowly when there's something heavy on the other end. Like an anchor.'

In the morning it was the large trees that became the windlasses. All the oxen were detached from the wagons and the two back wheels were locked with a chain run through them and attached to the wagon bed so that they couldn't turn. Then the oxen were hitched to the back of the wagon. They weren't used to this and pulled back, which helped slow the wagon down. Meanwhile heavy ropes were tied to the backs of the wagons and wrapped around large trees. Under James's orders the ropes were let out bit by bit as each wagon, one by one, was slowly lowered down the hill.

Cornelius loved it. 'A piece of engineering perfection!' he said, beaming. 'You see how a machine can change our lives!'

Everyone and everything made it safely down the hill, which was remarkable. Henry was panting with the effort. I looked at him laughing with the other men, all of whom were sweating but delighted.

'He's grown so much,' said Kate, smiling, seeing me looking. 'Your Da would be proud.'

When we reached the foot of the hill, Henry made us turn round and look back at it.

'It's so steep!' he marvelled. 'You would think it impossible for any wagons to have come down it.'

'Well done, Henry,' said Kate, and he blushed with pride.

I was so glad that he didn't fight with her any more.

Now we entered a beautiful vale covered with fine grass and flowers of nearly every variety. The sides were lined with majestic ash trees.

'Ash Hollow,' replied James when Toby asked for the name of this place.

How we had struggled to get this far, and how everyone needed rest. At last the air was clear and calm. The mosquitoes left us alone and thousands of birds welcomed us with their song.

'Listen!' called Jack from inside the wagon. 'That's—'

'A meadowlark!' called out Jeni. She turned and grinned at me. How thrilled we all were that Jack was well enough to pay attention.

A beautiful flute-like sound rang out across the grass. Cool streams prattled about and there was the most wonderful scent of wild roses, which grew everywhere under the majestic ash trees. There must have been fifty rose bushes to each ash tree. The place looked like a fairyland for it was alive with gooseberry and currant bushes, cherry trees and every variety of wild flower.

'This,' declared Cornelius, 'is a wonderful place!'

'It's like paradise,' sighed Bea, and so it was.

Near the mouth of the hollow there was a small log cabin. It had been put up the past winter by some trappers. No one lived there, and now it acted as a sort of unofficial post office. On the outside walls were all manner of handwritten advertisements – descriptions of lost cattle, horses, etc. – while inside, in a recess, dozens of people had left letters addressed to others in almost every quarter of the globe, with requests that those who passed would convey them to the nearest post office in the States. I know Kate left another note. Maybe it was for Da but she wouldn't say. I left one of my printed notices, but I was leaving them less and less frequently. I couldn't print any more, and the further we travelled the harder I found it to believe that Da would ever find us.

We moved on into the hollow, where at last there was plenty of good firewood and clean water. It was what we had dreamed of as we trudged endlessly beside the creaking wagons on the sun-drenched prairie.

Cornelius began to sing:

> *'A rose tree in full bearing*
> *Had sweet flowers fair to see:*
> *One rose beyond comparing*
> *For beauty attracted me.'*

Soon everyone joined in, and it was a happy band of people who camped for the night. Fiddles came out of cases and there was dancing by the campfires. Cornelius got Bea up to dance, and I can still see her red hair leaping about her shoulders as she enjoyed the music.

'It's like being back in Ireland,' said Henry. 'Do you remember the party we had for your birthday, Slim?'

'Uncle Aedan played the fiddle,' recalled Toby.

I realized I hadn't thought about anything as ordinary as a birthday in months. 'I think it must be soon,' I said.

Cornelius and Bea wandered over to us, all hot and happy from dancing.

'What?' he asked.

'My birthday. My Uncle Aedan gave me a fishing rod for the last birthday I had at home.'

Cornelius smiled. 'I don't have a fishing rod because all I need is my magic rubber bands and a couple of pieces of wood.' He got some rubber bands out of his pocket and looked about for some wood. He found a small piece that was hollow as well as straight.

'Sharpen the stick to a point, Slim,' he instructed. 'Like you're making an arrow.' I got out Da's knife and set about my work. Meanwhile Cornelius attached a band to the hollow piece of wood. When my arrow was finished, he slotted it inside the hollow and put the rubber band around the blunt end of the stick. With one hand he held the end of the arrow while the other held the wood. He pushed them apart and the rubber band began to stretch.

'Now watch!' He let the stick go and it shot up into the air before landing about twenty feet away.

'There's a lot of power in that,' said Cornelius, as happy as a little boy with his new game. 'You could catch a fish if you're quick.'

Me, Henry and Toby had a competition to see who could hit a tree trunk on the edge of the glade which lasted for ages.

It was a happy night. Card games were secretly set up

310

behind wagons and there was a lot of jolly chatter. Louise, Jeni, Bea, Kate and Mrs Meadows had a sort of tea party and asked other women from the train to come and join them. The men gathered in groups, lots of them still arguing the case for oxen or horse being better for the trip. I think even drink was taken because there was a lot of silliness.

Every night I had to carry water back for everyone, and that evening it was such a pleasure to drink from the springs. We drank and drank. The water seemed so fresh and clear but it was to be our undoing. We did not know – we couldn't know – that there was sickness in the water.

Reverend Goudy got to his feet, which made lots of people sigh.

'Don't tell me it's the Sabbath again,' groaned Jeni.

'I'll drink to that!' declared Buddle, getting out a bottle of something called 'sweet vitriol' which he was very fond of.

The Reverend's wife, Parenthia, tutted, which made Louise decide she'd drink some too.

'We must at least make time for Eli to give a sermon,' said Parenthia sternly.

'Don't know why,' argued Jeni, counting the stitches on her knitting. 'It's not like he stops yakking the rest of the week.'

'We must keep the Sabbath!' insisted the Reverend, starting one of his coughing fits. No one wanted him to be upset as it made him sick so Buddle tried to make peace.

'Why don't we say that we will observe the Sabbath day when circumstances permit,' he suggested.

Everyone agreed to that but no one could agree on what those 'circumstances' might be. Soon everyone went back to mending wagons, harness, yokes, shoeing animals, etc. Cornelius was showing Bea how to remove and polish the mirrors of his spyglass.

'You have to do it continuously as they get tarnished in the open air,' he explained.

'It's a beautiful thing,' marvelled my sister.

Cornelius beamed with delight. 'It certainly is. I got it from Jacob Blattner, a marvellous mathematical instrument-maker on Chestnut Street in St Louis. Why, he . . .'

Cornelius continued about Mr Blattner for some time. I could not think why Bea was suddenly so interested in spyglasses.

All around us women were busy: some washed clothes, some boiled a 'big mess of beans' and others did their mending, while Eli stood in the centre holding a service and no one except his wife and Mrs Honeyman paid much attention. Henry was checking the tongue of the wagon till late and I was sent to see if the woods held any mushrooms. We were all busy. Everything, however, stopped for the sickness.

The first person to fall ill was the mother of five small children. Why she was alone with so many kids, I don't know. We had all stopped asking each other why we were making the trip a long time ago. The woman became sick while sitting by the campfire. She began to retch and Reverend Goudy paused in his thought about the Good Samaritan.

Parenthia was sitting next to her and shrieked as the woman lay down on the ground, shaking. The Reverend rushed over. I thought he was trying to help, but instead he grabbed his wife and quickly got her away. The two of them moved to the very edge of the camp. We could hear them praying while Bea and Louise tried to help the sick woman. Within the hour she was dead.

The grown-ups tried to keep what was happening from us, but we all heard the word 'cholera' whispered over and over. It was in the water, and it caused crippling pain that hit without warning. There was violent retching and diarrhoea. Sophie Walker was struck down with it, and then lots of her children. It was Louise and our own Bea who did most of the nursing. None of the women were ever elected to anything in the wagon train but everyone knew who to turn to when there was trouble.

'We need the roots and herbs the Indians use for sickness,' declared Louise.

'And who on earth knows about that?' asked the Reverend.

'I do,' said Louise.

That was when she took over. She pulled some roots out of the ground and showed us all what to look for.

'How do we know she has any idea what to do?' grumbled some of the men.

'It's better than just dying,' replied the women.

Everyone who was well enough began to gather roots to make medicine.

'Reckon your sweet vitriol kept us well,' said Louise to Buddle, who seemed fine.

'Can I have some?' asked Toby, who was getting scared of all the sickness. 'Too strong for you, my boy,' muttered Buddle.

Bea had learned such a lot from Ma that she had almost become the doctor for everyone, but she didn't know the local cures. Louise showed everyone how to brew up the root till it was black as coffee.

'Only use water we brought ourselves in barrels,' ordered Louise. 'Don't touch the stuff from the springs here. Slim, dig up some more.'

I pulled at a plant she pointed to. 'What is it?' I asked.

'Injun fizic,' said Louise, 'but don't tell folks that or they'll be stoopid and not drink the darn stuff.'

The hot drink she showed us how to make tasted terrible, but Louise made everyone drink it. She had taken charge now and the whole train did as she said. A lot of the children had to have their nose held while it was poured down their throat as it smelled so bad. Hero became sick. She got diarrhoea, which we knew could kill her. Kate spent all her time trying to make her well. She lay completely still in Kate's arms and didn't even cry.

Tears flowed down Kate's face. 'I can't lose another baby. I just can't,' she kept whispering.

I didn't feel well but I wasn't as sick as the others so I didn't say anything. I was older than Hero, and Ma had told me I needed to be a big sister to her, so I carried on looking for roots to make the medicine.

Jack had started to show signs of the sickness too and Bea was worried.

'He's not strong enough to cope,' she said.

I climbed up into the wagon and sat with him, whispering, 'You can do this, Jack. You are the strongest man I know.' But he didn't answer.

The illness was swift to take people from us. Many were so frightened of the cholera they refused to help bury the victims. The rest did what they could. A line of women held up their skirts to give some suffering soul a little privacy but the illness had no mercy. Parenthia became very sick. Louise took her fizic and held her while she drank it.

The Reverend, however, seemed fine.

'You could help some of the others,' suggested Louise, but Eli Goudy stood by and watched and said nothing.

Our guide, James Long, who had been with the train from the beginning, died and that made everyone panic.

'We won't know the way,' they cried.

'What is to become of us?'

'We shall be lost out here!'

So now everyone was scared, both of dying of the terrible sickness, and of how we would manage if we lived.

Then old Mrs Meadows passed away. It was awful. Louise and Jeni wept over the old lady. 'It's my fault,' sobbed Jeni. 'I thought the trip would help her, but instead it's killed her.' We all cried for Mrs Meadows, and maybe we cried for our own mother too.

Cornelius and Henry helped Louise get ready for the funeral. They cut down a cottonwood tree and split the trunk into planks. They borrowed a plane from the carpenter and carefully made the best coffin they could. Henry, Toby and I helped dig a grave a short distance from the camp, under an oak tree on the right-hand side of the trail. I could hardly dig I felt so angry and scared. Hot tears poured down my cheeks. I'd had enough. It was all too much to bear. Someone found a large boulder. Louise smoothed the surface with a chisel before carefully engraving Mrs Meadows' name and the date.

Bea put on her fine bonnet with the roses and Kate made us all wash our faces. We did our best to have a service, but the Reverend, who might finally have been useful, would not come near. He was too afraid to stand by the coffin so we made something up.

Louise spoke and said, 'The Indians who live out their lives on these plains say that no one is dead who lives in the hearts of those they leave behind. Jeni's mother is in all our hearts and so she will live on. This is a beautiful place and we shall remember her here, resting for eternity.'

Then we sang a hymn everyone could remember. I couldn't sing. It was a beautiful place but I wouldn't want to be left behind here. I thought we were finished, but Henry surprised us all by saying, 'She liked Shakespeare, Mrs Meadows. I used to read to her so I thought I might say a little . . . out of respect. She was nice. I liked her.'

Jeni nodded and Louise whispered, 'Thank you.'

Henry stepped forward and cleared his throat. I thought he would read from the book but instead he spoke from memory.

> *'Like as the waves make towards the pebbled shore,*
> *So do our minutes hasten to their end . . .'*

He carried on speaking. I didn't understand what he was saying but it sounded beautiful. His whole face changed as he spoke. He looked older and somehow handsome in a way I had never noticed before. I think everyone thought that because they stared at him as if hypnotized.

'Mrs Meadows would have been pleased,' muttered Buddle, clearing his throat so that he didn't cry.

'And Da,' whispered Bea, who never spoke Da's name.

After Henry spoke the grave was closed and the green turf of the prairie carefully laid over it.

Jeni was so sad and Louise did her best to hold a proper wake. She brought out the precious china plates she had been hiding in old Mrs Meadows' mattress and we had dinner on the grass. It felt so odd using a plate but Louise insisted everything be done properly. Jeni smiled at the plates as if she had always known.

'It doesn't matter how old you are; it is hard to miss your mother,' said Buddle.

Henry and Toby sat together, leaning against a wagon wheel, while Hamlet lay with his head on Toby's leg. Kate was trying to get Hero to take some Injun fizic. The baby seemed a little better but I could still see the worry on Kate's face.

'Your Shakespeare was wonderful today, Henry,' said Jeni. 'Thank you.'

'We lost so many,' sighed Louise. 'I don't know what we'll do without a guide.'

'I thought this was supposed to be a good place?' whispered Toby to Henry.

Henry put his arm round him and replied,

> *'Oft expectation fails, and most oft there*
> *Where most it promises.'*

Kate looked up from what she was doing. 'Henry, how have you been learning all that Shakespeare?'

Henry blushed. 'I like it,' he said. 'Reading it is fine but I like it when you say it out loud. It sounds good.'

'Do you know the rest of that quote?' asked Kate.

Henry nodded and continued,

'. . . *and oft it hits*
Where hope is coldest, and despair most fits.'

'What does that mean?' asked Toby.

Kate smiled. 'It means something good will happen when we least expect it.'

I hoped she was right. We could do with something good. Bea went to look after the five small children who had lost their mother.

'The youngest is just six weeks,' she said, shaking her head.

'How is Jack?' asked Buddle.

Bea shook her head. 'He doesn't wake and his breathing is not good.'

I went to sit with Jack. He was sleeping. I laid my head on his giant shoulder, remembering when he had been ill on the boat from Ireland. He had got better then.

'You got better then,' I whispered, reminding him. 'So you know how to do it.'

We couldn't stay in that sad place, but no one was sure what to do next. James had told us that 'Ash Hollow was the gateway to the high plains'. We knew that beyond lay the broad prairie, which we would have to cross before we began the long climb up to the mountains. The trouble was, without James to guide us, no one knew the exact way. The Walkers had recovered and now set off on their own. They couldn't wait to get away but we didn't feel as confident.

Louise gathered everyone together. 'Right, who has any information about the way forward?' she asked.

'There are landmarks,' replied Cornelius. 'I've read about them. Rocks that look like a courthouse, and one which is a giant chimney you can see for miles. We'll head for them.'

Cornelius' spyglass meant he could see for miles, so without any voting he began to lead the way. The land stretched far away to the west. There were no signs and no tracks as we moved on, making a wagon road through the high grass. I think everyone was afraid.

At some point a small group of wagons heading back east came towards us. Parenthia had recovered, and now she and her husband turned round too and left. They went back where they had come from. We waved goodbye. No Indians had been baptized, but at least they took the five orphans with them as they rushed to save themselves.

CHAPTER FOURTEEN

We left behind a small row of graves with the names of people we had come to know. Beside them Kate left a message for anyone following, warning them about the water. Chronicle and I went back to the 'post office' and left a note there too. We knew that the slower travellers were still behind us and we didn't want them to get sick too. 'Why did no one do that for us?' Bea fumed.

'Not everyone is kind,' sighed Jeni.

Now we had no guide but Cornelius; Henry and Buddle were determined we could manage. They called a meeting, and this time Louise was included in the discussion. A plan was made to keep heading west and look for the great rock Cornelius had read about. We were a much smaller group now and lots of people were scared. They came to Toby to ask advice about their animals and to Bea for help when they were unwell. Hero was getting better and Jack had managed to sit up and drink some tea. It was good to hear Henry suggest, 'Let's lead the way. Let's show everyone that we are not afraid.'

Leaving the hollow, we passed a Sioux Indian encampment. Our clothes were ragged now and a few people stopped to buy leggings and moccasins made of deer and antelope skin. Mrs Honeyman refused to 'wear such things' but she could have done with them. Her once fine dress was faded and torn, and Algernon had long ago lost his jacket and shirt.

The Sioux lived in lodges, which were a kind of house made of buffalo skins stretched over about twenty poles in the shape of an umbrella. Through the opening flap you could see that there was about a ten-foot space inside, with buffalo skins laid out for carpet. In the centre a fire burned, its smoke curling up to a hole at the top.

'Genius!' declared Cornelius, who liked any invention. 'See that, Bea,' he called to my sister as he looked inside one of the lodges. 'The hole for the smoke is fixed on two poles which you can move depending on the wind. It stops the smoke coming back down inside. We need a drawing of this.' Bea sat down to capture it.

Some of the Indians looked strange. They had painted faces, which Buddle said was to keep insects from biting, and some of them wore clothing abandoned by other wagon trains. One young brave wore a bonnet and carried a parasol trimmed with lace. Others wore white robes or shirts of buckskin, with matching pantaloons and moccasins embroidered with porcelain beads in bright colours. The light copper-coloured skin of the women was so beautiful that Bea hardly knew where to look for things she wanted to draw.

'One of the most powerful tribes of Indians on the continent of America,' declared Buddle with respect. 'You don't want to fight a Sioux; you ain't gonna win.'

'They don't want to fight us. They want sugar, coffee, whiskey,' said Louise, 'so everyone needs to find a little something to give as a gift.'

Some of the men still grumbled about Louise being allowed to have a say in what we did, but they knew she had saved us at Ash Hollow so they kept quiet. Louise wasn't the only woman in charge. The Sioux were packing up to leave and it was clear that their women were also telling everyone what to do. Some of the Indian women looked very old and thin but they did the hardest labour in the camp. They were taking down the lodges, fastening the long poles to each side of their packhorses, so that one end dragged behind on the ground. Then they attached short crosspieces to make a frame for their belongings. The tiniest children were placed in cages of willow, and these too were placed on the frame behind their horses.

They called the children *wakanisha*, which Buddle told me meant 'sacred', and they were clearly the centre of everyone's attention.

'Shall we get you such a cage, Hero?' teased Kate as she carried my little sister through the encampment.

'You see,' boomed Buddle to Louise, 'the women are in charge and everything is working like clockwork.'

Toby was thrilled to see that the Sioux had white wolves trained as dogs, and they loved his pig. Children naked except for a bit of cloth about their loins swarmed around him. Everyone was busy. The chief wanted to speak to Louise and Bea. He had heard about the illness in Ash Hollow. The Sioux had had it too and he wanted to know what medicine they had used.

Toby was quite the centre of attention as he got Hamlet to walk on his hind legs, pretend to be shot and then play dead. The Indian children were all clapping their hands when suddenly Hamlet took fright at something, I don't know what, and ran off squealing.

'Hamlet!' shouted Toby, but the pig wasn't listening. Toby and I chased after him, but he was so fast we couldn't catch him. We ran to the edge of the encampment where there were some abandoned lodges. I don't think we should have been there, but Hamlet ran inside and Toby went in after him. Inside there were maybe half a dozen dead Indians. They were laid on the ground, wrapped in robes of buffalo skin, with their spears, saddles and camp kettles all piled beside them.

Toby shrieked, terrified.

'Dead people, dead people!' he shouted, pointing at them.

'It's all right. They can't hurt you. They're like Mrs Meadows, that's all.'

We were both breathing heavily, and despite what I had told my brother I was afraid to move. I put my arm round him as we backed away from the dead Indians.

'Cholera?' whispered Toby.

'Maybe,' I agreed.

We carried on searching for Hamlet. In the next lodge we found a dead young Indian girl laid out by herself. She was about my age but dressed in amazing clothes. Her leggings were of fine, elaborately decorated scarlet cloth. She had a new pair of moccasins beautifully embroidered with porcupine quills and her body was wrapped in stunning buffalo-hide robes. Hamlet had come to rest beside her and he sat looking almost respectful.

'Sorry, sorry . . . um . . . Indian person,' Toby managed.

He was afraid and didn't want to get too close, so I slipped a rope around Hamlet's neck and got him to come out of the lodge.

'Thank you, Slim,' gasped Toby.

It had been too much for him, and he ran off with his pig.

I could hear him scolding Hamlet for his bad behaviour as they raced away.

I looked at the dead girl. I had seen such a lot of death, but this was the first time it was someone the same age as me. Where had she gone? If I died, would Ma be waiting for me? I thought about Da. I shut my eyes and tried to see him laid out in fine clothes like this, but in my heart I just knew that I had not said goodbye to him. Not yet. He was alive. I was sure of it.

I was deep in thought when I left the lodge. Too deep to notice someone come up behind me. The next thing I knew an Indian about my height and dressed like one of the braves jumped on me from behind. I crashed to the ground and, without thinking, began to defend myself. We wrestled and fought. I hadn't realized how full of fury I was and I pummelled him with all my might. He was strong and the battle raged for some minutes until at last I managed to get the upper hand. I flipped him over onto his back and sat across his chest, pinning him down with my hands and knees. It was only then that I realized it was a girl. She was dressed in pantaloons, her face painted bright red and a great tail feather in her hair, but it was definitely a girl.

'Ssh,' she said urgently, looking up at me. Then she turned her head slightly to one side, and to my horror I saw the biggest brown-patterned snake right beside us. It was maybe five foot long. I couldn't really tell because it was curled up. What I could see was that its tail finished in a series of ridges.

'Rattlesnake!' whispered the girl.

I had heard of these. They could kill you if you were bitten. We had disturbed the thing and now it slowly raised its head up until its wide mouth and beady eyes were level with mine.

'Slow,' said the Indian girl, and I thought that 'slow' was probably a good idea. We did not want to startle the vicious creature. I was still lying on top of her. I silently indicated a direction away from the snake with my head and she nodded. Clinging together, we rolled quietly away from the snake before slowly getting to our feet. I thought we should run, but instead the girl raised her hand to make me stand still. Then she looked around before picking up a stick about four feet long. From a pocket she pulled a short piece of string and tied one end to the stick and the other into a slip knot. I had no idea what she was doing and I didn't like to ask in case it made the snake look at me.

Standing as far away from the snake as possible, she slipped the loop over its head and round its neck, then gave a little jerk, which drew the slip knot tight and lifted the dangerous creature right off the ground. It wriggled but was powerless to strike.

I realized I had been holding my breath but now I was cross. 'What did you jump on me for, you idiot?'

'I'm not an idiot,' she said in very good English. 'You are. I was trying to save you from the snake.'

'Oh, well, thank you,' I managed gruffly.

She reached into the lodge and picked up a tube made of the bark of a sapling which was hanging there. Carefully she lowered the snake into the tube.

'You're going to eat that?' I asked, amazed that she was keeping it.

She shook her head. 'Don't be silly. I'll let it go somewhere it can't hurt us.' She stopped and looked at me. 'You're a good fighter for a white girl.'

I think I was pleased that she thought so but I just nodded.

'It was Wakan Tanka,' she said.

'What was?'

'Wakan Tanka who saves us. He is the great mystery who protects us.'

As far as I could understand Wakan Tanka was their god. The girl was called Mapiya, which I learned later meant 'sky' or 'the heavens'. Mapiya took me to meet her horse. It was a sort of yellow colour and very strong.

'What do you call him?' I asked.

'Horse,' she said. Buddle would have approved.

'Why don't you give him a better name?' I asked.

'Why don't you race me?' she suggested, leaping onto Horse. I ran to get on Chronicle, and soon we were galloping away across the prairie. For more than a year I had done nothing but work and worry, travel and feel tired. I couldn't remember the last time I had just had fun for no reason. Fun with a girl of my own age!

We raced up a high hill, with small rocks shooting out from under the hoofs of the horses as we went. Mapiya won easily and jumped off, laughing, to let the rattlesnake go. It slid off into the coarse grass and we watched it leave. It hadn't killed us and I was glad we hadn't killed it either. Enough death. In the distance little prairie dogs sat yelping at us from the mouths of their burrows on the dry plain. I don't know if you've seen prairie dogs. They're a funny sort of ground squirrel about the size of a young puppy. Suddenly an antelope leaped up from its hiding place among the sagebrush, gazed at us, and then, lifting its white tail, streaked away like a greyhound. It was beautiful.

When we got back to the camp there was a lot going on. The Indians were getting ready for an attack against another group called, I think, the Snakes and the Crows. The Sioux men had arrows strapped to their back and bows in their hands. One was teaching Henry how to use a bow, and despite only having one eye my brother proved a natural shot. The Sioux would take the women and children to a safe place where they left them in the care of old men to wait until the war party returned. Mapiya was desperate to be allowed to go and fight with the men. She was dressed for it. She wore Indian boy clothes, carried a bow and arrow, and strapped to her lower back was a large hunting knife. But no one was interested in a girl or what she wanted. It wasn't just her. When it came to war, none of the women had a say in what was happening.

The chief was sitting on the ground with some of his men. In a small circle with him sat Buddle, Cornelius and Henry. Buddle was handing out tobacco.

'We have all lost a great deal,' agreed Buddle. 'Cholera doesn't seem to mind where people come from or how much money they have.'

'We have all walked in the shadow of death,' said Cornelius.

The chief shook his head. 'There is no death. Only a change of worlds.'

Cornelius asked the chief for directions and he carefully drew a map on the ground with a stick. He then sent his medicine man to look at Jack. The man made up some ointment to put on Jack's wound. Kate gave out presents and there was a lot of handshaking. It was all very friendly but Cornelius and Henry were keen to get moving. There was talk of Crow war parties in the area.

Everyone seemed happy to have spent time together. There was certainly no trouble at all between us and the

Indians. The wagon train was just getting ready to leave when the Honeymans' son, Algernon, noticed that one of their horses was missing its halter. He looked around and saw it sticking out from under the short cloak worn by an Indian brave.

He went straight over to him and demanded, 'Give me that halter.'

But the brave stood silent and pretended not to hear. Algernon was only eleven but he was becoming quite a fighter. The Sioux boy was about the same age but he clearly thought of himself as a warrior and was not about to give in. Algernon grabbed the end of the halter and yanked it. The leather and metal harness fell to the ground with a sound loud enough to get everyone's attention. In a flash the brave had grabbed his bow and reached for an arrow. Algernon realized he was in trouble, so he ran for the family rifle on the side of their wagon. He pulled it down and immediately turned to level the gun on the Sioux boy. In the blink of an eye other Sioux were ready to defend their own. Now they too put arrows to bowstrings, which made lots of our men grab their rifles. The women from the train raced to get the kids into the wagons and there was general panic.

Algernon stood with his gun aimed, his finger on the trigger. Slowly the brave pulled back the string on his bow, ready to fire.

CHAPTER FIFTEEN

It was Mapiya who stepped in between the two boys and held up her hand.

'Slim?' she said, and I moved to stand with her. No one was going to cause trouble for my new friend. Watching both boys, she carefully bent down and picked up the halter. She handed it to Algernon and then put her hand on the end of his rifle and forced it down towards the ground. As she did so, the brave slowly lowered his bow and arrow.

'Algernon!' called Mrs Honeyman, racing to his side.

'He started it!' declared Algernon.

'We did not ask you to come here,' said the brave angrily. 'This is our land.'

'Get more presents,' said Buddle urgently to Kate, who brought some cloth and sugar from our wagon. She handed them to the chief, who took them silently.

Mrs Honeyman took Algernon away, but we could all hear her scolding him.

'You don't lose your temper like that! Think of the trouble you could have caused. Why, you could have started a war with those Indians. I have told you not to mix with the people on the wagon train, but I didn't think you needed telling about Indians!'

'Catch up your teams!' called Buddle, keen to get away.

I could see Mapiya pleading with the chief about something, and once our train was ready to set off I was surprised to find her riding alongside.

'I show you the way,' she said quietly.

'You're going to guide us?' I asked, and she grinned.

'Come on then!' I called, delighted, and we both kicked our horses on as we raced off to the front of the wagon train.

We were heading for Fort John. The Sioux would meet there too and the chief had let Mapiya ride with us. Even though she was young she had been to the fort many times and knew the way well. It was not perhaps what anyone had expected, but now our wagon train was led by a young Indian girl.

We rode on, passing hill after hill and hollow after hollow. The land was dry and parched. None of the plants looked familiar. I remember the sagebrush along the way smelling of turpentine. The sun and the thin air made everyone squint. Things seemed to glimmer and quiver in the snaky heat waves that filled the plain. In the distance we saw forests and ponds where none existed. We dreamed of lakes which could never quench our thirst.

'They're called "mirages",' explained Cornelius. 'Our eyes conjure things which don't exist in the heat.'

Off to our right we heard Mrs Honeyman take fright at a clump of sage, which she was sure was a horde of Indians.

Once I cried out: 'Look, Jack! Sailing ships!'

And sure enough we thought we saw them sailing ahead of us on calm waters, but as we got closer the lake turned into a low fog and the ships into a couple of abandoned wagons. Jack didn't wake and we walked on. I was worried about him, but having Mapiya with us helped. She and I spent our days racing on our horses or playing games.

The endless shimmering valley had a hypnotic effect and everyone walked as if asleep. I can still hear the creak of the harness, the crack of the bullwhips, the bellowing of the oxen, the shouts of the drivers, and the rustling of wagon covers in the wind. The sound of thunderstorms in the distance was, Bea said, 'the sound of the elephant brushing us with his tail'.

Now when we passed people on the trail no one even looked up. We went by one wagon on which everyone was asleep and the horses seemed to move without anyone telling them to. The days of fighting each other in silly races were long gone. The mosquitoes were the worst they had been. They bit us so badly that Kate said we all looked as though we had the measles. I remember the skin on one of my ears was quite raw. Mapiya showed Bea how to make some liniment, which helped a little.

The grass turned brown and short. Prickly-pear cactus, thin-bladed yucca and prairie-dog towns appeared in the sandy soil. By midday the heat was always unbearable. The calls of the men to their animals sank to mumbles and the train hardly seemed to move under the brilliant blue sky as we tried to find shade for our 'nooning'.

We were looking for something called Chimney Rock, which Cornelius had read about. It was Toby who saw it first. Cornelius had let him use the spyglass and we thought he must be mistaken when he called out, 'Chimney Rock! Chimney Rock!'

'It's another mirage,' said Jeni wearily, not even looking up from her knitting.

Cornelius put the spyglass to his own eye and began laughing.

'No! Chimney Rock indeed!' he declared. 'And no mistake!' The air was clear that day, and soon we could all see it.

'Is that it? Is that it?' people shouted to each other as

they walked. No one had seen a picture of what it was supposed to look like, but there on the horizon was a huge upright rock, several hundred feet high, sticking up just like the chimney of a furnace. It cheered everyone, for now we knew that we were on the right path. Beyond the rock lay Fort John, where there would be fresh supplies.

'And buildings!' said Bea, clapping her hands in excitement.

Buildings. I had almost forgotten that people lived in such things.

I rode up beside Buddle as he walked along with Dog and his mule.

'How far away is that rock, Buddle?' I asked.

He shook his head. 'Guessing at distance is the most complete hornswoggling game that a man ever undertook. Might be as much as forty mile.'

He was right. It was a 'hornswoggling game' to guess any distance in those rough, barren prairie hills and valleys. You could travel three days towards a point on the horizon and it would seem no closer. The end of the sky moved further and further away each day. Even the stars at night seemed closer to the ground than we had ever seen them. We walked for days wondering if the desert would ever end. Everyone was weary, and many of us were overwhelmed by the empty openness. According to my marks on the wagon, we had been travelling for seven weeks. The landscape spread out and a wagon seemed a speck on the endless roll of the grasslands.

The chimney stood out against the sunset, and the next morning it was there again. The pace was slow. There was plenty of time to memorize the landscape.

'It's a land where all men are equal,' declared Cornelius. 'The speed out here for a president or a pilgrim is exactly the same.'

'Look, a giant castle,' called Toby. We thought it was another vision, but a great rock high above the plain did look like an impressive building. It was as though it had huge domes on the roof.

There was column after column of sand and stone in massive bluffs shaped by the wind. Huge rock formations 400 feet tall lay before us like storm-carved castles.

'That must be what they called the Courthouse,' Cornelius announced with delight. 'I met a man in Independence who told me I would see a large rock in the distance like a castle from a fairy story. I seem to recall that a stream runs round the southern base. Can anyone see a large rocky bit beside the Courthouse – same height but not nearly as big?'

'Yes!' cried Toby.

'That's called the Jailhouse.'

Mapiya and I raced towards the rocks on our horses. It felt as though at last we were making progress.

No one was worried about Indians while Mapiya was with us but Buddle seemed anxious.

I heard him talking to Henry.

'Keep an extra lookout,' he was saying. 'They say there are horsemen who have been following us for some miles. We don't want any trouble.'

The next morning the wind blew white sand and dust through the air. It drifted in heaps like freshly fallen snow in a furious storm. There was a terrible smell of something rotten in the air.

The Courthouse had been the first in a chain of reddish sandstone cliffs. It was impressive, but Chimney Rock was grand beyond all description. It looked tall enough to touch the sky.

'It's like an old tree with no limbs,' said Cornelius.

'The smoke stack of a steamer,' declared Jack, managing to sit up for long enough to take in the view. I grinned at him. He was getting stronger every day. I dared to hope he would make it.

'Most remarkable thing I've seen since we left Missouri,' declared Louise.

Beyond the rock lay a range of mountains.

'Be climbing up before you know it,' said Kate.

Some of the men went to the foot of the chimney and climbed up as high as possible to carve their names there.

'Let's scratch our names too!' I suggested, so Mapiya and I carved them together into the rock.

Toby had a fight with Algernon Honeyman over a pile of buffalo chips.

'Those are mine!' cried Algernon.

'You thief!' shouted Toby, and we all raced over to find out what was happening. We never got to the bottom of who tried to steal from whom, but Algernon threw a chip at Toby and caused his face to bleed.

'I think you'll live,' said Bea, cleaning the wound. 'If you don't, at least we can enjoy telling everyone you were killed by buffalo poo.'

We all laughed, even Toby, and that felt good.

Algernon was becoming quite the ruffian on the trip.

'He was such a neat child when we met him!' exclaimed Kate to Bea, and they agreed the journey didn't seem to be doing him any good at all. Kate asked me to walk him back to the Honeymans' wagon so he couldn't get into any more trouble.

Mrs Honeyman was standing by the back of their wagon. She smiled and me and said, 'Would you like to come into my parlour for tea?'

I didn't know what she meant.

'I can't stop,' she carried on. 'I need to dress for dinner.'

I walked away but I could still hear Mrs Honeyman. 'Do come and walk with me; there is the most marvellous moist coolness underneath the big elm which borders our pond in the east pasture. The brook positively sings falling into it.'

That night dark masses of clouds, which had been rising from the west all afternoon, broke into a great storm. The rain poured down in torrents, and once more we woke shivering and wet. The buffalo chips were too wet to be of any use so there were no hot drinks and everyone was grumpy. But then the sun came out, and no matter how brilliant Bea is at painting, no matter how many words I learn, I don't think any of us will ever be able to describe how beautiful it was. The land was washed clean and we marched on with the sun on our backs. *Nanpisa*.

The landscape was full of spectacular rocks and bluffs, each one looking like the finest building anyone has ever built or even imagined. In places it was like a vast city of high castles and wide streets, a fairy-tale vision of towers, churches and forts. As the sun sank behind the western range of hills it gave the sight a golden hue.

'A more beautiful or majestic scene it is not possible to conceive,' sighed Cornelius, and everyone agreed.

'It's as if the wand of a magician has passed over a city and converted everything to stone,' marvelled Bea.

'I could die here and be sure that I wasn't far from Heaven,' sighed Jeni.

Jack was starting to be awake more, and he joined us

for supper each evening. He was too weak to walk, but every day I could see he was improving.

The next morning Cornelius, who was walking alongside our wagon, suddenly leaped up beside Bea and declared,

> '*Though sluggards deem it but a foolish chase,*
> *And marvel men should quit their easy chair,*
> *The toilsome way, and long, long leagues to trace,*
> *Oh! there is sweetness in the mountain air,*
> *And life that bloated Ease can never hope to share.*'

'Is that Shakespeare?' asked Henry, wide-eyed.

Cornelius jumped down before the wagon shook him loose. 'No, Lord Byron. Great poet. You like poetry, Henry?'

Henry smiled and nodded but he was distracted by a sound coming from our wagon. The axles needed greasing, and now they added a torturing shriek to the high-pitched singing of the wheels and the scrape of the iron tyres on stone or rubble. The wheels had finally had enough of the dry air, and without warning one of our tyres' wheel spokes suddenly pulled out of its frame and the wagon came to a halt. It was happening to a lot of people. The same brittleness could snap the metal 'hounds' – the side bars that connected the tongue and the front of the wagon to the back. Sometimes a wagon would just collapse. We stopped to fix the wheel, and as we did so, the Honeymans drove right past us without offering to help.

Henry was furious but Bea calmed him down.

'Mrs Honeyman is not well. Let it go,' she said.

No one would say it, but I think Mrs Honeyman had gone a bit mad.

To be honest, the sickness at Ash Hollow, the tiredness, the deaths we had seen and the near trouble with the Sioux had made everyone more and more anxious. If dust swirled on the horizon, people would rush to corral the wagons, and one night when the guard fired his gun by accident, all the men ran up with their weapons ready.

We passed two graves, but no one even mentioned such things any more. Mapiya led us steadily on through the knee-high grasses and past great patches of yellow plains wallflowers. We saw a few other people. Once we met a supply wagon heading to Fort John, but it was in a hurry and didn't stop. We passed another group of discouraged pioneers who had turned round and were heading east. Their cattle had stampeded in a storm. With one wild and mad rush, 250 head of oxen had crashed over the wagons, trampling one man to death and wounding several others. The cattle had run off and now all the poor people wanted to do was 'go home'.

Home. I hadn't thought about home for such a long time. I didn't know what that was any more. We couldn't go

back to Ireland or New York. I wondered if we would ever
have a home again. Bea had done lots of drawings of what
we had seen and people we had met. She pinned them to
the inside of our wagon cover to make it more like home,
but it was hard to imagine any life other than the endless
walking.

I'm not sure how we kept going. There was terrible
flying sand and dust. Sometimes it was so bad it filled our
lungs, mouth, nose, ears and hair, and covered our faces so
that we could hardly recognize each other. The immense
sun, the endless wind and the gritty, never-ending dust red-
dened and swelled our eyes, inflaming the sockets.

Cornelius produced a pair of goggles.

'I just remembered! Bought these in St Louis. Fine pair.
Best thirty-seven and a half cents I ever spent.'

He bowed and presented them to Bea, who pretended
she didn't care, but she wore them just the same. Since Mrs
Meadows' funeral she had taken to wearing her rose-
covered bonnet all the time. With the hat and the goggles I
hardly knew her.

'You look like some kind of bug under a microscope,'
teased Toby, and Cornelius got an earful from Bea for
laughing.

I suppose we all would have looked odd to anyone who
had known us in Ireland. Our skin was burned almost

black. Louise took a can of tomatoes and put the juice on our cheeks.

'Won't you need it for food?' asked Toby, wriggling as she did it, but Louise shook her head. 'No point in eating if your skin has come off.' You wouldn't think it but the juice did help.

We passed many prairie-dog towns.

'Seem to prefer city life,' remarked Buddle as we passed a large yelping group. Our wagon wheels disturbed them in their underground homes and they would pop out, sitting up straight on their hindquarters near the burrow, and give a funny little bark. They didn't stay long. If the slightest thing alarmed them, they would drop back into their holes.

Ahead, a great sandstone hill, bright orange in the evening light, rose 800 feet high, with ridges like the floors of a great castle in the air.

'*Me-a-pa-te*,' said Mapiya.

'What does that mean?' asked Toby.

'The hill that is hard to get round,' replied Mapiya, and we all laughed because it described it perfectly. 'I think the white man calls it "Scotts Bluff",' she added.

I wrote that down in my leather book.

'Named after an unlucky traveller whose bones were discovered here,' said Buddle. 'Abandoned by his friends when he was sick, he managed to drag himself sixty miles to this very spot before dying. Terrible thing.'

Kate nodded. 'Never leave anyone behind,' she declared.

'We left Da behind,' I said, and everyone went quiet. I looked at Henry and I think he knew I blamed him.

'Slim,' he whispered to me, but I turned away.

The days were hot and the nights were cold. Apart from Toby, who slept soundly curled up next to Hamlet, we began to find it hard to sleep at night. Jack took up all the space in the wagon so we found spaces to stretch out underneath it, under bushes, trees, bits of tarpaulin. Anything, really. The animals were restless, chomping, snorting and whinnying, while all manner of coyotes howled in the dark. We were all tired of the wild wind, the long slow marches, smoky camp-fires and the same food over and over. Sometimes we had all weathers in one day. A pair of oxen died from the heat while everyone sniffed from the fierce cold the day before.

'There is no going over *Me-a-pa-te*,' said Mapiya. 'Much too steep. We must go south.'

She and Horse led us up a long climb to a natural gateway in the great bluffs. When we got to the top at last, we had our first real view of the mountains. It was a spectacular sight, with the great Chimney Rock and the vast Laramie Peak still visible.

'It's beautiful,' sighed Bea.

'It's terrifying,' whispered Kate.

I thought it looked wonderful.

For weeks we had crossed over vast plains with no

features at all. Now this huge mountain appeared to reach above the clouds.

'It's good to have something to aim for,' said Louise positively.

'How far?' I asked Buddle, expecting him to grumble in reply.

He never liked to guess at distance, but he squinted as he looked at the mountain.

'About seventy miles,' he replied.

That meant something to me now. I knew we still had several days of walking to do.

We passed six or seven newly made graves and camped about three-quarters of a mile from the Platte, where we got good water and grass but no fuel of any kind. Even buffalo chips were impossible to find so we had hard biscuits for supper. For the first time we saw mountain sheep, climbing amongst the rocks as if they were dancing. There were black-tailed deer and antelope, and a great herd of elk suddenly appeared. There must have been two hundred of them, their antlers clattering as they walked forward in a dense throng. Seeing us, they broke into a run, rushing across the open land and disappearing amongst the trees and scattered groves.

'Might be Indians disguised, eh, Toby?' teased Henry.

How different was our feeling about Indians now. I had learned such a lot from Mapiya. Her father wanted her to learn how the 'white man' lived so, just like Nashobanowa's daughter Emily, she had been sent away to the city to learn English. She loved to chat, but more than anything she loved all the Indian ways. She had not liked life in the busy town.

'I missed my father and mother too much,' she said as she showed me how to make a bark tube for a snake.

'I miss mine,' I said.

She nodded. 'You will heal.'

I wasn't sure I wanted to.

It was Mapiya who taught us to catch the antelope, which were so swift you wouldn't have thought it possible. They ran in herds of up to thirty and came towards us like the wind before stopping a short distance away. There they would stand and look at us, before running full pelt round to our other side like prairie birds flying across the grass.

'Do you have red cloth?' asked Mapiya.

Kate gave her a piece which Mapiya tied to a stick. Then she went a little distance away from the train and hid behind some brush. She held the stick up and waved it so that all you could see was the red cloth like a small flag waving in the breeze.

The antelope circled near out of curiosity and, when the time was right, out shot an arrow from Mapiya's bow.

'Look at that!' cried Henry, delighted.

How delicious it was to have such lovely meat. Louise was good at cutting it up and we shared it with everyone.

All through the day Mapiya and I raced across the plains on our horses. Neither of us had saddles or even proper reins. Just a bit of rope for a halter and a blanket to sit on. There was nothing Chronicle wouldn't do for me now.

'Race you to the front of the train,' Mapiya would call, and she would set off without waiting for me to start. I'd hardly kick my heels at all, and my wonderful horse would stretch out as we chased after her. It was an incredible feeling.

'That's your best friend now,' said Louise with a smile.

'I really like Mapiya,' I replied, and she laughed.

'I meant the horse,' she said.

At night the wolves on the prairie made a horrible yowling. They each made the sound of five dogs so you thought there were hundreds of them around the camp. At dawn the coyote would give a grand chorus of yelps. We often saw wolves galloping alongside the train too. They were larger than any dog, with teeth the size of shears, and they would grab any animal which strayed too far from the train. We didn't shoot them.

'Too many of them, too few bullets,' said Buddle.

Now we descended once more towards our old friend

the Platte River. It was empty country, broken by deep chasms and ravines. We had to pass over plains of cactus, whose thorns dug into the feet of our animals. Malvolio had never looked unhappier. The river was narrow here and the banks were sandy and barren. We needed, as Buddle said every day, 'to just keep the wheels moving' along the sandy valley floor, but it was hard.

At last we began to see the buffalo we had heard so much about. They moved in great herds, some quietly eating grass while others marched along, bellowing. They made a roaring noise as they tramped along half a mile away. The first one I saw up close was an old buffalo which some of the men had killed just for sport. He was too old to eat so they left his body in the shallow water where he had been drinking.

'I don't think you should kill them if you're not going to eat the meat,' I protested.

One of the men laughed. 'There'll be buffalo aplenty long after you and I are both dead,' he declared.

I looked at the dead animal. He was huge. Much bigger than our oxen. Maybe ten or twelve feet long, with a shaggy coat. He had weighed thousands of pounds but was brought down by a bullet. His dead eyes stared up at me from the water. I wondered if I could shoot such a thing.

Louise had really helped me, and I had practised a lot with

my guns so that I became very good at hunting antelope. Now I felt ready for something bigger.

'What does buffalo meat taste like?' I asked one night.

'Tender and juicy,' said Buddle, who had eaten it before.

'But not fatty,' added Mapiya.

'I bet I could shoot one,' I said.

'Bet you can't,' replied Henry, and the bet was on. Henry should have known better than to challenge me!

The next day he borrowed Louise's horse on the promise of bringing her and Jeni a buffalo steak each, and Mapiya took me and Henry out onto the plain.

'Remember,' she explained as we rode, 'no point aiming at the buffalo's face. He has years of sand and dirt there, and it makes a mat in the hair several inches thick. You need to hit close to the front legs. About a third of the way up the body. That is where the life lies.'

Henry put our rifle in a pocket called a 'scabbard' on the horse and I loaded my pistols. Mapiya showed us how to gather up a rope, coil it and put it on a saddle.

Buddle watched us getting ready.

'You be careful out there, young people. I think I saw strangers nearby last night. Stick together.'

We didn't really listen but waved to him. Then we were off, galloping across the prairie with the familiar smell of sage in the air. Birds rose from the ground as we raced ahead. We didn't see any buffalo for ages. Then we rode up a small hill, and there they were. Maybe three hundred of them. The place was black with them. My heart was pounding, but I was not the most frightened of our group. Chronicle did not like the look of this at all. He and I had been having a wonderful time together for quite a while, but now he stopped and would not go on, no matter how much I tried to encourage him.

'Come on, Chronicle,' I repeated. 'What is the matter with you?'

I think Henry and Mapiya thought it was funny. I sat there kicking my horse uselessly, and they rode off across the plain.

'We're supposed to stick together!' I yelled, furious with them.

I didn't know why Chronicle was being so stubborn. It wasn't like him and I was very cross.

'Chronicle!' I began in a stern voice. 'This is not what you do any more. You and I—'

Then, across the still of the plain, I heard a terrifying sound. It was as loud as the great railway we had taken in New Jersey. I didn't know what it was. Perhaps a dreadful storm was moving towards me. I turned and felt as though my breath had left my body.

The army of buffalo were stampeding. All the hundreds of creatures were moving in one vast mass, like a thunderous black cloud, racing towards the wagon train.

'Hero! Toby! Bea! Kate! Jack!' I could hardly speak. They were all in the path of the stampede. I was paralysed with fear. I looked around for Henry and Mapiya, but they had ridden away and I couldn't see them. Down at the distant camp I saw that someone had called the alarm, for the wagons were being driven into a circle. A few of the men were firing towards the crazy herd, but it made no difference. The huge creatures boomed along with their beards almost sweeping the ground, their long tails sticking straight out behind, their great brawny necks and high humped shoulders covered with long flowing hair, their eyes rolling and fiery. The ground shook. For a moment it seemed as if all the buffalo from the four corners of the globe had gathered to make this charge. I had to do something, but I was alone.

I could see that the stampede was being led by one especially powerful bull.

'Chronicle!' I said loudly.

It was almost as if he nodded. As if he had known all along that we would be needed. Maybe he had heard the buffalo long before me and that was why he'd stopped.

I barely touched his side with my heels and we were off, chasing after the leader. I don't know if I planned it, but I think I knew I had to distract him away from the wagons.

The sea of buffalo made the earth quake and judder. The sound grew louder and louder as I got closer. It felt as if the soil beneath me would crack and swallow us all. I could feel Chronicle straining with every muscle. The herd was quick but he was quicker. The dust was terrible. It cut into the back of my throat, and for a moment I couldn't see where we were going at all, but if anything Chronicle sped up. I was choking but still we galloped on. I could hardly breathe so I let go of the reins with one hand and reached to pull my red handkerchief up over my mouth, but just then my horse swerved to avoid some brush. My whole body slipped to one side and I had to grab Chronicle's mane to stop myself falling. Now I was clinging on for dear life. My body hung down against Chronicle's side, and I could almost touch the buffalo as we sped past. I pulled with all my strength. I thought my chest would burst with the strain, but at last I was back upright and holding the reins. I could feel Chronicle's heart pounding as we passed the younger bulls at the back of the pack, then some of the older ones, until at last we were racing alongside the old bull in charge. I don't know if he saw us. His shaggy head was down as his hoofs hammered across the ground. He was huge and terrifying, but we were only fifty feet from the wagons and he showed no signs of slowing down. I knew what I had to do. With a nudge from my knees, Chronicle pulled across the buffalo's path. I felt his snorting breath on my leg and I thought he might just run right through us, but instead he swerved. He veered off to the right and through the haze of dirt and dust I could see that at last he was leading the herd away from the wagon train. I wanted to make sure he didn't turn back, so I reached for one of my pistols, but I couldn't get him in my sights. We galloped on. I didn't want to shoot him, just scare him. I managed to fire, but the first shot just bounced off his thick hide. On we galloped, over the prairie and away from the wagons. I kept firing, but every shot seemed to rebound from his head as if from solid rock. I don't know how far we chased the herd. It must have been miles. Chronicle was exhausted and began to slow. The wagon train was a long way off now. At last I felt it was safe and brought Chronicle to a halt. My wonderful horse was panting and heaving. We had saved the wagon train.

But now the bull slowed down. Instead of being scared of my gun he turned and stopped. The herd too came to a shuddering halt and the old bull stood there, his breath heaving, fury in his eyes. A second later he charged straight towards me. Chronicle was quick. He leaped to one side and we escaped the bull's sharp, curving black horns. The buffalo stopped once more and turned his massive body towards me. He was madly pawing the ground, his bloodshot eyes full of both rage and distress. I had clearly had some success with my shots, for he was bleeding.

The giant creature lowered his huge shaggy head to

charge. I had had twelve bullets in my two guns. I was pretty sure I had one shot left, but there was no time to think. It all happened so fast. I didn't think we could outrun him. I felt bad, but I remembered Mapiya's advice.

I raised my pistol and fired about a third of the way up his body, between his front legs. The last bullet left my gun and the old bull looked at me almost as if he were surprised, then he slowly sank rather than fell to his knees – front legs first, then the back ones – and he just stayed there. He looked dead but he didn't roll onto his back. In the distance the rest of the herd had calmed and stood in the tall grass, unsure what to do next.

Chronicle was still breathless. His sides heaved and his back was dark with sweat. I had ridden so hard that I too felt as if I were soaked in warm water. Every muscle in my body shook and my lungs felt full of sand. Still the bull seemed to be kneeling. I wasn't sure what to do. The herd had calmed and even looked a little bewildered by what had happened. Slowly I slipped down from my horse's back, my legs almost crumpling beneath me with exhaustion. I hugged Chronicle while his breath came in great billows like a steam train. The old bull was still kneeling, which was odd. I was still scared, but as I walked towards him I could see that he was definitely dead. Even kneeling he was taller than me. A magnificent creature. I was sad for him, but glad that no one in the wagon train had been hurt.

The wagon train! I needed to get back or they would worry. I looked around to see where I was. I might as well have looked for landmarks in the middle of the ocean. How many miles I had run, or in what direction, I had no idea. The prairie rolled in steep swells and pitches. The grass was so high that I could barely see over the top of it. Even the giant dead buffalo was easily hidden. There wasn't a single distinctive feature to guide me.

CHAPTER SIXTEEN

The sun beat down on my head. It was too high above for me to be able to work out which way was east and which was west.

'The sun rises in the east and sets in the west,' I repeated to myself. I knew that. I knew if it were morning the sun would be in the east and if it were afternoon it would be to the west, but it was midday and the brilliant light was right above my head. Then I realized that even if I worked out which way was west, I wasn't at all sure which direction the wagon train lay in. I couldn't decide whether I should head west and hope to catch them as they travelled on or wait where I was and hope someone came to find me. I had no water with me and didn't know how long I would last.

Chronicle had calmed now and he pushed me gently on my shoulder, as if trying to help. I got back on him, thinking I could see better from higher up. I tried to pick a landmark

357

on the horizon, something to head towards as a marker, but I could see no trees or rocks that would help. I was so lost. I thought about Mapiya with the red cloth and the antelope. I had my red neckerchief on, so I took it off and looked on the ground for some kind of stick. There was nothing, but some of the grass was long and tall. I got off Chronicle again and tied the red cloth to the tallest, strongest grass I could find.

'Chronicle,' I said, explaining my plan to him, 'we are going to ride straight that way' – I pointed into the distance – 'while I count to a hundred and see if we can see anything. If we don't, then we will ride back to my red scarf and try a different way. All right?'

Chronicle seemed fine with the plan so we set off. We had tried three different directions when I saw the horsemen. Buddle had warned us about strangers lurking near the train. The prairie was full of stories about people who'd had everything stolen from them. Everyone was warned that there were men out there who were up to no good. My heart pounding, I leaped off Chronicle, pulling on the reins and persuading him to lie down in the grass beside me. It wasn't easy, and he lay looking at me bewildered as I put my arms round his neck to keep him still. As we lay there, we heard the sound of a horse galloping towards us. I buried my head in Chronicle's mane, but whoever it was had found us. The approaching horse stopped and someone leaped from its back.

'Slim!' called a familiar voice.

It was Mapiya! Mapiya had come to save me.

'I'm here,' I replied, getting to my feet.

She ran to me, signalling frantically. 'Get down,' she said urgently, 'someone's coming.'

She pulled her horse down and then grabbed me, almost throwing me to the ground. We lay there between Horse and Chronicle.

'Where's Henry?' I whispered.

'He went east to look for you while I went west. We heard the buffalo and thought something might have happened.'

I was so glad to see her, but now the fear rose up in me again. We could hear someone approach on their horse. Whoever it was stopped and got off. Now there were heavy footsteps flattening the grass near us. The sun suddenly darkened. It was as if a great cloud had blown in front of it. We looked up. There were two men. One in a grey, wide-brimmed hat and the other behind him bareheaded. They stood over us.

'It's all right,' I heard the one behind say, but the man in front waved him away. The sun was behind the man in the hat so we couldn't see his face, but we could see light glimmer off the barrel of the gun he was pointing right at us.

'Get up!' he ordered.

I was beginning to learn that guns were no fun at all. I had no bullets left and I was terrified. Mapiya moved slowly as she got to her feet. She pushed me behind her and I saw that she was carefully reaching for the knife she kept behind her back.

'We have nothing you want,' she said steadily.

'Let go of the child!' the man ordered.

Mapiya shook her head. 'No,' she said firmly. 'You can have the horses but she stays with me.'

'Let go of the child,' he repeated. 'You will not hurt her.'

'What?' said Mapiya, surprised. She stopped reaching for her knife and spoke calmly. 'I'm not hurting her. She's my friend. I'm Mapiya. This is Slim Hannigan.'

'She's your friend?' said the man, lowering his gun. I peeked out from behind Mapiya's back. There was something familiar about that voice.

'Patrick, it's all right,' said the man behind him, whose voice also sounded as if I knew him.

Just then both men moved and their faces came out of the shadow. It was the most wonderful sight in the world.

'Da?' I dared to ask. 'Da, is that you?'

The man with the gun nodded but he could not speak. He shifted his head again. Now the sun lit the side of his face and I could see it was my father. I could see it but I couldn't take it in. It was like one of those mirages we had seen so often on the trail. I had dreamed of finding my father and could not believe that he was standing in front of me.

'Slim,' he said, choking with tears.

'You know him?' asked Mapiya, wondering what on earth was going on. I nodded. Slowly Mapiya let go of her knife and her face began to crease into a great smile. She turned to me. 'Is that your father?'

I nodded again, tears streaming down my face, but I couldn't move. It was too happy a thought.

'Well, go to him!' she laughed, almost pushing me away.

'Oh, Da!' I cried, running at the man fast enough to knock him over.

'It's Da! It's Da!' I yelled, laughing and crying at the same time. 'It's my Da!' I shouted to the heavens. He was so much thinner than before and his beard and hair were long, but it was my beloved father. I could never forget his eyes.

'I knew you weren't dead, Da, I knew it. I told everyone. I wanted to wait. We made posters. We couldn't get a boat to go back. No one would take us back and we didn't know what to do so we—'

Da was crying too. 'Shush now, little one, I have you now,' he soothed as he held me tight. 'I'm here now. I found you. Thank God, I found you.'

'But how?' I cried. 'How did you find me out here?'

'He followed his heart,' said the man with Da. It was only then that I realized who it was.

'Nashobanowa!' I cried, and had to run to him too. We hugged and cried and carried on so long that now Mapiya started crying.

'Curse you, I never cry. Don't you tell anyone I cried,' she ordered, wiping tears of joy from her eyes.

'Nashobanowa, what are you doing here?' I demanded, not knowing who to ask questions of first.

Nashobanowa smiled. 'You brought my daughter to me, so when I met your father I knew I had to take him to you.'

My wonderful Choctaw friend looked just the same but Da was quite different. His hair curled down past his ears, but you could just see the scar on his cheek which I remembered so well. His face was burned like mine. He wore Indian clothes and shoes, but it was still my Da. He held me by both arms and looked at me.

'Look at you, Slim,' he said as tears ran down his face. 'Look how tall you are, and brown, and like a . . . well, like a cowboy. Are you all right? Is everyone all right? Henry and Bea and Toby, oh and the baby . . .'

'We're fine. We're all fine. Jack got shot but he'll be fine too, and Kate is with us, and then Buddle is in charge because James died in the sickness and—'

Da put his hand up and laughed. 'Well, there's certainly a lot of tales to tell. Let me get my wagon and—'

'You have a wagon?' I said in amazement.

Da nodded. 'I probably have a story or two to tell you too.'

He led us to a small wagon with a neat white cover not far away, with two horses tied to the back, grazing. The wagon was led by two oxen which stood patiently waiting, with no idea of the wonderful thing that had just happened. Mapiya and I climbed up to drive with him. I leaned against him as Mapiya pointed out the way and Nashobanowa rode alongside leading Chronicle and the other horses. I don't think I have ever been happier.

It was an amazed group who greeted us.

'There she is!' yelled Kate, who had been frantic with worry. She ran towards us and then stopped in her tracks. She put her hand across her mouth, which had opened wide with surprise.

'No, it can't be!' she whispered. Then she turned and yelled louder than I had ever heard her yell before. 'Bea! Henry! Toby! Come! Come quick.'

Henry had been frantic looking for me. He came running with the rifle. Toby appeared with Hamlet at his side and Bea raced across with the baby. Cornelius was next, running into view and holding his spyglass, which he had been using to search for me.

'What is it?' cried Henry.

'It's . . . it's . . . your Da!' replied Kate, amazed at the sight.

'And Nashobanowa!' cried Toby.

Well, it's hard to describe the celebration that greeted

our arrival. Da could barely breathe for Toby hanging on him. Kate ran to get Hero from the wagon. I thought Kate was going to hug Da too, but instead she made sure he held the baby, who had grown so much in the months we had been separated that he could hardly believe it.

'Some of the men wanted to make us leave without you, Slim,' wept Bea. 'We didn't know what had happened but we couldn't do it again and Buddle wouldn't allow it. Louise went searching. So did Henry and Cornelius.'

Just then Louise galloped into the corral. She smiled when she saw me, jumped down and gave me a hug. Buddle came over, and Jeni too. It was the greatest celebration.

'Da, these are our friends,' I cried. 'This is Louise and Jeni. Louise taught me to shoot and I'm afraid Jeni's mother died but Henry did such a nice reading from Shakespeare and Buddle has a new leg because we found a table which Cornelius sawed a bit off and—'

'Everyone, this is my Da!' shouted Toby, jumping up and down. 'And my Indian friend Nashobanowa!'

There was so much to tell Da and we all spoke on top of each other.

'We couldn't leave anyone behind,' Bea kept repeating. 'We wouldn't have done it, Slim; we wouldn't.'

'Slim killed a buffalo all by herself,' added Mapiya, while everyone congratulated her on finding me.

'I had to,' I muttered, 'but I didn't want to.'

I looked at Nashobanowa and he smiled. In all the excitement I reached for his hand and he squeezed it.

'I have oxen called Malvolio, Balthazar and two Dromios,' explained Toby over the sound of the whole wagon train whooping and cheering. Da's return was wonderful for everyone. How we needed some good news!

'Back from the dead, Mr Hannigan, are you!' declared Cornelius, grasping Da with a firm handshake. 'I couldn't be more delighted!'

Nashobanowa was introduced to everyone and was slapped on the back and hugged for bringing him to us.

'We tried to find you!' said Toby, jumping up and down.

'We did, Da, we did!' I insisted.

Da nodded. 'I knew that. I found this in Independence.'

He reached into his pocket and pulled out a folded piece of paper. He opened it out and showed us one of the posters we had made.

'And while I was reading it, I met this grand fellow Nashobanowa who has led me to you. Although you did make it easy for us, for I also found this . . .'

He reached into another pocket and pulled out another folded poster with his picture on it.

'And this one and this one . . .'

Da held up the drawing Bea had done of him.

'It's no wonder you weren't able to find me,' he laughed.

'You made me far too handsome!' He smiled and ruffled Toby's hair. 'And I got your messages.'

'Messages?' asked Henry.

'All along the way,' said Da, 'pinned on buffalo skulls, and once in a little room in a place called Ash Hollow.'

Kate blushed. 'I may have left the odd note just in case,' she murmured.

Da looked at her. 'There were more than forty of them.'

Kate face went even redder. 'Well, sure, and it's a dull journey without much to do, Patrick,' she explained.

'We printed the posters ourselves!' I said proudly, but then I remembered about the printing press and I thought how disappointed Da was going to be.

'Oh, Da . . .' I began.

He looked at me and hugged me once more. 'Ssh, now, Slim. I know you have a story to tell and I want to hear it, but let me tell you something that will brighten your heart. Sure and Nashobanowa and I were riding after you when we found an ox all by itself.'

'He was lonely,' said Nashobanowa, enjoying the story.

Da grinned. He was so happy. 'Then Nashobanowa found another, and now we had a pair. Next – and who would have thought it? – someone had left a wagon behind, and I thought, well, now, Patrick Hannigan, you've a wagon and a pair of oxen, why not put them together?'

Da walked backwards along the side of his wagon, drawing us all with him.

'We got to a place called . . .'

'Ash Hollow,' said Nashobanowa. He turned and gave a slight bow to Kate. 'Thank you for your note about the water. You saved many lives.'

Da was getting excited. 'There was so much abandoned that I began to think everything we needed could be found. And I was right, because the very next thing I came across was . . .'

We all waited in suspense. Da swept open the cover at the back of the wagon, and there stood our printing press.

'A printing press!'

How we cheered and laughed and hugged.

'We need a party,' declared Louise, who immediately organized for Mapiya to lead a few people back to the dead buffalo to cut it up for steaks. 'No point in that grand old fella dying for nothing,' she declared.

Jack was awake enough for Da to visit him. He still wasn't fully well and slept most of the time but Bea said he was healing.

'He saved Toby's life,' said Kate. 'A bad man tried to shoot him and Jack threw himself between them.'

'No!' gasped Da.

'But he's on the mend,' I added.

Da wept again, thanking Jack with all his heart.

That night we had such a feast and everyone talked on top of each other. There was so much to tell.

It seemed that when Da fell into the river at the Ohio Falls, he hit his head on a rock.

'It was young Liam Byrne who saved me,' he explained. 'He grabbed me and swam me to shore against all that rushing water. I was knocked out and stayed that way for some weeks, but the boy got me care and waited till I was better. I owe him my life.'

I think Bea felt bad.

'I wasn't nice to him,' she said.

'He hadn't been good to us,' soothed Da, 'but he made up for it. I asked him to come with us, but he said you wouldn't want it, Bea.'

'Where is he?' Henry asked.

'He stayed in Louisville,' replied Da, 'where the accident happened. He's a good boy. He'll cope. Then I went to Independence, as it seems everyone heading west does, found your picture and Nashobanowa and . . .'

'The old wolf walks again!' added Nashobanowa, and we all cheered.

Buddle got out some sweet vitriol to celebrate and there was singing and dancing. Then Cornelius got to his feet and declared, 'This is a night of unparalleled delight, but we forgot a matter of momentous importance! Today, ladies and gentlemen of the prairie, the wagon train, our wagon train, was threatened by a terrible stampede, a stampede like an earthquake. We were saved not by our guns or our ingenuity but by a slip of a girl who had the courage of a tiger. Ladies and gentlemen, I raise my glass to Slim Hannigan!'

'Slim!' everyone cried out.

Sitting by the fire, I leaned against Da while Nasho-banowa smiled at me. I thought it was the happiest day of my life.

CHAPTER SEVENTEEN

As soon as Da and Nashobanowa turned up, everyone seemed happier and brighter. The buffalo I killed was so big that we weren't able to eat it all so the rest of the meat was cut into ribbons. Nashobanowa showed Kate and Bea how to drape it over the wagon bows so that it dried in the air. He fastened ropes from the front to the back along the side of the wagon, which was now decorated with slices of meat dangling from strings like a coarse red fringe.

Bea shook her head at the sight. 'It's ridiculous,' she said. 'It's meat drying but I like it. It looks so . . . I don't know . . . festive.'

'They call the meat "jerky" when it's dry. You'll be glad to eat it when we run out of food,' said Louise, watching us work. Nashobanowa smiled at her as he strung up more pieces. I was so happy to see him, but not everyone in the wagon train was pleased. We already had Mapiya leading the way and some people were mean about another Indian travelling with us.

'Typical Hannigans!' I heard some say, but we didn't care.

'Will you come all the way?' I asked Nashobanowa.

He looked thoughtful. 'You are in my heart, Slim – your family too – so I shall get you safe to the place you need to call home. Then I will return to my Emily to see out my days.'

I clapped my hands. 'One last adventure!'

'Indeed,' he agreed.

Da sat long into the night talking to Buddle, Kate, Louise and Jeni about how far we had come and how much further there was to go. Now Mapiya didn't have to guide us by herself. Both Da and Nashobanowa had suggestions about what to do next.

'I've a map,' said Da. 'Nashobanowa and I travelled a long way with a German family called Wagmute and they gave us a copy when we parted. It shows a shortcut which we might use.'

He laid it out for everyone to look at. I remember that the adults looked worried all the time, but I wasn't worrying about anything now that we had Da with us. All I wanted to hear were stories about his journey. He talked about the trail and how so many things were abandoned on the way. As you travelled, you could find mounds of bacon, beans and rice.

'No need to pack a thing,' he said, delighted by his good fortune. He looked at the jerky drying in the wind. 'I'd have taken it all if I had known we might run out of food.'

The first morning Da was with us I think he was amazed at what we could do. Without thinking I lit the fire and got the water, Toby sorted the animals, Henry packed the wagon, Kate made bread using a tent peg and Bea cooked bacon in the Dutch oven.

'Look at you all,' he said in amazement as he bounced Hero on his knee. 'What have you done with my children, who knew nothing of this life?'

'Bacon and bread?' called Kate.

'Sounds wonderful,' said Da.

'Not if it's every day,' I sighed, and he laughed.

Hamlet ran past playing with Dog.

'Doesn't Toby mind about you eating bacon?' whispered Da to Kate. 'I mean, with his pig and all?'

Kate smiled and whispered back as she winked at me. 'We haven't told him where bacon comes from.'

Jack sat up in the back of the wagon and drank some tea Nashobanowa had made for him. He was pale and had lost a lot of weight, but Da made him laugh, and both Bea and Louise said that was the best medicine of all.

Suddenly life was happy again. Funny things happened.

For example, I remember we came across a temporary camp of Dakota Indians. For several acres the land was covered in Indians and what seemed like hundreds of dogs in all sizes and colours.

Da clapped his hands with delight and held Hero up to see the sight. A wide shallow offshoot of the river was alive with boys, girls and young squaws, splashing, screaming and laughing in the water. No lodges had been erected but the women had made shelters from the sun by stretching buffalo skins over some poles.

We crossed the creek with our wagons, dragging our things in a slow, heavy procession and made a halt. Our women made coffee and biscuits.

'Now what?' asked Toby.

'Now we wait,' said Nashobanowa, leaning against a wagon wheel and sipping his drink.

After a short while a huge bloated Dakota man came over to our wagon. He rode a little white pony which could barely stand up under the weight. He was one of the fattest men I had ever seen.

'He is rich,' whispered Mapiya to me.

'How do you know?'

'He has more than thirty horses.'

'You'd think he could get one that fitted,' said Toby, and Da sniggered.

The man rode up and shook Henry by the hand. Then

he began making a series of most earnest signs and gestures, his oily face full of smiles, and his little eyes peeping out with a cunning twinkle from between the masses of flesh that almost obscured them. I knew nothing about such sign language but Mapiya sat watching.

'He wants your horse, Slim,' she explained.

I stood up, furious at the thought.

'How dare he!' I exclaimed. 'He's mine. Chronicle saved my life. He wouldn't want to be ridden by anyone else! Nashobanowa gave him to me!'

Mapiya began to giggle, and even Nashobanowa tried not to laugh. 'Well, it might be worth it. See his daughter, the one in the white?' Mapiya pointed at a pretty girl with beautifully decorated clothes and horse. 'He says Henry can marry her if he gets the horse.'

'I am not marrying her!' said Henry, bright red at the thought.

I don't know which idea I was more shocked about – my horse being given away or Henry being old enough to get married.

'Well, Henry!' called Da. 'You're seventeen. Time to be thinking of a wife.'

'Perhaps marriage is in the air,' said Nashobanowa quietly. I didn't know what he meant but I thought Kate blushed and Bea spilled her coffee.

Henry didn't marry the girl and I didn't give up my

horse, but we parted as friends with the Dakota. We were all in a holiday mood now. There were only a few miles to Fort John. This would be the first settlement we had reached – or 'civilization', as Bea insisted on calling it.

She made Buddle stop the train.

'We have to make ourselves a little bit presentable,' she insisted. 'These people live in buildings. They don't travel in a wagon. They'll think we are terrible people to arrive so . . . untidy.'

Bea was almost mad with excitement and ran around the whole wagon train checking that everyone had smartened themselves up. None of the men had shaved for weeks, but now small mirrors were produced and hung in trees for them. Henry and Jack both had big beards now. Henry carefully helped Jack shave and it made him look better. Kate and Bea combed our hair, which hurt, and Jeni said Louise had to put on a skirt. I didn't have one so at least I escaped that. It was hard to get clean, for the water of the Platte in this part was so thick with mud it looked exactly like a cup of chocolate, but everyone did their best.

It was quite a sight when at last we reached the fort. We hadn't seen any building for so long that at first this seemed like yet another fancy of the mind. The walls were about twelve feet high and made of a cracked mud brick called 'adobe', which had seen better days but was so exciting for us. It felt like a great gala day. A cannon fired from the walls and Bea jumped.

Cornelius grabbed her and laughed.

'It's a welcome!' he explained. 'We are welcome!' He jumped up onto our wagon, spread out his arms and shouted to anyone who would listen, *'Arm! Arm! It is – it is – the cannon's opening roar!'*

'I'm not sure it's us who's being greeted,' said Kate, who I don't think had stopped grinning since Da had returned. As for Da, he was like a small boy, so pleased with everything. He grabbed Kate in his arms and danced about with her. It made us all smile.

It was impossible to know who the cannon had been fired for. There were dozens of other wagon trains ahead of us.

'Look, there's the Walkers!' cried Toby, and sure enough we could see Christopher and Sophie Walker walking in, surrounded by their large family. Everyone wanted to get to the fort, but we couldn't just drive up and walk in. Nothing was ever that easy on the trail. The waters of Laramie Creek stood between us and the fort. We were just below the building, but the stream, swollen with the rains in the mountains, was too rapid for us to cross. Once more we were so close to where we wanted to get to and yet so far away.

Mapiya led the way about a mile upstream before she

found a suitable ford. Her horse, bracing his feet, slid into the water with the greatest calm. She looked at Nashobanowa.

'Here,' she said. 'We cross here.' And he nodded. He was impressed with her guiding skills and I was proud of her.

I rode up beside Mapiya, and Chronicle easily slipped in and out of the water while we checked the current. Nashobanowa sat on his horse watching.

'That horse is your friend, Slim,' he said. 'It is good.'

I don't think any praise ever pleased me more. 'Thank you, Nashobanowa, and thank you for sending him to me. He has protected me.'

Nashobanowa nodded and smiled. 'I know.'

Da was amazed at how we had become what he called 'seasoned travellers'. I helped Louise and Jeni block up their wagon bed, double their teams with ours and lash fast the cargo while Henry, Toby and Kate dealt with ours. Bea got Jack down from the wagon and stood waiting till everyone was ready to cross. Once the wagons were sorted we all headed into the water, where it almost boiled against my saddle, but we were through. Jack was definitely stronger. I thought he would be scared of the water, but he stepped gently in and began crossing all by himself.

'Look at you, Jack!' yelled Henry, impressed.

Jack grinned as Toby shouted, 'Maybe being shot is a

cure to help you not be scared of other things!' We all laughed.

Once more poor Buddle's mule nearly went down in the current. We watched it scrambling over the loose round stones at the bottom, but without a thought Toby waded in, grabbed the frightened animal and brought it safely back. What a lot we had learned. Safely across, we rode up a steep bank and at last headed for the gateway of Fort John. A huge adobe-brick blockhouse had been erected above it to defend the entrance but there was no way we could reach it.

The Sioux had gathered in their hundreds outside the fort, getting ready for their battle with the Snakes and Crows. There were so many of them that they blocked the way. Their horses had also grazed all the grass from the plain surrounding the fort. It meant we had to camp miles away, so it was a while before we managed to walk into the fort.

Mapiya's family were waiting. I think I had almost forgotten that she didn't really belong with us.

'I go now,' she said.

I didn't want to say goodbye.

'You saved me,' I said.

Mapiya smiled. 'You wrestled me and you won.'

She took a feather from her hair and gave it to me.

'We will see each other again,' she said with absolute certainty. 'We shall ride together once more.'

My experience with Nashobanowa meant that I knew this was probably true, but it was difficult and I was sad. We hugged and she left us to be with her family.

Henry was watching. He came over and put his arm round my shoulder.

'I keep losing people,' I said.

He squeezed me close to him. 'You'll never lose me,' he said, but he was wrong. We didn't know then but going into Fort John would change Henry's life for ever.

CHAPTER EIGHTEEN

Inside the fort, three sides were lined with sheds where goods were kept and workshops for fixing wagons, shoeing horses, etc. The fourth side was a two-storey building with a small balcony. It wasn't much.

Bea had been more excited than anyone. She had brushed off her hat and combed her red hair into a ponytail. She almost ran to get inside and it's possible she was a little disappointed. I think she had imagined Fort John to be rather grander than it was. Mostly it was just a very plain place full of old traders and trappers.

Mr Honeyman called them 'French Indians!' and Mrs Honeyman kept telling everyone she couldn't go into the fort because she was expecting a visit from the mayor.

The Indians were only allowed in the fort during the day. Tall men wrapped in their white buffalo robes strode about the place or lay full length on the low roofs of the buildings. Many squaws in brightly decorated costumes also rambled about surrounded by whooping children.

Jack had tired himself walking to the fort so he hobbled inside with his arm round Henry's shoulders. Then he sat in the sun enjoying all the activity. He and I were easily pleased.

Someone gave us a piece of peach pie.

Jack sat staring at it. 'Look, Slim! Pie! Peach pie!'

After weeks of endless bacon and bread it was the most delicious-looking thing we had ever seen.

'You take the first bite,' I encouraged.

Jack slowly lifted the pie to his mouth and bit into it. A sigh escaped from his whole body as his mouth slowly allowed the peaches to sink onto his tongue. A small piece of filling dribbled from his lips and he rushed to catch it, not wanting to waste any. I think it took us half an hour to share that one piece of pie. It was so good and we didn't want to the moment to end.

'Are you getting better, Jack?' I asked when we were finished.

'I'm going to Oregon with you, Slim,' he replied firmly, 'and nothing is going to stop me.'

There was only one building everyone wanted to visit at the fort and that was the traders' store. It was the only reliable post office within three hundred miles. It also had supplies for sale, but the prices were astonishing.

Buddle stood spluttering in the middle of the shop.

'See that! See that!' He pointed to some tobacco on a shelf. 'That'd be a nickel in St Louis! Cost a dollar here! A dollar!'

'It is terrible,' agreed Kate. 'Sugar is a dollar fifty a cupful and flour is one dollar. We paid two cents in Independence.'

'Six hundred and seventy-two miles,' said Cornelius.

'What is?' I asked, still reeling from the pie.

'How far we've come from Independence in Missouri. I've been checking my roadometer.'

We stayed for a couple of days while everyone tried to make some order after weeks of travel. Mothers heated water in kettles and washed all the clothes. Kids were made to have baths and wash their hair. Each wagon wheel was taken off. Lots of the spokes were damaged now. They had shrunk and come loose. The tar buckets that usually swung on the axle were taken down and each wheel greased. Some men traded their horses for Indian ponies, thinking they might be better in the mountains ahead. Others replaced their worn-out boots with moccasins.

Jack loved going to the fort. I think the coming and going of all the people reminded him of a dock with ships loading and unloading. He was beginning to walk now but Buddle made him a stick.

'He'll always be a little lame,' said Louise.

'But he's not dead,' I said.

I too felt excited by all the new people who came and went every day, but every spare moment I had I spent with Da. I was so happy to have him back. I didn't care where he went if I could walk beside him. We were together at the main gate when I saw a great wagon pulling up. There were hundreds of Indians camped outside but the wagon slowly made its way through the crowds like a royal train, confident of its welcome. Everyone stood aside to let it pass because this was no ordinary wagon, this was magnificent. The people on it were not shy. A large man with a bright red face was sitting in the driving seat blowing a trumpet as he urged the horses on. A young man rode alongside on a small pony, calling out, 'Come and see! Come and behold!'

The driver pulled up outside the fort, wound the lines round the brake handle, gave one last blast on his brass horn and leaped down from his high seat. They made such a noise that lots of people ran out from inside the fort. Henry hurtled out and came to stand with us.

As far as I could make out there were three women inside the wagon. As soon as it stopped they leaped up to roll back the wagon covers. Then, with the help of the young man who'd jumped off his horse, they lowered one side of the bed and quickly made what looked like a small stage with whale-oil lamps along one edge and curtains made of red and blue blankets. The older man jumped up onto the wagon bed, threw out both arms and declared, 'Ladies and gentlemen, boys and girls – indeed, Indian people as well if you have money – welcome, welcome! This very evening we' – he waved his arm to include the women and the young man – 'the Dematinee Strolling Players, will present "Scenes from Shakespeare".'

'Shakespeare!' sighed Henry, as if someone were offering free gold.

'The very thing we need!' shouted Da with delight.

'A show!' I marvelled. 'Right here?'

'Henry, tell your Da about your own Shakespeare reading,' prompted Kate, but Da didn't hear her as he was busy walking up to the wagon to get a closer look.

'I will, I will,' said Henry, pointing to the man up on the wagon bed who was still speaking.

'The chief aim in life,' continued the man in a loud voice, 'is the pursuit of life, liberty and happiness, and all three shall lie upon this stage tonight!'

With that he leaped down and began handing out leaflets about the Shakespeare show and how one might get tickets. Everyone needed a little fun, so it was not long before many seats for the evening had been sold, even though there would be no real chairs, just a space on the ground, but everyone wanted to make sure they were close enough to hear.

Henry and Da went over and introduced themselves.

'His name is Sir Hugh Magnum Dematinee,' Henry explained to us excitedly over lunch. 'There's him and his wife, Sarah, and their two daughters, Patience and Virtue. They do Shakespeare!'

'Did you tell him we named our animals after Shakespeare?' asked Toby excitedly.

Henry grinned. 'No, but I will. A show!' I had never seen him so excited. 'Isn't it marvellous?'

Kate smiled and we all agreed it was.

'But,' said Da, 'they've a little trouble. The young man in their troupe is very good at riding ahead and putting up posters but he can't learn the lines. Sir Hugh finds it very difficult. It's not as though this place is full of actors.'

'Do some Shakespeare for your father, Henry,' asked Kate, but just then Jack called for Da to help him get back to the wagon and it didn't happen.

Da bought tickets for us all, and it was in a holiday mood that, early that evening, we trekked along to watch the show.

'Have you seen Shakespeare before?' Da asked Nasho-banowa.

My Indian friend nodded. 'Emily loves it,' he replied.

'Where's Henry?' asked Da as we all sat waiting for the show to begin.

We'd none of us seen him since lunchtime. The lights

were lit on the small stage, and the curtains drew back and the show began. They did a lot of different scenes, but Sir Hugh played each part about the same. He had an incredibly deep and loud voice which he used to bellow the words at us. His wife, on the other hand, turned out to be an amazing queen called Cleopatra. I didn't understand all the words, but when she died I found I was sobbing. In fact, her death was so good she had to do it again. Then Sir Hugh declared, 'And now Hamlet, the great Prince of Denmark, will tread these boards uttering words which we must all have considered at some time.'

'This will be good!' exclaimed Da, delighted.

Then Kate gasped. 'Look!'

Out onto the stage, dressed in a fancy velvet shirt we had never seen before, strode our own Henry. The whale-oil lights lit his face from below.

'Henry!' said Da, amazed. Henry looked young and very pale, like the boy I had known in Ireland. It was a large crowd which gathered, and as he looked out I saw him freeze. He opened his mouth to speak but nothing came out.

'Go on!' shouted someone from the crowd, but still Henry didn't speak. He swallowed hard and his knees began to shake. Da stood up and caught his eye. Da nodded and stood quite still until Henry began.

'*To be or not to be* . . .' he said quietly, and the audience, which had become restless, hushed.

Once he had started there was no stopping him. He was wonderful. Tears ran down Da's face and he reached out to grab Kate's hand.

I was so proud of Henry. I kept grinning at everyone and wanting to tell them that he was my big brother.

How we all celebrated afterwards!

'You're an actor!' declared Da, slapping Henry on the back with more delight than I had ever seen. 'And not just any actor, a Shakespearean one! Shakespeare!'

Sir Hugh was very impressed. 'He has natural talent, your boy. Welcome to join the Dematinee Strolling Players at any time. A fine life on the road. A fine life indeed!'

Henry couldn't stop grinning.

Kate shook her head at him. 'All that drama you caused in New York,' she said. 'Who knew it was because you were really an actor!'

How we laughed. It was so good and we were so happy. Da was back and we were laughing all the time! It was wonderful, but it wouldn't last.

CHAPTER NINETEEN

I think all Da wanted to do was talk about Henry and his acting, but there was work to be done. We couldn't stay any longer at the fort. We needed to get moving, but some wagons were beyond repair. These were either made into carts or just abandoned in favour of putting everything people owned on the backs of pack mules. Before we could head off there was also washing, mending, reloading and cooking, so we were all non-stop busy.

Louise was determined that we should be prepared for the next part of our trip, so she spent all her spare time in the fort getting anyone who knew anything about the journey to tell her what they knew, while Bea drew maps of what they said. Bea marked the points we should look out for, which had names like Independence Rock and Soda Springs. The people on the wagon train knew each other well by now, but it was clear that we would not all be carrying on together. Despite how far we had come, some gave up the dream there, and turned round and went home. There was a meeting at which Da explained that Nashobanowa had offered to take Mapiya's place as our guide.

However, instead of being pleased, some people carried on grumbling.

'Well, the Indian can guide,' said Mr Honeyman, 'but he can't be in charge.'

Cornelius frowned. 'I thought Buddle was in charge. He's the captain.'

'Everyone says the next part of the journey is the hardest,' continued Mr Honeyman, 'so we need someone... younger and fitter.'

'Fine,' said Buddle, who was clearly hurt by the suggestion that he couldn't manage. He stomped off while the men of the wagon train gathered to vote. It was then that Cornelius made a startling proposal.

'Buddle has done a grand job, but now I think the men should step back,' he suggested. 'The truth is, we all know it is the women who run this train, and I think of all of them Louise is the one I would trust to get us through. She saved us before and she can do it again. Who else has been trying to get us a new map?' No one said anything. Cornelius raised his hand in the air, as he often did when he was at his most determined, and declared, 'I vote that Louise become the new captain.'

I agreed, but the idea caused an uproar.

Da thought it was splendid, but a lot of the men did not want to vote for a woman. This made the women angry.

'Oh, you men are fine when food wants making and fires want lighting, aren't you?' fumed Jeni. 'We women will do for that, will we, but we can't have a say about who is in charge?'

Bea was furious too. I looked at her and realized how much she had changed. She looked strong, and her face, browned by the sun, was not that of the quiet shy person who had left Ireland. In fact, all the women had had enough and were ready to stand up for themselves.

'We women work as hard as anyone on this wagon train,' said Kate. 'I don't see why we shouldn't vote.'

'It's America,' declared Jeni. 'We're supposed to be a democracy.'

'I would never have voted for democracy,' replied Mr Honeyman, 'if I thought that meant women voting.'

'Everyone should vote, all of us, men, women and children,' said Da. 'We're all in this together.'

So we did all get to put our hands up, and Louise won with no trouble. Jeni was so proud she never stopped beaming. Louise was taken aback at first, but she soon took it all in her stride. She came over to look at our preparations. 'The next inhabited place is Fort Hall and they say that's more than five hundred miles away,' she warned, 'so make sure you think about every single thing you bring with you. If you're too heavy, we won't get to the mountains before the snow.'

'Our press is very heavy, Da,' I said after Louise moved on to check on others.

'We made it this far,' is all he would say, but I heard him talk about it with Kate.

It was Jack who refused to leave it behind. 'Democracy, Mr Hannigan,' he said, pointing to the press. 'That's what that is. We shouldn't have left it before and we shouldn't leave it now.'

No one argued with him. The press was coming with us.

Fort John was the place where everyone began to lighten their load.

'Beware! Weight is the great enemy of all wagons,' Louise warned everyone. 'It slows you down!' She and Jeni argued about their china plates coming with them.

People abandoned all sorts of things. One morning Jack came across a great pile of bacon which had just been left behind. It looked very nice but we didn't dare take it as it would slow us down.

The morning we were to leave, no one could find Buddle. We searched everywhere, until at last I found him inside the fort, lying on the ground with his thumb through the handle of a whiskey jug. He was slurring his words. 'Ah, the Hannigans! I am a little hipped this morning,' he declared, 'but the day will no doubt right it.'

He had been doing what was called '40 Rod drinking', and he was not, as Henry said, at his best.

'Is he well?' asked Kate.

'Drunk as a pigeon,' said Da, smiling, as he watched Buddle raise himself up on one forearm and a crooked elbow. The jug had been empty for some time but that didn't stop him every now and then swinging it back to his mouth just in case a drop had been left behind.

We loaded him onto our wagon, and it was to the sound of Buddle singing that once more we headed west.

'He's sad,' said Da.

'He doesn't sound sad,' I said as Buddle began a new verse of a song.

'He will,' said Kate. 'It was hard, no one voting for him.'

I think most of were sad to leave the fort. We were tired and liked the feeling we'd had for a few days of being settled. There was a strange silence in the train, interrupted only by the sound of gnats and mosquitoes flitting around us.

Bea looked back at the fort.

'It's our last link with civilization,' she wailed.

'We are outside the boundaries of Uncle Sam,' agreed Jeni.

'But closer every day to Uncle Niall!' I said.

'Forward, Bea, look forward. The future is ahead of you,' encouraged Cornelius, riding alongside us.

Louise gave the signal, and once more we headed out. We travelled up the south side of the Platte, enveloped in familiar clouds of dust but refreshed from our stop at the fort. Jack was well enough to sit in the driver's seat of our wagon and keep an eye on our animals as Toby walked alongside.

The landscape became drier. Louise ordered the drivers to spread out so that we were twenty wagons wide and one long to try and avoid 'eating dust'. Ahead lay Register Cliff, one of the landmarks on Bea and Louise's new map.

It wasn't long before our lead ox and Toby's favourite, Malvolio, began to limp.

'We should leave that ox behind,' said Mr Honeyman, pointing to him. 'It's slowing us down.' Toby sobbed at the thought.

Malvolio was getting lame by travelling over the hot, sandy and stony roads. We came across a dead ox by the roadside and Nashobanowa showed us how to help our animals. He cut a piece of hide from the dead animal and cut it into four squares. He took these and placed each one, flesh side out, over Malvolio's feet. Then he drew a string round each hoof, tight enough to hold it on the foot like a cushioned shoe. It worked, and we all walked on.

Not everyone was so lucky. There were those who'd lost all their animals and we saw one man pulling his own wagon.

There were so many things cast off along the side of the trail it was like walking through a giant shop. Bags of beans, salt, chests, tools of every description, clothing, trunks, kegs, buckets, stoves, ox chains and yokes.

'Like a defeated army retreating,' sighed Cornelius.

'Couldn't we just stop and live here?' asked Toby. 'There's so much stuff.'

'Nothing would grow here,' said Louise as she pressed us all on.

Buddle went back to not shaving, and most days he just sat in the back of our wagon looking out silently as we trundled along.

Cornelius found an anvil, bellows and even a large pyramid-shaped container made of metal with a great hook on top.

'Well, ain't that a thing!' He smiled. 'That's a diving bell. It has no bottom to it so a man can get inside and go under the ocean to have a look. Can you imagine such a thing! The fish swimming about your head!'

'Wouldn't he drown?' asked Jack, obviously thinking of how scared he'd be.

Cornelius shook his head. 'No, the pressure of the water keeps the air trapped inside the bell. Science, Jack! You can't beat it.'

We stood in the driest place on earth that you could imagine and Bea drew pictures of a happy Cornelius posing next to a diving bell. I couldn't think why anyone would want to carry such a thing such a long way.

'What dream did they have?' wondered Da.

Drivers unscrewed metal braces from abandoned wagons to replace their own, which were cracked and worn. They got rid of their own spoiled bacon and replaced it with good abandoned meat.

We were thirsty, but a lot of the water we came across was bitter with salt and something Cornelius called 'alkali'. It was undrinkable. Under our feet insects like giant fat crickets were everywhere. In some parts the ground was black with them, and you could hear them being crushed by our animals at every step.

Henry went off buffalo hunting with some of the other men.

'We'll bring back steaks for everyone!' they called as they rode away, but even Nashobanowa couldn't find any.

'The buffalo are smart,' he said when they returned empty-handed. 'They stay away.'

The trail was much more rugged and tortuous now. There were hills and canyons and too many obstacles which had to be 'got round'. Patiently Nashobanowa led the way and I often rode alongside him. At Register Cliff, a great wall of sandstone, we stopped to chisel our names into the soft stone as others had done before us. Bea put Ma's name there too.

'She needs to travel with us,' she said.

'Yes,' agreed Kate, and looked at Da.

He smiled softly, and I remembered how ill he had been after Ma died.

We travelled on, and at last we said goodbye to the Platte River. The river that we had followed for hundreds of miles now turned to the south and became impassable. At somewhere called Bessemer Bend we crossed the water for the last time. We had so often travelled over open spaces that it seemed incredible, but now there was a bottleneck of emigrants trying to get across the river. The year before some people had started a ferry at the bend, made up of eight dugout canoes with timber across for a platform. They could take one wagon at a time for a dollar.

'Nashobanowa, should we do this?' called Louise from her horse.

Nashobanowa nodded. 'The water is difficult. Some animals are weak. The ferry is best.'

Everyone grumbled but everyone paid.

We had to wait our turn so we spent the time hunting and fishing. We had trout for dinner, and it was quite a feast. Kate found an abandoned piano and sat down to play by the river.

Nashobanowa beamed and clapped his hands with delight. 'Like my Emily! She plays too!'

Da was so happy. 'Why, Kate, I had no idea!' he exclaimed. 'The talent I live amongst! You with your playing

and Henry with his acting! Why, we could make money!'
With that happy thought he began to bellow out the song
she was playing:

> '*Let Fate do her worst, there are relics of joy,*
> *Bright dreams of the past, which she cannot destroy,*
> *Which come in the night-time of sorrow and care,*
> *And bring back the features that joy used to wear.*
> *Long, long be my heart with such memories fill'd,*
> *Like the vase in which roses have once been distill'd.*
> *You may break, you may ruin the vase if you will,*
> *But the scent of the roses will hang 'round it still.'*

I remember that. The strange sight of a piano being
played by a river in the middle of nowhere. It sounded
wonderful.

'Life is good,' whispered Nashobanowa, 'when it has
music in unexpected places.'

Kate was flushed with excitement as we all applauded.
Da grabbed her hand and made her take a bow. I wasn't
sure I liked him holding her hand. I was fond of Kate, but
he should have been holding Ma's hand, and I . . . It was
very confusing.

On over the river to miles and miles of tough, barren
land. There were ravines and rattlesnakes, treacherous slopes
and squabbling. Louise spent most of her time getting people

to stop fighting over tiny little things when actually they were angry about soaking wet blankets, cold breakfasts after rainy nights, long hours without drinking water, and exhaustion.

We struggled through a horrible mix of burning sun and drenching rain as Nashobanowa quietly guided us on. Oxen and mules stopped and dropped in their tracks. Both the Dromios had to be left behind. Toby was desperate about it. He wept and wept, but Da kept telling him, 'Someone will find them and be glad of it.' We still had Balthazar and Malvolio and our wagon still moved, which was something. All around us animals died and wagon wheels snapped. We were slower, but still we walked on.

The order we travelled in caused the most trouble, until Louise announced, 'I have made a list of all the wagons. You will go in this order today, then tomorrow whoever was first will go to the back and work their way back up the line each day so it is fair. Everyone will have a job and you will all stop arguing.'

'Why didn't we do that in the first place?' I asked.

Cornelius smiled and replied, 'Because the women weren't in charge then.'

Every time Louise made a new decision Jeni stood behind her holding her gun, which seemed to help everyone get on with things.

There was no arguing when we reached the top of

somewhere called Prospect Hill. Now there was silence because from here we could see a giant valley ahead, and beyond that the Sweetwater Mountains. Everyone sighed at the beauty.

'It is our destiny to own this land,' declared Mr Honeyman.

'What is the destiny of the Indians who had it in the first place?' asked Nashobanowa quietly.

Da put a hand on his shoulder. 'It is a fine question, my friend, and one we must not forget.'

We were excited to see the Sweetwater River. Not that it was much of a river. Just a small shallow stream flowing gently over yellow sands, but it had such a wonderful name. We ran to it and lay down to take a large gulp.

'Urgh,' said Toby, 'it's not sweet at all.' It was bitter and disappointing.

'Don't matter,' called Louise. 'It will lead us home just the same.'

The valley which the river had carved would lead us to the high Rocky Mountains. First, however, it took us to Independence Rock, where we arrived on my birthday. The rock looked like a huge grey whale from a distance. I was fourteen, but no one cared about that as much as they did that it was American Independence Day. Jeni organized a little ceremony, where a salute of a couple of rifle shots was made, followed by Henry reading aloud the American Declaration of Independence. There was dancing and singing, and it was nice to have a sort of party. That night a baby was born in the wagon train and the family named her Ellen Independence.

Wood was scarce but the buffalo chips were excellent. They kindled quickly and the heat was fine, but they burned fast so you needed a lot. They looked like rotten wood and you needed two or three big loads to cook a meal.

By now we were spending most of our days looking for food but the day we got to Independence Rock was a sort of miracle. Louise had directed all the wagons into a corral when suddenly several large flocks of quail flew right into the camp. Some fell on the wagons while others landed in the dirt in the centre. Jack and all the boys ran about catching them with their hands. What a feast we had!

The rock itself was huge. It was the shape of a not-very-even loaf of bread covered in cracks and creases. It was light grey and as long as a city block in New York. The high part seemed smooth and slick enough that a person could slide off it. The lower surface was covered with the names of travellers, traders, trappers and emigrants; they were engraved and painted in every colour you could imagine, scrawled on almost every part you could see, including some so high up from the ground you wondered how anyone had got there. A man with a chisel offered to carve our names into the rock for a dollar each, but Kate said we had better things to spend our money on, so Jack got the tar bucket and carefully spelled out all our names in black on the side of the rock.

Buddle had been here before and we saw his name. Up until now he had been grumpy, but he had a story to tell and couldn't stay angry any longer.

'That was a terrible day,' he claimed. 'I was carving my name when I was captured by Indians!' He turned to Nashobanowa, adding, 'No disrespect. I'm just telling the story as it happened.'

Nashobanowa was used to Buddle by now and just smiled.

'What happened?' asked Toby, wide-eyed.

'They sold me back to my friends for tobacco and whiskey,' replied Buddle.

'No one you know would have swapped their whiskey for you,' declared Louise, and we all laughed.

There was no track at all now. In some places the plains were thick with sagebrush and greasewood shrubs growing nearly waist high to a man. Nashobanowa said we had no choice but to break a road through the brush so Louise set the strongest teams at the front and changed them over every day. There were days when the sage plain seemed to extend to the ends of the earth.

Death continued to follow us. A young man who had joined us at Fort John accidentally set off his gun and killed a blacksmith who was also new to the train.

'How terrible,' said Kate.

'Yes,' agreed Louise. 'We needed him to fix the wagons.'

Everything now was about being practical. Louise issued a new order prohibiting guns being carried uncapped or primed to stop anyone else dying by accident.

At a place called Devil's Gate the river ran through an amazing gap in a rocky mountain wall. The water had cut a narrow gorge through a ridge of granite. It was impossible for wagons to negotiate the chasm, so we would have to go round, but we camped above it and lots of people walked over to have a look. It was beautiful. There were towering cliff faces with the river flowing gently between. The view from the top was spectacular, but there was also a grave up there of a woman called Caroline Todd.

I turned to talk to Da but he was walking with Kate. I looked at them smiling together.

Nashobanowa stood quietly beside me. 'You miss your mother?' he asked.

I nodded.

'Your father too. It is good that he has someone to talk to.'

And I suppose I could see that he was right.

We fell into a routine of hard walking and exhausted sleeping. I think I believed it would be like that till we got to Uncle Niall's, but one night I was sitting with Louise and Jeni. We were having a nice time when Jeni suddenly looked up and pointed at a raven or possibly a crow – anyway, a black bird – flying near the camp.

'There is going to be a death,' she said quietly.

Louise was cross with her.

'Don't be such a darn fool,' she said. 'You and your mother's coffee grounds and your black birds predicting the future. It's all nonsense.'

Louise got up from the fire in a temper, but Jeni was right. I remembered Mrs Hughes on board the *Pegasus* saying something similar before the sickness took Ma, and I worried about the family but it wasn't us who suffered tragedy. It was after Devil's Gate that the Honeymans fell to pieces.

The walking was often boring. We had been doing the same things day after day for weeks and weeks, and everyone had had enough. Then one afternoon I heard Mr Honeyman cry, 'Get down!'

Algernon was more easily bored than anyone. We had all been marching along when he decided to try and stand on the tongue of his family's wagon. He stood with his feet on the piece of wood that attached the wagon to the animals and then leaned forward to rest his hands on the rumps of the oxen ahead.

'You'll fall!' shouted Mr Honeyman while his wife talked loudly to herself and paid no attention. Just then the wagon hit a rut and Algernon lost his footing. He was shaken from his place, and in a moment was under the giant wooden wheels. The animals didn't know to stop and just kept pulling the heavy wagon over him. How he screamed. Blood spurted from his leg. Mrs Honeyman hadn't noticed any of it, but the sight of the blood made her hysterical. She began shrieking too. It was terrible.

'They never helped us. Not once,' muttered Henry, but nevertheless we all did what we could.

Kate wrapped the boy's leg in linen. Bea gave him laudanum, while Da and Henry made a sort of trough out of planks to hold his leg still. Cornelius helped hold it all in place with his wonderful rubber bands. Then Algernon was laid in the back of the Honeyman wagon on a bed of blankets.

A few days later it was clear that things had got much worse. As we travelled, we heard Algernon calling out to his mother, 'There are worms crawling in my leg!'

Louise stopped to look and, sure enough, there were maggots swarming all over him. They were disgusting. The wound was open and raw, and inside wiggled hundreds of small brown worms.

'He has gangrene,' said Buddle in a matter-of-fact voice. 'It's a kind of infection. He needs a doctor.'

Nashobanowa and Louise both agreed. The leg would have to come off or Algernon would die.

But no one knew how to do such a terrible thing and there was no doctor. Buddle was the only one who knew about cutting legs off. He had lost his own leg years ago but he wasn't much medical help. When he was asked how it was done, he shrugged.

'I cut mine off myself with a bowie knife. Sealed up the blood with a red-hot bullet mould.'

Buddle liked to exaggerate, so no one knew if that were true.

'Whiskey helped,' he added.

Cornelius sat down with Bea and drew what he knew of how the leg attached to the body.

'We need something to dull the pain,' he said. 'I read an article about a man called Dr Crawford Long, I think. About four years ago he used something called "anaesthesia" to make a man sleep while he operated on him. That would be good.'

'What is that? Anaesthesia?' asked Bea, who was fascinated by all medicines.

Cornelius thought for a moment.

'Ether!' he remembered. 'Isaac Mulford! The doctor I met in New Jersey.'

'What does it do?' I asked.

'Makes you sleep.'

'I have sweet vitriol,' suggested Buddle. 'That makes me sleep.'

I ran to get it from Buddle's things and helped pour some into a mug for Algernon. He didn't want to drink, but

Bea persuaded him while Nashobanowa prepared some special tree bark for the pain afterwards.

Meanwhile Louise directed me, Henry and Toby to make a sort of tent to protect Algernon from the sun while the cutting was happening. Henry banged a peg into the ground with a hammer and accidentally hit Toby's foot by mistake. He hadn't really been paying attention to anything since his acting show at the fort.

'Ow!' shouted Toby.

'Oh, Toby,' muttered Henry. 'It's not as bad as Algernon.'

'Henry, be nice to your brother!' called Kate without thinking. We had all got used to her keeping us together.

Bea was worried. 'How I wish I had bought the sharp knife I was offered in St Louis when I was buying medicine.'

Louise had a butcher's knife which she used to cut up buffalo, which would have to do. Someone else provided a carpenter's handsaw and a shoemaker's awl, which is a kind of large needle. Cornelius said they would use it 'to take up the arteries'.

Algernon was clearly in a terrible state.

'It looks like death to me,' whispered Jack, and I thought about the bird Jeni had seen flying overhead.

Algernon was carried to the tent, and I realized that Louise had got us to put it up so that none of us could see the horror of what was about to happen. Louise, Cornelius, Bea, Kate, Buddle and Nashobanowa went in to do the job.

At the last minute they called Da in too to hold Algernon down in case the sweet vitriol didn't work.

Mrs Honeyman was frantic and quite mad.

'He isn't dressed for this. He has no tie,' she said as she paced up and down. No one could get on with anything, except Buddle who sat carving a large piece of wood.

'The boy will need a new leg,' he declared.

The screams from the tent were worse than the ones we had heard from Jack when his bullet was removed. They went on and on, until at last there was silence, which seemed even worse.

I don't know how long we waited but it felt like hours. Da appeared first. He had his arms round Kate, who was weeping. Everyone was covered in blood.

'He's alive,' said Da, 'but it was terrible. Truly terrible.'

Even though we all knew how important it was to keep travelling, Louise held a vote and everyone agreed to wait a day or two for Algernon, to get a bit stronger.

'I should have been nicer to him,' wept Toby. I went with him to see Algernon, but the boy was sleeping.

'He can't be moved. Not yet,' said Jeni, who was nursing him, so we rested, which was something no one was used to. We lay about sleeping so deeply that when Louise finally gave the call to move no one really stirred. Nashobanowa had gone ahead to look for the route, but it appeared no one was going to follow. We were too tired, and stopping had only made it worse. The whole train had come to a halt.

'I can't,' moaned Bea, lying stretched out on the ground as if she would never move again. Henry was leaning against a wagon wheel, and he too appeared to have lost all will to walk any further. The sun glared down on us with a pitiless, penetrating heat. The distant blue prairie seemed to quiver under it. We couldn't eat because no one had the energy and besides, our rifle, which was strapped to the side of the wagon, was too hot to use for hunting. There was a dead silence through our camp and all around it, unbroken except for the hum of gnats and mosquitoes. Jack, resting his forehead on his arms, was asleep under the cart.

Even Kate, who was always trying to be so positive, just sat on the ground with Hero in her arms. Just then my baby sister wriggled free and got to her feet. She had done plenty of crawling, but now, for the first time, she wobbled to an upright position and took her first steps. She was slow at first, but after a moment she gained speed and began walking towards the sun.

'I think she's heading west,' said Da, smiling.

'Well, we'd better follow her then,' replied Kate, slowly getting up. She put out her hand to me and we all got to our feet. Thus it was that the youngest member of the family kept us going. We began to walk, and slowly the rest of the train followed.

We walked on, not knowing what lay ahead or thinking about what was behind us. Without meaning to, we had left a trail anyone could follow. We couldn't be sure that Da had found all the notes which Kate had left, and our names were engraved on both Register Cliff and Independence Rock. It would not have been hard to work out which route we were taking.

CHAPTER TWENTY

Life got more and more difficult. We had been sold a barrel of flour and one of biscuits at Fort John, but when we opened them we found all the food was spoiled.

Once more the dust was intolerable. It would rise so thick that sometimes you couldn't distinguish the oxen from the wagon. There was nothing anyone could do. No matter how Louise tried to organize the wagon train, nothing helped. Then a wind would get up and hurl dust and sand at us like fine hail. It could be so strong that it stung our hands and faces. Henry got sand in his only good eye, and for a few days couldn't see at all. Hardly any of us bothered to wash any more, although Kate would go on about it and try to get a cup full of water behind our ears when she could. All the men had beards now. None of them shaved. A group of them got together and voted to give up and go back. They announced this to Louise, but she just laughed. None of the women paid any attention to the vote so we just walked on.

We had very little to eat and hardly anything to burn. We were no longer fussy about what might make a fire – dry prairie grass, driftwood, someone else's abandoned wagon, even the straw inside an abandoned horse collar. One evening we burned a beautiful bookcase but not the books that were in it.

'My heart would break if we set fire to books,' said Da. 'I think I'd rather die.' We were so happy to have him back that no one touched a page of the abandoned books.

During the day the landscape sizzled with heat and there was no sign of life other than the incessant drowsy humming of mosquitoes. I began to feel unwell. My head hurt and sometimes I couldn't see well. I didn't say anything because we were none of us quite right. Even Cornelius lost track of the miles behind us and how many there were in front. The roadometer clicked away but no one counted any more.

One night we were woken by a terrible squealing. I found it difficult to wake up. I don't think I had really been well since Ash Hollow. Toby leaped up, and half asleep we all went to find out what was happening. Mr Honeyman was standing with a knife drawn facing Buddle's yellow dog, who was snarling at him. Behind Dog stood Hamlet, looking wide-eyed and terrified. Jack was so much stronger now. He had managed to leap from the wagon and was in front of Mr Honeyman when I finally got there.

'What's going on?' Jack was demanding.

Dog bared his teeth at Mr Honeyman, who continued to hold his knife aloft.

'The pig needs to die,' he declared.

'What?' demanded Toby. 'No!'

My little brother ran at Mr Honeyman just as Cornelius appeared round the corner.

Cornelius grabbed Toby by the arm and held him close.

'What is this?' he asked, taking in the scene.

Da joined us, and then Kate and Bea. Now there was a group of us standing there. I noticed for the first time the incredible change in Mr Honeyman. He had been the smartest dressed man I had ever met, but now he looked destroyed. His once-neat beard was a great mass of untidy growth. His tie was long gone, as was his jacket. His trousers were torn and his shirt covered in dirt. He looked wild. He had been the best prepared of any of us, but it had done him no good.

Mr Honeyman took a deep breath and tried to be reasonable.

'My son needs meat,' he said firmly. 'He needs the pig. Toby, I thought you were his friend. Do you want Algernon to die?'

Da shook his head. 'That pig is part of my family and you will not touch him!'

'I will give you a hundred dollars for it!' declared Mr Honeyman in desperation.

Henry could not see well, but still he stepped forward. 'Mr Honeyman,' he began, 'I'm glad you've a hundred dollars. That's a marvellous thing and maybe it will be useful to you one day, but not here. Now I suggest you take your green bills and go back to look after your boy.'

Mr Honeyman shook with rage, and from then on Toby would not let Hamlet out of his sight.

'Well, that's told him, Hamlet,' Da said to the pig. 'Now, if you could help find us something to eat, that would be most kind.'

Hamlet snorted and went to curl up with Buddle's dog. We all made friendships that trip, but some were stranger than others.

Cornelius tried to solve our lack of food by inventing a rather clever bird trap. Bea helped him design it. I noticed that they were spending more and more time together. The trap was a small box made of boards set up on some triggers. Cornelius laid down a small piece of the meat jerky attached to the triggers. If a bird pulled at the bait, then the triggers would let the box fall and catch it. We put the box out each evening, and in the morning Jack would go and check if we had caught anything.

One morning I saw from a distance that Toby was

standing by the box. He had Hamlet by his side and they were both looking at the bird that was trapped inside. We were so hungry and I was so pleased that I began to run towards him. Toby opened the box, put his hand in, and the bird sank its talons into his skin. It wouldn't let go. It used its beak to peck away at his hand. Toby tried to hold the bird's head with his other hand. He pulled it towards him and I thought he was going to bring it to Kate for cooking, but instead he suddenly let it go. The poor frightened thing flew straight up into the sky.

'Toby, what are you doing?' I asked.

Toby looked down at his hand, which was bloody from the pecking. 'I could feel its heart beating,' he said. 'It looked so sad. I just couldn't do it.'

We had reached Shoshoni territory, and once more everyone was worried, although, as Kate kept saying, 'No Indian has so far given us cause for alarm. Quite the contrary, they have been our friends.'

Nevertheless, at night we could hear the steady beat of their drums in the distance and sometimes the chant of a song. It made people nervous.

'They're going to war,' said Buddle.

'But not with us,' replied Nashobanowa.

'How do you know?' I asked.

He looked at Louise and smiled. 'Because you travel with Shoshoni.'

414

I was confused and said to him, 'I thought you were Choctaw, Nashobanowa?'

He smiled and replied, 'I am, but Louise is not.'

We all looked at Louise, who looked at Jeni. Jeni nodded, before Louise said, 'My mother was Shoshoni.'

I gasped and then I chuckled. Henry laughed too.

'So the whole time Nervous Bob was worried about Indians, he was travelling with one?' I asked.

Louise nodded.

'Why didn't you say?' said Kate.

Louise shrugged. 'No one asked.'

'People are idiots,' I said firmly, and Da nodded in agreement.

Louise put her arm round me and pulled me in for a hug. '*E aisen ne tei*,' she said.

'What does that mean?' I asked.

'You are my friend,' she said quietly.

The next day Louise took everyone to a Shoshoni camp and it was lovely. They had some medicine for Algernon and made a feast for all of us. Nashobanowa said it would be good to sit and rest.

It was so calm sitting by the fire. Everyone ate roasted meat with wild fruit and vegetables, but Jack and I didn't eat. I didn't feel well. Jack was better but his leg would never be the same. He sighed as we sat there.

'What is it, Jack?' I asked.

'I'll never climb rigging on a sailing ship again,' he said sadly. He reached into his pocket and pulled out the magic box his father had left him.

'When we get to Oregon,' he said, 'all I have is this, and it's nothing. It's not magic. It's just not anything. You are all Hannigans. You have each other.' He put the box away and declared, 'I've changed my mind. I'm not going to go to Oregon.'

'What?'

Jack shook his head. 'I'll wait till we see some people who've turned round and are going back. I'll go back to New York with them and return to the docks. I can't go to sea, but maybe I can find work near the water.'

'Jack!' I said, shocked. 'They have water in Oregon! I've seen it on the map! We won't let you go. Not after all this.'

'It's nothing to do with you, Slim!' he snapped.

He got to his feet and limped away. I was so upset. Jack had never spoken to me like that. My head was spinning and I wanted to cry. I didn't know what to do so I went to find my real friend, Chronicle. He was tied to a small tree a little way off, eating what grass he could find. He whinnied as I approached and made it easy for me to leap up onto his back. Riding was so familiar now. Like sitting in a comfortable chair. As usual he seemed to know what I needed. I hardly had to touch his sides before he turned away from all the people and headed out where we could be alone on the empty prairie. Leaving everyone at the Shoshoni camp, at first we ambled along, but then I kicked my heels into Chronicle's sides and we raced off. As we sped across the land, I realized how used to it all I was now. What a lot I had learned. I knew how to hunt, fish, light a fire, ride a horse. I was the cowboy I had once dreamed of being.

It was good that Chronicle knew what he was doing. I didn't realize how weak with the sickness I had become. We were a mile or two from the wagon train when I found that I could hardly hang on. The ground grew dim before my eyes, the trees seemed to sway to and fro, and the prairie to rise and fall, so that I thought for a moment that I was back on the ship *Pegasus* passing over the swells of the ocean. I stopped Chronicle by a small stream and got off to take a drink.

Sweat poured down my face. I felt light-headed with fever and I couldn't get enough air. I knew I needed to return to the wagon train but I didn't think I could get back on my horse. The blood pounded in my ears and I could hardly stay upright. I reached for the rope around Chronicle's neck and, as I did so, a shadow loomed across our path.

'You! Stop right there!' came a familiar voice.

If I thought I had felt unwell before, now it was much worse. I looked up, and there right in front of me, seated on a great black stallion, was Parker Crossingham.

CHAPTER TWENTY-ONE

The sky was darkening but there was enough light to
see my old enemy clearly. He no longer wore the great
black cloak with the scarlet lining that had been his uniform in Ireland, but he still looked terrifying. He was
wearing American clothes – a black hat and a dark jacket –
but there was no mistaking the terrible man from Ireland
who had made our lives such a misery. Parker Crossingham
had been Lord Cardswell's agent, the man who had bullied
us for rent when we had no money, the man who had pur-
sued Henry to have him arrested, and the man who had
caused us to flee to America when he tore down our home.

'You, boy!' he demanded. 'Which wagon train is this?'

That's when I realized – he didn't recognize me! I was a
year older, I wore trousers and I suppose my face was different. He thought I was a boy, and I didn't want to give him
a chance to change his mind. I pulled my hat down low over

418

my face as if shielding it from the setting sun. I thought I was going to be sick but I lowered my voice as much as I could.

'All sick,' I said gruffly. 'Everyone dead. I'm sick.'

I think he could see I was sweating.

A look of disgust passed over his face.

'What's your name?' he demanded.

'Wagmute,' I replied, coming up with the first name I could think of. I realize now it was the name of the German family Da had said he and Nashobanowa had travelled with.

'I'm looking for a family called Hannigan. From Ireland. Nasty people.' Crossingham spat on the ground as he said it, and then reached into a pocket for one of his terrible cigars.

'All German here,' I claimed in a voice I hoped sounded at least a bit German.

I didn't think I could keep this up, and besides, he terrified me. Without thinking I used the last of my strength to leap onto Chronicle. My great horse didn't need any instruction from me as we raced off across the prairie. I could hear Crossingham yelling at me and then chasing after me on his horse. I raced ahead, and as I reached the edge of the Shoshoni camp I could hear him cursing as he stopped his horse. He didn't dare follow me into the Indian camp. I galloped on and leaped off my horse beside the circle of gathered men. By now my head was spinning and I tried to say what was happening, but actually all I did was faint.

I don't know what happened next. I was mad with

fever. I felt soft hands on my brow and I was sure it was Ma. The others told me later that I'd cried out for her and once I'd sat up shouting, 'Parker Crossingham!' but they thought it was part of the sickness and gently laid me back down in the wagon.

We moved on, and in the heat of my illness I thought we were at sea again. I felt the waves lift me up and smash me back down. I called Jack's name and I think he answered, but soon I was asleep again. I slept, and Ma was there looking after me. She held me tight against the crashing sounds and whispered stories in my ear. I was so happy to have her back again.

I was ill for some days and couldn't warn anyone about Parker Crossingham. The wagon train travelled on, climbing gently up to the South Pass of the Rocky Mountains. This was the backbone of America – the dividing ridge that separates the waters of the Atlantic and the Pacific oceans on either side of the great continent – but I didn't see it. Da told me the climb up was so gentle and the 'gap' in the mountain so wide that it would have been easy to forget what a goal everyone had achieved.

Jack began to write in my notebook so that 'I didn't miss a moment', so I have some idea of what they saw and how they travelled.

'The Pacific side of the continent!' exclaimed Cornelius. 'Why, you take a jug of water, pour it on one side, and it would make its slow way to the Atlantic Ocean. Pour it on the other, and water would flow to the Pacific!'

'This is where Oregon begins,' agreed Buddle.

'Then we will say goodbye soon,' whispered Kate.

'Goodbye?' said Da, and Kate nodded. 'I am going to California to my sister, and the trail there parts soon from this one.'

Henry told me I didn't miss much. He said everyone knew the South Pass was important but it wasn't spectacular. There was no dramatic gorge or high ledge, just a broad, grassy valley so flat that you couldn't tell you had passed from one side to the other.

'Work still to do,' called Louise, and everyone just rolled down the western slope to look for water.

I didn't see the sun glittering off the snow-capped peaks of the Wind River Mountains, whose tower-shaped summits rose up to our right. Everyone thought the journey had been difficult, but they had no idea what lay ahead. Behind us there had at least been fresh grass and sometimes buffalo, while ahead were deserts, dry land, few streams, little grass and no buffaloes at all.

There were no trees either. The craggy land was made of sand and clay. Nothing grew here. It looked brown and dead and endless. It stretched on and on under the great canopy of blue sky. The walking was hard on everyone's feet, human and animal.

'How far have we travelled?' I called to Cornelius.

He shrugged. 'No idea. Maybe three hundred miles.'

Everyone drank from a small river which Bea had marked on her map as 'Pacific Springs', and marvelled that the water now flowed west. We had walked about a thousand miles since Independence, though now I just slept. We were in danger but I couldn't warn anyone.

There was grass for the animals amongst the willows on the bank of the Little Sandy River, and wild sage to make fires. The family ate antelope and sage hen, which Henry was now quick to catch with his bow and arrow.

Everyone was exhausted and fancied they saw lakes and streams of running water bordered by waving timber in the distance, but there was nothing; it was a barren and arid desert. At night it was cold and people woke with frost on their blankets or buffalo robes.

I began to come to when the train reached the Big Sandy River. It was evening and I was in the back of the wagon. I remember opening my eyes to find Jack sitting beside me scribbling in my notebook. I had dreamed of Ma for days, and as I awoke I called out for her.

'Ma! Jack, get Ma for me!'

Tears rolled down his big face. 'Ssh,' he said, putting down his pencil and stroking my head.

'Where is Ma?' I asked again.

He shook his head, and it was only then that I remembered

she was dead. Now we both wept as he put a hand gently behind my head and helped me to drink some water.

'How long have you been there?'

'A few days,' he replied.

'You sat with me?'

Jack shrugged. 'You sat with me on the boat when I was sick and when I was shot.'

I was weak and it took a while for me even to sit up. I could see everyone gathered around the campfire where Louise had called a meeting. She was explaining what the train had to decide.

'This place is where we decide who is going to part ways,' she was saying. 'South is Fort Bridger and the route to California. We can go that way, but those of us who are bound for Oregon ... Well, Patrick Hannigan has a map which shows there is a cut-off to shorten the distance to Fort Hall by some fifty or sixty miles.'

'Let's do that!' called some of the men.

Nashobanowa nodded. 'We can, but there is no water. No water for fifty miles until we reach the Green River.'

'It's a fifty-mile "water scrape",' agreed Louise, 'but I reckon we can do it if we do most of our travelling by night. It'll take three days. If we go south, it's seven days longer but much safer.'

Now the old arguments began again about whether California or Oregon was a better place.

'You don't want to go to California,' said Henry. 'Why, it's a foreign country. They speak Spanish and it has a very hot desert.'

'That's not a good reason, Henry,' scolded Da mildly, 'although I don't think you should go.'

'Oregon has trees and rich soil,' I heard Bea chip in; she now seemed to have an opinion on all sorts of things.

'And a better climate,' said Cornelius, agreeing.

I realized they were all talking to Kate. Kate had been with us for so long I had forgotten that she was always planning to go to California and not to Oregon with us. She had a sister there, but I couldn't imagine our family without her.

Jack helped me climb down from the wagon. I hadn't eaten for days and was very weak. He put his arm round my waist. He led me to the fire and helped me sit down. Everyone got up as we approached.

'Oh, Slim, how wonderful!' said Kate, tears pouring down her face.

'Thought we might have lost you, little one,' said Da, trying not to cry.

Nashobanowa hugged me and everyone fussed as I sat down.

'Hero!' I cried.

She was running! I watched her race towards me with her arms out and realized how far we had come.

Everyone hugged me, and I was about to tell them about Parker Crossingham when a wagon rolled up and a booming voice called out, 'Well met! Well met, fair fellows! Good even and twenty!'

'It's Sir Hugh!' cried Henry, more excited than I had ever seen him.

It was Sir Hugh Magnum Dematinee and his family with their wondrous theatrical wagon, which could become a stage in no time.

'A show! A show!' cried Toby.

'Well, I'm not sure there is a sufficiently large audience . . .' began Sir Hugh, but no one was listening. Everyone rushed to help them unpack and soon the lights were lit and everyone sat waiting for a performance. Henry was persuaded to give his speech from *Hamlet*. Sir Hugh and his wife did a marvellously funny scene from *Twelfth Night*, and then Henry joined the whole family to do the mechanicals play from *A Midsummer Night's Dream*. I was weak and lay against Da while Toby hugged Hamlet and kept an eye out for the Honeymans, who were missing. How we all laughed. I was so happy to be with everyone. I realized I still hadn't told them about Parker Crossingham but I didn't want to spoil our happy evening with news about our old enemy.

The next morning there was sadness in the air. Our wagon train had travelled together for months. We all knew each other so well. We had been scared and tired together. We had fought and laughed. Now we had to say goodbye and separate.

I found Toby sitting by the morning fire stroking Hamlet.

'Algernon is dead,' he said quietly.

Nashobanowa tried to comfort us. 'The prairie makes quick and sharp work of death,' he said. 'Better to die here, in the open air, than stifle in the hot air of a sick chamber.'

Bea nodded but no one spoke. No one wanted to cook or talk or anything, but there was work to do.

Mr Honeyman seemed broken, and Mrs Honeyman stared into the distance and said nothing.

'We're going back,' he said. 'I cannot go on one more step towards that infernal place.'

I looked at Jack. He had said he would return to New York if he found a way, but I didn't want him to.

Kate was leaving too.

'It was always the plan, Bea,' she said, as my sister sobbed while helping to pack Kate's things. 'I was always going to my sister in California.'

Bea nodded but could not speak. Da too was silent, as silent as he had been in New York after Ma died.

Kate finished packing and we could hardly bear it. She would travel with a family from Pittsburgh until she could find a wagon train heading to where her sister lived. She hugged us all. Tears poured down her face as she kissed baby Hero one last time. It was all she could do to hand her to Bea.

'Goodbye, little Slim,' she said, turning to me. 'Your Ma would be so proud of you. We would never have made it without you. *I* would never have made it without you.'

Now I sobbed and flung myself at her. She held me tight until Da gently pulled me away. Tears flowed down all our faces as we stood watching her climb onto the wagon. Kate turned to wave goodbye one last time, and they headed off. We stood watching, unable to speak, and then Bea did something I had never seen her do.

'Are you mad, Da?' she exploded.

'What do you mean, Bea?' he asked.

'You're supposed to be a clever man, but honestly! You love Kate – we all do – and you shouldn't let her go. You should run after her and marry her or you're . . . you're an idiot!'

'Bea!' said Toby, shocked by our usually calm big sister's words.

Bea put her hands on her hips and turned to him. 'But I'm right, aren't I?'

I had never thought about it. Of course she was right.

'You do love her, Da!' I cried. 'And so do we. Bea's right. You are an idiot, Da, if you let Kate go.'

'But what about your Ma?' he asked.

Bea's voice softened. 'She would be pleased for you. She

427

wouldn't want you to be alone. She loved you and so does Kate.'

Da turned to my big brother. 'Henry?' he said.

Henry smiled and quoted, '*She's beautiful, and therefore to be wooed; She is woman, and therefore to be won.* Go on, Da!'

Da stood watching the wagons disappear towards California. He seemed to be having a million thoughts all at once. He looked to Nashobanowa, who said quietly, 'It is a Choctaw tradition for the man to chase after his bride.'

Da grinned, and then he nodded as if he had made his mind up.

'May I borrow your horse, Slim?' he asked.

As usual, Chronicle didn't need telling and was all set to go. I swear that horse could speak English. Da leaped onto his back and raced off.

We all stood waiting, but he travelled too far into the distance for us to see what was happening. It felt like ages, until at last Cornelius saw him through his spyglass.

'He's walking . . . He's leading Chronicle because . . .' he began.

'Because?' said Bea impatiently.

'Because . . . Kate is on his back!'

How we all cheered and whooped.

Da was like a shy schoolboy when he returned with his prize.

'Well, I can't think why, but she said yes!' he shouted when he was close enough to call.

Kate and Da couldn't stop smiling.

Louise and Jeni stood watching, and soon a whole crowd had gathered cheering the good news. We missed Ma, but Kate was so much part of the family now that her marrying Da was perfect.

'I don't know what I shall tell my sister,' Kate kept saying.

Buddle shook his head. 'I've seen women so delicate that they were afraid to ride for fear of the horses running away with them,' he said, 'afraid to sail for fear the boat should over-end, afraid to walk for fear the dew might fall, but I never saw one afraid to get married.'

Louise clapped her hands to bring some order amidst all the excitement. 'We have to collect water and be gone by tomorrow so you'd better get the wedding done tonight,' she declared.

'Tonight?' gasped Kate. 'But I look such a mess,' she said, 'and my apron is filthy from the buffalo chips.'

Louise was very practical. 'This is not a journey where we have time for a long engagement,' she said, and everyone agreed. 'So let's get the job done.'

Now everyone rushed around. Pretty things were found for Kate's hair and a clean apron was produced. Jack and Henry helped Da have a shave and got a comb for his hair. Toby gathered some flowers while I set up a great fire for the ceremony. Jeni and a few of the women even managed to make a sort of cake. The sun was setting as Kate and Da stood before the whole wagon train. We didn't have a minister so Buddle did the honours. Bea was the maid of honour, Toby and Henry were Da's best men, and I was allowed to walk Kate 'up the aisle'. It was beautiful. Louise and Nashobanowa laid out a small rug on the ground where Da and Kate sat together. They handed them food, which they each took a small bite from. Then they got up, and Louise wrapped the small rug round both their shoulders so that they stood arm in arm. Nashobanowa spoke in Choctaw and then in English, 'Always face the future together,' he said, 'and always face each other with respect. May the Creator bless noble children to share. May they live long.'

Then Da spoke. 'This trip,' he began, 'indeed this day, has been something even a great storyteller could never have imagined. I'm not at all sure that if we'd understood what this journey would be like, we would ever have set one foot out before the other. Every day is hard for everyone . . .'

Da paused and many thought about the friends they had waved goodbye to or people we had lost along the way. Da choked back a tear and continued.

'But I don't want us to forget that there is also joy in this adventure. The finest thing in my life was finding you all again. I have seen such sorrow . . .'

Da's voice cracked a little and he paused. Kate reached

430

out and took his hand. She held it and smiled, encouraging him to go on.

'Such sorrow,' he said, 'that I thought there would be no more happiness, but today this beautiful woman, Kate Kavanagh—'

'Kate Hannigan!' I called out, and everyone laughed.

'That sounds nice,' said Kate.

Da grinned. 'Kate Hannigan has become my wife and it has made me believe in new beginnings. It has made me believe that even in this dry desert flowers can bloom. Thank you all for being my friends, and thank you to my wonderful family for . . . for everything.'

Then there was singing and fiddle playing. It seemed Da and Buddle both knew a funny song called 'Lord Lovel and Lady Nancy', which made everyone laugh.

It says something about life on the trail that Algernon had been buried the very morning Da and Kate's wedding took place.

I went to see if the Honeymans wanted some cake. On my way I found that Louise and Jeni had emptied their wagon and made a bed in it. I asked them what they were doing as they piled all their belongings onto the ground.

'We need a "shivaree",' explained Jeni. 'Find something to make a noise!'

A 'shivaree', I now know, is a very loud thing indeed. After the ceremony Kate and Da were bundled into the empty wagon, at which point everyone from the wagon train took hold and ran the wagon half a mile out onto the prairie. All the men, women and children had found 'something to make a noise'. There was the banging of cans and pans, and the shooting of guns and shouting. It went on for ages until Louise said it was time to go. We left Kate and Da out alone on the prairie.

As we walked back we could see by the light of a lantern that Mr and Mrs Honeyman were sitting by Algernon's grave. It was unmarked and lay between the furrows the wagon wheels had dug into the trail.

'Does no one care about his grave?' asked Toby.

'It's not because no one cares,' explained Buddle. 'Out here you have to hope that the constant passing of the wagons will wipe away the scent and keep the poor boy safe from animals that might try to dig him up.'

Jack stopped and stared at where Algernon lay. His death had upset him more than anyone had expected.

'Tomorrow we will move on,' said Bea, 'and this place will be empty again.'

'Algernon will be here,' Jack said.

'But no one will know,' replied Toby.

'Life is short,' said Nashobanowa, 'so we must live now.'

That night we sat under the stars together. Cornelius was playing with Jack's magic box when Jack suddenly announced that he had decided to go back east with the Honeymans.

'No!' cried Toby.

I was too shocked to say anything.

Toby had no such problem. 'Why?' he demanded.

'I'm not a Hannigan,' said Jack. 'I don't have anything. What kind of a life will I make? I don't know anything except the sea.'

'That's not true,' I almost shouted. 'You know about printing. We'll start a newspaper. You and me. We'll make one in Oregon just like we did in New York.'

'But it won't be mine,' argued Jack. 'I don't have any money. I don't have anything.'

'You have us,' I insisted.

Jack looked at me more seriously than I had ever seen him. 'I was sent to sea when I was ten. My father died and I never knew my mother. My uncle didn't want me so he sent me to work. I have no family. You are my friend, Slim, but it's not the same. I nearly died twice, and when I actually do' – Jack looked to the lights where the Honeymans sat beside Algernon's grave – 'there will be no one to . . .'

Jack stopped speaking. I didn't know what to say. Jack was my friend and I couldn't lose him. There had been too much loss already.

CHAPTER TWENTY-TWO

The next morning Kate and Da returned so happy from their night on the plains. Henry had been helping the Dematinees pack up. Then he came to talk to Da. He looked nervous and he was ages getting to the point.

'They want me to go with them,' he said at last.

'Who do?' asked Da, confused.

'Sir Hugh Magnum and his family,' mumbled Henry, almost as if he were embarrassed. 'They're going to make a theatre in California eventually, but meanwhile they're on the road and they want me to . . . well, act. They think I can act.'

Da looked stunned. 'Leave us?'

'Henry!' I cried. 'No!'

Henry looked at me. 'I'm sorry, Slim. I don't want to leave you, except that I feel like I've found my place. When

I'm on the stage and I speak those words, something inside me sings. I don't know—'

'You can't go!' I said, standing up and grabbing his arm. 'You said you would never leave me. You promised. We shook hands!'

'I know, Slim, I'm sorry, I . . .'

'Ssh, now, Slim, let him go.' Da reached out and pulled me to him before turning to Henry. 'You're a man now and a fine actor, my son. There is no better job than making people laugh and cry. I'm proud of you.'

Da reached out to Henry and they solemnly shook hands.

Saying goodbye to Henry was one of the hardest things I had ever had to do. We had been through so much and we didn't know if we would ever see each other again. He hugged me, weeping and saying, 'Kate was right. We'd never have made it without you, Slim. You're the very heart of the Hannigans.'

'Don't cry, Henry. Save that for when people are paying money for it,' said Da, trying to be cheerful.

'You'll be a great actor and one day we'll come and see you in a fancy theatre!' cried Toby, excited at the thought.

Henry smiled and nodded. 'You will. I promise.'

Da gave Henry the book of Shakespeare and told him to 'go and bring pleasure to the masses'.

Louise and Jeni gave their spare horse to him as a present.

'You're as close as we'll get to family,' said Louise gruffly as she handed him the pony. Cornelius made him a new slingshot and Kate and Bea sewed him a shirt to start his journey in. He left as the sun rose. There was no time to grieve.

'Let's move,' shouted Louise.

Everyone was busy filling anything that could hold water to take with us across the desert. I knew Jack hadn't slept well and neither had I. He packed his few things slowly. I had seen him talking to Mr Honeyman.

'You have to come with us,' I was saying as Kate and Da packed up the wagon.

'And why might he not?' asked Kate.

'He says he's not a Hannigan,' said Toby, getting right to the point.

'Jack?' said Da.

Jack looked embarrassed. 'You've been good to me, but when Algernon died I realized . . . I mean . . . I don't have anyone. My father said he would look after me in Oregon but it's nonsense. He's dead. I have nothing. He won't be there when I arrive. I should go back to be by the sea. To where I belong.'

'Are you saying it's because you're not family, you're not a Hannigan?' asked Da, trying to understand.

Jack nodded.

'Well, that's a quick fix,' said Da. 'I need a new son now that Henry has gone off to be an actor. What do you say, Kate? Too soon to start a family together?'

Kate smiled and said, 'Nashobanowa said the Creator would bless children for us to share, Patrick.' She turned to Jack without any further discussion and asked, 'Would you like to be our boy, Jack?'

Jack swallowed hard and looked at Da with a shy grin. He nodded, so Da put out his hand and, shaking Jack's, said, 'Welcome to the family, Jack Hannigan.'

'Should we sign something?' asked Bea.

'Good idea!' declared Da, so Bea made a beautiful certificate and we all signed it. Da bowed and handed it to Jack. And that was that.

'I'll never let you down, Mr Hannigan,' said Jack seriously.

'Well, you will,' replied Da, 'unless you call me "Da".'

Everyone was so happy and I didn't want to spoil it, but I knew I had to tell the family about Parker Crossingham.

'We need a family meeting,' I said. Jack headed off to sort something and I called to him, 'That means you too, Jack Hannigan!'

He beamed as we all sat down together, but he was soon looking worried. I explained to Jack and Kate what a terrible man Parker Crossingham had been in Ireland.

'But that's all behind us,' said Da.

I shook my head. 'No, Da, he's here. I saw him. The day we were all with the Shoshoni. He was looking for us at the wagons. He didn't recognize me. Thought I was a boy . . .' Toby sniggered but I ignored him.

'You had a fever, Slim,' said Kate. 'Are you sure it was him?'

'You know we have all imagined things out here in the desert,' added Da.

It made me angry. 'It was him. We spoke. He smoked a cigar. He is after us. I tell you, he won't give up.'

Da looked at Kate and they both frowned before Da shrugged and said, 'This is America. He can do nothing to us here.' With that he got up and started loading the water into the wagon. It was clear he didn't want to talk about it any more.

The Honeymans left that morning. As they turned back to the east their whole wagon, the one which had been the finest and most expensive of all, simply broke in half.

I think Cornelius felt responsible. It was his wind wagon that had caused the first damage. He rushed to help. He and Jack managed to make a cart from the broken pieces which could be pulled by a single ox. When they finally left, Mrs Honeyman was raving. Her pink dress was brown with dirt and ripped everywhere you looked. No one felt it right to say goodbye.

We set off. I wanted to believe Da about Parker Crossingham – that either I hadn't seen him at all, or if I had, he wouldn't bother us – but as we travelled on, I noticed he kept looking over his shoulder.

'Are you all right?' I asked him.

Da smiled and replied, 'And why wouldn't I be, my lovely Slim?' Then he quoted,

> '*Away, away, from men and towns,*
> *To the wild wood and the downs—*
> *To the silent wilderness*
> *Where the soul need not repress.*'

Da began to whistle and I knew he was trying to show me that everything would be fine. I hoped he was right.

Jack grinned at me, and however terrible the trip across the cut-off was, he kept grinning. He loved his certificate. He put it inside one of the *McGuffey Readers* and kept getting it out to have a look.

The cut-off proved to be one of the toughest parts of the journey so far. For the first time we even missed the stink of buffalo dung. We still needed fire and there were no trees. Nashobanowa helped us wrench up knots of sagebrush, which burned so fast there was never enough. Chronicle became ill. I could tell straight away. His eyes looked dull as lead and I should never have tried to get on him. Instantly he staggered and fell flat on his side. He got back on his feet after much effort but just stood with a drooping head.

I panicked. 'What's wrong with him?'

Buddle and Nashobanowa both shook their heads.

'Snakebite maybe, or eaten something rotten,' suggested Buddle.

'Let him walk without you,' said Nashobanowa.

So I walked beside him, willing him to be better.

We were not following any tracks now. Nashobanowa led the way, while Cornelius scouted ahead. He would often ride back, and the two of them would stop and whisper with Louise. I suspected sometimes the three of them were just having to guess which way was best.

About halfway across the desert our biggest barrel of water broke. We went over a nasty bump, the wagon cracked down and the whole barrel fell apart. Water poured out as we watched in horror.

'Don't just stand there!' yelled Louise, running forward with a tin cup to catch some of the precious liquid. We all raced to save the drink, which was more valuable than all the riches on the earth. Without it we would die.

'Where are our bowls?' cried Bea, but we had thrown away almost all of them at Fort John because of the weight. Jack grabbed cups and Da came running with the Dutch oven, but the water gushed so fast from the barrel that it had spread across the ground before we could catch it.

'My hat!' cried Toby. He took his hat off and began scooping water into it to give his animals, but the rest lay on the ground, doing no good to anyone.

Now we would have to keep what was left for ourselves and not let the animals have any more. No one slept well and all the animals were tired at sunrise. They had had no food for a day and a half. Buddle gave our team a dose of vinegar and molasses but they were weak and nearly mad with thirst. When we saw the Green River they went crazy. Malvolio would not wait to be unyoked. He led an uncontrollable stampede to water.

'Malvolio!' shouted Toby helplessly, but our usually obedient ox was too thirsty to listen to instructions from anyone. The giant animal charged towards the water, and Balthazar, who was yoked beside him, had no choice but to go too. Toby ran, shouting with all his might, as the wagon bounced and flew in the air behind them. Pieces flew off it as Balthazar fell and the wooden tongue was ripped right off. Malvolio reached the water and began drinking in great gulps, while behind him both the wagon and Balthazar lay broken.

Fortunately no one had been riding in the wagon. We all ran to Balthazar as Louise galloped up on her horse. She leaped down and pulled out her gun. Without a word she fired a single shot and our ox was dead. She looked up into Toby's shocked face.

'I'm sorry,' she said. 'His leg was broken.'

'It was the kind thing to do,' explained Buddle, putting his hand on Toby's shoulder. Everyone stood there in a state of shock until Cornelius began gathering pieces of wood to fix our wagon once more.

'Get the nails, Jack,' ordered Da. 'Toby, catch Malvolio again.'

We all got to work but no one spoke.

Our wagon was now a rickety mess pulled only by our last ox. We were sad, but perhaps we understood Malvolio's madness. What a relief it was for us all to have cold, fresh water that wasn't muddy and didn't smell. There was trout in the river, and plenty of firewood. We caught deer and wild ducks.

'We could just stay here,' said Toby, fearful of being somewhere without food. He did not want anyone to suggest eating his beloved pig.

Louise shook her head. 'The tops of the mountains ahead are white,' she said. 'We don't have long. Light snows have already fallen.'

Talk of snow was everywhere. One night Buddle told the story of the Donner party – a group from Illinois who'd set out two years before to go to California. There had been twenty wagons and eighty-nine people led by two brothers, George and Jacob Donner.

'They set out too late,' warned Buddle, 'got snowbound

and were trapped for months with hardly any food. Nobody found them till late February. There were just forty-seven folks left and they were half starved. They only survived because they had eaten . . .'

'What?' asked Toby breathlessly.

Buddle lowered his voice to a whisper. 'Some of the people who died,' he said.

If Toby had thought of staying put before, now he just wanted to get going, but the going was slow and hard. There were rivers to cross with freezing cold water. Wagons got stuck on the stony river beds and the chill of the water made the oxen's hoofs soft. Some developed such tender feet that they could no longer pull the wagons. The sound of a gunshot putting an animal out of its misery became commonplace.

I caught Jeni on her knees praying out loud to be shown the way.

'Don't tell,' said Louise, coming up behind me. 'Be strong, Slim.'

'I am,' I said. 'We have Wakan Tanka on our side. He is Mapiya's god and he will watch over us.'

Louise nodded. 'Well, if we have all the gods, then we can't go wrong.'

Everyone made traps for food. Nothing was wasted. Cows died and Nashobanowa used their heads for bait. One night Cornelius caught a fox, which tasted surprisingly nice. Toby didn't want to eat it, but in the end his hunger won.

We knew we were on the right track when we reached a place on the Bear River called Thomas Fork Crossing. Someone had built two bridges there, and it felt like civilization. We were all happy to pay a dollar a wagon if it meant we didn't have to get back into the water.

The rain fell and it felt as cold as a raw November day. Now the land fell away into the steepest and longest hill we had yet encountered. Going up was tricky but coming down was worse.

'What do they call this?' I asked Buddle.

'Big Hill,' he replied. I thought it was a joke, but I found out later that was actually its name.

We began to see some small farms starting. At last there were people who had decided to stop and stay.

'Soil's good,' said Da. 'Make good potatoes.'

The nicest place we stopped at was called Clover Creek. It had beautiful flowers. I know that because I still have Bea's drawings of their bright pink and purple heads with delicate grasses whose wispy white hair blew in the breeze. Everyone was exhausted but the sight made us a little more cheerful. Sometimes our evenings even finished with music and singing. I remember those nights. The sound of the tinkling bells on the cows, the bushes and grass covered with washed clothes; men in groups, chatting or reading, others rambling across the meadows and hillsides, and some bathing, fishing and playing games.

Nashobanowa turned us north, and at last we felt we were heading in the right direction. We made a small detour to visit Soda Springs because we had heard from others that it was amazing. Water spouted from the ground and tasted fizzy.

'Iron and carbon dioxide,' explained Cornelius, who loved the science. Everyone else just liked the taste.

'Like flat beer,' declared Buddle.

Some of the springs belched out water more than others. Toby took a bet that he could squelch one by sitting on it, but all that happened was he bobbed up and down on the steady stream of water.

How Da laughed at him. 'Toby, you'll be pounded into beefsteak,' he declared.

There was also hot water, which pumped up in places, so lots of the women did laundry. Puffs of steam issued from the earth like the noise from the escape pipe of a boiler on a paddle steamer.

We walked on. Jeni didn't need to pray any more nor Cornelius to use his spyglass to look ahead. We could find our way just by the smell of dead cattle. One time Louise's horse stepped into a hornets' nest. She was thrown out of the saddle with her foot still stuck in the stirrup. She got dragged over rocky sand and sagebrush, and was badly bruised. For a few days Jack took charge of getting the train ready in the morning. He limped up and down giving orders. I was so proud of him and I could see Da was too.

'That's my boy!' called Da, and Jack beamed. It was ten days from Big Hill to Fort Hall. By the time we arrived we were a ragged army with broken wagons and not even half the animals we had set out with. The fort was a square, shabby place of mud brick. The walls were solid on the outside, except for a gate or two, and portholes. Inside the square court there were houses on all four sides.

Cornelius smiled at Bea, who couldn't stop grinning. 'Welcome to civilization.'

Again traders were selling goods at ridiculous prices. There were sad-looking Indian squaws stretched out on piles of buffalo robes; Mexicans, armed with bows and arrows; long-haired Canadians and trappers, and American men who could be spotted by their brown clothes and the bowie knives displayed at their sides.

We felt relieved to have arrived. So far Parker Crossingham had not tracked us.

'He's far behind, I'm sure,' said Da confidently.

But he wasn't. He was there. Standing in Fort Hall as we walked in.

CHAPTER TWENTY-THREE

Parker Crossingham stood in the open centre of the fort, all in black except for a narrow red string tie with a silver skull at his neck. He was not alone. Behind him and slightly to one side stood Nervous Bob.

'There they are!' said Bob, pointing, his eyes filled with hatred. 'I told you I could find them!'

We had all walked in together, but now we stopped in dead silence. Jack, Kate, Nashobanowa and Cornelius had no idea who this man was so it took them a moment to realize that the rest of us were not moving. I think the whole fort came to a stop. Everyone could smell trouble ahead.

Crossingham was smoking his usual cigar when we entered. He looked at us and smiled as if he had laid a very successful trap. He took a great puff of the cigar, blew out the smoke and then threw the thing to the ground, grinding the stub into the dust with the heel of his boot. His black boots had silver spurs and as he slowly walked towards us they jingled in the silence.

'Well . . .' He half laughed as he spoke. 'If it isn't my favourite Irish runaways, the Hannigans. I have to say, I think you made it almost too easy for me to find you. Signing your names at Register Cliff, was it? And Independence Rock?'

'I'm sorry, Da,' I cried, feeling it was my fault. 'We didn't know. Everyone was doing it.'

'You can do nothing here, Crossingham,' said Da firmly.

Now Crossingham laughed out loud. He stepped right up to Da. He was taller and looked down on him.

'Do you hear that, Bob?' he asked Nervous Bob, who had followed close behind. 'Says we can do nothing. Isn't it funny how two people can have such a difference of opinion? Have you met my friend Bob? He doesn't seem to like you lot.'

Crossingham reached into his pocket. I thought he had a gun and I pulled mine from my belt, ready to defend the family.

Crossingham looked at me. 'I see you've adopted a German boy as a guard. Curious choice.' Instead of a gun he pulled out a folded piece of paper.

'I have an arrest warrant for' – he glanced at the paper as if to check – 'one Henry Hannigan from the court in Dublin itself. A warrant for deportation for "crimes against the state". The Americans won't want a criminal on their shores now, will they? I'm sure they'll be glad that I want to rid them of such' – he practically spat the word – 'vermin.'

'Henry is not with us,' declared Da, fixing his eyes on Crossingham's. 'You won't find him.'

Just then we noticed the young man from the Dematinee Strolling Players walking across the courtyard with posters in his hand.

'Look!' whispered Jack urgently to me. 'Henry's name might be on those!'

Parker Crossingham was looking at all of us. 'Where is Margaret?' he suddenly demanded.

'Margaret?' asked Kate.

'Ma,' I whispered back. 'She was Margaret or Peggy.'

Da kept looking Crossingham in the eye and said nothing.

'She died,' I said loudly. 'Now leave us alone!'

Da was right that words can be more powerful than anything. Parker Crossingham looked like a man who had been punched in the stomach. I knew he had once loved Ma very much and it showed in his face. Until I told him, it was clear that he hadn't known she was dead. He swallowed hard, and for a moment he was silent.

Da said nothing. Instead he turned and began to walk away.

'Let's go!' said Kate, shooing us along to follow him.

As he walked Da leaned towards Toby and whispered, 'Quick! Take Jack with you and make sure there are no posters up anywhere for Henry's show here in the fort. We don't want your brother found.'

Toby grabbed Jack by the hand and they raced off.

Da paused outside the store door. Crossingham hadn't moved. He took a slim holder from his pocket and removed a cigar. Then he bit the end off, spat it out and put the cigar carefully in his mouth as he continued to stare at us.

'I don't think the law in Ireland can reach this far,' whispered Cornelius to Da. I knew he was trying to help but no one was sure he was right. Maybe the Americans wouldn't want someone who seemed to be a criminal to stay here.

'He'll never find Henry,' soothed Kate, although she too sounded unsure. 'They headed south. A long way from here.'

'No. Only to perform at Fort Bridger,' I said, 'and that's not far! After that, who knows where? If there are posters going up, then they will be heading this way.'

Da nodded. 'It's not like Sir Hugh Magnum keeps himself quiet.'

'Maybe I should go and look for Henry,' I suggested. 'Warn him.'

Kate shook her head. 'No, Slim, you are not going anywhere. I couldn't bear it.'

'I could find him,' offered Nashobanowa, but we needed him to guide us. We knew we would never make it to Oregon on our own.

None of us knew what to do. Meanwhile we had urgent work to get on with. Malvolio's last charge towards the water of Green River had pretty much finished off our wagon. It had never been that strong to begin with and now it was literally falling apart at the seams.

Da, Cornelius and Jack spent hours trying to see if it could be repaired. There was a blacksmith's shop with a furnace and an anvil and they went to get advice. I tagged along. The beat of the hammer and the roar of the fire made me long for home. If I closed my eyes I could take myself back to Uncle Aedan's shop in Ireland.

'Do you think Uncle Aedan and Aunt Eimear are all right?' I asked Da.

He smiled at me. 'We shall send for them,' he replied. 'One day we shall send for them.'

I liked that he said that, but I don't think either of us believed it.

Everyone who knew anything about wagons shook their heads at the state of ours. We had no money for a new one but Louise and Jeni were sure it didn't matter.

'I've asked around,' said Louise, 'and most folks say no one can make it to the Pacific Ocean from here with any kind of wagon.'

'Everyone says the way is too difficult and everyone ought to swap to mules anyway,' added Jeni.

Louise nodded. 'Besides, the snow is coming and we can make more speed with mules. No one wants to die in the Blue Mountains.'

No one wanted to die at all.

Toby led our faithful Malvolio down to the river. He was sore-necked, sore-footed and exhausted. Toby unhitched him for the last time and we all had a tear in our eye as we said goodbye. Toby hugged and hugged him, saying, 'Thank you for helping us. You stay here now, Malvolio. You can have a rest. No more work now.'

We turned to leave. Toby began sobbing and Malvolio gave a great bellow.

'He needs me!' cried Toby, and Da had to put his arm around him to lead him away.

'He will have a good life,' promised Nashobanowa, ruffling Toby's hair, and I hope he was right. I like to think that grand beast, who did so much for us, lived out his days grazing by the riverbank.

Mr Grant, who was in charge of the fort, was offering to buy wagons but he gave almost no money for them. We got a little for the scrap metal so Kate had to sell the last of her cloth and Jack his nails. It was enough to buy just four mules from some Mexican traders. The men had also brought buckskin shirts, pantaloons and moccasins to trade. My boots had quite fallen apart and I would have loved some moccasins but we had no spare money.

As I looked at the shoes for sale I saw Crossingham standing with one foot up on a ledge. He had on brand-new, shiny black boots. Slowly he took a white handkerchief from his pocket and gave the boots a quick polish. Then he looked straight at me and gave a horrible smile. Everywhere we went Crossingham followed and watched us. Bob was his constant shadow.

'I think we shall all be barefoot,' declared Kate as her own shoes fell apart. 'Why, how nice to feel the mountains under our feet!'

The mules were all in a large corral. Most of them were young and had never been used for work before. Catching them was hard, and leading them out of the pen even harder. Sometimes half a dozen men would be hanging onto the ropes attached to one mule, who was kicking them away. Buddle showed us how to use a 'nose stick', a loop of rope attached to a stick. Buddle managed to get the loop round the upper lip of the animal and then twist the stick to tighten it. No matter how vicious and stubborn the mule was, it would give in.

Getting them to let us place our stuff on their backs was another matter. The Mexican showed us how to divide our things into packs, which were put together in two parts and lashed on with rope. The mules were always the same about this in the beginning. At first they would stand stock-still and then, as soon as everything was in place, they would rush madly off, kicking till they were free of their load.

Bea was busy trying to sort out what supplies we needed for the journey. No one even discussed the printing press. That was definitely coming with us, but we couldn't take so many other things and she dashed about getting advice on what was essential. The first day we were there she was carrying a small frying pan which she had swapped for our Dutch oven, when she bumped right into Crossingham. She was startled and dropped the pan with a gasp. He took off his black hat and tipped his head towards her.

'Looking for me, Miss Hannigan?'

Bea was flustered. She bent down to get the pan but so did he, grabbing her arm as he did so.

'Let her go!' demanded Cornelius, racing across the centre of the fort.

Crossingham laughed and put both his hands in the air, saying, 'Why, if it isn't a knight in shining armour!'

Cornelius took Bea away, but Crossingham called out to my sister, 'You come with me, Beatrice, and we can forget the whole matter with your brother!'

After that Crossingham haunted her. He always said the same thing – that Bea could protect all of us by going away with him. It made Cornelius so furious. In the end he wouldn't let her go anywhere without him by her side. At night as we made our camp you would see the light from the end of Crossingham's cigar as he stood nearby watching us.

Lots of people swapped their horses for new animals. Chronicle was still not well. Nashobanowa put a special liniment on him every day and helped me massage his legs, but it didn't look good. I had found a nice tree for shade and some grass for my horse when we first arrived. He lay on the ground under the wide branches, looking weak.

'Maybe he should stay here,' suggested my Choctaw friend gently, and I lost my temper.

'Chronicle is not doing anything except going with me,' I shouted. 'He is my friend and I thought you were too.'

Nashobanowa didn't say a word and I was sorry straight away that I had got angry. Tears filled my eyes and I turned away in time to see Nervous Bob walk past muttering, 'Damn Injuns!'

We might have been hundreds of miles from a town but the place was busy. There were about five hundred Snake Indians camped near the fort, but they soon headed off to fight battles with the Sioux.

'I don't know why we can't all just get along,' murmured Kate, who was endlessly trying to wash all our clothes and sort our things. Crossingham's constant hovering had made Bea afraid. She had become so strong on the journey, but now she sat in the wagon, hopeless at helping.

Kate kept making lists of food. There were two Mormon

families making butter and cheese. It looked so tempting but we couldn't afford it. We had very little left to eat – just some bacon and a little dried buffalo meat – so Kate spent a little of our money on some flour, but it was a dollar a pound, which was some of the most expensive we had ever seen. Mr Grant of the fort was growing corn, peas and fine potatoes.

Da crouched down to look at the plants. 'You think we'll grow our own potatoes again, Slim?' he asked, gently stroking the leaves in wonder.

I looked at the green leaves and remembered Ireland and how the potatoes had failed us.

'We wouldn't be here if it weren't for the potatoes,' I said, thinking about all that had happened. I didn't know if I would ever want to grow them again. The truth is, I couldn't imagine being in one place long enough to grow anything. I had stopped imagining life ahead. For months I had dreamed of being in Oregon and making our newspaper; now all I thought was that we should run. Run away from Crossingham.

Nashobanowa was ready to guide us once more, but he had never been this far west. He had done his best to get directions but mostly it involved following the trail of the people who had gone last year.

'I can follow a trail,' he reassured us, but everyone was becoming jittery.

There were people who, having arrived at the comfort of the fort, did not want to continue. They were full of terrible warnings.

'The snow will get you. You'll die of eternal cold.'

'There'll be no food! Death by starvation!'

'The Blackfeet Indians want nothing but blood!'

Da and Kate said they had 'no time for such nonsense', but I knew they talked about it between themselves.

One morning Kate had sent me to buy another half-pound of flour. I was just walking into the fort when I nearly got knocked over by a horse and rider leaving at high speed. I looked up to see Nervous Bob galloping away from the fort. Parker Crossingham stood leaning against the fort gates as I passed by.

'You must miss Henry,' he declared. 'That must be awful.' Crossingham took off his black hat and began brushing it carefully with his hand. It was fancy, with a silver band and I could see it was very expensive. I hated him. I hated his hat.

I tried to ignore him and carry on walking, but he grabbed my arm and pulled me close to his face, sneering, 'Good job for you that I know where he is, your brother. He's giving a little show south of here as a matter of fact. My friend Bob is going to bring him home for a touching Hannigan reunion. Won't that be nice?'

I felt sick. I pulled myself away from Crossingham and

ran as fast as I could to tell Da. He was standing with Kate as I reached him. 'We have to save Henry!' I cried, telling them what had happened.

Kate put her hand to her mouth and whispered, 'Oh no!' She turned to Da. 'What shall we do?'

Da shook his head in despair. The truth is, no one knew what to do. I realized that all the adults had become agitated since we'd arrived at the fort. Even Louise, who had always been so calm, was not her usual self. I think it was because Jeni kept saying, 'We have to set off now or we'll be too late!'

Da did not know what to do. He didn't dare let any of us go after Nervous Bob but he wanted to protect Henry.

'Oh, Kate,' I heard him agonize, 'I want to warn Henry, but I can't leave the rest of the family again. I need to look after you all.'

Cornelius ran into the Walkers from Missouri, the large family who we had met so many weeks ago.

'We're going that way,' said Mr Walker; 'the way the theatre people went. Let us look for your son. We can manage. You know we will take care of him.'

It was the best option we had. We had to trust him.

'We don't really know them. They're practically strangers!' said Kate.

'No,' said Nashobanowa, 'they are just friends who we don't know so well yet.'

'We have to leave!' urged Louise.

I ran to the shady spot where Chronicle had been resting since we arrived. I was relieved to see that he was on his feet, though his head still hung down. I put my arms around his neck and hugged him close.

'We have to go now, Chronicle, so you have to be well. You have to come with me.'

I couldn't bear to leave him behind, but I wasn't at all sure he could manage any more. As I stood there, Chronicle gently lifted his head and seemed to give a little shake. Then I swear he looked at me, and it was as if we understood each other. I reached for his mane, and for the first time in ages pulled myself up on his back. I settled myself with his reins and he almost nodded before we slowly walked towards the others.

Once more we set off, and yet again our group was smaller than before. Our train had split into three smaller groups – there were the ones who headed south like the Walkers, others who were going to continue with their wagons, and those of us with just mules would go ahead alone. There was Buddle, Louise, Jeni, Cornelius, Nasho-banowa, the Hannigans and a family from Michigan who had just joined us.

'Let's see now!' declared Cornelius, trying to make Da smile. 'What is this new wagon train made of? Two old women, an Irish family with a printing press, a family from Michigan, a mad inventor, a Choctaw Indian man, a pig called Hamlet, a dog called Dog, some mules, a horse with a limp, a couple of milk cows and a man with a wooden leg.' Cornelius clapped Da on the back. 'Why, it's the travelling troupe of your dreams, Patrick!'

Da did smile but I could see how hard he found it.

Again we set out over the burning sands and through trackless deserts. We started out with all our belongings balanced on the back of our mules, and within a mile everything was swinging under their bellies. We'd no sooner righted one pack than the next one would be heading for the ground. I swear the mules were laughing at us, but if they weren't, then Parker Crossingham was. He rode alongside us, keeping a slight distance but never out of sight.

It made Bea crazy. 'Maybe I should go with him!' she began to say, which made Da furious. 'Then you have to tell him to leave us alone, Da!' she pleaded.

Jack wanted to deal with it, but it was Cornelius who rode over to Crossingham and demanded to know what he wanted. The terrible man just shrugged and said he was 'heading west like everyone else'.

Cornelius came back shaking his head. 'There's nothing we can do,' he sighed. 'We can't stop him following us.'

He was right, and so we walked on and Crossingham followed, winding along the track, sneering at us continuously and making everyone feel afraid.

'I should have gone after Henry,' Da kept repeating.

Kate tried to soothe him but I could see that my father was wretched at the choice he had had to make. Protect us or Henry.

Before long we began to follow the Snake River, and once more life became routine. Day after day we crossed valleys and rolling hills covered with sagebrush. Nashobanowa, Louise and Cornelius did their best to guide us, but there was not much to go on in terms of 'following people who had gone before'. Sometimes you could see the marks of wheels or broken bushes where wagons had pushed their way through. Sometimes there was nothing but the droppings from horses or mules. Jack became very good at finding a way forward. Nashobanowa and I rode ahead as scouts to see if we could work out which way to go. Chronicle was stronger every day. We would look for water to camp by, and the sight of ashes from other people's fires was always comforting.

One morning we met some Bannock Indians. They carried bags made of salmon skin and Kate traded bread for a beautiful piece of pottery.

'We can't eat that!' complained Toby, but Da smiled at the dish Kate had purchased.

'We're not dead yet, my son. We can still appreciate beauty,' he said.

Neither Louise nor Nashobanowa could speak their language so we couldn't talk to each other. Cornelius tried to make a map on the ground and ask the way. He built little mountains of earth with pebbles for rocks and twigs for trees, but no one was sure what anyone was saying.

'We'll follow the river,' declared Louise, and Nashobanowa agreed.

The walk along the Snake was dry and level, but thick with sagebrush and greasewood. We were all barefoot now and everyone had to keep stopping to sit down and pull the thorns of prickly pear out of our now bare toes. The river cut a deep groove more than a quarter of a mile deep in the plain and the slope down to it was very steep. There was plenty of grass, and one night the few cattle we had were grazing on the slope. Two of the Michigan boys, whose names I forget, were rolling rocks down the slope into the river. Sometimes the splash threw the water thirty feet high. You could see it was fun, but the boys were not thinking about the cows. Toby ran towards the animals just as one of the boys started a stone the size of a cannonball in the direction of a young calf grazing near the foot of the slope. Toby cried out for the animal to get out of the way but it was too late. The poor calf was killed as if it had been hit by lightning and everyone was very cross.

Louise and Nashobanowa had decided we would take a route via something called Goodale's Cut-off, which followed traditional Shoshoni and Bannock paths, north of the Snake River plain. It cut miles off the journey but we crossed terrible land which Cornelius said looked like the 'craters of the moon'. It was something called 'lava', which he explained is black rock from a fire deep in the earth.

'Looks like hard black vomit to me,' said Jack.

'Bad luck to the man who is such a sinner as to have to seek refuge in such a country as this,' muttered Jeni.

Crossingham's shadow continued to fall across our path.

Sometimes he would call out to Da, 'Maybe we could come to a deal? Let me have Beatrice!' Or, worse still, he would call out in a rage about Ma. 'You killed her, Patrick Hannigan! You killed that beautiful woman. She should have been mine!'

'Ignore him, Patrick,' counselled Kate, and we walked on.

'What's that about?' asked Cornelius.

I shrugged. 'A long time ago that man wanted to marry my Ma,' I explained.

'But she chose your father?' asked Cornelius. I nodded. 'Good choice,' he said.

There was a terrifying place called the Devil's Backbone. It was a very narrow ridge with a drop of a thousand feet into a gorge on the left and a sheer cliff face on the right down to the Snake River, which was so far away it looked like a ribbon about four inches wide. The path was narrow and crooked.

There was arguing. The Michigans didn't like something about the route Louise and Nashobanowa had chosen.

'Don't know why you trust those Indians,' grumbled the man, so once more we split into a smaller group. Now all that was left was my family, Louise and Jeni, Cornelius, Buddle and 'that Indian'.

I looked at Nashobanowa, who had been the best friend in the world to all of us, who had brought Da to us. How could anyone talk about him like that?

Everyone was exhausted. Buddle found the walking impossible and Jack was often out of breath. I think his leg hurt but he wouldn't say.

In the valley carved by the Boise River at last we found some calm. There was shade and firewood and salmon in the water. There were mobs of rabbits to catch and eat, but one morning Da found that someone had taken our rifle from the side of our cart. It meant I had the only guns and was sent out each day to bring home meat. I had become a good shot and Jack would come with me to gather up our supper. We could see the Rocky Mountains in the distance as we gradually climbed. It was good, but we never stopped feeling threatened.

At night Cornelius would tell us stories about the railway he said would one day cross the plains, but no one believed him. He was just trying to distract us. We ate fruit from black hawthorns which was delicious and sweet. We hadn't had fruit for so long, but Jeni said she'd heard a woman had died from eating too many.

'Every pleasure we find has pain in it,' moaned Bea, who hated the journey more than ever.

We met other Indian tribes – Walla Walla, Nez Perce and Cayuse. They were all different and no one was unkind. We traded a little scrap iron with the Cayuse for *yampa* – some small white roots half an inch thick or less, and twice as long. Nashobanowa showed Kate how to bake the roots in the ground under heated stones or make them into bread. 'Nez Perce' meant pierced nose. Buddle said they had been named by Canadian trappers but it was a poor name because, to Toby's disappointment, not one we met had a hole in their nose. They showed us how to gather 'camas', which were the shape and colour of an onion and could be boiled like a potato. We met Walla Walla people who had many cows. I think some of them had never seen white children and women. They wanted to see everything, look in everything, and they wanted tobacco. Some of the women had amazing woven hats shaped like upside-down pots on their heads. They carried babies encased in sacks made of a dressed hide with a board attached to support the back of the child.

'It's called a papoose,' explained Buddle as the little round chubby faces of the babies stared at us.

'They're like the cocoons of some kind of insect,' marvelled Cornelius.

At night, as our campfires burned, Indians would often appear with a noiseless tread. You could see them standing with a blanket round their shoulders, watching but not coming near.

I think we thought it was more Indians when we heard a horse approach late one night. Someone was cursing and shouting. Da went to look and we could hear him shouting, 'Let him go!'

Jack, Toby and I, followed by Bea and Kate, all raced to the sound of his voice, only to be stopped in our tracks. Nervous Bob had caught Henry. My poor brother looked terrible. He was filthy. His wrists were tied together in front of him with a long rope which was attached to Bob's saddle. Bob kicked his horse along, dragging Henry, who ran behind, struggling to stay on his feet. Parker Crossingham rode alongside laughing. He pulled up in front of us so sharply that dust and dirt flew up at us. He had a rifle which he pointed at Da. He leaned down and practically spat in my father's face.

'I told you I would have my revenge,' he declared.

'No court in the land will let you take my son,' shouted Da, lunging at him, but Cornelius arrived just in time to hold him back, afraid the terrible man would shoot.

Crossingham laughed, a short bark of a sound. 'Court? You think I will bother with a court? There is no law around here for hundreds of miles.' He jumped down from his horse holding up his rifle. 'This, oh, and this!' From the side of his saddle he produced our rifle, the one which had gone missing and which he had clearly stolen from us. 'These are the law!' He pointed both guns at Da. 'You ruined my life, Patrick Hannigan, and now I, Parker Crossingham, am your worst nightmare.'

'No,' called a voice in the dark, 'you are mistaken.'

Out of the gloom rode an old man with white hair. He had a pure white horse and I knew him immediately. It was Lord Cardswell.

Da gasped.

'I, Parker Crossingham,' said Lord Cardswell, 'am *your* worst nightmare.'

'Who is that?' whispered Toby.

'That,' I said with pride, 'is our grandfather.'

CHAPTER TWENTY-FOUR

Lord Cardswell had a gun, but it was a small pistol and no match for a rifle. Another horse appeared out of the darkness. It was Ma's sister, Esther. She looked thinner than before and was covered with the layer of dust that we all carried, but still she looked noble.

'It's our grandfather and Ma's sister!' I cried with such delight that Hero began clapping her hands, thinking something wonderful was happening.

'Our grandfather?' said Toby in disbelief. I realized I was the only one who had met them before.

'Yes!' I cried. 'Our grandfather and Ma's sister, Aunt Esther.' I turned to Bea, grinning. 'She's lovely.'

I think no one knew what to say.

Aunt Esther rode forward until she stood right in front of Parker Crossingham.

'What are you doing, Parker?' she demanded quietly,

and I could see right away that this was not a woman to be trifled with. I was thrilled.

Crossingham seemed unnerved by the appearance of my aunt and grandfather. He had worked for the Cardswells, but that was back in Ireland.

'What . . . what . . . what am *I* doing?' he replied haltingly. 'What are *you* doing? What are you doing here?' he finally managed, still pointing the rifle at Da's head.

'I came to protect my family,' replied Lord Cardswell. 'Put the gun down, Parker, and let the boy go.' Grandfather pointed to Henry, who still stood shaking at the knees and tied to the rope from Bob's horse.

Crossingham shook his head. 'Margaret is dead, Lord Cardswell. Do you know that?' he snapped.

Esther gasped. 'Is it true?' she whispered.

Da nodded.

'He killed her!' yelled Crossingham, pointing at Da with the gun.

'That's not true!' protested Henry, his voice weak and exhausted.

Hero had been dancing about clapping her little hands. She had no idea what was happening. Just then Kate picked her up and stepped forward. 'Slim, is this really your grandfather?' she asked me.

'Yes!' I said, delighted by how things were turning out. 'This is Lord Cardswell.'

Kate gave a slight curtsy as she said, 'No one killed Peggy, sir. I was there. I'm sorry to say she died giving birth. On the journey. It was terrible, but she brought this beautiful child into the world. I'd like you to meet your youngest grandchild. This is Hero Hannigan.'

She held my baby sister up for Lord Cardswell to take. His face was a terrible mix of emotions. He looked so sad and yet so determined. He reached down for Hero and pulled her up onto his horse. He looked at her for a moment and then hugged her as if he would never let her go. Hero gurgled with delight.

Bob didn't seem at all certain what to do. He toyed with the rope as if he were going to let Henry go, but I could see he was afraid of what Crossingham might do to him.

Then my grandfather turned back to Crossingham. 'I learned too late that you had torn down Margaret's house. That you tormented her family. It has to stop now.'

'Should I let him go?' muttered Bob to Crossingham, nodding at Henry.

'No you should not!' shouted Crossingham. He grabbed for the rope and pulled it hard so that Henry fell to his knees. Bob didn't know what to do. He sat on his horse, wide-eyed, with Henry still attached but lying on the ground.

'You should have let me marry Margaret!' Crossingham was in a rage now, shouting at my grandfather. 'You should have let me marry your daughter!'

Lord Cardswell sighed. 'Margaret was never going to do anything other than what she wanted. I should have respected that.'

'Well, respect this!' Crossingham said, suddenly clicking back the triggers on both the rifles and pointing them at us.

'I don't think so,' said a woman's voice. Louise stepped forward, pointing her gun at Crossingham.

Parker Crossingham laughed. 'An old woman!'

'No,' came another voice. 'Two old women!' Jeni joined her with her gun ready.

Crossingham still sniggered but he took a step back. As he did so he fell, for he had not seen Buddle come up behind him, ready to trip him with his wooden leg. Crossingham dropped both rifles, and I moved towards him with both my pistols drawn.

'You wouldn't dare fire those,' said Crossingham.

'I wouldn't bet on it,' I replied. 'That's my family you're messing about with.' I took careful aim and shot his stupid black hat clean off his head. He scrambled backwards in the dust looking wild-eyed and frightened. He tried to reach his horse but the gunfire had frightened the animal and it turned to run off in the night.

'This is not the end!' cried Crossingham as Louise aimed her gun at him. He turned to run, and as he did so Toby got out his slingshot and aimed a rock right at his backside.

'No, but that's your end!' he shouted with delight as Crossingham scampered to get away.

Nervous Bob was still standing there holding onto Henry. Any courage he had now disappeared. He looked the same nervous man we had always known.

Da turned to him and said quietly, 'My son, please.'

It was hard to know what Bob might have done but he was faced by a lot of determined people. He slowly let Henry go, and when Jeni cocked her rifle he gave a slight scream before riding off into the dark as fast as he could. One day we would see him and Crossingham again, but not in this story.

How Lord Cardswell and Esther fussed over us. How sorry my grandfather was about how we had been treated and how sad about Ma's passing. He hugged Hero and me, squeezed Toby to him, and shook Henry's hand so hard I think it hurt.

'I'm sorry, Lord Cardswell, if I did not behave well,' said Henry.

The old man shook his head. He would not hear of it.

'I was the fool, Henry. I should never have treated your Ma as I did, or indeed any of the people who lived on my land.'

'Are you really my grandfather?' asked Toby.

Lord Cardswell smiled and nodded. 'I am.'

'I'd better call you that then,' said Toby, and we all agreed.

Then Grandfather stood in front of Da, put his hand out and said, 'I have been a foolish old man, Patrick Hannigan, and I apologize. I only wish Margaret had been here to see me try to put it right.'

Da swallowed hard and put his hand out too.

The sun was rising by the time all the talk had died down and Louise called order.

'Might as well get going. Miles to cover, miles to cover,' she shouted.

She was right. More rivers to cross, more land to walk, but now we did it with our aunt and grandfather riding with us.

At Farewell Bend we said goodbye to the Snake River. Ahead a huge climb up a rocky bluff tested our final reserves of energy. They call it Flagstaff Hill now, but then it was just another terrible obstacle in our way. The ground was littered with loose rocks and all the men had to help Jack drag the printing press on a cart behind them. Kate could hardly get her breath.

'Air is thinner up here,' explained Louise as she and Jeni helped her keep going. Behind us lay the harsh, dry canyons of the Snake, but as we finally reached the top we all took a deep breath, for ahead lay the most wonderful view – rolling country and endless places for pasture. We had not seen anything so lush and green since we left Ireland.

'Look at those magnificent trees,' sighed Da. Huge

banks of them lay before us, reminding me of the forest at home where I would wander with Ma picking mushrooms.

'I wish we could stay here,' I said.

'I want to stay here,' said Bea.

Nashobanowa smiled at us all. 'You can. This is it. This is Oregon. Welcome home.'

'We did it!' marvelled Henry.

Jack put down the handles of his cart. He was sweating from the effort of the climb, but now he couldn't stop grinning. 'We made it! Slim! We made it!' he shouted, and began to dance about. He picked Hero up in his arms and threw her high in the air so that she laughed with delight. Cornelius grabbed Bea by the waist and began to whirl her round. Jeni and Louise clapped their hands and wept as Aunt Esther hugged me to her. Toby ran to Grandfather and hugged him, making the old man smile with delight.

This was the place, exactly as we had imagined it.

'Soil that will grow trees like these will grow anything,' declared Da as he put his arm round Kate.

'Have we done it? Can we stop?' asked Toby.

Nashobanowa shook his head. 'Not quite.'

Da nodded in agreement. 'This is the territory of Oregon, but we have a ways to go before we get to Uncle Niall's.'

'Don't you worry, Toby. The end is in sight!' declared Louise.

'Our future,' sighed Kate.

'A new beginning,' promised my grandfather.

But we also saw the Blue Mountains in the distance. We could see a white blanket of snow on the high points as they rose above a layer of cloud. They looked beautiful, but terrifying too. It was cold now and we all shivered.

We had been so excited to be in Oregon, but now the climb up the mountains was terrible. Sometimes it was so steep it was as though we had to go up winding stairs. In some places the land was almost straight up over our heads and the animals seemed to dread it as much as we did. No sooner had we gained a foot on the mountain than a steeper, more dreadful path was ahead of us. The hills were covered with rocks from the size of your fist to giant boulders. At night heavy frost covered everything and ice formed in the water buckets.

In the day it was warm and we sweated and strained, but there was no time to dawdle.

Jeni became tired and bad-tempered. 'What are we doing? We'll get there and we'll have nothing. No house, no clothes, no food. I'm sorry, Louise. I'm so sorry.' Jeni began to cry, and no amount of coaxing from Louise could make her feel better.

It was as if we all just realized what we had done. We were thousands of miles from our homes and relatives, without money or anywhere to live, amongst strangers in a new land. More time was spent shedding tears than sleeping that night. It was Grandfather who kept us going. He was easily the oldest but had become the most determined.

'I missed the life I could have had with my family back in Ireland and none of your moaning is going to stop me having it in Oregon. Keep going. I do believe we will reach the promised land.'

The journey had changed Grandfather. He was not the grumpy man I had first met at the grand house in Ireland. He was interested in everything and everyone. I asked him endless questions about his life and his house. He and Nashobanowa got on so well, while Aunt Esther, Bea and Kate could never seem to have enough chat.

It turned out that Grandfather had travelled the world. One night he sat with Jack, who showed him his magic box.

'I know these!' said Grandfather. 'They're marvellous.' He began to play with the box. To us it looked just as it had always done, a nicely decorated piece of wood about the size of a brick, but Grandfather thought differently.

'As a young man,' he continued, 'I travelled in China.'

'China!' exclaimed Toby, his eyes wide with amazement. I was cleaning my guns and sat back to enjoy a good story.

Esther smiled as she and Kate cooked our supper and Bea drew pictures. Grandfather seemed to find a little indent in the box. He pushed it and a piece of the wood slid to one side.

476

'Oh my goodness,' breathed Jack. 'It moved! Slim, something opened!'

'Not open yet,' said Grandfather, carefully turning the box over in his hands.

Cornelius was watching.

'Yes,' continued Grandfather, 'I recall sailing to Pagoda Island, to a place called Mawei. You would like it, Jack; it is the cradle of Chinese seamanship, and the site of marvellous giant rocks with magnificent Chinese names, such as "Double Turtle Guarding Door", "Five Tigers Defending Gate" and "Warriors' Leg".'

As he told the story, Grandfather continued to turn the box over and find small new pieces of wood which slid and moved.

'Sailors have been trading there with lands across the ocean before most of China knew that seas existed,' he went on. 'The authorities gave me a house built of boards over the river, which flooded twice a day. I had very little to do but I did have one of these.'

Grandfather held up the box, which now had many slim sections of wood that had moved about the basic shape. Jack couldn't speak. He sat with his mouth open, not daring to move as Grandfather played with the magic box. Esther and Kate put down their cooking things to watch, Bea stopped drawing and Da gave up cutting the meat he'd been dealing with as we all began paying attention to the strange moving wood of the box.

'What do you think, Cornelius?' Grandfather asked.

Cornelius thought for a moment before tapping a piece on the side.

'That one,' he replied.

Grandfather nodded. He had wonderfully delicate fingers. Gently he pushed against one side of the box and a tiny bit moved. Then he turned it and pushed another, and something else moved. He did this about a dozen times, until at last one side of the box slid open to reveal a secret compartment, inside which lay a piece of folded paper. We were all amazed.

'It is magic,' sighed Jack, his face alive with wonder.

'Yes,' agreed Grandfather. He opened the piece of paper and looked at it. Then he peered at Jack.

'Where did you get this, Jack?' he asked.

'His father,' I couldn't help replying. 'His father left it to him. Said it would look after him if he could get to Oregon.'

'And so it will.' Grandfather handed the paper to Jack, who began to read.

He shook his head as if it didn't make sense.

Bea took it from him and tipped it towards the fire so she could see better. 'Oh my,' she said.

'What is it?' I asked.

'It's called a deed,' answered Grandfather. 'It means

Jack owns land. A great deal of land in Oregon. This piece of paper, Jack, means that you are very rich indeed.'

This was what Jack's father had left him. Not a wooden box but a place to make a home. A new beginning.

I was so happy for him. 'You can do whatever you want now, Jack!'

'He *did* look after me,' said Jack in wonder. How pleased we all were.

Da laughed. 'Well, I'm glad I adopted you now! And there was me thinking you had no money at all! Now you can look after all of us!'

We were close to our journey's end. All that lay between us and our new life was the Columbia River rapids. The river led all the way to the town of Portland. It was where Uncle Niall lived but it was not going to be easy. Two great rocks held the entire flow of the river between them and there was no way to continue down the riverbank. The only way to reach Uncle Niall's home was down the river, but it had great high perpendicular banks and vast rocks, with water tumbling so fast it was white and furious.

'Eighteen hundred miles and now this,' marvelled Cornelius.

Bea shuddered at the thought of travelling on the wild river. 'We are so close,' she said. 'Is there no other way?'

Nashobanowa went to see what he could find out.

'It's the most dangerous water on the whole trail,' declared Louise as we all waited and looked at the foaming water.

The grown-ups chatted among themselves, but I heard Kate say that this was the place where so many had died trying to finish their trip. She was scared. We all were.

Nashobanowa came back with some Chinook Indians.

'They have a raft,' he explained. 'They can take us downriver.'

The raft was long and made of logs lashed together. The trip would take two days but the cost was terrible.

'It's the last of our money,' worried Kate.

'That is no longer a concern,' said Grandfather as he pulled coins from a purse.

'The men say there is a way across the land but it is far and hard,' said Nashobanowa. 'They say this is the best.'

'What about the printing press?' Jack asked.

Even I, who really loved the printing press, could see it was too big and heavy for the raft.

In the end it was decided to make a cover for the press and leave it behind until Da could return for it with a wagon and horses in the new year.

I didn't like it, but Da said it would be fine, and Jack persuaded me that it was a good plan.

'I will buy the finest wagon and return for it in the spring,' he promised.

The Chinook men, wearing basket hats made of finely

woven spruce root, were brilliant at balancing themselves on the raft and putting our few things on board. The log boat was about forty feet long, and Nashobanowa helped them load up. When he was finished he turned to help me get on. He put out his hand but I turned away. It was all too much and I began to weep.

'I can't go! I can't go,' I kept repeating.

Da moved to find out what the problem was, but Grandfather said, 'Let me!' He gently pulled me to one side as I sobbed.

'I can't leave my horse. Chronicle! He's my friend. I can't. I'll have to ride! Go the long way!'

'Hmm,' said Grandfather, and went to speak to the men in charge. I don't know what he said to them, but I suspect we were the only people who ever made that journey down-river with a horse on board. Chronicle was persuaded to lie down so that he wouldn't fall overboard, but he was heavy, and once he was on the raft the water ran three inches over the logs. I loved my family so much in that moment because no one ever said a word about it.

The river was hell. We had struggled with water before but this was the worst. There were whirlpools which looked like deep basins in the river. Great waves splashed and rolled over the raft, thick with foam. It leaped from wave to wave, sometimes slipping into a trough and then mounting a crest with perfect ease, dashing spray into our faces when we were in rough water. Close to the riverbank loomed ugly cliffs of rock, black and forbidding, some rough and barren, others thickly set with timber and brush.

At night we camped on the shore – sometimes the south side and sometimes the north. As if we had not had enough, now everyone had fleas. They crawled all over us and every person squirmed, desperate to change their clothes.

At a place where the water threw itself over something called 'the Chutes' everyone had to get out and walk. We were all exhausted but Esther began to sing 'Home, Sweet Home' and one by one we all joined in.

Sometimes we saw Indians in canoes made from a single log with two or three people in them. We had just seen such a boat disappearing round a bend ahead when we heard the rapids. The boat began to rise and fall and rock from side to side. As we made the turn we could see breakers ahead extending in broken lines across the river and the raft began to be carried along so fast. Our Indian pilot squatted low. I can see him now, with his old red hankie round his head and long black hair down his back. He concentrated and no one said a word. Foam-crested waves swept across the bow. We were about twenty yards from the right-hand shore. On the opposite side we saw another boat, not a raft exactly, more something made from a wagon bed. Their pilot chose a different way forward and, as we watched, it disappeared in wails of confusion and shrieking. The whole boat crumbled into giant pieces, tipping all the passengers into the water. We saw men and boys struggling against the torrent. Da, Henry and Cornelius all wanted to jump in and help, but it was clear no one could reach them. Our pilot tried to come ashore but there were steep rocks all along the bank and the water dashed against them.

'They came all that way to die,' whispered Bea.

Now we saw bedding and furniture floating by. One man clung to a feather bed, which carried him safe to the foot of the rapids, but we saw no other survivors. The boat had been taken into a whirlpool; swallowed in a roaring circle of water. That night a windstorm of cold rain fell down on us. We were heartbroken and exhausted.

The next morning we made our final journey on the river. No one spoke as the Chinook pilot pulled in to the shore for the last time to let us off. We were a miserable-looking party. There was not one of us who owned an entire outside garment. All our clothes were rags, our bodies exhausted, and I don't know how much we were able to take in of the paradise we had arrived in. We walked into the Willamette Valley and found everything we had hoped for. The land was fertile, the climate gentle, the growing season long and the timber abundant.

'A veritable Eden,' declared Louise, and Jeni nodded, too tired to reply.

'Well worth the journey,' said Cornelius, looking at Bea,

who smiled. He put his hand out to her, and after a moment she took it as we walked on.

It was almost like one of our fanciful sights from the desert when we first saw houses along the way. I think we had almost forgotten that such things existed. It had been so many thousands of miles since we had seen anyone living like that. The houses were made of properly cut wooden boards with real windows. Some of them were painted, and Bea wept at the sight. We had spent so many months sleeping in the open; now I couldn't believe that there were homes with fireplaces and beds. We had endured so many hours repairing wagons with wire, scraps and luck. Now we heard the sound of a sawmill churning out as much wood as anyone could ever want. We had eaten terrible things cooked on buffalo chips, but gradually we began to see stores with food for sale.

'Now what?' asked Henry.

'I'm not sure,' said Da, but then he clapped his hands and laughed. 'No! I do know! Slim has a map!'

And I had! I had carried it all the way from Ireland. A map drawn by my Uncle Niall and sent to us all that time ago so that we might find his house.

I got it out, and we all stood round looking at it and trying to make sense of what we could see. What a ragged bunch we were as we slowly walked along, looking for the signs he had drawn. Chronicle walked beside me, as did

Louise and Jeni. They had come to Oregon for the health of Jeni's mother, and now they were not at all sure what to do next.

'Stay with us,' urged Kate, and so along they came.

'We'll make a plan,' said Da. 'We'll all make a plan together.'

'I have land,' said Jack. 'We can all live there.'

I held the map out as we walked. I could see that Bea and Cornelius might be inseparable now and I guessed there would be another wedding soon. Henry walked with us, but I knew he would leave us one day to find his actor friends again. Toby whistled as Hamlet trotted along. They too had adventures ahead. Jack strutted along with a new-found confidence. I tried to imagine what might lie ahead for all of us, but before I could dream too much I saw that Jack had stopped in front of a small log cabin with windows on either side of a neat front door. I looked at my map and looked again at the house. I could hardly breathe.

'Do you think this is it?' I asked quietly.

Jack checked the map once more and nodded.

We had arrived.

Nobody moved. We had finally reached our destination and none of us could quite believe it. We had travelled thousands of miles across terrible water and deserts. We had been in fear for our lives and had lost our beloved mother. There we stood, a shabby, worn-out group, unable to walk one more step. One day there would be many more stories to tell. How we would struggle in the months to come; how we would get back our printing press and say goodbye to some of those we loved. But all that was in the future. Right now we were in Oregon. At Uncle Niall's house.

We stood in silence until Toby said, 'We never did see it.'

'See what?' asked Da.

'The elephant.'

We all laughed.

Da smiled and ruffled Toby's hair. 'You're right, but I'm not going back to look for it.'

He looked at Kate.

'Go on, Patrick,' she said quietly.

He looked so tired, but he smiled and gently pushed a strand of Kate's dark hair back from her face.

'No,' he said, before turning to me. 'You do it, Slim. We would never have made it without you.'

I looked at Nashobanowa and he smiled.

'You are home now, Slim,' he said quietly.

I didn't think I could move, but Chronicle, my wonderful horse, my wonderful friend, gently nudged me with his nose. I took a deep breath and went to the door of the house. I looked once more at my ragged family. We had changed beyond all imagination but we had survived. I raised my hand to knock. I knew that whatever happened next, this would not be the end of the story.